NEW YORK REVIEW BOOKS
CLASSICS

THAT AWFUL MESS
ON THE VIA MERULANA

CARLO EMILIO GADDA (1893–1973) was born in Milan, where he spent a "tormented childhood and even more miserable adolescence." He earned a degree in engineering, volunteered to fight in World War I, and was taken prisoner by the Germans. After the war, he began to write while working as an engineer in countries as far afield as Argentina. *Acquainted with Grief*, Gadda's first novel, set in an imaginary South American country, appeared in 1938. His masterpiece, *That Awful Mess on the Via Merulana*, was serialized after the war, but only published as a book in 1957. Both novels, like much else that Gadda wrote, were left incomplete. Among Gadda's other notable works are essays, film and radio scripts, a travel book, and his journals from the World War I.

ITALO CALVINO (1923–1985) was an Italian writer and novelist. His works include *The Road to San Giovanni*, *If on a Winter's Night a Traveler*, *Invisible Cities*, *Marcovaldo*, and *Mr. Palomar*.

WILLIAM WEAVER is celebrated for his numerous translations from the Italian, including Umberto Eco's *The Name of the Rose* and novels and stories by Italo Calvino. Weaver's translation of Pirandello's *The Late Mattia Pascal* is also published by NYRB Classics.

THAT AWFUL MESS
ON THE VIA MERULANA

CARLO EMILIO GADDA

Translated from the Italian by
WILLIAM WEAVER

Introduction by
ITALO CALVINO

NEW YORK REVIEW BOOKS

New York

THIS IS A NEW YORK REVIEW BOOK
PUBLISHED BY THE NEW YORK REVIEW OF BOOKS
435 Hudson Street, New York, NY 10014
www.nyrb.com

Published in Italian as *Quer pasticciaccio brutto de via Merulana*

Library of Congress Cataloging-in-Publication Data
Gadda, Carlo Emilio, 1893–1973.
  [Quer pasticciaccio brutto de via Merulana. English]
  That awful mess on the Via Merulana / by Carlo Emilio Gadda ; introduction
by Italo Calvino ; translated by William Weaver.
    p. cm. — (New York Review Books classics)
  ISBN 978-1-59017-222-3 (alk. paper)
  I. Weaver, William, 1923– II. Title.
PQ4817.A33Q413 2007
853'.912—dc22

                                    2006036813

ISBN 978-1-59017-222-3

Printed in the United States of America on acid-free paper.
10 9 8 7 6 5 4

INTRODUCTION

by Italo Calvino

IN 1946, when he started *That Awful Mess on Via Merulana*, Carlo Emilio Gadda intended to write not only a murder novel, but a philosophical novel as well. The murder story was inspired by a crime that had recently been committed in Rome. The philosophical inquiry was based on a concept announced at the novel's very outset: nothing can ever be explained if we confine ourselves to seeking one cause for every effect. Every effect is determined by multiple causes, each of which has still other, numerous causes behind it. Every event, a crime for example, is like a vortex where various streams converge, each moved by heterogeneous impulses, none of which can be overlooked in the search for the truth.

A view of the world as a "system of systems" had been expounded in a notebook found among Gadda's papers and published after his death. Using his favorite philosophers, Spinoza, Leibniz, and Kant, as a starting point, the writer had constructed a "discourse on method." Every element of a system contains within it another system; each individual system in turn is linked to a genealogy of systems. A change in any particular element results in a breakdown of the whole.

What matters most is how this philosophy of knowledge is reflected in Gadda's style, in his language, which is a thick amalgam of folk expressions and learned speech, of interior monologue and artistic prose, of various dialects and literary quotations. The same philosophy is also apparent in the narrative, where the slightest details are enlarged until they occupy the entire frame, concealing or effacing the overall design. And so it happens in this novel, where the murder story, little by little, is forgotten. We seem about to discover the murderer's identity and motive when the description of a defecating hen demands our attention more strongly than the solution of the mystery.

The seething cauldron of life, the infinite stratification of reality, the inextricable tangle of knowledge are what Gadda wants to depict. When this concept of universal complication, reflected in the slightest object or event, has reached its ultimate paroxysm, it seems as if the novel is destined to remain unfinished, as if it could continue infinitely, creating new vortices within each episode. Gadda's point is the superabundance, the congestion, of these pages, through which a single complex object—the city of Rome—assumes a variegated form, becomes organism and symbol.

For, again, this book is not meant to be only a detective novel or a philosophical novel, but also a novel about Rome. The Eternal City is the true protagonist of the book, with its social classes ranging from the middle bourgeoisie to the underworld, the voices of its various dialects surfacing in the melting pot, its extroversion and its murkiest unconscious. In this Rome, the present blends with the mythical past, Hermes and Circe are invoked in connection with the most plebeian vicissitudes, and characters who are domestic servants or petty thieves bear the names of Aeneas, Diomedes, Ascanius, Camilla, Lavinia, like the heroes and heroines of Virgil. The ragged, brawling Rome of the neorealist cinema, in its golden age when Gadda wrote the novel, takes on a cultural, historical, mythical dimension that neorealism ignored. And the Rome of art historians also plays a part, in references to Renaissance and Baroque painting, descriptions of the feet of saints and their huge big toes.

A novel of Rome, written by a non-Roman. At the time he wrote *That Awful Mess,* Gadda knew Rome only from having lived there a few years in the 1930s, when he had worked as director of the Vatican's thermoelectric plant. He was in fact Milanese and closely identified with the bourgeoisie of his native city, whose values of concrete practicality, technical efficiency, and moral principle he saw being swept away as another Italy—conniving, raucous, and unscrupulous—prevailed. But even if his stories and his most autobiographical novel, *Acquainted with Grief,* are rooted in the society and dialect of Milan, it is *That Awful Mess* that brought him to the attention of a wider public, a novel written to a large extent in Roman dialect and where Rome is seen and comprehended with an almost physiological penetration, in its most infernal aspects, like a witches' sabbath.

Gadda was a man of contradictions. An electrical

engineer, he tried to master his hypersensitive, anxious temperament with a rational, scientific mentality, but he simply exacerbated it instead; and in his writing he gave vent to his irascibility, his phobias, his fits of misanthropy, which in his everyday life he repressed behind the mask of ceremonious politeness belonging to a gentleman of another age.

Critics considered him a revolutionary in his use of language and narrative form, an expressionist, a follower of Joyce. He had this reputation from the beginning in the most exclusive literary circles, and it was renewed when the young members of the avant-garde in the 1960s acknowledged him as their master. But in his own literary taste, he was devoted to the classics and to tradition (his favorite author was the sage, calm Manzoni), and his model in the art of the novel was Balzac. His own work displayed some of the fundamental gifts of nineteenth-century realism or naturalism in its portrayal of characters, settings, and situations through their physical substance, through material sensations as, for instance, the tasting of a glass of wine at the dinner with which the book opens.

Fiercely critical of the society of his time, animated by a visceral hatred of Mussolini (seen in his sarcastic description of the emphatic set of the Duce's jaw), Gadda shied away from any kind of radicalism in politics; he was a moderate man of order, respectful of the law, who looked back with nostalgia toward the sound administration of an earlier time; a good patriot, he had been a conscientious officer in the First World War, had fought, and had suffered. This was a fundamental experience for him, though he never got over his indignation at the harm done by incompetence, expediency, velleity. In *That Awful Mess,* which takes place in 1927, during the early years of Mussolini's dictatorship, Gadda does not confine himself to a facile caricature of Fascism: he conducts a minute, extensive analysis of the effects on the daily administration of justice caused by a failure to respect the separation of powers as envisioned by Montesquieu, to whom there is explicit reference.

This constant desire for concreteness, for verification, this appetite for reality are so strong in Gadda's writing that they create a kind of congestion, hypertension, blockage. The characters' voices, thoughts, and sensations, the dreams of their unconscious, are mingled with the author's omnipresence, his fits of impatience, his sarcasm, and the fine network of cultural references. As in the performance of a ventriloquist, all these voices coincide in a single speech, sometimes in the same sentence, with shifts of tone, modulation, falsetto. The structure of the novel is stretched out of shape from within by the excessive richness of the material and the intensity with which the author charges it. The existential and intellectual dramatic force of this distortive process is implicit: comedy, humor, grotesque metamorphosis are natural means of expression for this man whose life was always unhappy, tormented by neurosis, by the difficulty of relations with others, by the anguish of death.

Gadda did not intend that his formal innovations would overturn the structure of the novel; he envisioned constructing solid novels that observed all the rules, but he never succeeded in carrying his plans through to the end. *Acquainted With Grief* and *That Awful Mess* seem to need only a few more pages to reach their conclusions. In other cases, he dismembered his novels, breaking them into short stories, and it would not be impossible to reconstruct the originals by piecing together the various fragments.

That Awful Mess recounts the police investigation of two criminal cases, one trivial and the other inhuman. Both take place in the same apartment house in the center of Rome within the space of a few days: a widow, eager to be consoled, is robbed of her jewelry; a married woman, disconsolate because she cannot bear children, is stabbed to death. An obsession with infertility is central to the novel: Signora Liliana Balducci surrounded herself with girls whom she considered adopted daughters, but then, for one reason or another, they become separated. The figure of Liliana, dominant even as victim, and the gynaeceum atmosphere that surrounds her seem to open the prospect, full of shadows, of femininity, a mysterious force of nature in the face of which Gadda expresses his perturbation in scenes where contemplations of woman's physiology are joined with geographical-genetic metaphors and to the legend of the origin of Rome, where the rape of the Sabine women insured the city's continuity.

A traditional antifeminism that reduces woman to a procreative function is expressed with great crudeness: is this merely the method of Flaubert recording *idées reçues,* or does the author himself share this view? To see the problem more clearly, we must bear two circumstances in mind, one historical and the other personal to the author. Under Mussolini, the first duty of the Italians, inculcated unremittingly by official propaganda, was to present sons to the Fatherland; only prolific mothers and fathers were considered worthy of respect. In the midst of this apotheosis of procreation, Gadda, a bachelor oppressed by a paralyzing shyness in any female presence, felt like an outsider, and he suffered an ambivalent feeling mingling attraction and repulsion.

Attraction and repulsion animate the description of Liliana's corpse, her throat horribly cut, in one of the most elaborate scenes of the book, like a Baroque painting of a saint's martyrdom. Officer Francesco Ingravallo conducts his investigation of the crime with a special interest: first because he knew, and desired, the victim, and second because he is a Southerner, steeped in philosophy and moved both by scientific passion and by sensitivity toward all that is human. It is Ingravallo who theorizes about the multiplicity of causes that concur to produce a single effect, and among these causes, as if reading Freud, he discerns always *Eros* in one form or another.

If the police officer Ingravallo is the author's philosophical spokesman, Gadda identifies himself with another character on a psychological and poetic level. Angeloni, a retired government official and a tenant in the building where the murder takes place, becomes so embarrassed when questioned that he immediately falls suspect, although he is the most inoffensive of souls. An introverted and melancholy bachelor, Angeloni is given to solitary walks along the streets of the old center of Rome. A man subject to gluttony, and perhaps other temptations, he orders hams and cheeses from food shops which are delivered to his home by boys in short trousers. As the police track one of these boys, a suspected accomplice in the robbery and perhaps also in the murder, Angeloni lives in fear of being accused of homosexual tendencies and, overly protective of his respectability and privacy, he becomes entangled in reticences and contradictions that result in his arrest.

But greater suspicion is focused on a nephew of the murdered woman, who must explain his possession of a gold pendant containing a valuable stone that belonged to the victim. This investigation soon shows every sign of being a false lead. The inquiries about the robbery, on the other hand, seem to garner more promising information, as they move from the capital to the Alban Hills (and thus become the responsibility no longer of the urban police but of the *carabinieri*) in search of a gigolo-electrician, Diomede Lanciani, who had visited the eager widow. In this rural setting we rediscover the traces of various girls on whom Signora Liliana lavished her motherly attentions. And it is here that the *carabinieri* find, hidden in a chamber pot, the jewels stolen from the widow.

The description of the jewels is not simply an outburst of virtuosic writing; it adds to the rich depiction of circumstances—beyond the linguistic, phonetic, psychological, physiological, historical, mythical, gastronomic, and others—yet another level, a mineral, plutonic level of hidden treasures, bringing geological history and the forces of inanimate matter to bear on the sordid story of a crime. And it is around the possession of these precious stones that the knots of the characters' psychology or psychopathology are tightented: the violent envy of the poor, along with what Gadda calls the "typical psychosis of the frustrated woman" that led Liliana to bestow gifts on her protegées.

We might have been brought closer to the solution of the mystery by the first version of the novel, published in installments in a literary review in Florence in 1946, but the author suppressed a crucial fourth chapter when the novel was prepared for publication in 1957, precisely because he did not want to show his own hand too clearly. In this chapter, Ingravallo questions Liliana's husband about his affair with Virginia, one of his wife's "adoptive daughters." The sapphic atmosphere enveloping Signora Liliana and her gynaeceum is underlined, and the girl's character reveals lesbian tendencies, as well as amorality, cupidity, and social ambition (she had obviously become the man's lover to blackmail him later); there is evidence of a fit of blind, violent hatred as she utters obscure threats and slices into a roast with a kitchen knife.

Is Virginia the murderess then? Any doubt this raises is resolved by the posthumous discovery and publication of a film treatment that Gadda seems to have written at about the same time as the first draft of the novel. Here, the plot is developed and clarified in every detail, and we learn that the jewel thief is not Diomede Lanciani but Enea Retalli, who, rather than allow himself to be arrested, fires on the *carabinieri* and is killed. This treatment was ignored when Pietro Germi made a film from the novel in 1959 without Gadda's collaboration, and it was never considered by producers or directors. Their indifference is not surprising: Gadda had a rather ingenuous notion of writing for film and relied heavily on dissolves to reveal characters' thoughts and further the action. It makes interesting reading as a sketch for the novel, but it creates no real tension either as action or as psychology.

In other words, the problem is not "who done it." From the first pages of the novel, we are told that what determines a crime is the "field of forces" that emanates from the victim's situation as it relates to the situations of others in the complicated web of events: "that system of forces and probabilities which surround every human creature, and which is customarily called destiny."

Rome, March 6, 1984

Translated from the Italian by William Weaver

TRANSLATOR'S FOREWORD

There is hardly anything about Carlo Emilio Gadda that is not contradictory. Stately and courtly, he lives in a lower-middle-class apartment house in Rome, where the yelling of children, the clatter of dishes, and the laundry hanging on the balconies contrast violently with the cloistral austerity, the shy solitude of the writer's quarters. And this solitude, the timid elegance of his speech and manner are, in turn, a surprise to one who has read his most famous book, *Quer pasticciaccio brutto de via Merulana,* a teeming canvas of Roman life, many of whose characters speak the city's expressive, but not always elegant dialect. The contrasts are, to a supreme degree, present in the book itself, a pastiche—as its title implies—of languages and dialects that has been compared to the work of Joyce.

Via Merulana, the locale of much of the story, is also an unlikely setting for a great novel. It is the least romantic street in Rome: a long, straight thoroughfare with square, solid, ugly buildings, constructed for the square, solid bourgeoisie of half a century ago, already a bit down-at-the-heels in 1927, the year in which the novel's events take place, and still more down-at-the-heels today. A street no tourist ever sees, except to pass along it hastily en route to some monument of the neighborhood like Santa Maria Maggiore or the church of the Santi Quattro Incoronati, both mentioned often and tellingly in *Il pasticciaccio* (as the novel is familiarly called).

Gadda himself, the poet and chronicler of Rome, is not a Roman; and this most Roman of novels was written, some years after the events it describes, in Florence, where the author lived between 1940 and 1950. Born in Milan in 1893, Gadda has lived not only in Rome and Florence, but for long periods in Argentina, France, Germany, and Belgium. Officially he was—until the years in Florence—an engineer, but this profession was also a part of the disguise behind which the writer and thinker operated.

A soldier in the First World War (and a prisoner in Germany), Gadda had already begun filling notebooks with his round, precise hand. These notebooks, in part, appeared in his first published volume, *La Madonna dei filosofi* (1931), and, more completely, in his *Giornali di guerra e di prigionia* in 1955. His first articles had appeared in the distinguished Florentine literary magazine *Solaria* in 1926, and in *Solaria*'s successor, the review *Letteratura*, he published installments of his two novels, *Il pasticciaccio* (1946) and *La cognizione del dolore* (1938–41).

Gadda's first published volumes were collections of short stories which came out in small—almost clandestine— editions. Some of the books were published, wholly or partly, at the author's expense. But despite this secret manner of revealing his works, Gadda soon attracted the attention of the Italian critics and of a small but devoted band of readers. And, in time, those critics and readers included editors of two of Italy's leading publishing firms, Garzanti and Einaudi, who, after the Second World War, began to bring out Gadda's *opera omnia* in a more accessible manner, attracting new readers and renewed critical attention. And it was the influence of the Italian critics and publishers which brought about Gadda's being awarded the Prix International de Littérature at Corfu in 1963 for *La cognizione del dolore*.

This prize came as something of a shock to the Italian literary world—where Gadda, though considered the country's most significant prose master, was still more or less a coterie possession—and as a complete surprise to critics and readers in other countries, where Gadda's name was known, at most, to a few specialists of Italian literature. A piece of Gadda's journalism (journalism, always, of a very unorthodox nature) had been translated into English for a special number of *The Texas Quarterly*, but otherwise his work had been totally ignored. A story of his then appeared, in English, in the review *Art and Literature* in Paris, and an article on his work was translated for a recent Italian number of *The London Magazine*. The present translation of *Il pasticciaccio* follows translations into French, German, and Dutch.

La cognizione del dolore is an unfinished work, and so, in a sense, is *Il pasticciaccio*. Gadda's short stories—which now number several volumes—are frequently not stories at all, but fragments of other, unfinished longer works. Unfinished, but not incomplete. Even the briefest of Gadda's fragments has its own curious wholeness; and if the "murder story" aspect of *Il pasticciaccio* remains unresolved, one feels—at the end of this long, apparently ambling work— that it is better *not* to know who is responsible for the death of Signora Liliana. The reader feels that he has probed deeply enough already into the evil and horror of the world and that yet another, worse revelation of it would be more than the reader, the author, and the protagonist Ingravallo could bear. Though students of Gadda's work might not agree, one also suspects that his novels were born to be fragments, like certain imaginary ruins in Venetian painting, perfect parts of impossible wholes.

Il pasticciaccio occupies in contemporary Italian literature the position that *Ulysses, Remembrance of Things Past,* and *The Man without Qualities* occupy in the literatures of their respective countries; but as these three works do not resemble one another, so Gadda' s novel resembles none of them. Joyce and Gadda have this much in common: a fascination with language, and a revolutionary attitude towards the use of language in fiction. From the time of Manzoni on, the "problem of language" has been a central theme in all Italian discussion of the art of writing; the literary language that Manzoni fixed and made national was, for some authors, both a guide and a strait jacket. And, even in the last century, Verga and other novelists were working towards bringing the language of daily life into fictional descriptions of daily life. The dialect theater helped create the dialect novel.

But *Il pasticciaccio* is not a dialect novel. Gadda uses the language of his characters to help portray them: his detective, Ingravallo, speaks a mixture of Roman and Molisano; the Countess Menegazzi lapses frequently into her native Venetian. The author himself, when writing from his own point of view, uses all of these, but also uses

xviii

Neapolitan, Milanese, and occasional French, Latin, Greek, and Spanish expressions. At the same time he expoits all the levels of Italian, spoken and written: the contorted officialese of the bureaucracy, the high-flown euphemisms of the press, the colorful and imaginative spiel of the vendors in Rome's popular market in Piazza Vittorio. And at the same time, Gadda's vast erudition, in such disparate and recondite fields as philosophy, physics, psychology, and engineering, is frequently evident—all of this fused into a single, difficult, rich, yet flowing style.

Grim as its story sometimes is, and bitter and bleak as the author's attitude towards the world may be, *Il pasticciaccio* is basically a satirical work. And the targets of Gadda's satire are scattered: at times his lighthearted whimsy touches some friend's foible or attacks the pretensions of some innocent public figure (like the poor President of the Italian Touring Club who campaigned for more road signs); at other times, with Swiftian *saeva indignatio*, Gadda lashes out at the Fascists, their followers and their dupes, the destroyers and despoilers of life.

Another Gaddian contradiction: his ferocity is counterbalanced by his timidity, and often his attacks are so thoroughly veiled as to be incomprehensible to all but the author himself (even his victim remains unaware). This quality gives, at times, a curious allusiveness to his prose and lifts what would be a personal vendetta to a larger, more universal level.

The reader will note that Gadda does not hesitate to accept as his own the verbal difficulties or spoonerisms of his humbler characters. The Romans are notoriously bad at getting names right (as any foreigner whose name contains a "w" will well know), so that detective Ingravallo may also be called Incravallo, Ingravalli, or Incravalli, and the hapless Countess Menegazzi's name is mispronounced so often that it becomes hard to remember how it really should be spelled. There is confusion even in place names, and one locality, mentioned often in the latter part of the book, is called, indifferently, Torraccio and Torracchio.

The Romans are also fond of giving people titles. An accountant named Rossi is never called Signor Rossi, but always Ragioniere (accountant) Rossi. Thus any official, however minor, is known as Doctor, whether or not he has a university degree. And Ingravallo, being a southerner, is known not only as Doctor Ingravallo but also as Don Ciccio.

When it originally appeared in *Letteratura,* this novel was enriched by many long and discursive footnotes which Gadda removed when *Il pasticciaccio* came out in book form. For the benefit of non-Italian readers, the translator has added a certain number of footnotes of his own to this English version. *Il pasticciaccio* takes place under the stifling years of Fascism, so that there are many references, direct and indirect, to the personages, the ukases, the slogans and customs of the regime, references which even to the Italian reader (especially if he is under thirty) are obscure.

A word on the special problems of this translation. The question of rendering dialect in another language is a particularly tormented one. Several years ago an American poet made a brave, but disastrous attempt to re-create the Roman-dialect sonnets of the great Gioacchino Belli in Brooklynese. The result was ingenious, but wholly lacking in the wit and elegance of the original. To translate Gadda's Roman or Venetian into the language of Mississippi or the Aran Islands would be as absurd as translating the language of Faulkner's Snopeses into Sicilian or Welsh. So the English-speaking reader is therefore asked to imagine the speech of Gadda's characters, translated here into straight-forward spoken English, as taking place in dialect, or in a mixture of dialects. Other aspects of Gadda's language were easier to transpose, but in a few cases, where untranslatable puns underlie a passage, the translator has inserted an explanatory footnote.

The present translation was made from the seventh Garzanti edition of the novel (October 1962), which contains a few variants on earlier editions, variants made by the author, of course. The translator wishes to express his thanks to the author, for help and encouragement, to his friend Ariodante Marianni, who explained a number of Roman terms and customs, and to the critic and Gadda scholar Giancarlo Roscioni, who read the translation in manuscript and generously furnished innumerable elucidations and suggestions. Of course, the translator himself assumes full responsibility for the final result and, especially, for the general approach to the daunting, but infinitely rewarding task.

WILLIAM WEAVER

Rome, January 15, 1965

THAT AWFUL MESS
ON THE VIA MERULANA

I

EVERYBODY called him Don Ciccio by now. He was Officer Francesco Ingravallo, assigned to homicide; one of the youngest and, God knows why, most envied officials of the detective section: ubiquitous as the occasion required, omnipresent in all tenebrous matters. Of medium height, rather rotund as to physique, or perhaps a bit squat, with black hair, thick and curly, which sprang forth from his forehead at the halfway point, as if to shelter his two meta-physical knobs from the fine Italian sun, he had a somnolent look, a heavy, lumbering walk, a slightly dull manner, like a person fighting a laborious digestion; dressed as well as his slender government salary allowed him to dress, with one or two little stains of olive oil on his lapel, almost imperceptible however, like a souvenir of the hills of his Molise. A certain familiarity with the ways of the world, with our so-called "Latin" world, though he was young (thirty-five), must have been his: a certain knowledge of men: and also of women. His landlady venerated, not to say worshiped him: for and notwithstanding the unfamiliar complication of every telephone trill and every sudden telegram, and night calls, and hours with no peace, which formed the tangled texture of his time. "All hours! He works around the clock! Last night he came home at daybreak!" For her he was the "distinguished, single gentleman, government employee" she had long dreamed of, the gentleman preceded by a discreet "to let" in *Il Messaggero*, evoked, extracted from the infinite assortment of single gentlemen by that lure of "spacious and sunny" and despite the stern, closing injunction: "no women allowed"; which, in the language of the *Messaggero*'s advertisements can offer, as everyone knows, a double interpretation. And besides, he managed to persuade the police to overlook that ridiculous little matter . . . yes, that fine for letting rooms without a license . . . why, when they divided it up, that fine, between City Hall and the police . . . "A lady like me! Widow of Commendatore Antonini! All Rome knew him, you might say; and everybody who knew him had only the highest regard for him. Now I don't say this because he was my husband, rest his soul. And they take me for a common landlady! Me? Rent out my rooms to just anybody? Merciful Heavens, I'd rather throw myself in the river."

In his wisdom and in his Molisan poverty, Officer Ingravallo, who seemed to live on silence and sleep under the black jungle of that mop, shiny as pitch and curly as astrakhan lamb, in his wisdom, he sometimes interrupted this silence and this sleep to enunciate some theoretical idea (a general idea, that is) on the affairs of men, and of women. At first sight, or rather, on first hearing, these seemed banalities. They weren't banalities. And so, those rapid declarations, which crackled on his lips like the sudden illumination of a sulphur match, were revived in the ears of people at a distance of hours, or of months, from

4

their enunciation: as if after a mysterious period of incubation. "That's right!" the person in question admitted, "That's exactly what Ingravallo said to me." He sustained, among other things, that unforeseen catastrophes are never the consequence or the effect, if you prefer, of a single motive, of *a* cause singular; but they are rather like a whirlpool, a cyclonic point of depression in the consciousness of the world, towards which a whole multitude of converging causes have contributed. He also used words like knot or tangle, or muddle, or *gnommero*, which in Roman dialect means skein. But the legal term, "the motive, the motives," escaped his lips by preference, though as if against his will. The opinion that we must "reform within ourselves the meaning of the category of cause," as handed down by the philosophers from Aristotle to Immanuel Kant, and replace cause with causes was for him a central, persistent opinion, almost a fixation, which melted from his fleshy, but rather white lips, where the stub of a spent cigarette seemed, dangling from one corner, to accompany the somnolence of his gaze and the quasi-grin, half-bitter, half-skeptical, in which through "old" habit he would fix the lower half of his face beneath that sleep of his forehead and eyelids and that pitchy black of his mop. This was how, exactly how he defined "his" crimes. "When they call me . . . Sure. If they call *me*, you can be sure that there's trouble: some mess, some *gliuommero* to untangle," he would say, garbling his Italian with the dialects of Naples and the Molise.

The apparent motive, the principal motive was, of course, single. But the crime was the effect of a whole list of motives which had blown on it in a whirlwind (like the sixteen winds in the list of winds when they twist together in a tornado, in a cyclonic depression) and had ended by pressing into the vortex of the crime the enfeebled "reason of the world." Like wringing the neck of a chicken. And then he used to say, but this a bit wearily, "you're sure to find skirts where you don't want to find them." A belated Italian revision of the trite *"cherchez la femme."* And then he seemed to repent, as if he had slandered the ladies, and wanted to change his mind. But that would have got him into difficulties. So he would remain silent and pensive, afraid he had said too much. What he meant was that a certain affective motive, a certain amount or, as you might say today, a quantum of affection, of "eros," was also involved even in "matters of interest," in crimes which were apparently far removed from the tempests of love. Some colleagues, a tiny bit envious of his intuitions, a few priests, more acquainted with the many evils of our time, some subalterns, clerks, and his superiors too, insisted he read strange books: from which he drew all those words that mean nothing, or almost nothing, but which serve better than others to dazzle the naive, the ignorant. His terminology was for doctors in looneybins. But practical action takes something else! Notions and philosophizing are to be left to scribblers: the practical experience of the police stations and the homicide squad is quite another thing: it takes plenty of patience, and charity, and a strong stomach; and when the whole shooting match of the Italians isn't tottering, a sense of responsibility, prompt decision, civil moderation; yes, yes, and a firm hand. On him, on Don Ciccio, these objec-

6

tions, just as they were, had no effect; he continued to sleep on his feet, philosophize on an empty stomach, and pretend to smoke his half-cigarette which had, always, gone out.

For the 20th of February, Sunday, Feast of Sant'Eleuterio, the Balduccis had invited him to dinner: "At half-past one, if that's convenient for you." It was, the signora said, "Remo's birthday"; and in fact, at the City Registry, Remo had been inscribed as "Remo Eleuterio," and baptized as such at the Church of San Martino ai Monti, so as to mark the day of his birth. "Two names that have a nasty ring to certain ears nowadays,"* thought Don Ciccio, "both the first and the second." But for a guy like Balducci, who didn't give a damn about anything, they were a downright waste. The invitation, like the last time, had been issued by telephone two days ahead, a call "from outside" at the Collegio Romano Station, or rather, to give the street address, Santo Stefano del Cacco. First, in a melodious voice, the signora herself had spoken to him: "This is Liliana Balducci"; and then the old goat took over, Balducci, following up. Don Ciccio, after having kept the Sabbath with a visit to the barber's, took the signora a bottle of fresh oil from home. The Sunday dinner was happy, in the light of a marvelous afternoon, with confetti still littering the pavements, and an occasional carnival mask, a toy trumpet, an azure Cinderella or little devil in black velvet. The men talked about hunting: of expeditions and dogs: of guns:

* The name Remo (Remus) Gadda imagines as being disliked by the Fascists because of their cult of Romulus, founder of Rome. Eleuterio is the Italian translation of the Greek name which means "free." It's unlikely that many Fascists gave these names any thought.

then about the comedian Petrolini: then about the various names they give the mullet all along the Tyrrhenian coast, from Ventimiglia to Cape Lilibeo: then the scandal of the day, Countess Pappalodoli, who had run off with a violinist; a Pole, naturally. Only seventeen. The story went on and on.

When he came in, Lulu, the little Pekinese bitch, a ball of fluff, had barked, and angrily, too; well, when she stopped growling, she had sniffed his shoes at length. The vitality of those little monsters is incredible. You feel like petting them, then stamping them. They were four at table: he, Don Ciccio, the husband and wife, and the niece. The niece, however, wasn't the same one as last time, that is to say on the Feast of San Francesco, this one was much younger, barely emerging from childhood. The other niece —the one on San Francesco's day—was only a niece after a manner of speaking: she looked like a peasant bride, her head crowned with black braids; strong and broad, she'd fill up a whole bed by herself: those eyes! and what a front! what a behind! Something to make you dream at night. This new one was a little girl with a pigtail hanging down her back, and she went to the sisters' school.

Don Ciccio, despite his somnolence, had a quick memory, infallible even: a pragmatic memory, he used to say. The maid, too, was a new face, though she vaguely resembled the first niece. They called her Tina. While she was serving, a wad of drained spinach deviated from the oval plate onto the candid whiteness of the immaculate tablecloth. "Assunta!" the signora cried. Assuntina looked at her. In that moment, both maid and mistress seemed extremely beautiful to Don Ciccio; the maid, harsher, had a severe, self-confident expression, a pair of steady, luminous eyes, two gems, a nose that made a straight line with the forehead: a Roman "virgin" of the age of Clelia; and the mistress, such a cordial manner, such a lofty tone, so nobly passionate, so melancholy! Her skin was enchanting. Looking at her guest, those deep eyes with a light of ancient nobility seemed to see, beyond the poor person of the "officer," all the poor dignity of a life! And she was rich, very rich, they said: her husband was well-off, traveled thirteen months the year, always tied up with those people up there in Vicenza. But she was even richer in her own right. To begin with, only real gents could afford to live in that huge building at number two hundred and nineteen: a few super high-class families, but above all people who were new to business, those who a few years ago had been called profiteers or "sharks."

And in the neighborhood the building itself was called by the poor people the palace of gold. Because it was as if the whole place right up to the roof were crammed with that precious metal. Inside, then, there were two staircases, A and B, with six floors and twelve tenants each, two per floor. But the triumph of it all was the third floor of stairway A, where on the one side lived the Balduccis, real class, and opposite the Balduccis there was a great lady, a Countess, also with a pile of money, a widow with a hard name to pronounce, Signora Menecacci, *many cash,* you might say, wherever you touched her there was a cache of gold, pearls, diamonds, all the most valuable stuff there is. And thousand-lire notes like butterflies: because money isn't

9

safe in banks, you never know, and when you least expect it, they can catch on fire. So she had a dresser with a false bottom.

This, more or less, was the myth. The ears of Officer Ingravallo, which, under his crisp, black mop, rejoiced in a spring-like vitality, had seized it like that, in the air, like the ravings of ravens, or of Merulanian *merli*, after every whirring, from bough to bough of the spring. It was on every mouth, for that matter, and in every brain, one of those notions that become, thanks to a collective imagina-ion, compulsory, fixed ideas.

During the dinner Balducci had assumed, towards Gina, a paternal manner: "Ginetta, please, another drop of wine..." "Gina, fill the guest's glass ..." "Gina, an ashtray ..." like a good Papa; and she would answer promptly, "Yes, Uncle Remo." Signora Liliana then looked at her, content, almost with tenderness: as if she saw a flower, still closed, a little chilled by the dawn, now opening and shining before her eyes in the wonder of the daylight. The daylight was the male, baritonal voice of Balducci, the voice of the "father," and she, wife and bride of Papa, was therefore the Mamma. With great solicitude and a certain anxiety she followed the pretty hand of her still slightly hesitant ward in the act of pouring: glug, glug, golden Frascati, judging by the sound: the crystal decanter was heavy; the frail little arm seemed almost unable to hold it. Officer Ingravallo ate and drank soberly, as usual: but with a good appetite and a healthy thirst.

He didn't think, he didn't believe it opportune to think of asking anything, either about the new niece or the new maid. He tried to repress the admiration that Assunta aroused in him: a little like the strange fascination of the dazzling niece of the previous visit: a fascination, an authority wholly Latin and Sabellian, which made her well-suited to the ancient names, of ancient Latin warrior virgins or of not-reluctant wives once stolen by force at the Lupercal, with the suggestion of hills and vineyards and harsh palaces, and with rites and the Pope in his coach, with the fine torches of Sant'Agnese in Agone and Santa Maria Portae Paradisi on Candlemas Day, and the blessing of the candles: a sense of the air of serene and distant days in Frascati or the valley of the Tiber, taken from the girls drawn by Pinelli among Piranesi's ruins, when the ephemerides were heeded and the Church's calendars, and, in their vivid purple, all its high Princes. Like stupendous lobsters. The Princes of Holy Roman Apostolic Church. And in the center those eyes of Assunta's, that pride: as if she were denigrated by serving them at table. In the center . . . of the whole . . . Ptolemaic system; yes, Ptolemaic. In the center, meaning no offense, that terrific behind.

He had to repress, repress. Assisted in this harsh necessity by the noble melancholy of Signora Liliana: whose gaze seemed to dismiss mysteriously every improper phantom, establishing for their souls a harmonious discipline, like music, that is: a texture of imagined architectures over the ambiguous derogations of the senses.

He, Ingravallo, was very polite, he was even a kindly uncle, with little Gina; from her throat, still rather long beneath her braid, came that little voice composed of yes and no, like the few, lamenting notes of a clarinet. He ignored, he chose to ignore, Assunta, after the maccheroni, as is only right in a guest who, also, has good manners. Signora Liliana, from time to time, might have been thought to sigh. Ingravallo noted that two or three times, in a whisper, she had said Hm. When hearts heave a sigh, then sorrow is nigh, as the saying goes. A strange sadness seemed to fill her face in the moments when she wasn't speaking or wasn't looking at the others at the table. Was she in the grip of some idea, some worry? concealed behind the curtain of her smiles, her polite attentions? and her talk, not studied or contrived, but yet always very courteous, as she adorned her guest with it? At those sighs, that way of passing a dish, those glances that sometimes wandered sadly off and seemed to breach a space or a time, unreal, only sensed by her, Ingravallo seemed little by little to take notice, to divine respective indications not so much of a basic disposition but of a present state of the spirit, a growing disheartenment. And then, a casual word or two, from Balducci himself: that hearty husband, all business deals and hares, now chatting so noisily, thanks to generous Frascatian inspiration.

He thought he could guess: they have no children. "Et cetera et cetera," he had then added once, in speaking with his colleague Doctor Fumi, as if alluding to a well-known phenomenology, an experience that was clearly defined and in public domain. He knew Balducci as a hunter, and a lucky hunter. Hunter *in utroque*. In his heart of hearts Ingravallo reproached him for a certain masculine vulgarity, a way of bragging, of laughing a bit too loud though always kindly, a certain egoism or egotism, a bit like the common womanizer: and with such a wife! One would have said, if one had felt like fantasticating, that Balducci had not evaluated, had not penetrated all her beauty: all that was noble and recondite in her: and then . . . children had not come. As if because of a gamic incompatibility of their two spirits. Children descend from an ideal compenetration of the parents. But she loved him: he was the father in her image, the male and father, in virtue if not *in facto*, in possibility if not in act. He had been the possible father of hoped-for offspring. Of his fidelity, perhaps, she was not even sure: as for that, she felt that her unfulfilled maternity might justify some venatorial wandering of her husband, some curiosity, some extravagance of the male and possible father, desirous at every turn, like all males. "Try with another person!" What she would never have even dared imagine for herself (matrimony is a sacrament, one of the seven granted us by Our Lord), she didn't want, no, for him: even Don Corpi said it was a bad thing, on the part of a Christian husband: but after all . . . one must be patient in all things: prudent and patient. Don Lorenzo Corpi was a good soul whom one could trust completely. And "prudence" was one of the four cardinal virtues.

All this Ingravallo had partially sensed and partially filled out with some hints of Balducci's, or with these gentle "moments" of her sadness: and the name of Don Corpi, Don Lorenzo, Don Lorenzo Corpi often shone, too, in Signora Liliana's conversation. To hell with Don Lorenzo! One would have said that in every big man she venerated . . . an honorary father, a potential father, even in Don Lorenzo, yes, despite his black cassock, despite the sacramental incompatibility, of the two sacraments which were . . . divergent.

Even in Don Lorenzo. Who must have been something of a tower of strength, that mule. One of those men, to judge from certain remarks of hers, who have to stoop every time they go through a door. At least he must have had the δύναμις of a father. Don Ciccio was rather well-versed in such matters: a vivid intuition, and dating from his years of puberty: opened afterwards to all the demotic encounters of his race, "fertile in works and brave in arms" (to quote D'Annunzio): native genius rather than systematic course of reading. From the dense teeming of generations, from police station guard rooms, from Latium to Marsica, from Picenum to Sannium, or even to his own Molisan hill: hard mountains, hard heads, hard luck! And the holy, unremembering validity of the matrixes. Among his people, rich in children, he had been able to distinguish the facts of prolification from those of non-prolification. What began to amaze him, nonetheless, was that the reservoir of Balducci's nieces was brimming with such buxom or such sweet nieces: or at least, this present one was sweet, while the others simply stupendous. In the time that he had been seeing this couple, he had already met three or four. And there was another thing: once a niece was off the scene, it was as if she had died. She never came to the surface again. Like a consul or the president of a republic, when his term has expired.

Don Ciccio was about to glimpse the bottom of the last,

so-to-speak, chalice—an extra-dry white, five years old, now, from Cavalier Gabbioni Empedocle and Son, Albano Laziale, something to dream of even at the station, the wine, the glass, the father, son, and holy Lazio—when the burden of his private opinions on the affective (he even said erotic) concomitant causes of human events led him to consider, obviously, that a niece in such conditions wasn't an ordinary niece, a Luciana or an Adriana, who comes today to the city to stay with Auntie and Uncle, then goes away, then comes back, then telegraphs, then leaves, then reaches home, then sends a postcard with love and kisses, then is in town again from Viterbo or from Zagarolo because she has to see the dentist again, and so on and on.

"This here's a more mixed-up kind of a niece," he muttered to himself, with that white wine back in Porta Paradisi still tickling his *velum pendulum*. Yes, yes. Behind that noun "niece" there must be hidden a whole tangle . . . of threads, a cobweb of feelings, of the rarest and most . . . delicate nature. She. He. She, out of respect for him. He, out of regard for her. So she dug up this niece, after years: suffering and weeping at night, and during the day candles to Sant'Antonio in all the churches of Rome: and hopes, taking the cure at Salsomaggiore, and other cures at home, and examinations by Professor Beltramelli and Professor Macchioro. And with each new candle, a hope. And with each new hope, a new doctor.

She dug up this Gina, poor Ginetta! But before Ginetta the story had quite a different direction, a different flavor. A strange thing, indeed it is, thought Ingravallo.

Virginia! (her image was a flash of glory, a sudden

thunderbolt in the darkness): and before Virginia, that other one from Monteleone, what was her name? And the maids! Of course they flutter off like sparrows at the first rustling caprice: but the Balduccis, seriously! you might say, had a new one every month. A thought came to him, and a disrespectful word: it was the wine.

Signora Liliana, since she couldn't dish up any of her own . . . And so every year: the change of niece must have been, in her unconscious mind, a symbol, in place of the one she failed to dish up herself. As for his mother, who had had eight, the real child every new spring. Those born in May are children of August. "A good month!" Don Ciccio thought, "even for cats: the racket they make around here, some nights."

Year after year . . . a new niece: as if to symbolize, in her heart, the successive births. *"Jedes Jahr ein Kind, jedes Jahr ein Kind . . ."* that German used to sing to him in Anzio: the one who looked like a seal.

And he, he, the hunter (Ingravallo looked at him), what does he feel, what does he experience, inside, when the niece arrives in his house, the niece whose turn it is? What had he thought of the various . . . nieces?

For her, from the Tiber down, there, there beyond the crumbling castles, and after the blond vineyards, there was, on the hills and mountains, and in the brief plains of Italy, a kind of great fertile womb, two swollen Eustachian tubes, streaked with an abundance of granules, the granular and greasy, the happy caviar of the race. From time to time, from the great Ovary ripened follicles opened, like pomegranate seeds: and red grains, mad with amorous certitude, descended upon the city, to encounter the male

16

afflatus, the vitalizing impulse, that spermatic aura of which
the ovarists of the eighteenth century wrote their fantastic
treatise. And at Via Merulana two hundred and nineteen,
stairway A, third floor, the niece re-burgeoned, in the best
of cores, there, in the palace of gold.

The niece! The Alban niece, flower of the eternal Sabellian people. The afflatus of the predators. Yes. There was
no need to seize those Sabine women . . . so radically!
waiting for the night's mediation, the warm flesh of dawn.
The Alban women, nowadays, came down to the river-
banks on their own. And the river flowed on, and on, overcoming all din, to reach, at the sea's edge, the inexorable,
waiting eternity.

But what about him? Signor Balducci? What did he, the
hunter, think of the Alban niece, the Tiburtine?

The bell rang. Lulu raised hell again. Assunta had gone
to the door. After some discussion, in the other room, a
young man entered, dressed in a gray suit, not inelegantly
cut. He was made to take a seat. "Another cup, Tina, for
Signorino* Giuliano." He was introduced at once; he introduced himself: "Valdarena." "Ingravallo," grumbled Ingravallo, barely detaching himself from the chair, and
barely clasping, almost reluctantly, the hand which the
other man extended to him. "Signor Valdarena . . ." Liliana
said, dealing with the coffee, the cups. "A cousin of my
wife's, Balducci explained, ruddy-faced.

There was, painful as it is to admit, in Don Ciccio a
certain coldness, a kind of prickly jealousy towards the

* The title "signorino," now disappearing from Italian usage, was
given—usually by the women of the family—to unmarried men, young
or old. The word, when used by Ingravallo, has a slightly contemptuous
nuance.

young, especially towards handsome young men, and even more so, the sons of the rich. This sentiment, for that matter, did not go beyond the admissible limits of an internal phenomenon, it would never have influenced his behavior as a police officer; he, no, he was not "handsome"; and he wasn't even able to console himself with that proverb he had heard in Milan from a girl at the prophylactic dispensary in Via delle Oche: "Real men are always goodlookers."

He felt already, in his heart, a dismay, a voice, *una voce poco fa* . . . which already whispered in the cells, he himself couldn't have said whether in the cells of the brain or of the heart, but perhaps it was the effect of the dry white of Signor Gabbioni and his son, a rather nervous wine, a voice that was trumpeting awfully: "This is her boyfriend," like the fierce tom-tom of those headaches which used to grip his temples.

He didn't know why, but he thought, or he imagined, that the young man was one of those boys who wants to get ahead at any price: he too: the kind who are rather "attached," that is to say, seduced by the idea of the old cash, which for that matter, say what you will, doesn't do anybody any harm. Coming in, the signorino had eyed the furniture and the knickknacks, the fine cups, and the silver pitcher, and that silver sugar bowl, remnant of the old Umbertine glitter, a souvenir of the seven fat kine, with a gold acorn and two little silver leaves on the lid. Yes: to pick it up with. He had accepted a fingered cigarette from Balducci (who opened the gold cigarette case under his chin with a sharp click): and he was smoking it, now, with a kind of restrained voluptuousness and, at the same time, with an elegant naturalness.

Ingravallo was then seized by a strange idea, as if he had drunk poison, it was Gabbioni's dry wine: he had the idea that this "cousin" was paying court to the Signora Liliana in order to . . . yes, of course! . . to win financial favors from her. The thought infuriated him: with a secret, dissimulated fury, a suspicion, naturally. A treacherous suspicion, however . . . which made his temples ache, a suspicion of the most ingravallian, most donciccian nature.

On the right ring-finger, on the white hand with the long, gentlemanly fingers, which he used to shake his cigarette, the young man had a ring: of old gold, very yellow, magnificent: a bloodstone mounted on it: an oval bloodstone with an initial carved in it. Perhaps the family seal. It seemed, to Don Ciccio, behind the veil of words and politeness, that there was some coldness between him and Balducci . . . "Giuliano is all eyes, all full of attentions towards his lady cousin," Ingravallo thought, "gentleman though he is." After a dutiful handshake, he hadn't even glanced at Gina. He gave the dog only a casual pat: and instead of its angry yip! yip!, the nasty thing, she shifted to some sinking growls, like a little storm, retreating, and finally she was quiet.

Signora Liliana, though with some badly repressed sighs (on certain days) under the shifting clouds of sadness, was . . . was a desirable woman: everyone noticed her looks, as she walked along the street. At dusk, in that first abandon of the Roman night, so crammed with dreams, as she came home . . . there, from the corners of the buildings, from the sidewalks, tributes, individual or collective, blossomed in her direction, glances: flashes and shining youthful looks: at times a whisper grazed her: like a passionate murmur of the evening. Sometimes, in October, from that changing of colors, from the warmth of the walls there emanated an improvised pursuer, a Hermes with brief wings of mystery: or perhaps from strange cemeterial Erebuses, risen again to the living, to the city. One more brassy than the others. And more of a dope . . . Rome is Rome. And she seemed to feel sorry for the ass, so gloriously driven after his fortune by those great sails of ears; with a glance, half-disdainful, half-pitying, between gratitude and scorn, she seemed to ask him: "Well?" A woman who seemed veiled to the desiring, her timbre sweet and profound, her skin stupendous: lost, at times, in some private dream: with a knot of handsome chestnut hair which burst from her brow; she dressed in admirable style . . . She had ardent eyes, helpful, almost, in a light (or with a shade?) of melancholy fraternity . . . At Assunta's sing-song, somewhat boorish announcement, "It's Signorino Giuliano," it seemed, to Ingravallo, that she had given a little start, or blushed even: with a "subcutaneous" flush. Imperceptibly.

When the two policemen said to him: "There's been a shooting in Via Merulana, at number two hundred and nineteen: on the stairs, where the sharks live . . ." a jet of curious blood, anguished perhaps, flooded his right ventricle. "Two hundred and nineteen?" he couldn't help asking, though in an absent tone. And he relapsed at once into that kind of remote somnolence which, in him, was also his official's mask. Meanwhile the chief of the investigations squad had come into his room. He carried his *Messaggero*, still unsavored, and a petal, a single white petal, in his buttonhole. "Almond blossom," Ingravallo thought, questioning his superior with his eyes, "The first of the season. So now he can even afford flowers, eh?" "Will you go over to Via Merulana, Ingravallo? Take a look. It's nothing much, they tell me. And this morning, with that other business of the Marchesa in Viale Liegi . . . and then the mess here in the neighborhood, in Via Botteghe Oscure; and then that other nice little bunch of posies, the two sisters-in-law and the three nephews; and on top of it all, we have to straighten out our own business, and then, and then . . ." he put this hand to his forehead, "all we needed was the Under Secretary on our back. I'm fed up to here, I tell you. So do me a favor, eh? and go on over."

"All right, I'll go," Ingravallo said, then muttered, "I'll go," and he took his hat down from the peg. The badly fitted peg came loose and fell to the floor, as it did every time, then rolled for a bit. He picked it up, stuck its withered root into the hole, and with the sleeve of his forearm, as if it were a brush, briefly smoothed his black hat, along the band. The two policemen went after him, as if by tacit command of the chief commissioner; they were Gaudenzio, known to the underworld as "Blondie," and Pompeo, alias "Grabber."

They took the PV bus* and got off at the Viminal, then changed to the tram for San Giovanni. So in twenty minutes or so they were at number two hundred and nineteen.

The palace of gold, or of the sharks, if you prefer, was there: five floors plus mezzanine. Worm-eaten and gray. To judge by that grim dwelling and its cohort of windows, the sharks must have been a myriad: little sharks with yawning stomachs, that's for sure, but easily satisfied esthetically. Living underwater on appetites and phagic sensations in general, the grayness, the lofty opalescence of the day was light, for them: that little bit of light which was all they needed. As to the gold, well, yes, maybe it did have gold and silver. One of those big buildings constructed at the beginning of the century which fill you at first sight with a sense of boredom and canarified contrition: you know, the precise opposite of the color of Rome, of the sky and the gleaming sun of Rome. Ingravallo, you might say, knew it by heart: and in fact, a slight palpitation seized him, as with the two policemen he approached the familiar structure, in his official, investigative role.

In front of the big, louse-colored building: a crowd: circumfused by a protective net of bicycles. Women, shopping bags, and celery stalks: a shopkeeper or two from across the street, in his white apron: an "odd job" man, also in an apron, striped, his nose the shape and color of

* The initials PV and BM—which will be encountered later on— are indications of various bus lines in the Rome of 1927.

a wondrous pepper: concierges, maids, the little daughters of the concierges shouting "Peppiiino!" to boys with hoops, a batman saturated with oranges, trapped in his great net bag, and crowned by the ferns of two big fennels, and packages: two or three important officials, who in that hour ripe for the higher ranks seemed to have unfurled their sails: bound, each of them, for his personal Ministry: and a dozen or even fifteen idlers, headed in no direction at all. A letter carrier in a state of advanced pregnancy, more curious than all, with his brimming bag which smacked everyone in the ass: some muttered goddamnit, and then goddamn, goddamn, one after the other, as the bag struck them, in turn, on the behind. A gamin, with Tiberine seriousness, said: "This building here, inside it, there's more gold than there is garbage." All around, the stripe of the bicycle wheels, like a *sui generis* skin, seemed to render impenetrable that collective pulp.

Assisted and virtually preceded by his two men, Ingravallo cleared a path for himself. "The cops," somebody said. "Hey, kid, make way for old Grabber . . . Hi, Pompeo! Did you catch the thief? . . . Now here comes Blondie . . ." The door to the building was ajar, guarded by a corporal from the San Giovanni Station. The concierge had seen him pass and had called on him for help: shortly after the event and just before the arrival of the two men of the squad, that is to say Gaudenzio and Pompeo. She had known the corporal for ages, because of the reports she had to turn in on the tenants' moves. The deed had been done an hour before, a little after ten: an incredible hour! In the entrance hall and in the porter's lodge there was another little crowd, tenants of the building: the women's chatter. Ingravallo, followed by the concierge herself and by the other two, as well as by the comments of all, "the cops, the cops," climbed up to the third floor, stairway A, where the robbed woman lived. Below, the great chattering continued: the unleashed, fluted voices of the females, emulated by an occasional masculine trombone, which from time to time even drowned them out: like the cows' bent cervixes by the bull's great horns: the crowd's mind gathered the clover of the initial eyewitness accounts, of the "I swear I saw him's"; began to weave them into an epic. It was a robbery, or to be more precise, a case of breaking and entering, *manu armata*.

It was a rather serious affair, to tell the truth. Signora Menegazzi, a moment after her fright, had fainted. Signora Liliana had "felt unwell" in her turn, as soon as she came out of the bath. Don Ciccio collected and transcribed then and there what he could skim from the explosive jet of this first account: he began with the concierge, granting Signora Menegazzi time to comb her hair and deck herself out a bit: in his honor, one would have said. He had paper and fountain pen, and omitted the *"Gesù, Gesù,* officer dear . . ."* and the other interjections-invocations with which the "signora" Manuela Pettacchioni did not fail to flavor her report: a dramatic tale. Her porter-husband, a doorman at the Fontanelli Milk Company, wouldn't be home until six.

"Gesummaria! First he rang Signora Liliana's bell . . ." "Who did?" "Why, the murderer . . ." "What murderer are you talking about, since there's nobody killed . . .?" Signora

Liliana (Ingravallo shuddered), alone in the house, hadn't gone to the door. "She was in the bathroom . . . yes . . . she was taking a bath." Don Ciccio, involuntarily, passed a hand over his eyes, as if to shield them from a sudden, too-dazzling brightness. The maid, Assunta, had left a few days earlier for her home: her father was sick, as maids' fathers often are, "especially the way things are nowadays." Gina was at school all day, at the Sacred Heart, at the sisters'; where she had lunch and sometimes even a snack. So, "you see," nobody answered, "it's obvious, of course" then that the criminal rang at Signora Menegazzi's door; yes, right there, on the same landing, just opposite the Balduccis': the door facing, there. Oh! Don Ciccio knew that landing well, and that other door!

La Menegazzi, her hair arranged, came on stage again, with a faint cough. A great lilac scarf around her neck which, at the front, seemed scrawny and withered: a languid tone in all her traumatized person. A rather unexpected negligee, a mixture of Japanese and Madrileno, a cross between a mantilla and a kimono. A bluish mustache on her rather faded face, her skin pale, like a floured gecko, her lips made of two hearts, joined, enamelled in a strawberry red of the most provocative shade, gave her the appearance and the momentary formal prestige of an ex-madam or ex-habituée of some brothel, now a little come down in the world: if, on the other hand, that neo-virginal, stern touch, and the devotion-solicitude typical of the *virgo intacta* hadn't placed her, beyond precautionary suspicion, in the romantic roster of the nubile, as well as of the respectable. She was, in fact, a widow. The mantilla-bathrobe overlapped the foulard, or rather foulards, not one but two, also powdered and vaguely modulated in their hues, so that the first merged into the second, and the second into the delicate petals— or perhaps butterflies—of that somewhat Castilian kimono. She superimposed her report on that of the concierge, straightening out, correcting. She spoke up, a tremor in her voice, her poor voice, a hope in her eyes. Not perhaps the hope of seeing her gold objects again, but the certainty . . . of the protection of the law, so validly personified by Ingravallo. On hearing the bell, Signora Menegazzi had let out her usual "Who is it?": she now repeated the tone, worried and whining, which she adopted every time the doorbell trilled. Then she had opened. The murderer was a tall young man in a cap, a mechanic's gray overall, or at least so it seemed to her, his face dark, with a greenish-brown woolen scarf. A handsome boy, yes, a good-looking sort. But somehow he immediately made you feel afraid. "What was the cap like?" Don Ciccio asked, writing the while. "It was . . . why, to tell you the truth, officer, I don't quite . . . I can't quite remember what it was like. I wouldn't know what to tell you." "And you?" he said to the concierge: "When he ran off, ran right past your eyes? Didn't you see? Can't you tell me what it looked like, this cap? . . ."

"Why, officer dear, . . . I was that upset! How could I think about caps, at a time like that? You see . . . Now tell me yourself, frankly: when they start firing all these bullets, do you think a lady notices a cap? . . ."

"Was he alone?" "Oh, yes, alone, alone," the two women said, in unison. "Oh, officer," la Menegazzi implored, "you must help us, you who can help us. For pity's sake. *Maria*

Vergine! A widow! Alone in the house! *Maria Vergine*! What a nasty world we live in! These aren't men, they're devils! Ugly devils that come back from hell . . ."

La Menegazzi, like all women alone in the house, spent her hours in a state of anguish or, rather, of suspicious and tormented expectancy. For some time her constant fear of the doorbell's ring had become intellectualized into a complex of images and obsessions: masked men, seen in close-up, with felt-soled shoes: sudden, and equally silent, intrusions into the hall; a hammer brought down hard on her head, or her throat clutched by hands or strangled with a length of string brought for the purpose, preceded perhaps by horrible torture: a notion—or a word—this last, which filled her with unspeakable emotion. Mixed anxieties and fantasies: to the accompaniment, perhaps, of a sudden palpitation of the heart, the sudden creak, in the darkness, of some cupboard, its wood more seasoned than the others: fantasies, in any case, greedily anticipating the event. Which, after so much insistence, couldn't fail, in the end, to arrive. The long wait for house-breaking and aggression, Ingravallo thought, had created a compulsion not so much for her, her actions and thoughts, a victim already marked down, but a compulsion for destiny, for destiny's "field of forces." The prefiguration of disasters must have evolved into a historic predisposition: it had acted: not only on the psyche of the woman to be robbed-strangled-tortured, but also on the "field" of atmosphere, on the field of the external psychic tensions. Because Ingravallo, like certain of our philosophers, attributed a soul, indeed a lousy bastard of a soul, to that system of forces and probabilities which surrounds every human creature, and which is customarily called destiny. To put it simply, her great fear had brought bad luck to her, to Signora Menegazzi. Her dominating thought, at every trill, used to coagulate in that "Who is it?", a bleat or bray habitual in every female recluse whose *lares* are too weak to protect her. In her it was a moaning antiphony to the ring itself, to the doorbell's most domestic requests.

It turned out that the young man, as soon as Signora Teresina resolved to take off the chain and open up, had said he was sent by the management of the building to check the radiators, which he was to inspect one by one. In fact, some days before, there had been an argument over the radiators because, at centrally heated winter's official end, they were more tepid (towards the cold) than the tenants' desire to spend money.

The flame of all heating equipment, in Rome, was extinguished on the Ides of March, at times it was the Nones instead, or indeed, even the Kalends. During double winters with prolonged epilogues, as was the winter of Twenty-seven, the flame was fed for the whole month, then it was allowed to waste away in a prolonged languor not without discussion and diatribe among the opinionated tenants, vociferous in proportion to the event: among pros and cons, the penniless and the wealthy, the stingy careful ones and the carefree, urinators in hope and glory. As to the rooms on the upper floors of two hundred and nineteen, they could be numbered, beyond any doubt, among the most Romanly sunny of all Rome: for which reason, since in that early spring it was snowy-raining, the inhabitants quaked with cold.

The mechanic had with him neither bag nor sack: the implements of his position for the moment were not required. It was merely an inspection. The Signora Teresina added—but this Don Ciccio did not write down—that she was sure that young man . . . yes, the murderer, the mechanic . . . she was sure, and could have sworn it in court, was sure that the boy had hypnotized her (Don Ciccio stood there and listened, his mouth agape, with a sleepy manner) because at a certain point, while they were still in the vestibule, he had stared at her. "Stared!" she repeated, almost declaiming, enthusiastic at the stern fixity of that gaze: "his eyes were merciless, steady and hard," from beneath his cap, "like a snake's." And she had, then, felt her strength fail her. She told how, indeed, at that moment, whatever the young man had asked or commanded, at that point she would have done it, would have unquestionably obeyed him: "like a robot" (her very words).

"Maria Vergine! Hypnotized! That's what I was . . ." Don Ciccio, in his thoughts, couldn't help editorializing: "These women!"

And so it happened that he, the mechanic, was able to go all over the apartment. In the bedroom, glimpsing some gold objects on the dresser, on its marble top, he had scooped them up with one movement of his hand, opened with his other hand beneath it, like a bucket, the large pocket at his disposal, over his hip, in the overall.

"What are you up to?" la Menegazzi had screeched at him, not totally helpless despite her hypnotic condition. He, turning, had aimed a pistol at her face: "Shut up, you old witch, or I'll fry you to a crisp." Having taken the measure of her terror, he opened the drawer, the top one, where the key is . . . And he had guessed right. There was all her gold, her jewels: in a little leather coffer. There was the money. "How much?" Ingravallo asked. "I couldn't be absolutely sure. Four thousand six hundred, I think." The money in a man's wallet, dry and old: a memento of her poor husband. (Her eyes became damp.) And that boy, without a moment's hesitation, had already wrapped the coffer in a kind of dirty handkerchief, or maybe it was a rag, yes, it was, with a fever in his fingers: the wallet he had simply slipped into his pocket, so quickly! *Maria Vergine!* "In the pocket here . . ." and the signora slapped her hip with her hand.

"Devils. I don't know how they do it. The devils! Devils."

"Aw shut up," the young man had said to her in a grim, menacing voice, keeping his eye on her, his face almost touching hers. They looked like a tiger's, now, those eyes: the evil soul had seized its prey: he would have defended it at whatever cost. He sneaked away without any difficulty, like a shadow. "Keep quiet!": the terrible injunction. But instead, as soon as she had seen him go out, she had flung herself at the window, yes, that one, that very one, which looked down on the courtyard, and opening it, had shouted, shouted, the tenants said rather that she had screamed wildly: "Thief! Thief! Help! Stop him!" Then . . . She wanted to follow him at once, but she was taken ill, worse even than before. She had fallen, or thrown herself, on "her" bed: there. And she pointed it out.

Two hundred and nineteen, five floors plus the roof and the two stairways, A and B, with some offices on B, on the mezzanine: it was like a railroad station. The stairs, both of them easily climbable, and one darker than the other. Stairway A was a bit quieter than its counterpart: all real respectable on that side, *du côté de chez madame.*

From the combined and overlapping reports of the concierge and the other lady tenants more prompt in myth-making, whom Ingravallo questioned outside without writing anything down, and again later in the entrance hall below, behind the building's main door and at the little door, guarded first by the corporal, then by a policeman, one could finally reconstruct the event. And verify another circumstance, a fairly curious one, indeed. The delinquent had been boldly pursued. "Ah!" Ingravallo said. "Yes," too boldly perhaps. It seemed that in pursuing him, or pretending to pursue him, down the steps and into the hall, even before Signor Bottafavi of the fourth floor who had also chased him with a revolver, there had been first of all a young man, "yes, a young man." "No, not a young man, a kid . . ." What do you mean, a kid? He was this tall: he looked like a grocer's helper, with an apron all twisted around his waist, but he had sporty pants on, with heavy, long green stockings. "What! Green?" He had darted out, through the entrance, a little after they heard the two shots, two pistol shots on the stairs. And nobody had seen him afterwards. "Yes, I did! On the sidewalk! I was coming from Santa Maria Maggiore! He ran off . . ." The testimonial passion, striking fire in every soul, kindled an epos. All the women talked at once: a confusion of voices and sights: maids, mistresses, broccoli: enormous broccoli leaves came out of a crammed, swollen shopping bag. Shrill or infantile voices added denials or confirmations. All around, a little white poodle wagged its tail excitedly, and from time to time he barked too: as authoritatively as possible.

Ingravallo felt stifled, crushed by the tales and by their tellers.

After the shouts of the Signora Menegazzi, the two Bottafavis above, husband and wife, had come out on the landing in their slippers, also shouting, a lovely connubial soprano-baritone duet: "Thief! Thief!" Now they demanded suitable recognition of their courage, of their presence of mind. Bottafavi, indeed, with a big revolver, which he chose to display to Doctor Ingravallo, then to the others present: the women stepped back a pace: "Well, now don't start shooting at us!": the children craned their necks, lost in admiration. They had, from that moment on, a very high opinion of Signor Butt and Fiver, as they called him. He went on narrating, revolver in hand, but unloaded: barrel in the air. He re-created the events with great precision. At that moment, try as he might, he hadn't managed to fire it. Because the safety was on, a little pin in the seventh hole of the drum. And after so many years of that machine's absolute inactivity, he had forgotten that real revolvers—like his, precisely—had that damn safety! which, when it is down, prevents them from going off. So, at the height of things, the thief had slipped away, full tilt. "But didn't you fire two shots?" Ingravallo asked. "Why, officer, you think I'm some crazy kid? . . . Shooting for the fun of it like that?" "But you tried." "Tried. Tried is one thing. My revolver isn't the same as the kind crooks have . . . The ones that really shoot. This revolver here, officer, is a gentleman's weapon. I . . . I was a bonded guard when I was a youngster: and I think I know how to handle a gun better than the next fellow. I . . . I'm in full control of my nerves . . ." The thief had got away. By a hairsbreadth: "But next time he won't make it."

"And what about the boy?" "What boy?" "The grocer's boy," the women said. "Didn't you hear what these ladies said? They've been talking about it for an hour . . ." Ingravallo said. "Well, I don't have much to do with grocers: for things like that . . . that's the wife's department," the man answered self-importantly. Grocer's apprentices, obviously, couldn't compete with his revolver. No, he hadn't seen any boy, grocer's or other tradesmen's, butcher's or baker's.

And yet Signora Manuela had seen him, clear as day, running out of the entrance, after the thief. "No, no!" Signora Bottafavi said, supporting her husband. "No?! No, my foot, Signora Teresa dearie, you think I don't have eyes in my head? . . . Fine thing that would be . . . with all the comings and goings in this building . . ." Professoressa Bertola contradicted the Bottafavis' denial and, at the same time, corrected the affirmation of the concierge. She was just coming home. On Wednesdays she taught only one class, from eight to nine. She was just turning into the entrance when she saw coming out—and was almost run into by—that frightened seraph with an unbelievable shock of hair: his face distraught, his lips white . . . his lips were trembling, she was sure of that. She had lost sight of him because, immediately thereafter, she saw "that wicked young man" come out, the mechanic in the gray overall,

33

but it was a rather special overall, quite swollen, and with a package: "in other words, the murderer in person . . ." "And what sort of cap was he wearing?" Ingravallo asked. "His cap . . . why, to tell you the truth . . . the cap . . ." "What was it like? Tell us." "I really wouldn't know, officer." A moment before, yes, oh yes, she had heard the two shots: two thuds, which came out of the main door.

Now it was the concierge's turn to speak up again. The two shots, yes, first of all the two shots . . . everybody agreed on them. Then she had seen a kind of gray streak in the hall, a mouse scurrying off . . . "He looked like a mouse when they run off, when I chase them with my broom . . ." And then, after him, the grocer's boy. She could swear to it. When the boy went past, all in white, except for his pants, of course, well, the murderer had already gone by. The shots? Yes, of course . . . A moment before that son of a . . . had fired two shots. Still on the stairs, where they had resounded like two bombs. "Boom! Boom!" I tell you, doctor dear, I started having palpitations . . ."

The Professoressa chose to answer back. A row flared up between the two women. Signora Liliana, in the meanwhile, hadn't appeared: and Don Ciccio was happy about it: she! mixed up in a business of this sort!

He felt it was pointless to waste time trying to look for the projectiles, or the mark of the projectiles. Whether it was a Beretta 6.5 or an ordnance Glisenti 7.65 mattered little to him: it's quick work getting a pistol out of sight for a while. He knew this from past experience: all you have to do is entrust it to a partner, a friend.

He dismissed the tenants, male and female, maids and

shopping bags; without noticing, he stepped on the poodle's paw, and the beast unleashed a yelping that the Pope must have heard over in the Vatican. He ordered the main door closed, leaving a guard at the smaller door, the policeman who had taken over from the corporal. He went up, for another brief inspection, to the Menegazzi apartment; Pompeo, who was with him, followed; Gaudenzio hadn't even come down. He asked and looked to see if there were traces or, better, fingerprints of the murderer. The handles, the dresser's marble top, the waxed floor.

Signora Liliana finally appeared, very beautiful; she said she could make no guesses; she found kindly words for Signora Menegazzi and offered her hospitality. She confirmed, on being asked, that a short time before the two pistol shots, he had also rung her doorbell—quite timidly, for that matter. She was in the bath, and hadn't been able to open the door; perhaps she wouldn't have opened it in any case. In those days the newspapers had been talking a great deal about the "murky" crime in Via Valadier, then of that other one, even more "heinous," in Via Montebello. She couldn't dispel from her mind what she had read. And then . . . a woman alone . . . is always a little afraid of opening the door. She took her leave. Only then did Ingravallo think of his pea-green tie (the one with little black clovers and a quincunx pattern), and his Molisan beard, thirty-six or thirty-eight hours old. But the vision had filled him with bliss.

He asked again widow Menegazzi if, after sober reflection, she had an idea, a suspicion about anyone at all. Couldn't she furnish some clue? People who knew the

house? Acquainted with her habits and with the layout—
they had to be that, certainly, when you think of their self-
confidence. He asked again if there were any traces . . .
prints or whatever . . . of the murderer. (This term invented
by the myth-making crowd had by now settled also in his
ears, and forced his tongue to repeat the same error.) No,
not a trace.

Pompeo and Gaudenzio were made to move the dresser.
Dust. A yellow straw from a broom. A bluish ticket, slightly
crumpled, from a tram. He bent over, picked it up, and
unfolded it very carefully, his moonface bent over this
nullity: it seemed worn, almost. Tramways of the Castelli,
the suburban lines. Punched on the date of the preceding
day. Punched apparently (it was torn) at the station of . . .
of . . . "Tor . . . Tor . . . Goddamnit! The stop before . . .
Due Santi." "It must be Torraccio," Gaudenzio then said,
stretching his neck behind Don Ciccio's shoulder. "Is it
yours?" Don Ciccio asked the terrified Menegazzi. "No,
sir, it's not mine." No, she had had no visitors, the day
before. The maid, Cencia, a slightly hunchbacked little old
woman, came only part time, at two in the afternoon: to her
great disappointment: (her, that is, la Menegazzi's). And
therefore she herself straightened up her bedroom, since
. . . her poor nerves, ah! doctor! It was already in order,
in fact, when, suddenly breaking the silence "that terrible
bell" had unexpectedly made itself heard. And besides, in
her bedroom, *Maria Vergine!* how could they possibly
think—? In that sanctum of memories, no, no, she never
received anyone, never, absolutely no one.

Don Ciccio could believe this easily, but she had a tone

and a *"Maria Vergine,"* as if admitting that she could be suspected of the opposite. No, the maid wasn't from Marino, wasn't from any of the Castelli Romani . . . She lived, since time immemorial, in one of the most mangy hovels in Via de' Querceti, halfway along the street, under the behind of the Santi Quattro, with a sister, a twin, a little smaller than she, just a tiny tiny bit. For the rest, he must believe her, they were very pious women. Cencia had a weakness for sugar, true enough, and coffee, too, very sweet. But touch anything . . . no, no, she would never touch a thing without asking. She suffered from chilblains, on her feet and hands, oh yes; there were times when she couldn't wash the dishes, because they burned her so, her hands; she suffered very much, yes, that she did. But not this winter, no, bad as it had been, no sir; the winter before. Very, very pious; kept her rosary in her hand all day long: with a special devotion to San Giuseppe. Don Corpi, too, could furnish information, Don Lorenzo—you don't know him? . . . Ah, a sainted man, that he was: from Santi Quattro Incoronati; yes, because Cencia went to confession to him: at times she did some cleaning for him, lending a hand to Rosa, the titular handmaiden of the rectory.

Ingravallo had listened to all this with his mouth open. "Well? What about this ticket then? This ticket? Who can have left it here? Tell me. The murderer? . . ." La Menegazzi seemed to repel the diligence and the pertinacity of the questioning, unwilling to assume the burden of reflecting: all timid, all dewy with belated hope, in the dream and in the charism of the, alas, barely grazed, not experienced torturings. A polychromatic giddiness wafted from her lilac-colored foulards, her azure mustache, the kimono which was a warbling of little birds (they weren't petals after all, but strange winged creatures somewhere between birds and butterflies), from her hair which was yellowish with a tendency towards a disheveled Titian, from the violet ribbon that gathered it into a kind of bouquet of glory: above the vagotonic sagging of the epigastrium and of the faded face, and the sighs of the alas, avoided, brutalization of her body but not avoided robberization of her gold. She didn't want to reflect, she didn't want to remember: or rather she would have preferred to remember what had carefully not taken place. Her fear, her "disaster" had unhinged her brain, that modicum of her person that could be called brain. She was forty-nine years old, though she looked fifty. The misfortune had come in double form: for her gold, that exceptional appraisal . . . unequivocal in its judgment; for her, that title of *old witch*, and the barrel . . . of the pistol. "There was a time when you weren't such a scoundrel," she was inclined to think: of her guardian angel. No, she didn't know, she didn't want to: she was beside herself; she couldn't concentrate. But the one who still obliged her to speak was Ingravallo, as you might take some good tongs to pick up an ember which sizzles and pops and smokes and makes you cry. Until she ended, exhausted, by confirming that the boy, yes, that criminal, had taken the pistol from his pocket or wherever he had it, yes, right there, in front of the dresser, then that dirty handkerchief, or a mechanic's rag, perhaps, to wrap up the leather case . . . the jewel box, when he had taken it out of the drawer. With the pistol something else had come out, like a handkerchief, something crumpled, paper, probably. Oh no, she couldn't remember; the fright had been too much for her, *Maria Vergine!*; remember? . . . Papers? That boy, yes, it was likely enough, had bent over to pick them up. She could see the scene again confusedly: to pick up what? The handkerchief? . . . if it was a handkerchief. How can a person remember . . . so many details . . . when a person is so frightened?

Doctor Ingravallo settled the ticket in a wallet, went downstairs again, after barely fifteen minutes had elapsed. The stairs were dark. From below, the hall was light: even with the main door closed as it was, the hall received light from a window on the courtyard. Gaudenzio and Pompeo followed him. He looked for the concierge again; she was there, squabbling with somebody.

Since ninety per cent of the tenants, male and female, had withdrawn at his invitation, but only a few steps away, and with their ears pricked up, it wasn't difficult for him to extend his inquiry with a supplementary investigation concerning the mysterious grocer's boy, tacitly reassembling there in the hall the previously dismissed group or clump of humans and vegetables from which he was to press information about the events and, possibly, clarification of the person involved. It turned out that no tenant of the building, whether from stairway A or B, had received anything or was to receive anything, that morning, from any grocer of the capital. Nobody had opened a door to a boy with a white apron, at that hour. "It was all staged," a lady, friend of Signora Bottafavi, then suggested, though she was no friend of la Menegazzi and lived on the fifth floor. "You know, when one of them goes to rob a place, there's always another one outside to keep watch . . . The two of them . . . now you take it from me, doctor . . . the two were in cahoots . . ."

"Don't you ever see delivery boys in this building?" Ingravallo asked, in a tone of conscious authority and, also, annoyance. He drew back his eyelids, breaking his habitual tedium and heaviness: his eyes then received a light, a penetrating certainty. "Of course," la Pettacchioni then said, "why this building is like the Central Station . . . The highest type of people live here, people in trade, sir." The others all smiled: "the kind who don't like to eat just any old greens." "Then who did they deliver to? Don't you remember? . . . Who brought the fresh mozzarella to their doors?" "Oh well, sir, they came more or less for everybody . . ." she bowed her head and put her left index finger to the corner of her mouth: "just let me have a think." Now all of them were mentally groping for boys bringing mozzarella: a sudden fervor of hypotheses, arguments, memories: wicker baskets and white aprons. "Yes . . . Signor Filippo here," she sought him, with a glance: and as if she were introducing him: "Commendatore Angeloni, of the Ministry of National Economy," and she pointed him out, in the group. The others then moved aside and the designated man bowed slightly: "Commendatore Angeloni," he then ventured, on his own. "Ingravallo," Ingravallo said, who so far hadn't even been made a cavaliere, touching the brim of his hat with two fingers. The homage due the National Economy.

Signor Filippo, tall, dark of overcoat, with his belly somewhat pear-shaped, and his shoulders hunched and sloping slightly, his face between frightened and . . . and melancholy, and in its midst a big, rudder-like priest's or fish's nose, which could sound the great trump of the Last Judgment, if you blew on it—that was how it looked—though commendatorial and ministerial, yes; but in particular there was a something . . . a sadness, an insecurity, and with it also a kind of reticence in his eyes, as he looked at the officer, Officer Ingravallo, almost as if afraid of losing his berth . . . the next time the Ministry fell: which was not to fall, on the other hand, until Forty-three, the 25th of July. A strange old crow, my God, all bundled up, inside those lapels and that elegiac scarf: a Ministering cleric from that group of very black ones that nest, by preference, between San Luigi de' Francesi and the Minerva. Unnoticed by the absent-minded or hurrying passer-by, one foot after the other in the easy hour of the day they are used to stroll over their beloved little side streets, from the arch of Sant'Agostino and Via della Scrofa, along Via delle Coppelle or the Pozzo delle Cornacchie, up to Santa Maria in Aquiro. On rare occasions they venture, very slowly, along Via Colonna and enter, agoraphobes all, the cobbled Piazza di Pietra, disdaining the half-liter and the snobbish pizzeria of the Neapolitan: and then from that alleyway of Via di Pietra they may even reach the Corso, but it has to be Holy Saturday, at the very least, opposite the Enciclopedia Treccani, to the most inviting clocks and watches of Catellani, the jeweler. In Lent or low Sundays, mourning and flabby, they are content to flank Santa Chiara, under the globes of the two hotels, up to the elephant and his graceful obelisk, past the shopwindows of rosaries and Madonnas: very slowly, or else: equally slowly, they go back: a bicycle grazing them, they turn into the Palombella and hug the back of the Pantheon, by now, however, retracing their steps as if a bit disappointed by the dusk.

Commendatore Angeloni had moved to Via Merulana some years ago, after the demolitions in Via del Parlamento and Campo Marzio, where he had lived since time immemorial. He must have been a gourmet, judging at least by the little packages, the truffles . . . Packages which, as a rule, he delivered to himself, with great concern and all due respect, holding them horizontally and on his chest, as if he were nursing them: the kind of package from de luxe grocers, filled with galatine or *pâté* and tied with a little blue cord. And sometimes, for that matter, they also delivered them to his house, at two hundred and nineteen, at the very top; they "handed" them to him, as the Florentines would say. (Little artichokes in oil. Tunnied veal.)

"Signor Filippo here," Signora Manuela repeated. "Well, sometimes you've had one come, a boy with packages, and a white apron. I've never looked him in the face, so I couldn't come right out and describe him. But now that I think of it, the one this morning could have been yours, more or less. One evening, when I ran after him, he yelled down the stairs that he was going to your house, said he had to deliver some ham."

All eyes were trained on Commendatore Angeloni. The object of this attention became confused.

"Me? Grocery boys? . . . What ham?"

"Why, commendatore dear," Signora Manuela implored, "you wouldn't make me look like a liar, would you, telling me it isn't true in front of the officer here? . . . After all, you live alone . . ."

"Alone?" Signor Filippo rebutted, as if living alone were a sin.

"Well, is there anybody up there with you? Not even a cat . . ."

"What do you mean by saying I'm alone?"

"I mean that if somebody delivers food to your house, when it rains, or in the evening . . . well, it can happen, can't it? Can't it? . . . Am I right?" Her tone was conciliating, as if she had winked at him to say: what kind of mess are you getting me into, you fathead?

And apparently, it *was* a mess. Signor Filippo's embarrassment was obvious: that stammering, that sudden pallor: those glances so filled with uncertainty, even with anguish. Interest and suspense gripped them all: all the tenants looked at him agape: at him, at the concierge, at the officer.

The only sure thing, Ingravallo said to himself, was that the concierge hadn't seen the delivery boy's face this time, either: if he had been a delivery boy. She had seen his heels and also his . . . shall we say his back? That much, yes . . . Professoressa Bertola, now, she had seen his face: it was white, with white lips: but she hadn't seen him the other times. So she had nothing to say either.

The murderer, too . . . Signora Manuela had to admit finally that she wouldn't be able to recognize him again. No. She had never seen him before. Never. Like a thunderbolt it was!

And the two revolver shots, in that darkness of the stairs, hah, God only knows where they ended up.

Officer Ingravallo cut it short. He invited to the police station Signora Manuela Pettacchioni, concierge, and the Signora Teresina Menegazzi née Zabala, where clerks could type up and the ladies could sign further, if there were further, statements: the second of the above-named, in particular, had to make an official charge. The damages were rather great: the case was serious enough. It was a question of aggravated burglary, and for a value, if not a sum, fairly impressive in its total: about thirty thousand lire, more or less, between the gold things and the jewels (a strand of pearls, a large topaz, among others); and roughly four thousand seven hundred in cash, in the old wallet. "The wallet of my poor Egidio," la Menegazzi sobbed, on hearing herself summoned.

Commendatore Angeloni was asked, with all proper respect, to remain at the police's disposal, for further clarifications. Another nice euphemism. "Remain at disposal," meant, in effect, accompanying Don Ciccio on the various seesaw of trams and buses as far as the Santo Stefano del Cacco Station. In addition Signor Filippo had to skip his lunch.

"I'm afraid I couldn't, thank you," he said sadly to Pompeo, who suggested he break his nervous waiting with a healthy pair of sandwiches. "I haven't any appetite; this is the wrong moment." "Whatever you say, Commendatore. In any case, when you feel like it, Peppino Er Maccheronaro has a place here in Via del Gesù that really fills the bill. He knows all of us; we're good customers. Rare roast beef; that's Peppino's speciality." Signora Manuela, once she had completed, on Don Ciccio's desk, that horrible and interminable tangle that was her respected signature, Manuela Pettacchioni crossed the dim antechamber and decided to take her leave also of the bundled-up dignitary. She gave him a jovial greeting, loud and woman-of-the-people as ever: "Ta-ta for now, Commendatore . . ." And everyone stared at him. "Stiff upper lip, eh? There's nothing to it . . . and it's over before you know it." And she went out to catch the PV-1, all in a rush, wiggling her ass like a quail and clicking in perilous equilibrium on the heels of her good shoes which were like trampolenes, like an old sow on her trotters. "With all the mess he's in today, he won't feel much like eating artichokes . . . He won't even eat a crust, poor Signor Filippo . . . Santo Stefano del Cacco, of all places to end up. That's a place to keep away from!"

The Commendatore couldn't calm down. That tick-tock of the awful clock in the room, from one tick to the next, had hollowed the sockets of his eyes: he looked as if he had been dug up from his grave. He was questioned, in the early afternoon, by Ingravallo himself, who alternated blandishments and courtesy with rather heavier phases, falling victim, at times, to that "office torpor" which so usefully weighted his eyelids. Moments of vivacity and irony: bursts of what seemed sudden impatience: boredom, as if the red tape were stifling him: harsh parentheses. Deviti—Gaudenzio, that is—who was unobtrusively present throughout the interview at a little table in the corner, his head on the day's sheaf of documents, later told how, at the first bars of this duet, the harassed, intimidated Angeloni promptly and completely lost his bearings. It's a thing that happens to respectable people, to serious gentlemen, or to those who

45

obstinately make a show of being such, in certain situations which are not adapted to them. An incredible anguish seemed to have overwhelmed the Commendatore. It ended with him blowing his nose, red-eyed: he trumpeted like a widow. He insisted he knew nothing, thought nothing, could imagine nothing, concerning that shop assistant. He insisted painfully, against all normal usage, on that term "shop assistant." The more Ingravallo fell back on a folkloristic tone, between the Tiber and his native Biferno, the more he taunted by saying "grocer's kid" or "delivery boy," the more the other man withdrew like a snail into the pompous shell of high-flown terminology: which, however, was competely out of place, in that atmosphere of generic police distrust, like jellied eels and artichokes in oil. Via Venti Settembre, with its ministries, its clerks, its doormen, must in that implacable hour have seemed to him a paradise more teetering than ever: a distant Olympus, ruled over by a Quirites Commendatore, indeed Grand 'Ufficiale, but alas, hardly likely to succor him. What? Farewell, the magic papers of the sweet bureaucratic inanity? Farewell, the comforting warmth of the Central Administration? The "considerable" increments in the graph of fishing . . . for sardines? The duty exemptions on pickling? The stormy, yet beloved grumbling of the Excise Office, the holy reverberation of the Superior Court? Farewell? Alone, seated on a bench in the station house, with upon him all the hairsplitting of the homicide squad (so he thought) which made his eyes brim. His poor face, the face of a poor man who wants people not to look at him, but with that schnozz in the middle which constantly prompted opinions, unexpressed, from every interlocutor, his face seemed, to Ingravallo, a mute and desperate protest against the inhumanity, the cruelty of all organized investigation.

At times in the past, yes, they had sent some ham to his house. Who? Who, indeed. A difficult question. No, he couldn't put a name to him. He didn't even remember, perhaps, after all this time. He . . . lived alone. He didn't have any regular tradesmen he dealt with. He bought things here and there: today from one, tomorrow from another. From all the shops in Rome, more or less. A little in each, you might say. At random, wherever he happened to be. When he noticed a bargain, or saw they had good things. Perhaps only some little pastry, often. Just to satisfy a whim . . . A bit of marinated herring, perhaps, or a spot of galantine. But more than anything, he blew his nose, some cans of tomato sauce to have a little stock at home. It's convenient to have some on hand. And the things were delivered, of course, by the assistants in the shops . . .

He shrugged, his eyebrows relaxed, as if to say: What could be more obvious?

"You once told the concierge" (Don Ciccio yawned) "that you had bought some nice lean ham in Via Panisperna . . ."

"Ah, yes, now that you remind me of it, I remember it too, once . . . I bought a whole ham, a little one, a mountain ham, just a few pounds." The small weight of the ham apparently seemed to him a singular attenuating circumstance. "And, yes indeed, I had it sent to me at home. From the grocer in Via Panisperna, yes, the one at the very end, almost at the corner of Via dei Serpenti . . . He comes from Bologna."

The poor victim of the interrogation was now gasping. Gaudenzio was dispatched to Via Panisperna.

At a quarter to six, a second round of questioning. Signora Manuela reappeared, with la Menegazzi, summoned urgently, as well as Professoressa Bertola, pale, shivering slightly. The youth that Gaudenzio managed to collect at Via dei Serpenti was introduced, at the right moment. Fairly straightforward, and yet with an appearance not altogether limpid, black hair thoroughly greased and shiny, he questioned the officer with his eyes, then rapidly glanced at the others present.

"Is this your boy?" Don Ciccio asked the Professoressa.

"What!" she said, with a start, indignant over that "your." Don Ciccio turned to the concierge: "You recognize him? Is he the one this morning?"

"No, it's not him. The one this morning . . . I didn't see his face—how many times do I have to tell you? But he was just a kid, compared to this one."

Don Ciccio then addressed Commendatore Angeloni: "Is he the one who brought you the ham?"

"Yes, sir."

"What about you?" he said to the boy. "What have you got to say?"

"Me?" the youth shrugged, looking at the others, face by face. "What should I know? What do you want with me, anyway?" Don Ciccio frowned hard. "Mind your manners, young fellow. You have been invited to appear, in accordance with the law . . ." he was almost chanting: "Article 229 of the Procedural Code. Do you admit knowing the Commendatore, here present?" and, with his chin, he indicated Angeloni.

"He came to the store last year a few times: after that, he never turned up any more. Once I delivered a ham to his house, all the way up to his door, on Via Merulana. It was raining hard. I got soaked."

"Were you there only once, or several times? Do you know the house?"

"Me? . . . the house? I went there maybe two or three times, when there was something to deliver." The answer was prompt, and at the same time, embarrassed. A certain anxiety to get it over with.

"And you, Commendatore?"

"I can confirm this young man's statement. He came two or three times, in fact." He was making an effort, that was clear; he wanted to seem more tranquil. "I even gave him a tip . . ."

"Aha! You gave him a tip," Don Ciccio smoothed his forehead: he seemed to congratulate himself on this fact, and yet with an inexplicable irony. He concentrated again. He bent his head over the signed statements. He shuffled them a little. Again he questioned Signora Pettacchioni, nodding towards the boy: "Is this the boy that you told me shouted at you once . . . from the top of the stairs?"

"No, he's not that one, either. I'm sure. *That* boy could be the same as the one this morning . . . they were both smaller than this one. That one, Officer, had a politer voice, and he was wearing short pants, too, if it wasn't the same one . . ."

"This one has short pants, too."

"Officer! . . . but these are sport pants. That one was more of a kid, I tell you. This one looks ready to go off to the army. And besides, besides, when was it that this one came to Via Merulana? A year ago? The one I mean, it was maybe two or three months, at the most. It was just after All Souls' Day."

Ingravallo drew in his breath, as if he wished to arrive at some conclusion.

"For the moment, you can go." His eyes stopped on the young man. "But don't forget . . . this is no place . . . to start acting up . . ." The boy went out, followed by a slow, persistent, official gaze. Collecting his papers and, with them, the threads of the results, Ingravallo began:

"The Signora Pettacchioni, here present, if I've got it right, testifies that she has seen another delivery boy come to your house with hams . . . several times, a younger look-ing boy, it seems, I mean more resembling the one seen this morning, whom the Professoressa . . ." he pointed . . . "was able to see in the face, and is therefore in a position to identify. Am I right, Signora Bertola?" The latter nodded.

Angeloni breathed again. For a brief moment he assumed a moralist's tone: "Well, Signora Manuela is the concierge, after all. She . . ."

"She what?" said the occupant of the conciergerie, men-acingly. Angeloni withdrew into his shell again, like a snail, leaving only his nose exposed, outside the husk of his soul. He meant perhaps that, being the concierge, her mission was in fact that of keeping an eye on the people who passed by.

"What I mean is . . ." he became mixed up: he spoke with the slightly nasal tone of a paper trumpet. "Well, I've told you before, Officer. I just buy things where I happen to find them. What she says may be perfectly true. The day before yesterday they delivered some things to the house. A colleague of mine sent his maid, a friend from the Ministry of Economy."

"Maid? A nice-looking girl, at last!" Ingravallo grumbled. He set the statements in order, grumbled for another minute. The three ladies were dismissed.

"You mean, we can go?" la Bertola asked then, still pale.

"Yes, Signora. Please . . ."

Donna Manuela, with a trembling of breasts that filled her blouse completely, unleashed merulanian smiles: "Well, good-bye for now, Officer. And I leave our Signor Filippo in your hands. Take good care of him for me."

Don Ciccio, mute, remained standing, the statements on the table, face to face with the subject: like a dark shrike its wings half-opened, its prey not yet in its talons.

But he insisted still, under that black poodle-coat that he had on his head, stubborn as he was.

The Commendatore took refuge behind the barricade of "experience of this world."

"Ah, women," he whimpered, "if you expect *them* to put in a good word . . ." He was short of breath, gasping at times; his eye sockets were like two caverns: exhausted.

"What do you mean? What would this good word be, that upsets you so much? Let's hear. What's troubling you? Tell me. You can confide . . ."

"In my position, Doctor, what could I do? Go around Rome with a ham on my shoulder? If you ask me, it's just downright nastiness, trying to argue whether the one who fired the shots was a delivery boy or wasn't a delivery boy, or whether he was the lookout for that other one, or whether he wasn't. What do I know about it? You see? Just put yourself in my shoes for a minute. Could I let people say: we saw Commendatore Angeloni climbing up Via Panisperna with a cheese around his neck, and with two flasks of wine, one tucked under each arm, like a pair of twins, carried by their wet-nurse . . . ?"

Ingravallo swung his head up and down, his gaze rooted on the typed statements. He seemed to lose his patience. He raised his voice, separating his words and their syllables: "The con-ci-erge has stated: that the other delivery boy has also come to your house a number of times. The one that was more of a kid. Is that clear? Two or three months ago, which is hardly an eternity, whatever you say. And since I am interested in this kid, since they swear that he looks very much like the other one, the one this morning— am I clear? So, if you don't mind . . ."

"I understand. I understand," the Commendatore whimpered.

"Well, then, why don't you do me a favor? . . . I'm anxious to make his acquaintance, this kid's."

It was written that number two hundred and nineteen of Via Merulana, the palace of gold, or of the profiteers, or

of the sharks, as the case might be—it was written that
from it, too, a lovely flower was to blossom, as from so
many other buildings in this world, for that matter. The
great, scarlet carnation of "well, did you ever?" With
great murmurings of the tenants and of his colleagues
in the Economy, not to mention the whispers of Signora
Manuela, Commendatore Angeloni was kept at the police
station until nine o'clock in the evening.

From some faint hint, that is to say a word or two, from
the two policemen, and from Blondie in particular, via
Manuela—Menegazzi—Bottafavi—Alda   Pernetti   and
brother (Stairway A), or else via Manuela—Orestino Bozzi
—Signora Elodia—Elia Gabbi (Stairway B), it seemed,
or rather one guessed, that the police suspected in this business an indirect though, of course, involuntary (and moreover, hardly demonstrable) responsibility on the part of
Commendatore Angeloni: the prime mover of that coming
and going of ham-bearers to the house. "He doesn't want to
talk; and they're giving him the full treatment." The police
had got it into their heads that Commendatore Angeloni
must perforce know the grocer's boy who hadn't rung anyone's bell but had simply "flung himself down the steps the
minute we heard the shots": but for some special, incomprehensible reason of his own, the Commendatore was pretending to be completely taken by surprise. His whole attitude, his obstinate melancholy reticence, with those turns
of phrase which came to nothing, tapering off, vague

53

and dilatory, his timidity more or less feigned, calculated, those sudden flushes of the dripping nose, those imploring and shifting eyes, at first, then those two poor eyelets lost in two caverns of fear, a confusion at times real and at times strangely ambiguous had finally enraged the two officials: Ingravallo and Doctor Fumi, the head of the Investigation Squad. Naturally, they measured all the seriousness, and the slight grounds for their . . . distrust, based on such elusive indications, of that excellent Grade Six of the National Economy. A Grade Six of unquestioned morality, of unbesmirched reputation. "Hmph!" Don Ciccio thought, to console himself, "every mother's son is pure as the driven snow . . . till he has his first fling . . . with the police."

And besides, it wasn't a question of suspicion, not at all. He only had to explain himself, say what he thought, to talk, sing out, loud and clear. If he thought something, why didn't he spill it? It was obvious enough: the burglar had rung the Balduccis' bell by mistake: perhaps, in his nervousness, or because he had misunderstood the directions of a third party, insufficient directions. This idea of the mistaken door . . . Ingravallo couldn't get it out of his head: the two doors were exactly alike, a twohundrednineteenish brown color, both of them, the number high up, invisible, in view of the darkness (of the landings). Receiving no answer and recovering himself, he had then rung the door opposite, the correct one. Doctor Fumi took a different view: the character had rung the Balducci bell to make sure nobody was at home: Signora Liliana usually went out at that hour, around ten: Assunta, Assuntina, was away, at home, with her "poor old father" who was about to pass on: the non-diminutive Assunta with those tits and that monument of an ass! Gina was with the sisters, at school: Signor Balducci at the office, or rather, off on a business trip, as he often was, in Vicenza, or in Milan. When Signora Liliana was also questioned—and it was Don Ciccio who questioned her, with great respect, that evening, at her home—nothing emerged. She shuddered at the thought of their being alone, she and little Gina, so she had asked Cristoforo, her husband's clerk, to come to supper and spend the night, and she had settled him in the room of the absent maid. She couldn't stop offering him blankets or comforters: ". . . if you feel cold . . ." He was a huge man who could scare off a thief with a puff of his breath: a good man with dogs, rabbits, shotguns.

Countess Menegazzi had gone one floor heavenward, guest of the Bottafavis, who had a "made in England" lock on their door, which could be turned eight times, good enough for the front door of Buckingham Palace. Signor Bottafavi, indeed, when he had wolfed down certain favorite dishes, dreamed of it at night; he dreamed he had that chain on his stomach. It was on such occasions that he was heard to cry "help! help!" in his sleep. From which he was awakened by his own cries. He had cleaned the revolver: he had greased it with vaseline, taken off the safety: the chamber now spun like a reel: the barrel was ready to fire, at the slightest hint of an excuse.

Ingravallo was surprised not to hear Lulu bark and he asked for news of her. Liliana Balducci's face became gently sad. Vanished! Over two weeks ago now. On a Saturday. How? Who knows? Somebody probably put her in his pocket. In the little gardens in front of San Giovanni where Assuntina took the dog for a walk, that scatterbrained girl: and instead of paying attention to the animal, there were all sorts of idlers who paid attentions to *her*, to Assunta. "Such a showy sort of girl . . . And the way things are nowadays!" An inquiry among the garbage collectors, two ads in the *Messaggero*, questions and reproaches to Assuntina, implorations to more or less everybody, but of no avail as far as bringing her back was concerned, alas, poor Lulu!

Don Ciccio, the next morning, was in a terrible humor. It was raining and windy: a harsh, angry northeasterly wind that spun everything crooked, beginning with the priests' cassocks, and the soaked dogs. Umbrellas were powerless. So were the rainspouts of the buildings. From what Pompeo reported to him, it seemed clear that the jewels of Countess Menegazzi were proverbial in the whole neighborhood. Epicized, desired, summoned up at every moment by the envy and the imagination of the women, the kids. They had been fabulizing about them for years. Brides used to say, "Oh, I'd like to have this," and "I'd love to have that," and they touched their throats, or their breasts, or the lobes of their ears as if to toy with a jewel in their fingers, to caress the little seed of a pearl, and they added: "like Signora Menicacci," "like the Countess Menecacci." Because she was a genuine countess, she was.

On their stupendous lips that Venetian name swam against the etymological current, that is against the linguistic erosion that had been at work for years. The anaphonesis pierced the undertow with the perforating vigor of an eel, or of certain anadromous fish which can cover miles upstream, up, up, until they drink in again their natal lymph, at the mountain sources of the Yukon, or the Adda, or the Andean Rio Negro. From the latest transliterations of the parish ledgers they returned to the faint guttural of the origins, from Menegaccio to Ménego, to Menico, to Domenico, Diminicus, and the "possessive which was of all." Certain maidens little instructed in the deciphering of parish registers stumbled over the name with their Sabellian or Tiberine awkwardness, after two or three heaves, they paused at Menecacci,* the kids yelled it, as they rolled about in their games, and the two policemen of the squad, in the presence of Doctor Fumi, had frequent opportunity of pronouncing it, even they, with the most admirable non-chalance.

That name and those jewels, real or imagined, that pile of gold of the "countess" on the third floor of number two hundred and nineteen (stairway A don't forget, because B is a different thing entirely) all along Via Merulana and Via Labicana as far as Sant'Antonio di Padova and San Clemente and the Santi Quattro, had become an epos, now ennobled, which flashed and gleamed, like the flames from greasy paper. For ages. Months, or years. On one occasion, the misplacement of a ring with a topaz or towpats (some-body, out of spite, pronounced it top-ass), which la Mene-gazzi, or more properly, Menecacci had forgotten in the toilet, solely because she was vain as a goose and equally brainless: she left it, the ring, at Cobianchi's public baths

---

* One of the difficulties of the Countess' surname is that it is peril-ously close to several Italian obscenities, such as *cazzo, caca*.

at San Lorenzo in Lucina—you know the place, there around the corner from Palazzo Ruspoli, but sort of underground—and then miraculously she found it again, on the little glass shelf under the mirror of the basin, having previously lighted a candle to Sant'Antonio, having gone over to the church at San Silvestro for that very purpose, and only after lighting it, had she gone back to hunt: on that occasion, and on that same day, when the news became known, various women at numbers 217 and 221 had played the lottery, the Naples series, which specialized in miraculous matters, as everybody knows. In fact, a double combination came out, the very numbers, but at Bari. This can give you an idea of the reputation the countess' treasure enjoyed. *"Fama volat,"* sighed Doctor Fumi, his hand on a stack of red dossiers, *"fama volat."* It must have flown, on rapid wings, to the ears of that no-good thieving bum.

Of course, the police's first care, especially Officer Ingravallo's, to whom the papers were not ungenerous with the adjective "alert," had been to try to identify and possibly lay hands on the murderer, that is to say "the young man in a gray overall, wearing a cap, and a greenish-brown scarf." The most trusted informers in the light-fingered branch, suitably encouraged, had each made his ritual little trip: they had drained a glass here and there, had then expressed an opinion, one each, of course. They gave precise answers, as precise as the Sybils. In the vagabond branch . . . well, more than a branch, it's an ocean: "Turn loose the informers!" In the street-walking branch, and respective protectors . . . no: it was no use even of thinking of them.

The character, as la Menegazzi had described him, must have been a little crook from out of the city, a hick. Only that on Wednesday at nine, Doctor Fumi, glancing a little reluctantly and with a belated yawn over the list (of the lovely ladies pinched the preceding evening), let his eye pause on the information regarding a woman picked up on the Celian Hill, and identified as a . . . seamstress, no fixed address, from . . . from Torraccio. It was the list of the women picked up, after dark, by the various patrols of the "vice squad," which was also sent to him, by routine, for his information. The name of the place, Torraccio, glimpsed out of the corner of his eye, immediately caused him to reflect. He had the woman's card brought him. And the card repeated: Cionini Ines, aged 20, from Torraccio, un-married: at the "without fixed address" there was a little "x" which meant, yes, really without one: "profession" seamstress (trous.), unemployed domestic: "identification papers" a horizontal stroke of the pen, which meant: no. She had insulted the arresting policemen with the epithet "lousy." "Patrol: Celian-Santo Stefano, San Giovanni Station."

"What's this 'trous.' here?"

"Trousers, Chief. She must sew men's trousers, piece-work."

The policemen had caught her in the act. And the act could be classified as begging, four lire (the hard lire of those old days, however) which she had sought and obtained from a passer-by: with whom she had conferred then, standing, for a minute and a half, under cover of the dark-ness and of Santo Stefano Rotondo, from whom she had detached herself for a moment, at the approach of the fuzz: but the charitable gentleman had vanished just in time (from his point of view).

Doctor Fumi shook his head: a final yawn: he handed the card back to the policeman, the list was returned to its proper pile on the desk. Slim results, to tell the truth. Two or three random arrests, "in the usual places": which were, on this occasion, a dim café, a fifth-class brothel in Via Frangipane, and a park bench at Santa Croce. Three characters wearing caps: when your number's up, it's up. The third, in addition to the cap, also had ringworm.

II

T HAT morning—Thursday at last!—Ingravallo could
permit himself a little jaunt to Marino. He had taken
Gaudenzio along with him: then, however, he changed his
mind and, at the Viminale, dismissed him, urging him to
tend to some other minor matters.

It was a marvelous day: one of those Roman days so
splendid that even a Grade Eight government employee—
about to hump his way into Grade Seven, however—well,
even such a one feels something funny grab at his heart,
something pretty much like happiness. He really seemed
to be inhaling ambrosia through the old nose, drinking it
down into the lungs: a golden sun on the travertine or on the
peperino of every church's façade, on the top of every
column, where flies were already buzzing around. And for
himself, he had planned a whole program. At Marino,
there's something better than ambrosia. There's the cellar of
Sor Pippo, with a wicked white wine, a four-year-old rascal,
in certain bottles that five years earlier could have electrified
Prime Minister Facta* and his government if the Facta
factorum had been in a position to suspect its existence. Its

---

* Luigi Facta had been the ineffectual Prime Minister of Italy at the
time of the March on Rome. Mussolini made him a Senator in 1924.

effect was like coffee's, on Don Ciccio's Molisan nerves: and it offered him, moreover, all the verve, with all the nuances, of a first-class wine: the modulated controls— lingual, palatal, pharyngeal, esophageal, of a dionysiac introduction. With a couple or three of those glasses down his gullet, who knows . . . ?

In the two preceding days, on top of everything else— Via Merulana isn't the only street in this world—he had twice gone to the main office of the Tranvie dei Castelli: he liked to stretch his legs a little, around eleven, rather than tangle up his soul and his ears with the confused and groping reports of some subordinate. Gaudenzio and Pompeo were occupied elsewhere. "Those who want to go, go; those who don't want to, send . . ." The number and the series of the ticket, the hole on the date, the 13th, and the tear at the stop, Torraccio, had happily allowed him to establish the day, hour, car where the ticket was sold; he had also been able to interrogate the conductor who had sold it, summoned to the manager's office with the driver, the morning of Ingravallo's second visit. At Due Santi, Tor- raccio, Le Frattocchie, last Sunday, in the early afternoon, a number of people had got on: a crowd. It was impossible for the two men to remember everybody: some of them, yes, and they indicated the more easily recognized customers: not without some bickering between driver and conductor, confusing Sunday with the day before or the day after. The conductor, Merlani Alfredo, denied having seen a young man in an overall, blue or gray. "With a cap pulled over his eyes?" No. "With a scarf around his neck? A scarf?" Yes . . . that he had . . . "A kind of scarf or a big muffler of green wool? . . ." Yes, yes. "Green like dark grass." He warmed to the question. He had been struck by the fact, as he gave him the ticket, that the scarf was all wrapped around half his face, his customer's: "he had his chin inside," as if it were God knows how cold, the 13th of March, at Torraccio. No, he didn't have a cap. Bareheaded, yes, but with his head bent over, not looking you in the face: a great clump of hair, all rumpled up, and nothing else. He didn't know who he might be. No, maybe he wouldn't even recognize him again. That was all he could say.

It was eleven now. Officer Ingravallo was about to get on the tram, at the corner of Via d'Azeglio. The few cars at the disposal of the police were wandering over the seven hills, or busy in the forums and squares, or on the Pincio or the Gianicolo, idly, or perhaps to amuse those gentlemen of the era of the hejira, the big shots with the fezzes: or they stole a nap at the Collegio Romano, like so many hacks, but always ready to take the brass for a ride: you never know. There were great visits in those very days from the plenipotentiaries of Iraq and chiefs of the General Staff of Venezuela, a coming and going of people plastered with medals: poured out in shoals at Naples, down the gangways of every hoarse-voiced ocean liner.

These were the first explosions, the first tremors in Palazzo Venezia, after a year and a half of novitiate, of the Death's Head in frock coat or in morning clothes: the grim looks were already there, the vomiting stream of words: the period of the black derbies and the dove-colored spats was, you might say, about to come to an end: with those short little toad-arms, and those ten fat fingers that hung at his sides like two clumps of bananas, like a black minstrel's gloves. The glorious national destiny hadn't yet had room to show itself, as it would later, in all its splendor. Margherita,* the nymph Egeria now reduced to playing Dido Abandoned, was still launching the *Novecento*, the *neuf-cent*, modern art, the nightmare of the Milanese of the time. She attended the *vernissages*, the launchings, the oils, the watercolors, the sketches, insofar as a gentle Margherita can attend. He had tried on the *feluca*, five *felucas*. They fit him to a T. The glinting eyes of the hereditary syphilitic (also syphilitic in his own right), the illiterate day-laborer's jaws, the rachitic acromegalic face already filled the pages of *Italia Illustrata*: already, once they were confirmed, all the Maria Barbisas of Italy were beginning to fall in love with him, already they began to invulvulate him, Italy's Magdas, Milenas, Filomenas, as soon as they stepped down from the altar: in white veils, crowned with orange blossoms, photographed coming out of the narthex, dreaming of the orgies and the educatory exploits of the swinging cudgel. The ladies, at Maiano or at Cernobbio, were already choking in venereal sobs addressed to the strengthener of Italy. Journalists from Itecaquan went to interview him at Palazzo Chigi,† noted his rare opinions, greedily, down in a notebook, in all haste, so as not to miss a single crumb. The opinions of Lantern Jaw crossed the ocean, and at eight in the morning they were already a cabled article, *desde Italia*, in the *prensa* of the pioneers, of the far-flung merchants of vermouth. "The fleet has occupied Corfu! That man is the

* Margherita Sarfatti, one-time mistress of Mussolini and author of the fulsome biography, *Dux*.

† Mussolini, in 1927, was also Foreign Minister. His offices were in Palazzo Chigi.

64

salvation of Italy." The next morning the contradiction: *desde la misma Italia.* "Tail between legs." And the Magdalenes were at it: producing Sons of the Wolf for the Fatherland. The cars of the police remained "stationed": at the Collegio Romano.

It was eleven o'clock on March 17th, and Officer Ingravallo, in Via d'Azeglio, already had one foot on the tram step and with his right hand he grasped the brass handle, to hoist himself aboard. When Porchettini, all out of breath, overtook him: "Doctor Ingravallo! Doctor Ingravallo!"

"What do you want? What's wrong with you?"

"Listen, Doctor Ingravallo. The Chief sent me," he lowered his voice still further. "In Via Merulana . . . something horrible's happened . . . early this morning. They called the station, it was ten-thirty. You had just left. Doctor Fumi was looking all over for you. Meanwhile he sent me straight over there, with two men, to have a look. I kinda thought I'd find you there . . . Then they sent me to your house to look for you."

"Well, what was it?"

"You mean you don't know already?"

"How should I know? I was just going to take a little ride . . ."

"They cut her throat, they . . . sorry . . . I know she's kind of a relative."

"Whose relative? . . ." Ingravallo said, frowning, as if to reject any kinship with whomsoever.

"Well, a friend, I guess . . ."

"Friend? What friend? Friend of who?" Pressing together, tulip-shape, the five fingers of his right hand, he seesawed that flower in the digito-interrogative hypotyposis customary among the Apulians.

"They found the signora . . . Signora Balducci . . ."

"Signora Balducci?" Ingravallo blanched, gripped Pompeo by the arm. "You're crazy!" and he clutched it tight, until Grabber felt that a vise was crushing him, a machine.

"Sir, it was her cousin found her, Doctor Vallarena . . . Valdassena. They called the station right away. He's there too, now, in Via Merulana. I left instructions. He told me he knows you. He says," Pompeo shrugged, "he says he had gone to pay her a visit. To say good-bye to her, because he's leaving for Genoa. Say good-bye, at this time of the morning? I said. And he says he found her lying on the floor, in a pool of blood. Madonna! that's how we found her, too, on the parquet floor in the dining room, lying there, with her skirt all pulled up, in her underwear, you might say. Her head turned away, sorta . . . With the throat all sawed up, all cut up one side. You should see that cut, sir!" He clenched his hands, as if imploring, then passed his right hand over his brow. "And the face! I almost fainted! But you'll have to see it for yourself in a little while. What a slice! Not even a butcher could have . . . Just horrible: and those eyes! they were staring, wide open, staring at the sideboard. The face all drawn, drawn, and white as a clean sheet . . . did she have t.b.? . . . she looked like it had been terrible hard work, dying . . ."

Ingravallo, pallid, emitted a strange whine, a sigh, or the moan of a wounded man. As if he too felt faint. A wild boar with a bullet in his body.

"Signora Balducci, Liliana . . ." he stammered, looking Grabber in the eyes. He took off his hat. On his forehead, at the rim of the crisp black of his hair, a little line of drops: sudden sweat. Like a diadem of terror, of suffering. His face, usually an olive-white, was now floured with anguish. "Come on. Let's go!" He was damp; he looked exhausted.

When they reached Via Merulana: the crowd. Outside the entrance, the black of the crowd, with its wreath of bicycle wheels. "Make way there. Police." Everybody stood aside. The door was closed. A policeman was on guard: with two traffic cops and two carabinieri. The women were questioning them: the cops were saying to the women: "Stand aside." The women wanted to know. Three or four, already, could be heard talking of the lottery numbers: they agreed on 17, all right, but they were having a spat over 13.

The two men went up to the Balducci home, the hospitable home that Ingravallo knew, you might say, in his heart. On the stairway, a parleying of shadows, the whispers of the women of the building. A baby cried. In the entrance hall . . . nothing especially noticeable (the usual odor of wax, the usual neatness) except for two policemen, silent, awaiting instructions. On a chair, a young man with his head in his hands. He stood up. It was Doctor Valdarena. Then the concierge appeared, emerging, grim and pudgy, from the shadow of the hall. Nothing remarkable, you would have said: but as soon as they had entered the dining room, on the parquet floor, between the table and the little sideboard, on the floor . . . that horrible thing.

The body of the poor signora was lying in an infamous

position, supine, the gray wool skirt and a white petticoat thrown back, almost to her breast: as if someone had wanted to uncover the fascinating whiteness of that *dessous*, or inquire into its state of cleanliness. She was wearing white underpants, of elegant jersey, very fine, which ended halfway down the thighs with a delicate edging. Between the edging and the stockings, which were a light-shaded silk, the extreme whiteness of the flesh lay naked, of a chlorotic pallor: those two thighs, slightly parted, on which the garters—a lilac hue—seemed to confer a distinction of rank, had lost their tepid sense, were already becoming used to the chill: to the chill of the sarcophagus and of man's taciturn, final abode. The precise work of the knitting, to the eyes of those men used to frequenting maidservants, shaped uselessly the weary proposals of a voluptuousness whose ardor, whose shudder, seemed to have barely been exhaled from the gentle softness of that hill, from that central line, the carnal mark of the mystery . . . the one that Michelangelo (Don Ciccio mentally saw again his great work, at San Lorenzo) had thought it wisest to omit. Details! Skip it!

The tight garters, curled slightly at the edges, with a clear, lettuce-like curl: the elastic of lilac silk, in that hue that seemed in itself to give off a perfume, to signify at the same time the frail gentleness both of the woman and of her station, the spent elegance of her clothing, of her gestures, the secret manner of her submission, transmuted now into the immobility of an object, or as if of a disfigured dummy. Taut, the stockings, in a blond elegance like a new skin, given to her (above the created warmth) by the fable of our years, the blasphemy of the knitting machines: the stockings sheathed the shape of the legs with their light veil, the modeling of the marvelous knees: those legs slightly spread, as if in horrible invitation. Oh! the eyes! where, at whom were they looking? The face! . . . Oh, it was scratched, poor object! Under one eye, on the nose! Oh that face! How weary it was, weary, poor Liliana, that head in the cloud of hair that enfolded it, those strands performing a final work of mercy. Sharpened in its pallor, the face: worn, emaciated by the atrocious suction of Death.

A deep, a terrible red cut opened her throat, fiercely. It had taken half the neck, from the front towards the right, that is, towards her left, the right for those who were looking down: jagged at its two edges, as if by a series of blows, of the blade or point: a horror! You couldn't stand to look at it. From it hung red strands, like thongs, from the black foam of the blood, almost clotted already; a mess! with some little bubbles still in the midst. Curious forms, to the policemen: they seemed holes, to the novice, like red-colored little maccheroni, or pink. "The trachea," murmured Ingravallo, bending down, "the carotid, the jugular! . . . God!"

The blood had been smeared over all the neck, the front of the blouse, one sleeve: the hand, a frightful stream of a black blood from Faiti or from Cengio* (Don Ciccio remembered suddenly, with a distant lament in his soul, poor Mamma!). It had curdled on the floor, on the blouse between the two breasts: tinged with it, too, was the hem of the skirt, the underside of that up-flung woolen garment, and

* Faiti and Cengio are mountains where the Italian army fought bitterly and suffered severe losses in the First World War, and where Gadda's brother was killed. For a moment, here, Gadda identifies himself openly with Ingravallo and attributes his own bereavement to the fictional character.

the other shoulder: it seemed as if it might shrivel up from one moment to the next: surely in the end the mass would be all sticky like a blood pudding.

The nose and the face, thus abandoned, turned slightly to one side, as if she couldn't fight any more. The face! resigned to the will of Death, seemed outraged by those scratches, by marks of fingernails, as if he had taken delight, the killer, in disfiguring her like that. Murderer!

The eyes had become fixed in a horrible stare: looking at what, then? They looked, looked in a direction you couldn't figure out, towards the big sideboard, the very top of it, or the ceiling. The underpants weren't bloodied; they left uncovered two patches of thigh, two rings of flesh: down to the stockings, glistening blond skin. The furrow of the sex . . . it was like being at Ostia in the summer, or at Forte dei Marmi or Viareggio, when the girls are lying on the sand baking themselves, when they let you glimpse whatever they want. With those tight jerseys they wear nowadays.

Ingravallo, his head bared, looked like the ghost of himself. He asked: "Have you moved her?" "No, sir," they answered. "Have you touched her." "No." Some blood had been tracked around by somebody's heels, soles, over the wooden parquet, so you could see that they had put their feet into it, into that swamp of fear. Ingravallo became infuriated. Who did it? "You're nothing but a bunch of hicks!" he threatened. "Lousy goatherds from Sgurgola!"*

He went out into the hall and the vestibule: he addressed Doctor Valdarena, slumped on a chair, a kitchen chair, with

* Sgurgola is a small village not far from Rome, often used by Romans to indicate a backward locality, a place from which peasants come.

Pompeo who hovered over him like a kid sticking to his ma. The concierge wasn't to be seen; she had gone down to her lodge maybe; they had called her.

"Well, what are you doing here?"

"Doctor Ingravallo," Valdarena said, his voice serious, calm, and yet pleading, accepting the interrogation as an obvious necessity, looking the other man in the eye. "I had come to say good-bye to my cousin, poor Liliana . . . she wanted absolutely to see me before I left. I'm leaving the day after tomorrow for Genoa. I think I even mentioned it —that I was going to live in Genoa—when you were here, that Sunday, for dinner. I've already given up my room."

"For Genoa!" exclaimed Don Ciccio, absorbed in thoughts. "What room? . . ."

"The room where I live, Via Nicotera number twenty-one."

"He happened to be the first . . ." Santomaso, one of the policemen, said. "He was the first to come in here, any-way," Porchettini confirmed. "Then they called the station . . ."

"Who called?"

"Why . . . all of us together," Valdarena answered. "I didn't know where I was or what I was doing. There was me, a man from the floor above, all the women. The concierge wasn't here. Her lodge was shut up."

"You were the one who . . . who gave the alarm?"

"I came up: the door was open a little way. 'May I come in?' I asked. 'May I?' Nobody answered."

"Where was the concierge? You didn't see her, then? And did she see you?"

"No. No, I don't think so."

La Pettacchioni returned and confirmed all. She was on Stairway B, doing her daily cleaning. She began at the top, naturally. In reality, besom in hand, she had stopped first to chat a bit on the landing, with Signora Bolenfi of the fifth floor, Stairway B: the widow Elia Bolenfi née Gabbi from Castiglion dei Pepoli: (gabby by name and gabby by nature). Then she went on up, with her broom and her bucket. She went "just for half a sec" into the home of the general, Grand'Ufficial Barbezzi, who lived in the penthouse apartment: to straighten up a little. She had left the bucket outside, with the broom.

A little girl, who had gone up to the Bottafavis, the Felicetti's little girl it was, who always had to go and say "good morning" to the Bottafavis every day, after which they would give her a sweet, well, Signora Manuela showed her into the vestibule, and asked her was it true or wasn't it: and she, with a little simpleton voice, confirmed that it was true, that she'd seen only two women, who were coming down the steps. They had two shopping bags, one each, like they were going marketing. "They looked like they were from the country, to me, la Pettacchioni added, from her fund of wisdom.

"What women were they?" Ingravallo asked, absently. "Show me your hands!" he said to Doctor Valdarena. "Come over to the light." The young man's hands seemed perfectly clean: a white skin, healthy, warm, faintly veined: suffused with the warmth of youth: a signet ring of yellow gold, with a stupendous jasper, and in the jasper an initial: on the right ring-finger, it stood out, solid, imposing, ready to seal a letter, one would have said, a secret avowal. But the right cuff of his shirt . . . bloodstained! in the corner: from the gold of the cuff link to the cuff's edge.

"This blood here?" Ingravallo said, his mouth twisting with revulsion, still clasping that hand by the fingertips. Giuliano Valdarena blanched: "Doctor Ingravallo, believe me! I confess: I did touch poor Liliana's face. I bent over her: then I knelt on one knee. I wanted to caress her. She was cold! . . . Yes, it was to say good-bye to her! I couldn't help myself. I wanted to pull down that skirt of hers, my poor cousin! in that awful condition! But then I didn't have the courage . . . to touch her a second time. She was cold. No, no. And then . . ."

"Then—what?"

"Then I thought, I realized I didn't have the right to touch anything. I ran outside. I called. I rang the bell opposite. Who is it? Who is it? they said. It was a woman's voice. But they wouldn't open."

"They were right. Then what?"

"Then . . . I yelled again. Some other people came down . . . or came up. People came, that's all I know. They wanted to see for themselves, too. They started to scream. We called the police. What else should I have done?"

Don Ciccio stared at him, hard, and let go of the hand. His grimace of revulsion persisted, a slight contraction of the nose, of a single nostril. He reflected for a moment, still looking the man in the face. "How come you're so calm?"

"Calm? I can't cry. For years I haven't had any reason to. Not even when my mother . . . she married a second time and went to live in Turin. The tip of my cuff must have grazed the wound, her neck: I guess it had to . . . with all that blood! I have to leave day after tomorrow; I've already been given my instructions. I felt like I was leaving home, my own family. I wanted to see her and say good-bye, poor, poor Liliana. Poor . . . so splendid and unhappy, she was!" The others remained silent. Don Ciccio scrutinized him, sternly. "A caress! My God! I didn't have the strength to kiss her: she was so cold! Then I went out; I almost ran away. I was afraid of death, believe me. I called for help. The door was open, like a ghost had disappeared through it. Liliana! Lilianuccia!"

Ingravallo bent down and looked at the other man's trousers, at the thigh, the knees: on the left knee, a slight trace of dust.

"Where did you kneel down? With which knee?"

"Ah . . . by the buffet, the little one. Let me think now. With the left knee. Yes. To keep from kneeling in all that blood.

Don Ciccio glared at him, doggedly.

"See here, Doctor Valdarena, you've got to tell me every-thing the way it really was. Trying to use your imagination . . . at a time like this . . . in this place . . . you can figure it out for yourself, can't you? . . . it would be a bad mistake."

"Why, what do you mean? I'm telling you just what happened. Try to understand me."

"What's supposed to make me believe you, eh? Let's hear it. I'm all ears. You're the one who has to give us a trail to follow, in our investigation here. For your own good."

They reported to Ingravallo that Gina, the ward, had come back from the Sacred Heart at that very moment. On Thursdays school let out at one: for lunch. Balducci was supposed to get back from Milan the next day . . . or maybe from Verona. Ingravallo had a try with the young girl in tears, but he got nothing out of her: after her coffee and milk, before eight, she had said good-bye to her "Mamma," had received the usual morning kiss with the usual question: "Do you know your lesson today?" She had said yes and had gone out. For the present she was handed over to the neighbors, later somebody could probably take her to the sisters: now she went to the floor above, to the Bottafavis; la Menegazzi was too alarmed and upset to be of any help to the little one. A yellow wisp of mustache seemed bent back to her nose. She hadn't had time to fix her hair: what she had on her head looked like a wig made from corn silk and tied in ribbons. She said that this building had a curse on it. She invoked *Maria Vergine* with her eyes red, sunken, squeezed tight. She said, and kept repeating, "Oh, seventeen's the worst of all numbers." The little girl who had met the two women on the stairs could furnish no information concerning them. Her big eyes wide, "yes," she would say, or "no," poor kid, her lips numb with the fright she felt, seeing that big, black head of Ingravallo who, she decided, must be the man with the sack who carries off bad little girls when they won't stop crying. It was finally established that the two women had gone up to see the lawyer, Cammarota (fourth floor), or rather to see his wife, to take her two fresh cheeses: they were bimonthly suppliers of fresh cheese.

They tracked down Cristoforo, Balducci's clerk. The news shattered him, like a thunderbolt. He had gone out at seven-thirty, after a coffee-with-brandy which Signora Liliana had gently forced on him: he couldn't drink milk, it

75

never agreed with him. Yes, a little before Gina, who went off to the Sacred Heart at eight. He couldn't face the awful sight: "I can't look at her." He made the Sign of the Cross. Tears dribbled down the somewhat wrinkled skin of his face. He had been assigned some errands by Signora Liliana, poor lady: to pay a bill, to buy two brooms from the broom-maker, get some rice, wax for the parquet, take a bundle to the dressmaker. But first, however, he had had to go to the office: to open the office: dust off the desks. Officer Ingravallo wouldn't let go of him. In fact, he charged Grabber to have a fine old chat with him: in the meanwhile Giuliano was invited to remain at the disposal of the police.

The investigations continued on the scene of the crime in the early afternoon: with the main door of the building shut, the door of the apartment shut, with reinforcements of police, with Sergeant Valiani of the scientific office and with the armed intervention of the fingerprint bureau. The tenants and even the concierge herself were asked not to linger on the stairs, "to allow greater freedom of movement to the investigations," and to remain, on the other hand, insofar as possible, "within reach" of the squad. The coroner appeared after five-thirty. The attorney general's office had taken official cognizance of the crime shortly before four, via the various offices, via Doctor Fumi and the chief of police. The good Cristoforo, the variopainted Menegazzi, the little Gina, former artilleryman Bottafavi, and hand-some young Doctor Valdarena were heard alternately and simultaneously. But "the crime" remained shrouded in mystery, as the late editions said finally, in a paper which had managed to bring off the scoop, shouting the news along Corso Umberto. The reporters, wangle as they might, couldn't get past the door of the Balduccis. But at the smaller entrance to the building, however, they had caught Sora Elodia, of Stairway B, who, well, was rather jolly, as she usually happened to be, on Thursdays and Sundays. She was making eyes at the policemen, who only laughed in her face.

It was established that none of the building's tenants could furnish clues as to who might have been the author, or authors, of the crime. No one, except the little girl, Maddalena Felicetti, had encountered people on the stairs: not even Valdarena; nobody had seen him, either. He was a Doctor of Economic Science—Ingravallo was well aware of this—and employed by Standard Oil. For some time he had been stationed at Vado Ligure, then in Rome. Now he was preparing to move to Genoa, and also to be married. He was engaged to a Genoa girl, a snappy little brunette, whose photograph he produced: a certain Lantini Renata. Of excellent family, naturally. According to the excellent family, he "was terribly in love," our Doctor Valdarena, Signorino Giuliano. Balducci had spoken about it to Ingravallo, meeting him in Albano at the Cantinone tavern, with some jovial allusion to hot young blood, as well as the chronic lack, which afflicted the young man, of a few sheckels, which ought to stick to his fingers, at least in part; and yet money fluttered through them regularly, like butterflies from the fingers of an Apollo: the Apollos you see in the park, of marble. Balducci had dubbed him a "good-looking boy" (no need for references on this score): "with his degree in economic science," top grades and *cum laude*, too, but always broke, as is so often the case with those who want to teach others . . . how to handle the economy: a little short of the ready . . . shorter than a Roman cousin—not to mention a Genoese father-in-law—would have wished. "No, no, he isn't living off of short loans; but you know how it is, at his age, with all the temptations there are around: you understand, a boy like that . . . if he isn't hard up for money, he can't be very hard up for the other thing." Ingravallo was grim-faced, that evening, in Albano: the rosy-cheeked indulgence and, indeed, the male solidarity of Balducci, the husband, a toothpick between his teeth, to Don Ciccio betrayed too easy a digestion . . . of the product of Empedocle e Figlio, maybe. That carefree, after-dinner rosyness of the commercial traveler, the hunter with a pair of new boots . . . by God, it had finally exasperated him, he who came from years of poverty and hardship, from the barren Matese mountain, progressing to the procedures and the red tape of the law, a humble and dogged investigator of events, or of souls, in the law's name. He had glanced at Balducci: "the horns are growing on your head right now!" he thought. "An atoll of coral, that's what's growing on you." And instead he had sighed: "Ah, these women!" his face grimmer than ever under his astrakhan mop. And Giuliano, now, sat in the best drawing room. With two cops keeping him company.

A good-looking boy, the Signorino Giuliana, in there: rather lucky with women. Rather. Yes. They pursued him in swarms, buzzing around him; they fell on him, all together, nose-diving like so many flies on a honeycomb. And he was plenty smart too: he had a line, a hypnotizing mirror, a way all his own, so natural and, at the same time, so strange . . . that he charmed you with the greatest of ease. He pretended that he neglected his women, or even that he was bored with them: too many, too easy! and he had something much better in his grasp. He played the smart male, the you-bore-me role, at times, or the haughty; or the young man of high-class family in Via dei Banchi Vecchi, or the clever businessman who didn't have time to waste on chat. Depending. A matter of chance. According to his mood. Matching the suit he happened to have on. Following the inspiration of the moment. Depending on whether he had gold-tipped cigarettes or whether he was out of cigarettes altogether, or whether he had just bought some, but a pack of smelly Nazionali. He played the spoiled child. Sometimes he was as fickle as a weather vane. So he neglected them then, sure, the flirty ones. And that was what made them lose their minds. He granted his favors after much reluctance on his part, after infinite longing and swooning on the part of the victim, drawing out the mad abandon or exhausting any evasive indocility through an erogation of pseudo-symptoms (in reality, suggestions) alternating and contrasting, yesses and nos. He loves me, he loves me not. I want you, I don't want you. And, in any case, to the rare, predestined, and with mysterious deliberation, selected women, he conceded himself: like Divine Grace, the Eternal Health of Jansenius. At times, by contrast, with sudden violence: and to the total confusion of all plausibility. There! Just when everyone had turned the horoscope in a different direction. Boom! He plunged hawk-like on the most resistant hen of the whole coop: as if to punish her (or reward her) with this dazzling deviltry: to rescue her from some recondite weakness in her being, from some ignominy . . . existing prior to this magnifying election. In such case, the gratitude of the magnified could swell to the stars: like her fear, or even perhaps hope, of an encore.

Ingravallo, as you might have expected, even before the arrival of the coroner, in view of the way the events stood, had decided to take Valdarena in. Only later, the morning after in fact, the district attorney's office transformed his state of custody into temporary arrest and arranged for the respective warrant, after the arrest had in effect taken place, and with the subject of the warrant already in Regina Coeli Prison. Until late in the evening the chief and the two experts of the criminological bureau did not desist from their investigations, nor from photographing the deceased. They had brought everything they needed with them. There was no question of telegraphing Balducci, since his return was imminent, nor alerting the various police stations to have him traced: Milan, Padua, even Bologna, because he had to go also to Padua. Cristoforo, the widow Menegazzi, who couldn't stop cooing over the disaster, Bottafavi, Signora Manuela and her hubby, the one from the milk company, offered to go and meet him in a body at the station; he must be spared a shock, prepared in some way. The relatives? A telephone call at noon . . .

The relatives were officially "advised of the event" late in the evening, but Ingravallo, already that morning, had forbidden the men to let them in. Renewed investigation and precise autoptic observation both by the head man Don Ciccio and by Sergeant Valiani . . . well, to tell you the truth, they didn't amount to much. Oh, of course, some signs of theft. But no weapon was found. Still various drawers and such, when you looked in them, told you that there was something up. They apparently weren't so innocent, as they looked from outside. Weapons, no. And no clues to any, except for the red drops on the floor, and that blood . . . tracked by heels. Near the sink, in the kitchen, the tiled floor was wet, with water. A "very sharp" and completely missing knife was probably the instrument most capable of operating in that way. The drops, rather than from any murdering hand, seemed to have dropped from the knife itself. Black they were, now. The unexpected flash, the cutting edge, the brief sharpness of a blade. In her: alarm. Certainly he had first struck all of a sudden, then worked on the throat, insisting, and on the trachea, with ferocious confidence. The "struggle," if one had taken place, can have been no more than a wretched jerk, on the part of the victim, a glance, terrified and immediately imploring, the hint of a movement: a hand barely raised, white, to avert the horror, to clasp at the hairy wrist, the black, implacable hand of the homicide, his left, which already dug its nails into her face and threw back her head to free the throat further, to bare it entirely, helpless against the gleam of the blade, which the right hand had now produced, to wound, to kill.

A waxen hand relaxed, fell back . . . when the knife was already in Liliana's breath, tearing, ripping her trachea; and the blood, when she inhaled, flowed down into her lungs: and her breath gurgled out, coughing, in that torture, and it looked like so many bubbles of red soap: and the carotid, the jugular, spurted like two pumps from a well, plop, plop, half a yard away. Her breath, her last, sideways, in bubbles, in that horrid purple of her life: and she felt the blood in her mouth, and she saw those eyes, no longer human, on the wound: there was still work to be done: another blow: the eyes! of the endless beast. The unsuspected ferocity of the world . . . was revealed to her all of a sudden . . . brief years! But a spasm was depriving her of sensation, annihilating memory, life. A sweetish, tepid savor of night.

The hands, stark white, with their delicate nails, periwinkle color now, revealed no cuts: she hadn't been able, hadn't dared grasp the cutter, arrest the slaughterer's determination. She had submitted to the slaughterer. The face and the nose seemed scratched, here and there, in the weariness and pallor of death, as if the hatred had surpassed death itself. The fingers were stripped of rings; the wedding ring had vanished. Nor did it occur to anyone, then, to impute its disappearance to the Fatherland.* The knife had done its job. Liliana! Liliana! To Don Ciccio it was as if the world's every aspect were darkened, all the world's gentility.

The man from the criminological bureau said a razor was out of the question, because it makes a neater cut, more superficial, he opined, and in general, in such cases multiple cuts are required; since it has no sharp tip, and it can't be used with such violence. Violence? Yes, the wound was deep, all right, a horrible thing: it had hacked away half the

* At a later date, Mussolini, with great bombast, was to ask the wives of Italy to sacrifice their gold wedding rings to the Fatherland.

neck, just about. In the dining room, no, no clue . . . except for the blood. And, after looking around the other rooms: nothing. Only more blood: clear traces in the kitchen sink: diluted, until it looked like frog's blood: and many scarlet, or now black, drops on the floor, round and radiated, as blood characteristically behaves when you let it drip on the ground: like sections of asteroids. Those horrible drops indicated an obvious itinerary: from the abandoned encumbrance of the body, the still-tepid evidence of the deceased . . . Liliana! to the kitchen sink, to the chill, the ablutions: the chill which absolves us of all memory. Many drops in the dining room, there, of which five or perhaps more were contiguous to that other blood, to that mess, the stains and the largest pool, from which they tracked it all around with their shoes, those stupid louts. Many drops in the hall, a little smaller, and many in the kitchen: and some rubbed off, as if to erase them with the sole to keep them from being seen on the white, hexagonal tiles. The men had a go at the furniture: eleven drawers and cupboards, closets and sideboards they couldn't open. Giuliano, in the living room, was guarded by two policemen. Cristoforo had brought some sandwiches and a couple of oranges. All these big men kept wandering and tramping around the house. It jangled the nerves. Don Ciccio sat down, brokenhearted, in the vestibule, waiting for the magistrate. Then he went back in there again: he looked, as if in farewell, at the poor creature over whom the photographers were arguing in whispers, taking care not to stain themselves or their traps, their bulbs, screens, wires, tripods, their big box cameras. They had already discovered two

83

light plugs behind two armchairs, and had already blown a fuse two or three times, one of the three fuses of the apartment. They decided to use magnesium. They fiddled around like two sinister angels, full of a desire not to attract attention, above that terrifying weariness: a cold, poor derelict, now, of the world's evil. They buzzed around like flies, maneuvering those wires, snapping the shutters, agreeing in a whisper on steps, trying to keep from setting the whole kit and kaboodle on fire—these were the first hum of eternity over her opaque senses, that body of a woman which no longer possessed modesty or memory. They operated on the "victim" with no regard for her suffering, and unable to spare her ignominy. The beauty, the clothing, the spent flesh of Liliana were there: the sweet body, still clothed from their gaze. In the obscenity of that involuntary pose—whose motives, beyond doubt, were the skirt lifted back for the outrage, the parted legs, and above them, and the swell and furrow of voluptuousness to inflame the weak (and those sunken eyes, horribly open on to the void, fixed on an inane object, the sideboard)—death seemed to Don Ciccio an extreme decompounding of possibles, an unfocusing of interdependent ideas, formerly harmonized in one person. Like the dissolving of a unity which cannot hold out any longer, the sudden collapse of relationships, of all ties with organizing reality.

The sweet pallor of her face, so white in the opaline dreams of the evening, had given way through funereal modulations to a cyanosed tone, a faded periwinkle: as if hate and outrage had been too harsh, when encountered, for the tender flower of the being, of the soul. Shudders ran down his spine. He tried to reflect. He was sweating again.

From his pocket, mechanically, he took the tram ticket: from the right pocket of his jacket, where he had placed it that morning, and where it still rested, after all the day's grief: with half a cigarette and with a few crumbs: the elongated greenish-blue ticket of the Tranvie dei Castelli, with the hole at the 13th, and another hole, or tear, at Torraccio. He turned it over, then turned it back again. He went into the vestibule, into the master bedroom. He flung himself down in a chair, worn out.

He pondered, trying to put together the pieces of the evidence—disconnected as they were—to set in order the moments, the worn moments of the sequence, of the time that had been lacerated, dead. First of all: the two messes were to be connected, weren't they? The incredible burglary of that poor old parrot, la Menegazzi, that woman . . . that collection of spinach stains: and this horror, here. Same building, same floor. And yet . . . It seemed impossible. Three days apart?

His reason . . . told him that the two crimes had nothing in common. The first, well, a "daring" burglary, performed by a criminal very well-informed, if not personally acquainted with the customs and ways of number two hundred and nineteen, stairway A. "Stairway A, stairway A," he grumbled to himself, swaying his head imperceptibly, curly and black: staring at a point on the floor, his hands clasped, his elbows on his knees: "a burglary, all right, homemade."

With that unfindable grocer's boy as informer: hah, or as lookout. More likely lookout, since la Menegazzi, the old fool, hadn't the slightest idea: which means, when you come right down to it, still an accomplice. And with that flat toy trumpet, the Commendatore of the Economy, who had truffles delivered to him. "Commendatore Angeloni!" he sighed, with a certain emphasis. "He has a little weakness for artichokes. We'll have to look into that. And the country ham from Via Panisperna is another weakness. Down at the corner of Via dei Serpenti."

And the ring at the Balducci door? A mistake, surely. Or an alternative? Or a precaution? Rewarded with silence? In any case—this much was clear—a thief. Armed robbery, breaking and entering . . .

This other mess, for God's sake, was enough to drive you crazy! Who ever saw such a thing? Still, the robbery motive couldn't be overlooked here, either, not at all, not till Balducci got back. And then . . . then what? The drawers would tell their story. Yes, but . . . this was a different thing. The manner of the crime, that poor encumbrance in there, those eyes, the horrible wound: a motive, perhaps, a murkier one. That skirt . . . thrown back like that, as if by a gust of wind: a hot, greedy gust, blowing from Hell. Summoned by a rage, by such contempt, only the gates of Hell could have granted it passage. The murder "seemed, at this stage of the investigations, a crime of passion." Rape? Desire? Vengeance?

His reason told him to study the two cases separately, to get the feel of them, each on its own. The double number doesn't come up so rarely on the Naples or Bari lottery, and also in Rome it's frequent enough, so even here in the merulanian street, in this stingy phalanstery of two hundred and nineteen stuffed with gold, another fine double combination could turn up. The unwanted double of a pair of crimes. Bang. Bang. Without any connection other than the topical, that is the external, cause: the great fame of the sharks, and their evil gold. A fame omnipresent in the San Giovanni neighborhood, from Porta Maggiore to the Celian, to the ancient cloaca-swamp, the Suburra: where, however, the wine is icy, in summer. He looked at the ticket, again. He turned it over, twice. He scratched his nose lightly (extending his mouth like a tuber) with the thumbnail of his right hand, the back of the nail: a gesture habitual with him, and one of remarkable refinement.

III

THE next morning the newspapers reported the event more fully. It was Friday. The reporters and the telephone had been a nuisance all evening: both in Via Merulana and over at Santo Stefano. So, the next morning, the pack was in full cry: "Ghastly Crime in Via Merulana," shouted the newsboys, with their bundles knocking against people's knees: until quarter to twelve. In the local news, inside the paper, a bold headline over two columns: but then, sober and quite detached, the report itself: a terse little column, and ten lines in the continued column, "the investigation is being relentlessly pursued"; and a few other words, filler of purest New-Order style. The good old days were past . . . when for pinching a maid's bottom in Piazza Vittorio there was half a page of slobbering. The moralization of the Urbs and of all Italy, the concept of greater civil austerity, was then making its way. You might have said, in fact, that it was making great strides. Crimes and suggestive stories had abandoned forever the Ausonian land, like a bad dream dissolving. Robberies, stabbings, whorings, pimpings, burglary, cocaine, vitriol, arsenic bought for poisoning rats, abortions *manu armata*, feats of pimps and cardsharps, youngsters who make a woman pay for their drinks—why, what are you thinking of?—the Ausonian land didn't even remember the meaning of such things.

Relics of an age dissolved into the void, with its frivolities, and its clichés, and its condoms, and its Masonic screwing around. The knife, in those years—the dear old knife beloved of every cowardly killer and every smalltime gangster, the criminals and the traitors, the weapon of the tortuous alleyways, the pissed-on back streets—seemed truly to have vanished from the scene, never to return: except on the paunches of the new, funereal heroes, where it was now displayed, gloriously drawn out, a nickel-plated, or even silver-plated, spare genital. Now the new vigor was in power, of Lantern Jaw, the bowler-hatted Death's Head, the Emir with black fez, and with plume, and the new chastity of Baroness Malacianca-Fasulli, the new law of the rods tied in a *fascio*. Who would ever believe there were thieves, now, in Rome? With that humorless turkey cock in Palazzo Chigi? With Federzoni, who wanted to clap in jail all the neckers from the Lungotevere? Or everybody who did some kissing in the movies? All the randy dogs of the Lungara? With a Milanese Pope, and a Holy Year just two years before? And with the fresh brides and grooms? With the fresh chickens crowing all over Rome?*

Long files of black-dressed women, having rented the ritual black veil in Borgo Pio, in Piazza Rusticucci, or

* A typical Gaddian private joke. Pope Pius XI was fond of blessing newlyweds, referring to them as *sposi novelli* ("fresh bridal pairs") ; *polli novelli* is the characteristic Roman advertisement for fresh chickens. (Among Gadda's less well-known achievements is the construction, as engineer, of the Vatican Power Station for Pius XI. He also wrote the official description of it.)

Borgo Vecchio, trooped under the colonnade, swooned at Porta Angelica, and then through the gates of Sant'Anna, to go and receive the apostolic benediction from Pope Ratti, a Milanese of good background, from Saronno, a tough sort, the kind who get buildings built. As they waited to be formed into lines and led, after forty flights of steps, into the throne room, into the presence of the great Pope and mountain climber. All this to give you the idea that the Capital now incarnated, absolutely beyond any doubt, the city of the seven candelabra of the seven virtues: the city that had been invoked, through long millennia, by all Rome's poets, inquisitors, moralists and utopists, Cola not excepted (though hanged). Fat, he was.* In the streets of Rome not a whore was to be seen, at least not the kind with licenses. With the sweet thought of the Holy Year, Federzoni had confiscated the whole lot of them. The Marchesa Licker was off at Capri, or in Cortina, or had gone to Japan for a little trip.

"Sonovabitch . . ." grumbled Don Ciccio, clenching his teeth: they were the teeth of a bulldog, and a cuisine in which garlic was prominent kept them a gleaming white. His smartest men were being taken from him, one by one, sent to swell the ranks of that other squad, the political. And meanwhile he sat there snorting through papers.

* Cola di Rienzo (1312–54), medieval revolutionary figure who was executed. The words "fat, he was" are a quotation from a contemporary chronicle.

Now it was time to think of Mister Good-Looking, seriously, too. Good-looking. Yes, he was that, all right. And hard up for cash.

He seemed to remember a sentence of Balducci's, another evening at the Cantinone in Albano; it had issued forth with benign indulgence from that great ruddy face, while he was talking about a female cousin. "Women, of course, when they're in love . . ." He had pulled out his cigarette case. ". . . don't bother about petty details; they're generous-minded then." He had lighted Ingravallo's cigarette, then his own. "They're open-handed, not counting the change." Then and there Ingravallo hadn't paid much attention: a typically noble, after-dinner opinion. With him, Ingravallo, Doctor Francesco, to tell the truth, no woman had ever been open-handed, except perhaps, yes the poor signora herself: generous with her kindness, her goodness, a charming . . . inspiration. In her honor, once (he blushed) he had ventured to write . . . a sonnet. But he couldn't make all the rhymes come out right. The verses, however, even Professor Cammaruta had found perfect. "They're open-handed, oh yes, open-handed." Now, he felt he should convalidate that rather generic insinuation: perhaps, sure, women. "Don Ciccio! What if she had a private fund?" His thoughts were pursuing some anger, some vindictive bitterness. "Do they give money, along with all the rest?" No, no. He wanted to dispel this hypothesis. There were too many indications, no, Liliana Balducci . . . no, no, she wasn't in love with her cousin. In love? What're you talking about? Yes, to be sure, she had looked at him, openly pleased, that time, smiling at him, but . . . considering him a fine specimen of the family stock, the way you might smile at a brother. A young man, now he could understand, a young man who was a credit to them all; descended from the same grandfather, or rather, for him, great-grandfather. She, poor Liliana, was a cousin of his father. She had lost father and mother. Her husband was all she had left in the world. Hah! And Giuliano . . . a fine chip, struck smartly, from the same old block. Perhaps . . . yes, of course, they had played together as children, as cousins. The genealogy (Don Ciccio consulted a scrap of paper) had been compiled by Pompeo. "Her aunt, Aunt Marietta, wife of Uncle Cesare, was the grandmother of Giuliano. They grew up together, you might say. So with Giuliano, she always spoke like a sister. An older sister."

"How come she was a Valdarena, too, before she got married?"

"How? It's because her father and Giuliano's grandfather, Uncle Cesare, were brothers."

"Well, why drag this Marietta on me then? If they're related, it's through the men of the family, the two fathers . . ."

"Right!"

"Right, my ass! You've got to get this Aunt Marietta off my back now."

"She's the one that brought the signora up, when her mother died."

Ingravallo remembered, in fact, that Balducci had told him this: Liliana, when still a child, had lost her mother. Complications following childbirth, her second. And the baby, too! And so, and so . . . Then, that evening . . . that evening she had spoken to her cousin with that admiring indulgence, that touch of envy women always betray when they look at handsome young men . . . too sought-after by their rivals. And that was all there was to it.

"Ah! these women!"

It was one o'clock. He collected statements and reports, stacked the dossiers. In despair, he got up and went out.

"And yet," he was thinking, "Valdarena, the cousin . . . he was the one who gave the alarm. Is this a sign . . . an unmistakable sign . . . of innocence? Or at least, of an easy conscience. Conscience! But what about the cuff of his shirt? No, the whole thing wouldn't come clear. The story of that caress sounded made-up to him. Caress a dead woman! Or else . . . There are murky moments in the slow drip-drip of the hours: the hours of puberty. Evil crops up unexpectedly in sudden, horrible shards from beneath the tegument, from beneath the skin of gossip: a fine accountant's diploma, then a university degree. From beneath the covering of decent appearances, like a stone, it breaks the ground, and you can't even see it: like the dark hardness of the mountain, in a green field.

The handsome Giuliano! Too upset, he had seemed, too nervous, and too depressed, at the same time. He was on the verge of breaking down. He couldn't manage to maintain the proper composure. "How can you be so calm?" Don Ciccio had asked him: it was a trap. Anything but calm. "They're open-handed; they don't count the change. Ah!"

Liliana Balducci was very rich, Liliana Balducci née Valdarena. She had money of her own and, to some extent, she was mistress of it. An only child. And her father had had a gift for coining money. Even Doctor Fumi, in the vast din of this whole symphony, had picked out the theme, "the motive," the Leitmotif.

"Her old man knew his onions, all right. During the war, and during the post-war, too. He was a real, a no-bones-about-it shark. He had died, too, a couple of years ago, some time after the daughter got married. The apartment in Via Merulana was his property. Business deals, partner-ships, investments here, there and everywhere. Owner of this, part-owner of that. Lending money on mortgages, mortgaging to buy up. He must have been a real son of a bitch." He accompanied this sermon with some twirls of his right hand. Liliana had referred vaguely to her father's fortune, on San Francesco's day, during that happy meal.

As for the Valdarena relatives, Doctor Fumi had taken care of them. First Pompeo went to call: a long tramp it was, and no results. Then the sergeant: nothing. Finally the relatives themselves came to see Fumi. So he had given them the full treatment; he had handled them, in his way, touching them first here, then there, with great gentleness, swaying his head as if he were reciting a poem: with those eyes, with that voice of his, Fumi, if he had wanted, could have been a five-star criminal lawyer! A real tear-jerker!

Giuliano's mother no longer lived in Rome: a handsome woman, they said. Pompeo had codified the registerial information that had emerged relative to the relatives. A native talent, refined by excellent practice in the art and by the necessity for saving time, for abbreviating the long chains of procedural syllogisms, eye, ear and nose, at the service of the old gray matter, assisted by an occasional roast-beef sandwich, had made him a master of delineating with a few strokes, a couple of hard and fruitful knocks, the most entangled family trees of the whole repertory. And with the most edifying details.

When it came to women, especially, and exploiters of women, love, lovers, true marriages and false ones, cuckoldom and counter-cuckoldom, Pompeo was supreme, you might say. Certain smart-ass bigamists or polygamists, with all their troubles and poly-troubles, and with all the mess of the respective kids whom they sort of wanted sometimes and then maybe didn't want—well, in all that muck, he slipped in and out with the ease of a taxi driver. His necessary association with the underworld, his abbreviated investigation, obtained by his intuition of those "family status" questions, had brought him to such a pass that, on a moment's notice, he could give you all the "cohabitations," let's say, from Via Capo d'Africa to Via Frangipani, and as far as Piazza degli Zingari, at Via dei Capocci and Vicolo Ciancaleoni; and then down, past Piazza Montanara —not even worth mentioning—to Via di Monte Caprino, and Via Bucimazza and Via dei Fienili: the things that man knew! Or the neighborhood of Palazzo Pio, that other pesthole, and in all those alleyways behind Sant'Andrea della Valle, Piazza Grottapinta, Via di Ferro, and the Vicolo delle Grotte del Teatro: and maybe even Piazza Pollarola, even though the people there are classy, they still have some funny additions to the household, or a character or two around who isn't in the police's good graces. In those areas, in fact, he kept his trumps. There, he knew by heart all the couples, all their kith and kin, and all the ramifications that they sprung in the spring, whether the ramifications came in the shape of horns, or whether they appeared farther down on the body: the double couples, and the triple, the royal flushes, in all the possible combinations: birth, life, death, and distinguishing marks. He knew the dumps they rented, and when they moved out of one to go into another, the double rooms with kitchen privileges, the closets, the rooms let by the hour, the sofas and even the couches, with every flea that lives in them, individually.

So for Pompeo the Valdarena tribe was child's play. Giuliano's mother had left Rome to live elsewhere. Having married a second time, a certain accountant named Carlo Ricco of the Moda Italiana, she lived with the latter in Turin. The information on the children was good: they went to school and studied. Her classy relatives—well, it seemed she had "been somewhat cast off by them"; and they had made no effort, from Turin: but on the other hand "she had become estranged from her mother-in-law," or rather her "in-laws," as they were called, en masse: leaving her son to his grandmother. When you came right down to it, everybody was really satisfied, after all the rows and tears: because when she doesn't have cash, the best job a widow can find is to dig herself up another man who'll marry her. Giuliano had maybe been a little depressed and jealous of his mother, for a while he seemed kind of grumpy with everybody: then, as he grew up and developed, little by little, he had come around and seen reason: his mother was young and beautiful. And the depression of a kid like him ... He had soon found people who pulled him out of it.

His grandmother spoiled him rotten: this grandmother who was Liliana's Aunt Marietta.

Well, and then what? Things all started going wrong at once. Giuliano's mother, seven or eight months ago, was hospitalized in Bologna, stuck in a bed at San Michele in Bosco: an automobile accident, while she was on her way to Rome to visit the relatives—that's how much she disliked them, poor woman! They'd come by way of Milan. Both legs smashed: it was a miracle that she had saved her skin at all. There, traction and counter-traction, weights attached to one foot and to the other. And machinery of every shape and kind. For this reason, too, the signorino was a little dazed, and had been for some while: he was worried about his mother. And the womenfolk, all over him, sympathizing, poor boy! Going out of their way to see if they couldn't console him.

Liliana Balducci, then, was very rich. Daughter of a profiteer. So then what?

He, the young gentleman her cousin, his technique was that of the idler, the good-looker. Who has or can have his fill of women till they run out of his ears. But surely, too, inside, he must have had some fixed idea. A goal: surely he had one in his heart of hearts. Aha: he wanted her to be the one to want him. Now Ingravallo could see it clearly. Giuliano wanted to be desired. To give himself: but to condescend, to sell himself dearly. At the highest possible price. He tried to play it cool and handsome, like that, to act fancy-free. With all women. And even with her. Sure. He wanted to be fair to them all, her included.

And then when she had gone crazy, too, the way certain

poor creatures do lose their minds over certain animals in the right season (Ingravallo clenched his teeth), certain characters ripe for jail—then, the bastard! then, plonk, plonk, plonk, the rain of bank notes. Great big drops, too!

He—to summarize—he had to go to Genoa. His transfer had already been decided: it was imminent even, a matter of days.

The fine room in Via Nicotera 21, as confirmed by Signora Amalia Bazz . . . Buzzichelli, had really been given up, as of the end of the month. (That other nonsense, the pipeline that was to pump refined petroleum to Ferrania!)* There wasn't time left, now, for him to perfect his process of enchantment. And so? A blunt request? Refusal on the part of Liliana? Lack of money on hand? Or a grab at the gold, the jewels? That horrible object . . . for a handful of greasy paper? And the jewels?

Doctor Valdarena had been searched as soon as they brought him in; nothing had been found on him: nothing of a suspicious origin. But he had had plenty of time, between nine A.M. and twenty after ten, to go out and stash his loot in a safe place, and to come back (but, but the notion was a bit risky, to tell the truth) . . . after Cristoforo and Gina had gone off about their business, and before he had called for help, at ten-twenty . . . Well, yes, more than an hour had gone by, at the very least. The concierge Pettacchioni was busy up above, way up in the clouds. With her broom and bucket: and with her tongue, too, you could bet on that. At that hour, judging by Pompeo's report, she

* Ferrania is a small city near Savona. Mussolini had planned an oil pipeline there. It was never built.

98

liked to drop over to B, where her mainstay was la Bolenfi, or Sbolenfi, still in her slippers. Ingravallo, with one hand, rooting a bit among the papers: "Elia Gabbi, widow Bolenfi," he recited, with firm assurance.

Higher still than the widow, on the top floor, there was General Barbezzo. Ingravallo, promptly, plucked him out, too, from all that paper, like an old black hen, cluckcluck-cluck, might snap up a fat worm: with a single peck, never missing, even in a mountain of manure. Again he recited: "General Grand'Ufficiale nobleman Ottorino Barbezzi-Gallo, retired: age? hah! from Casalpusterlengo. To hell with him."

So he was a nobleman, as well. From what Grabber had hummed in an ear, a very distinguished gent, a widower, with his beard divided in two, looking like some de luxe brush: but his gout (according to Sora Manuela) made him suffer the torments of hell. Why, the doctors had for-bidden him to set his feet on the ground: celestified, per-force, into his own empyrean. A nice little collection to console himself: fourteen or fifteen of the finest bottles, kind that take your breath away, at one gulp. A perfect gentle-man, though: he wore two carpet slippers, that looked like elephant's feet. A gent. Sora Manuela, in the odd moments of leisure granted her from her concierge-ship, used to perform for him certain domestic services. She did little odd jobs . . . in the morning, too, while he was waiting for the maid to come; the maid came in late, at noon, but with the marketing already done. A man living by himself, and helpless like that! But she didn't want the tenants to know: and naturally, vice versa, all of them knew it. She claimed

99

she had things of her own to do, up on the roof. The roof, as all know, is the realm of the washing to be hung out. Well, on certain windy mornings up there, she seemed ready to fly away herself, like a plane from the launching deck of an aircraft carrier. With those four bombs she had attached to her, one pair fore and one aft.

"I'm up here. I'm hanging out the wash!" she yelled to the building's sleepers. She sang like a girl of eighteen. The kids, at times, called her from down below: from the fabled well of the courtyard. "Hey, Sora Manuè, somebody wants you! Come on down!" When they didn't go to school. Her husband was kept very busy, at the Fontanelli Milk Company. She came down, ker-plonk, ker-plonk, her cheeks flushed: that wind! all hundred and twenty-nine steps. With her breath smelling of anise. A breeze in itself! She descended, in a word, from heaven. A heaven of anisette. "Don Ciccio!" and Ingravallo turned the page. According to the more reliable, among the many and melodiously whispered rumors of number two hundred and nineteen, so promptly picked up by Grabber, it seemed . . . yes, in short, that she and Barbezzi-Gallo, from time to time, after a good swig of the old Barbezzi's gall, well it was only natural, they felt the need to exchange congratulations, glass in hand. The classics from his collection. Authentic Meletti anisette, a hundred and twenty lire the bottle, containing three-quarters of a liter. And for this reason, Napoleon himself with the whole Army of Italy, could go past the lodge, if the kids were off at school, as they were on that awful Thursday, and nobody would be seen.

The vigorous new forces, then effecting in Italian society

that profound renewal, were inspired by the ancient severity or at least by the severe faces of the Lictors, but the renewal also was flavored by their endowment of little clubs (staves tightly bound to the handle of the ax, not only emblematic). Now without wasting their strength in philosophizing (*primum vivere*), they devoted themselves to paving with the most verbose of good intentions the road to hell. Gassified into funereal menace, made Word (and Wind), they conspired with great impetus, in that whirlwind of air and dust they stirred up, to kiss the ass even of the clouds, destroying all separation of powers and also the living being generally known as the Fatherland: the distinction of the "three powers," which the great and modest sociologist of the slightly askew wig, observing the best institutions of the Romans and the wisest and more recent of English history, had isolated with such lucidity. Italy's new resurrection followed a not very clothed (as far as the human species was concerned) renaissance, with the pictorial or poetical forms which the world had hailed as indecent and, at the same time, masterful. And this rebirth clung, with an air of bringing it to the best possible conclusion, to a *risorgimento* a little too generous in squeezing pathos from the locks of its troubadours, shaggy or bearded, or generously mustachioed, or glorious in their muttonchops or sideburns, all in any case needing—to our taste—the radical attentions of a Figaro with drastic scissors. The effect that this above-mentioned resurrection extracted from its entrails, ruttingly eager at last to dispose of all the dispositions made disposable by political power, was the effect that is found every time: I mean every time that absolute power is assumed, conglomerating the three controls—discerned by Charles Louis de Secondat de Montesquieu with such clear thinking, in book eleven, chapter six, of his little treatise of roughly eight hundred pages on the *ésprit des lois*—conglomerating them, all three, in a single and triply impenetrable and unremovable mafia. In such an event *"le même corps de magistrature a, comme exécuteur des lois, toute la puissance qu'il s'est donnée come législateur. Il peut ravager l'État"* (did you get that? *ravager l'État!*) *"par ses volontés générales et, comme il a encore la puissance de juger, il peut détruire chaque citoyen par ses volontés particulières":* particulières to it, that is, to the above-mentioned corps. In our case, in the new ravage brought about by a too-fiery remembrance of the ancient cudgels (which, if anything, did their cudgeling in accordance with the law, and not in accordance with mob rule), the telephone was found ready and willing to lend, to the triply powerful mafia, the expert services of a liaison officer, controlled by the zeal and the hypersensitive ears of an official spy. Bureaucratic "urging" could assume that tone and, more, that harshly injunctive, or even imperious character fitting only to the *"homines consulares,"* to the *"homines praetorii"* of the neo-Empire that was being cooked up. The man who, through his strength, is sure to be right, never for a moment suspects he could be wrong by law. The man who recognizes himself as a genius, a beacon to all peoples, never suspects that he might be a candle to be snuffed out, or a quadruped ass. When one considers a depository, or a commissioner, of the renewed truth, one would never dare think him likely to pee new stupidities with each new day: into the mouth of those who are listening to him, agape. Ah well. The little cascade of official telephone calls, like every cascade with any self-respect, was and is unreversible, within a determined field of forces, the field of gravity, or the field of obsequiousness and pass-the-buckdom. And there was no need even to summon up two louts with two clumps of hair on their noses, and two huge shiny leather belts adorned with pistols and dirks, to make the ass-sitting subaltern aware, from the other end of the wire, on the spot, of what he had best answer, or how he should best proceed: "Prepared . . . always prepared to obey." Click. And so it happened after the crime, the first, at Via Merulana two hundred and nineteen, as soon as the second, the horrible murder, followed it. "The unjustified delay in the investigations, which" now must "assume a brisker pace," adapting themselves from one moment to the next to the impatient stampings of the *pausarius,* hammering at the prow, rather than the poop, and in compensation with all four hoofs. The economical Commendatore and, in his free time truffle-fancier, eighty-six hours after that nine P.M. of the Monday evening, was invited to show up again at Santo Stefano. After ninety-two, more dead than alive, he was sent back to blowing his nose in Regina Coeli: in the vast and least expectable of his handkerchiefs.

The poor Signora Balducci, according to the tenants' unanimous affirmations, seemed to have received no one in that house, the two last hours of her life! No one. Except her killer.

They hadn't heard any shouts, or noises, or thuds: not even la Menegazzi, who had been combing her hair, not even the two Bottafavis, husband and wife. Inquiries at the Roman office of Standard Oil, "conducted personally by Doctor Ingravallo," confirmed the fact of the transfer, to Genoa, decided upon some time ago, of Doctor Giuliano Valdarena. It had been settled that he would leave on Monday, March 21st, oh, give or take a day either way. As far as they were concerned, they had nothing but praise for the young man. A quick-witted employee, a good talker when he wanted to be, distinguished appearance: and basically, oh yes, a willing worker. He didn't have to be asked twice to take a taxi and chase after some client, some engineer, one of those who are always running around, constantly in motion, up and down the country, in trains. Some mornings, early, or some sultry afternoons, perhaps . . . Well, he was young. A little laziness, at times, on some sirocco days: the office atmosphere. But with the clients, for the most part, he hit it off just fine.

"It doesn't take much," Don Ciccio grunted to himself, "Where are they going to buy their oil, anyway? From the egg-man?"

He hit it off, yes. The competition, especially when it comes to oil for transformers, that's where the real money is, tended to knock down the prices, though within the limits established by the cartel, to exploit the profit margin . . . of the ten lire per quintal. He, well, he knew his way around: he had a kind of charm, his good manners, the appearance of a man who uses his head, who knows how to wait.

"You see, Doctor . . . er . . . Ingravallo, you won't believe it, perhaps, but a client is sort of like a woman. You think I'm joking, maybe . . . You have to know how to handle them. The patience it takes, sometimes! You have to wait, to know how to wait: stay there, under the stone bench, with your eyes looking sleepy, but ready to spring, like a tomcat in heat. And then there are times instead when you have to be cagey . . to make sure you get there before the next fellow, the competition, I mean. Believe me, sir, you have to keep working on them till they fall for you, at least a little bit, at least for half a day: *l'espace d'un matin.* Even when they drag along old Auntie to chaperone, the big holding company who pretends to sit in a corner and knit, but is keeping a weather eye on the ledgers: and maybe has a weakness, *her* weakness. She has her likes and her dislikes, too, just like some old women, some mothers-in-law . . . like times when you want to make the daughter fall for you, but you have to win the mother over first. That's how it is. There are the Platonic ones, mind you, and the romantic ones: the ones who dream in the moonlight, those who make a fuss over ten lire, those who hope and swallow everything, and those who like to drag it out. They make us hop, all right. Well, that's the way they like it: like a bunch of she-cats in February. Nothing you can do about it. It takes patience! Then there are the other ones, the brisk ones, who come straight to the point. I tell you, Doctor, you have to know how to handle them. Each in his own way. But, believe me, if we're going to work the way we should, first they have to fall in love! I don't mean with *us* exactly, we're just middlemen, although . . . not even a pretty doll would throw us away . . . what the hell . . . no, not us but . . . you might say, with Standard in general. They have to fall in love with Standard Oil, learn to trust Standard blindly, take what we give them! Because, we know what to give them, better than they do, the kind of bottle each one needs: this kind, and not that. Why, a world-wide organization like ours! I should hope so! Tens of thousands of gallons per year, in Europe alone, of the finest kinds of oil, that tells you something about Standard Oil, eh? Not something to kid about.

"Our great secret, you see, is the secret we like to tell everybody: the constancy of the specifications for each different kind of oil. Now, for example, take our unbeatable Transformer Oil B, Grade 11-Extra. You can ask about it here in Rome: Engineer Casalis of the Anglo-Romana Company, or Engineer Bocciarelli of the Terni." He assisted himself with the fingers of his left hand, thumb, index, middle finger, unrolling them one after the other, to list the merits of Grade 11-Extra; he reached his little finger, and remained there: "Absolutely waterless: this is the most basic essential; yes, the *sine qua non:* freezing point . . . extremely low: viscosity . . . 2.4 Wayne, at the outside: acid value, negligible: dielectric strength, amazing: flash point . . . the highest of all American industrial oils.

"Now, you tell me, what more can you ask from an oil for transformers? But then, as I said before, what really counts, more than anything else, is the *constancy of the specifications* in every grade: the characteristics that indicate the merit of a given oil . . . of our Transformer B, I mean. Always the same! Always! Identical, any time and any place: from one shipment to the next." He raised his voice. "Over a period of years! The world can come to an end, the phoenix can rise from its ashes, the Colosseum can catch fire . . . but Standard's Transformer Oil B, 11-Extra, is what it is, and remains what it is. Our client can sleep the sleep of the just, believe me. We know what he needs. And a lot of our clients have finally caught on to this themselves. It's easy enough for them to be unfaithful to us. But then what? Here you have a transformer that's cost you a million, let's say, and you wake up one fine morning and realize that you've been pouring tomato sauce into it, instead of oil. And when your transformer has burnt out on you, the first storm that comes along, then what do you do? You can kiss any operating economy good-bye! And it's good-bye to amortizement in fifteen years, or ten years! . . . Or in eight months, for that matter! . . . No, believe me, doctor, it isn't only the price that should determine the transaction, that's the bait . . . the bald fact of the amount: four, nine, six the quintal. No. The price . . . well, you know. Take a watch for example: you can find one for fourteen-fifty in some little store in Via dei Greci; but a good watch sets you back two thousand lire at Catellani's. You try to buy yourself a Patek Philippe, a Longines, a Vachéron-Constantin . . . for fourteen-fifty. Where are you going to find anybody who'll let one go for that? If you find me one, then that'll be the day I can make a present of my Transformer B 11-Extra at the price . . . at the price of some of the other stuff they've got on the market!"

He sighed, "Ah, well, so it goes." Ingravallo was in a

stupor. His eyelids had begun to drop forward like awnings over two shop windows: to fall down, halfway over the globe of each eye, in his poppy-seed attitude of state occasions: when the torpor of the office crowned him with a hebetude which was . . . almost divinatory. And instead, this divine occasion was being created by the stupidest source. A gusher! Oil! The people back in Apulia: oil is what they live on. But this other oil . . . he really didn't know how to get a grip on it.

"Make the client fall in love. That's the whole story. Hammer the truth into his head: the great nail of truth! That's all. Doctor Valdarena, when it comes to hammering, has shown plenty of talent. Then, when the day comes that they've fallen in love and have given our Transformer B a try, it's very hard, believe you me, for anybody else to seduce them away, to make them unfaithful to us! And all screwing aside, those who love us, follow us . . . as the Great Man says . . . so . . . How about a cigarette?" "Thanks." "So, I mean, they pay. They pay up, without saying another word."

"They pay. They pay," grunted Don Ciccio, in the solitude of his own, interior forum.

IV

AFTER twenty-two hours of general uneasiness Balducci arrived, on the 18th: unforeseen engagements, he stated. Meanwhile the police stations had been alerted: Milan, Bologna, Vicenza, Padua. It was, for Ingravallo and for Doctor Fumi, a real relief. If it had turned out that Balducci had skipped, the investigations would have had to be extended over half the peninsula, with a slow monsoon of telegrams.

And the mess, already fairly tangled up, would have become utterly snarled. But Balducci, miraculously unaware, got off the train at eight, the collar of his overcoat turned up, his face anything but ruddy at that moment and a bit smudged to boot: with his necktie loosened, and with a look as if he had slept, in discomfort and over interminable jolting, profoundly. He and the train had kept faith with the telegram, which for the rest had been vague. But the only through train coming into Rome Station at eight was the one from Sarzana: which at its final creak and the successive blocking of the breaks was on the dot, as clocks under the roof of the platform and beside the gate waited open-mouthed, observing the new orders from above, gloriously imparted from the Ass on high. The terrible news was broken to him with all due consideration and with all the most opportune toning down, right there by the train, as other travelers, at the windows, were still fighting over the porters, with shouts imperious or imploring, and the porters assumed the tone of their finest hour: Swiss and Milanese in arrival: good, sound luggage; it was broken to him by his wife's relatives who had come there on Ingravallo's invitation, some dressed in black, some merely in dark gray: Aunt Marietta at their head, with a black prayer shawl around her shoulders, like a mandrill's ruff, a necklace of little black beads around her neck, a hat like a teacher in a teacher's college, a face like an attorney general. Then, behind her, Zia Elviruccia, with her son, Oreste, the big boy with the big yellow teeth who looked so much like Uncle Peppino, who was, you might say, the spit and image of Uncle Peppino. A funeral face on him, too. There was also the sergeant, in uniform: Di Pietrantonio. When, little by little, they made him understand, Uncle Remo, what had happened, he, poor man, first of all, set his overnight case on the ground: the others, the heavy ones, had already been taken off by the porter. The news didn't seem to shock him so very much. Maybe it was sleepiness, fatigue after those nights in the train. Maybe he was kind of out of his head and didn't even hear what they were saying to him.

In the meanwhile the corpse had been removed and taken to the City Morgue, where they had proceeded to an external examination of the body. Nothing. When it was dressed and laid out, the throat was bandaged, with white gauze, like a Carmelite lying in death: the head was covered with a sort of Red Cross nurse's bonnet, without the red cross, however. Seeing her like that, white, immaculate, they all immediately took off their hats. The women made the Sign of the Cross. The coroner's office had witnessed the examinations, in accordance with the law, in the person of Judge Cavaliere Mucellato. Also the Attorney General's representative, Commendatore Macchioro, had paid her, so to speak, a duty call. The man in Palazzo Chigi had to have the last word, too, louder than all the others: "That evil murderer should have already been shot, six hours ago."

But Balducci hadn't read the papers.

On the body there was nothing, beyond the work of the knife, and those scratches, those fingernail marks.

Once he was at the house, poor Signor Remo was obliged to open drawers, unlock a reluctant cupboard or two. They hadn't been able to find the keys to some: and there were other keys, discovered at random, whose destination was still unknown. He tried them, he tried them again, here, then there, in vain. Nobody had gone into his little study. The desk, with "Marengo Universal" locks, seemed free from any tampering. He opened it himself: everything was in order. And so was the metal filing cabinet, where he kept certain papers: it was a little dark green, fired-enamel case, very neat and clean and new, which stood beside the half-empty wooden bookcases, half-filled with thumbed cheap volumes, and together, the two pieces of furniture looked like the young accountant fresh from the barber with the filthy-rich, dripping-nosed old woman whom he manages and robs and who is in love with him. The entire, mute examination was observed by the two ladies, the aunts, by Oreste, and the police sergeant Di Pietrantonio, in reality a top-sergeant, a policeman—one Rodolico—as well as by Sora Manuela. A moment later Blondie happened along. Doctor Ingravallo trusted Pompeo and the Blond Terror from Terracina: the others were a bunch of meatheads, at times, when you tried to drum a little psychology into them! Those two had sharp noses: they could catch on to people from their faces, after once glance: and usually without letting on. What was important to him, to Ingravallo, was, above all, the face, the attitude, *the immediate psychic and physiognomical reactions,* as he said, of the spectators and the protagonists of the drama: of this bunch of bastards and sonsabitches that people the world, and their women, whores and tramps and sows.

Bottafavi's aid was invoked, after a few vain tugs from Rodolico, who succeeded only in popping one of his buttons, where it wasn't immediately clear. The weapons expert came downstairs with a square-handled carpenter's box slung over his arm, containing a whole repertory of screwdrivers, saws, chisels, hammers, pliers, and a monkey wrench into the bargain: not to mention a goodly supply of loose nails, both straight and bent. In the end a smith was summoned, a veritable Don Juan when it came to locks: he had a bunch of hooks with an extra little twist in the end, and all he had to do was tickle the lock with one or the other, and it knew at once that it couldn't hold out. With him, locks were like virtuous women who suddenly go crazy. Balducci verified at once the absence of the best, the money and the jewels which the signora kept in a little iron coffer in the second drawer of the dresser: the coffer had disappeared, complete with contents. Not even the key was found: it stayed, usually, in an old velvet purse, black with embroidered forget-me-nots, in the mirrored wardrobe, tied by a fine little blue ribbon to the elite of its genteel and tinkling sisterhood. "The purse was . . . it used to be here. Let me have a look." He groped with his hand from below upwards in that perfumed heap of silk, of all those slips, those blouses, and those little embroidered handkerchiefs. Yes, yes. The purse, too, had disappeared. And also the two passbooks to savings accounts failed to answer Balducci's roll-call. "My God, they've gone too!" "What?" "The savings account passbooks, Liliana's." "What color were they?" "Color! One was in the Banco di Santo Spirito, and one in the Banca Commerciale." "In whose name . . . hers?" "Yes, Liliana's." "Were they made out to the bearer?" "No, personal."

The diminution of the little hoard (with the personal passbooks, however, there was no real danger) seemed to crush Signor Remo: even more perhaps, judging from outside, from *the immediate psychic and physiognomical reactions,* than the horrible news which had been brought to him at the station. It was a completely gratuitous, false impression, you might say: but none of those present managed to dispel it, not the (top) sergeant, nor Orestino: and still less Aunt Marietta and Aunt Elviruccia, embittered and malicious as they contemplated that gross man sunk in tribulations: "yes, yes, go out on your hunting trips now, now that the rabbit has run off," that huge man who went up and down the house, pulling out all the drawers of the furniture and looking into them . . . just in case a pin had been stolen.

Made grim and greedy, the aunts were, just thinking

about it, in the great fermenting that the latent avarice common to all the Valdarena relations had created in those hours of the incredible night with its troubled counsels, after the many-regioned voices of the police and the unquestionably Roman one of Sora Manuela in the telephonic shock of the preceding day: and now both of them, Aunt Marietta and Aunt Elviruccia, disappointed in the disappointment of a moment. Lilianuccia, eh? Not even a little souvenir left to her cousins? to her aunts? to her own Aunt Marietta, who had been a mother to her, you might say, since her real mother died? not even a little medal of the Madonna? with all that jewelry (You could have stocked a shop with it) that she kept under lock and key? Poor child, it had never occurred to her to make a will. When a person has to die like that, she can't think about it beforehand, she can't foresee such a thing. Madonna! it was enough to drive you crazy! What a world! What a world, indeed!

And besides they had Giuliano on their minds. That arrest, they felt, was an outrage: an offense against them, the splendid house of Valdarena, "a high-class family whose like you can't find in the whole of Rome"; a family of the most florid, the most solidly rooted: men, women, and kids. The thought of a girl like that, plunged into the devil's arms, with all her finest wedding presents, all her gold and jewels, leaving nothing to remember her by, not even a word of farewell! The idea, for the poor aunts!, was about to become a torment, heartache. Murdered that way. Rancor, horror, terror, a cry in the darkness! At the bursting out of a demoniacal tension which acts to lacerate in such a drastic way the folio certificates of one's civil

status, demos or parish, and the long, the many-eyed pre-
cautions of living—on such occasions, the human kin, the
gentes, tend to repeat, as a right, even if they don't achieve
it in fact, the thing lent. *Commodatam repetunt rem.* They
summon it back from the darkness, from the night. They
want it back, they want once more the flower! with its broken
stem, the quantum that has been lost from their life. Like
filings on the magnet, the tiniest fibers of their viscera are
polarized on the *tension of return.* They feel they must suck
back the gamic unit that has been expelled, the biological
unit, the person once alive, eternally alive, and sacra-
mentally alienated into marriage with some Tom, Dick or
Harry. They would like to control again the possibility,
the nuptial valency offered to another, to the husband (in
this case): to the brother-in-law or son-in-law given them
by the demos. And the gamic unit whose possession they
claim implies, at the same time, an economic quantum.
She was a splendid girl, and there was a coffer of jewels:
former and latter ripened by the years: by the slow, tacit
years. She was a girl with a little box; and they, the
Valdarenas, had entrusted her husband with the key: and
the right to make use of it, clickety-click: the sacrosanct
use. And Christ's coadjutor, at the church of the Santi
Quattro, had blessed the pact. With a wealth of *asperges
in nomine Domini:* without too much splashing, however.
She, beneath her orange-blossom crown, within her veil,
had bowed her head. So let him give back, back what was
wrongly taken, this fool of a hunter, this traveler in textiles.
How had he used her beauty? Or how wasted it? such
gentle beauty? and the cash? the grand old cash, equally

beautiful? Where had he stashed it away, the loot? Those gold pieces with the Gentleman King's ugly face on them? Those nicely round, bright yellow pieces of the days before this Puppet in Palazzo Chigi, yelling from his balcony like an old-clothes man. She had forty-four of them, Liliana had, forty-four gold marengos: which went clink-clank in a little bag of pink silk, a bag her grandmother had sent wedding sweets in.* And they weighed more than a pair of kidneys at Christmas. "And now where have they gone to?" the kinfolk thought. "What does he know about them, our hunter friend here?" *Manet sub Jove frigido.* To what marriage indeed has he reserved his wife, his bride's carnal and dowrial validity? What has he made of that tender flesh, this apoplectic salesman? and with that nice nest egg? which was so much a part of it? Yes, the tidy bundle! left her by a stubborn rumination of time, of the economic virtues of the lending clan? Thus, as she had inherited that tepid flesh from the accumulated vehemence of generations, after many a hard morning. Liliana's relatives seemed to be saying: "Oh! gentle bride, stuffed with nice cash! treasure of the years! Unexpected accrediting of the equinox! Let him cough up, that is to say, spit back, this hick of a commercial traveler! Let him not dare accuse Giuliano, splendid offshoot of the old stock, only because he has to face comparison with him now." Their minds, the minds of those two old bags Aunt Marietta and Aunt Elvira, pursued their private whims: "Giuliano, flower of the Valdarena clan! Replete with fertile days! Bud of life!"

* Reference to an Italian custom: recently married couples send sugared almonds in tulle bags to those who have sent—or should send —wedding presents.

There exists a dramatic region of every rancor, from the spleen and from the gall bladder inside the gnawing liver, to the very penumbras behind the household furniture where the *lares* officiate: the gods that see and remain silent, breathing in the dead odor of naphthalene in cupboards. But at the first appearance of the blade, they had trembled, unable to cry out: and in the room's opaque volumes, now, they were shocked and weeping, with the nerves of martyrs. Well, it was there, between the legs of the corporal and the locksmiths, when Manuela's globes had been shoved aside, that all those envenomed phantoms wandered. Erect and hard, the aunts awaited justice: Oreste didn't know himself how to behave.

Valdarena, at the Collegio Romano, had been subjected to repeated questioning: the alibis he had produced (office, clerks in the office) were watertight up until nine twenty, but not after that. He said he had been out, downtown. Out where? With whom? Clients? Women? Tobacconist? Two or three times he blushed, as if at a lie. He had even trotted out his barber, but then had immediately retracted this affirmation: no, he had had his hair cut the day before. Actually none of the tenants had seen him, at that earlier hour. Only at ten thirty-five, when he had called for help. The Felicetti kid: brought before him, face to face, denied having seen him on the stairs: the one who went to say good morning to the Bottafavis, who had met the cheese-bearers: "n . . o . . ." she said, with great tugging at her lips, so that she could hardly blurt out: "he . . . wasn't . . . there . . ." After which she went mute: and pressed by new and repeated questions, then by exhortation of every kind, she hung her head, in tears. She almost said yes, but she couldn't quite make up her mind: she wouldn't open her mouth. Finally, as big drops ran down her cheeks, it seemed to everybody that she wanted to shake her head: no. Her Mamma, kneeling beside her, face to face, patted her on the head, from which statements issue; she whispered in one ear, kissing her: "Tell the nice man, dear, tell the truth. Tell me, yes, now didn't you see this gentleman here, on the steps? See how blond he is? Like an angel, isn't he? Tell us, sweetheart, Mamma's baby doll! No, don't cry, your Mamma's right here with you, your Mamma who loves you to pieces. Here," two kisses smacked on the kid's cheeks, "you mustn't be scared of the officer. Doctor Ingravallo isn't the bad kind of doctor, those mean ones, who hurt my poor baby and make her stick out her tongue and say ah. He's a doctor in a black suit, too, but he's a good one!" and she squeezed the little stomach under the dress, as if to ascertain whether it were dry or damp: in certain cases, testimony is not necessarily unaccompanied by suitable outpourings of another nature. "Tell me, tell Mamma, there's my sweetie. Tell us, and Doctor Ingravallo will give you a nice dolly, the kind that shut their eyes, with a pink apron with little blue flowers on it." Then the kid hung her head still lower and said: "Yes." Giuliano paled. "And what was the gentleman doing? What did he say to you?" She burst out weeping, yelling desperately amid her tears: "I—want —to—go home! Home!" after which her Mamma blew her nose for her: and that was that, nothing more to be got out of her. Mamma, "Oh, I tell you!" insisted that she was an extraordinarily bright child, for her age: "you know how it

is . . . with kiddies, you have to know how to handle them."
To Ingravallo, on the other hand, she seemed an idiot, in every respect a daughter worthy of her mother.

The Pirroficoni case had not yet afflicted the pages of the city papers: the Death's Head in his diplomat's ceremonial hat twisting already, on the other hand, the peacock's feather of the suspect, to be able to stick it where he stuck his feathers: peacock's or of spoiled chicken that stank.

In any case it was wise, already in those days, to proceed with caution: Don Ciccio had a whiff of this, and Doctor Fumi as well, after public opinion—that is to say, the general racket—had taken possession of the event.

"To exploit" the event—*whatsoever* event Jove Scoundrel, big-cheese in the cloud department, dropped in your lap, plop—to the magnification of one's own pseudo-ethical activity, in fact protuberantly theatrical and filthily staged, is the game of the institution or person who wishes to endow propaganda and fisheries with the weight of a moral activity. The displayed psyche of the political madman (a narcissist of pseudo-ethical content) grabs the alien crime, real or believed, and roars over it like a stupid, furious beast, in cold blood, over an ass's jawbone: behaving in such a way as to exhaust (to relax) in the inane matter of a punitive myth the dirty tension that compels him to action, action *coûte que coûte*. The alien crime is exploited to placate the snaky-maned Megaera, the mad multitude: which will not be placated with so little: it is offered, like a ram or stag to be torn to pieces, to the disheveled women who will rip it apart, light of foot, ubiquitous and mammary in the bacchanal which their own cries kindle, purpled with torment and blood. In this way, a pseudo-justice assumes a legal course, a pseudo-severity, or the pseudo-habilitation of the finger-pointings whose manifest countersigns seem to be both the arrogance of the ill-considered magistrate's investigation and the cynobalanic* excitement of the anticipated sentence. Reread the sad and atrocious tale in *War and Peace*, book three, part three, chapter twenty-five: and understand the summary execution of the helpless Verestchagin, thought a spy, not being one; Count Rostopchin, governor of Moscow, play-acting on the steps of his palace before the grim, waiting crowd, orders the dragoons to kill him with their sabers, there, in the crowd's presence: on the fine old principle, by God, *"qu'il leur faut une victime."* It was in the morning, ten o'clock. "At four in the afternoon Murat's army entered Moscow."

Much more base and theatrical, *chez nous*, that Fierce-Face with his plume: nor can we grant him, as we can Rostopchin, the immediate attenuating circumstances of fear (of being lynched himself) and of anguish and rage and the pandemonium (total psychosis of the mob) and of the enemy approaching, after the brusque cannonades and the slaughter (at Borodino).

The hapless Pirroficoni was almost killed by the blows of an Italian of the same stripe: because they wanted to wring from him, in any way, in the "interrogation chamber," the truthful admission that he had raped certain little girls. He was stunned and pleaded no, there wasn't a word of truth

* *cinobalànico*, a word invented by Gadda, a Greco-Italian adjective created from an obscene Roman dialect expression meaning "badly done."

in it: but he was beaten to a faretheewell. O generous Manes of Beccaria!*

The Urbs, in the very period of his fits of public decency and of police-enforced Federzonism,† was to know (1926–27) several periodical stranglings of little girls: and on the meadows there lay traces of the remains and the torment, and the poor, slaughtered innocence: there, there *extra muros*, after the shrines of suburbicarian devotion, and the epigraphs of the ancient marbles and sacella. *Consule Federsonio, Rosamaltonio enixa: Damnato Shittonio dictatore syphlitico.*‡ Pirroficoni, the wretch! was master at that time of a mistress, rather plump not to say overripe, but somewhat difficult of access: fifth floor, a modern building: concierge in her lodge: husband, present and in working order ... in his carpet slippers: clusters of neighbors *ad libitum*, natural glossators superior even to Irnerius.§ Whence, that is, because of these factual premises, a pathetic up-and-down of autographs of various import thanks to a gentle maiden (thirteen years old) who bore them with some circumspection and with equal palpitation of the heart to their destination. And conversations in sign language and various finger

* Cesare Beccaria, Italian reformer and humanitarian (1738–94), author of the famous *Dei delitti e delle pene*. The Pirroficoni case was an actual event (as, for that matter, was the crime which inspired *Il pasticciaccio*).

† Luigi Federzoni was Mussolini's Minister of the Interior.

‡ A Gaddian parody of the Latin inscriptions on buildings all over Italy, a custom initiated by the Popes and continued with gusto by the Fascists, who were fond of translating their names and titles into Latin. Rosa Maltoni was the maiden name of Mussolini's mother.

§ Irnerius, teacher of law of Bologna, was the first great commentator on Roman law (1065–1125).

play from window to street: and vice versa. The expert and fingersome swain was arrested on the sidewalk, just when he was transmitting some of his signals with six or seven fingers (the hours of love) towards that window on the fifth floor (this, in the opinion of headquarters, was a "strategic feint"): and as he was entrusting a note for Madame, second stratagem, to her little messenger, a little maid, thrilled and frightened by her mission, her face all flushed. Pirroficoni had also given the child, as usual with him, a caress or two: this action, and his own blushing, were his perdition. On this splendid array of evidence the plumed Death's Head belched that "the Roman police in less than forty-eight hours etc. etc." And the cop, comforted by the lofty words of the Deuce, fell to with a will. The doubting intervention of some honest official saved Pirroficoni's bones, but not before they were sorely beaten.

Then it was Balducci's turn to be questioned: the afternoon of that same day, March 18th, at Santo Stefano del Cacco: for several hours: by the Chief himself: the coroner also took part, *pro forma*, "the police were still taking the initiative in the investigations." Ingravallo, this time, didn't really feel up to questioning him. A friend, after all! He didn't even want to watch. And besides, it was clear, they would touch on difficult matters: the delicate questioning was bound to end in the hairsplitting of a particular kind of interrogation, or else it would break out in disgusting crudities, an interrogation of the crudest kind. The relations between . . . Balducci and his wife: moods, her frame of mind. There came to the surface again that incredible story of the nieces: the strange "mania" of the victim, wanting a daughter at any cost. She would have bought one, second-hand, at the Campo de' Fiori market, all else failing. As to the dough, Doctor Fumi was quick to convince himself that the married couple, him and her both, were in an enviable economic position. With that ballast down in the hold . . . there was no rough sea that could rock the boat, no inflation scare.

The widower sketched out a list of their bonds, as best he could, from memory: his own as well as Liliana's: to facilitate the proof, he said, that when it came to him, they ought to consider him beyond all suspicion, even a momentary cloud. "Me? My own little Liliana? What? You're kidding?" His lips began to tremble, he burst into sobs which made his necktie jerk. When those tears were dried, he began summoning up his memory: with the aid of a little leather notebook, alligator skin it was: the kind real gents carry. He had brought it with him. Their holdings were noted down in it. Liliana kept a safe-deposit box at the bank, at branch number 11 of the Banca Commerciale, which had a safe-deposit service, a *caveau* of the most modern kind: at Piazza Vittorio, just opposite the market, under the arcades: right corner of Via Carlo Alberto. But then, there was another one at Corso Umberto, at the Banco di Santo Spirito. "Liliana's father, my poor old father-in-law, was a straight sort of man: a man with a real instinct: he didn't believe there was going to be any revolution, not this time, he said to me, and he said it was no good trusting corporations; first of all . . . because they're anonymous; you don't know their name or what they're up to, or where they are. Why, if one day it comes into their heads to say: this dope here, I think I'll screw him, then what can you do? You think you can track them down up there in Milan and say, hey, Signora Società Anonima, I want my dough back. The hell you say. No, no. Five-year bonds! he used to say. They're safer than gold! he said, because gold is up today and down tomorrow: but bonds . . . and a bit of consolidated, five per cent maybe, the sort of investment that lets you get your sleep at night. All stuff guaranteed by the government: the Italian government! It's like a granite building, the government, take it from me: there, nobody wants to screw you. What would they get out of it? And this new one, they say wants to do things seriously." Having quoted his father-in-law, at a sad smile from Doctor Fumi, Balducci reserved the right to produce detailed, exact lists. Himself. Liliana.

He furnished "unexceptionable" commercial references and bank references, then various clarifications about his position as a sales representative, in the textiles line, for certain producers up north. The question of cash, one might say, between him and his wife, simply didn't exist. "We never wanted for anything, not me, and not Liliana. Never any trouble, never a worry . . . no lack of ready cash, never, a loan . . . not even from today to tomorrow. Notes?" In their family they didn't even know what the word meant.

"Commercial bills, in my business: yes . . . you can't do business without them."

How was it, with all their means, that they lived there, among those wormy shopkeepers, retired merchants, commendatores making fifteen hundred a month?

"Well, the idea of having to move ... laziness. My father-in-law had bought the apartment, and had even lived there with Liliana before she was married. I met her there": and once again the poor man couldn't keep back his tears. His heavy voice shook: "we got married there! Me and Lilianuccia!" Doctor Fumi felt tears rising in his throat, too: like a level of water, rising in a well. Liliana's father, it was. He had a sharp eye, for a deal! "You know how it is, doctor ..." They had already known each other for a few years: business affairs. And then ... She, only child, her mother dead: a beauty! Ah, those were the days!

They had become engaged, they had been married in that house. Then, once they were husband and wife ... They were in love, they were company for each other. Their tastes were modest. They kept to themselves. "I didn't feel like working to work for the other fellow, that was it. One of these days we all have to die, and we had no kids. Like life was trying to spite us! And then ... the armistice after the war! And besides, by then we were all settled down, we were used to the place. There's central heating, even if it doesn't heat all that well, but still! It was good enough for us. There was a modern bath ... A few broken dishes, a few odd chairs. But who doesn't have them? Liliana didn't like having people around her too much. With that obsession of hers, to adopt a girl ... and that poor little animal, Lulu, who didn't want to move for anything! Her, too! What's happened to her now, poor animal? A bad sign!"

The war! All their worries about getting out of the draft! All the documents! A job! And yet, he had made it. Well, not exactly exempted, but more or less. A leather belt, a big revolver: "I was scary to look at": he shook his head.

"So I stayed in Via Merulana . . . Seventeen, after two years of being engaged, I said to myself, it looks to me like they're not going to stop this so soon. So to hell with it. If we're going to do it, let's go ahead. You probably remember what the apartment situation was then: with all those refugees! There was plenty of room at my father-in-law's: you couldn't find a thing anywhere else. So I moved in . . . with my father-in-law. There was nothing else to do. That house —it was like it was ours, I mean mine and Liliana's."

"It was your . . . er . . . nest, I understand."

"You understand: being able to loaf around in your shirt-sleeves whenever you felt like it." You long for a little peace and quiet, after work, after the trains, to do as you please: and not have to get involved with all your neighbors' messes.

And that melancholy of Liliana's. That kind of obsession. And then, with the Santi Quattro practically next door. "Why, Liliana, she'd never have let me take her away from Santi Quattro!"

So everything had sort of conspired to keep them where they were, in that awful building at number two hundred and nineteen. Now he regretted it . . . Anybody else, in their position, would have looked for something better. Now he understood: too late! A nice little place in Prati,* a little villa overlooking the Tiber . . . He sighed.

"And . . . the rest of it?"

"The rest . . . Ah, well, a man's only human. When you travel all the time . . . A little something extra here and there, of course . . ." Doctor Fumi was looking at him. But

* Prati, a section of Rome on the left bank of the Tiber, a fashionable residential district in the early years of this century.

in that direction . . . a moment of hesitation: a certain increase, however slight, in the natural ruddiness of the face.

Giuliano Valdarena had undergone three bouts of questioning in a single day, not counting the first one on Thursday, at the scene of the crime, in the presence, so to speak, of the victim's witnessing body. Three officials were following the course of things, three "bloodhounds"; including Don Ciccio, the most hounding of all. Then Fumi and Corporal Di Pietrantonio, or Sergeant, as may be. Precious hours and days: ideas, conjectures, hypotheses: which never came to anything. Valdarena and Balducci, cousin and husband, were brought face to face: the morning of the 19th, which was a Saturday: Balducci had gone to stay at the Hotel d'Azeglio. Grave, serious, the husband; more upset and anguished, Valdarena, more nervous. They looked at each other squarely, spoke to each other: they seemed to be meeting after years of separation, brought closer together in grief: each seeking in the other's face the horrible motive of the evil, not however attributing it to each other. Ingravallo and Doctor Fumi never took their eyes off the pair. No sign of animosity. Giuliano, restless at times: as if at recurrent gusts of fear. Their statements showed up no contradiction. They added little, virtually nothing, to what had already been recorded.

When Doctor Fumi was on the point of dismissing them, the visit of "a priest" was announced. "Who is it?" Don Lorenzo Corpi asked to be heard, because of an urgent communication he had to make, "regarding the painful case in Via Merulana." He had spoken to the corporal on duty. Fumi, with a gesture, sent the two from the room: Valdarena under guard. He asked Balducci to remain in the station.

Don Corpi was brought in. He removed his hat slowly, a prelate's gesture.

He was a handsome priest, tall and stocky, with rare strands of white amid his raven hair, and with a pair of owl's eyes very close to his nose: which, metaphorically, between such eyes, could be compared only to a beak. Decorously sheathed in his cassock, he bore in his left hand, along with the new hat, a black leather briefcase, the kind priests carry sometimes, when they have to visit their lawyer and let him know who has the right on his side. Black shoes, very shiny, long and sturdy, good for walking on the Aventine, as well as the Celian, with double soles. A man of remarkable appearance: and of exceptional robustness, judging from his walk and his movements, from the handclasp that he gave Doctor Fumi, and from the fullness of his cassock, above, and down to the waist, and from the flapping it made below, where it belled out in a skirt of strong cloth that looked like the Banner of Judgment.

After some slightly embarrassed or, at least, very cautious preamble, as the softer glances of Doctor Fumi led him on to speak, he said that: he had been out of Rome, visiting certain friends at Roccafringoli, at the very top of the mountains, at Monte Manno almost, which you reach from Palestrina on donkey-back, and having come back from there a mere twenty hours ago, "as soon as I heard of the terrible event," he had hastened to bring here the holograph will, entrusted to him by the "late lamented" Signora Balducci with her own hands, whom he had also "gone to visit" the evening before at the morgue, "may she rest in peace."

"At first," he stated, still deeply upset and horrified by the "thing," he had had reason to fear . . . that the document had been stolen from him. He had hunted for it all over the place, turning out all his papers, from all the drawers in his study: but he hadn't been able to dig it up. At night, all of sudden, it had come to him: he had deposited it with other envelopes and with certain . . . certain personal mementoes, in the Banco di Santo Spirito. In fact, this morning he had gone there, the moment they opened, just after he said the six o'clock Mass. His heart had been pounding, at times.

From that black calfskin case he took out and handed to Doctor Fumi—who received it with his very white hand —a white, fairly large, square envelope, with five seals of scarlet sealing wax. The envelope and the seals seemed to be in perfect order: "Holograph Will of Liliana Balducci."

The three officials, or rather Doctor Fumi and Ingravallo, decided to open it forthwith: and to read the "last wishes of the poor lady": dictating a report in the presence of Don Corpi and of four witnesses, in addition to Balducci, who had been called in again. Last wishes, which still must date back to a couple of months ago: last, since they had remained unchanged.

First of all, and by telephone, they consulted the royal notary Doctor Gaetano De Marini in Via Milano: 292.784:

who, according to Don Lorenzo, "must know about this matter." After some calling and recalling, finally he answered. He was deaf. A Neapolitan secretary assisted him at the receiver. Both of them were dumfounded. Balducci knew De Marini, to whose services both he and Liliana's father had on many occasions had recourse: but he "felt that he could rule out the notion" that, for her personal will, Liliana had gone to that old cockroach, likable and sly, but horribly deaf in the fortress of his competence.

To act as witnesses, two clerks and two policemen were called in. The ceremony was quickly carried out: it was noon, or almost: another morning had drifted by, without their resolving anything.

The will, as Doctor Fumi went on reading it aloud, in vivid accents, with Neapolitan resonances from the four corners of the ceiling, gradually revealed an unforeseeable turn: as if it had been drawn up in a state of particular emotion by a person whose pen was running away with him, a person perhaps not in full control of his faculties. From that soft, warm, suave reading, effectively conducted in the most harmonious Parthenopean tones, the listeners present realized, with mounting interest and with mounting wonder, that the poor Signora Balducci was leaving her husband heir to the lesser part of her substance, with some gold objects and jewels: the strictly legal share, so to speak: almost half. A conspicuous portion, on the other hand, fell to "my beloved Luigia Zanchetti also known as Gina, daughter of the late Pompilio Zanchetti and Irene Zanchetti née Spinaci, born at Zagarolo on the fifteenth of April, nineteen hundred and fourteen." To her, poor child: "since the inscrutable will of God has not seen fit to grant me the joy of motherhood."

Balducci didn't draw a breath: he made a face, as if he had been the guilty one. Or perhaps, more likely, it was the thought of all that good stuff (and how!) heading for Zagarolo. Until the ward reached her majority, the swag was to be assigned, to be administered, to some caretakers or executors, as it were, one of whom was Balducci himself, "my husband Remo Eleuterio Balducci, father in spirit, if not by blood, of the abandoned Luiggia." The mother of Luigia, according to the will, "was condemned by an incurable illness" (tuberculosis, probably complicated by priapomania): from time to time she went on a drunk in Tivoli with her lover a butcher: and it took plenty of pull to keep the carabinieri from sending her forcibly back to Zagarolo: given her "inability to support herself with her own means" and given the circumstances, too: a public scandal. The butcher, it was never quite clear how, managed to hush things up every time: almost certainly with the argument of the "prime fillet" (top quality): which is to say that, to the poor sick woman, his roast beef was much more salubrious than the all-too-thin air of Zagarolo, with the consequent unsatisfied appetite. At other times he beat her like a rug: she coughed and spat blood, poor thing, if not raspberry gelatin: "What did I do, after all?" She had gathered spring violets at Villa d'Este or some March daisies in Villa Gregoriana, just before you get to the waterfall. A future subject of the Mustached-Beast, armed with his Zeiss, exploring with that perfect binocular the whole slope of Venus Slut, inch by inch, from one blade of grass to the next,

Teuton fashion, all of a sudden, happens to see under the blazing sun a kind of spider, inhaling-exhaling: a strange clump in the shadow of a great laurel bush, the most Gregorian, according to his Baedeker, of all the bushes of Tivoli: a kind of back, in a kind of digger's jacket: with four legs and four feet, however; two of them upside down. And that back, so full of *Macht*, seemed gripped by an irrepressible agitation of an alternating nature, metronomic in its cadence. The binoculared seal then thought it his duty to report this to the management—*"Verwaltung, Verwaltung! . . . Wo ist denn die Verwaltung? drüben links? Ach so! . . ."*—which he long sought, in the sweat of his brow, and finally found: and where there wasn't a soul, because they were all home eating or enjoying a little after-dinner nap. Padre Domenico, the following Sunday, thundered at nine A.M. from the pulpit of San Francesco: what a pair of lungs! He had it in for certain shameless women, generally speaking, and he guaranteed them hell, the very bottom: a lodging adapted to them—he triptyched here and there with his head, his fist raised, as if one moment he were addressing Marta, then Maddalena, then Pietro, then Paolo. But everyone understood from his opening roar where he was going to end up: with those eyes bulging and that rage that looked as if he wanted to bite somebody, which then, however, calmed down, slowly, and went straight to strike the devil, where he got it all off his chest: and the devil, without a word, down, crouching, at the fear Padre Domenico inspired: then he climbed up gently towards "the beauties of nature so plentifully lavished by God's Providence on this, your Tibur" as well as the "miracles of art and our national generosity so wisely given to this ancient land by the provident hand of the Roman Pontiff Gregory Sixteenth, after the great telluric cataclysm of 1826 and the fearsome flooding of our own Aniene": when it came to the flooded Aniene he could share the local pride, being a native of Filettino, only a short distance from the river's source and 1,062 meters above sea level. "Today, alas contaminated," both miracles and beauties, "by the pestilential and stinking breath of Utter Darkness: which is always lying in wait: wherever he realizes that he can cause the loss of a soul, when he can wrest a soul away from its own salvation": even in the Villa Gregoriana.

Having reached the incurable illness part, Doctor Fumi stumbled, coughed: as if there had been a crumb determined to sidetrack into the trachea. Warming to his reading, at a certain point, he had swallowed some saliva the wrong way. Then, on and on, until that fit of coughing seemed about to unhinge his lungs.

His face barely flushed, but his veins swollen on the forehead: the whole machinery distended by a deflagration of inner charges, which however did not succeed in shattering it. He recovered himself: the others had slapped him on the back. Little by little he started up again, with his voice, after all, cleared. Now he seemed, as you listened to him, a defense lawyer, plunging into the grim tones of the peroration, with apparent calm, but portending the worst: waiting to explode at the demoniac motion: "of the abandoned Luiggia." A tidy sum, forty-eight thousand, to her cousin Doctor Giuliano Valdarena, son of Romolo Valdarena and Matilde née Rabitti, born et cetera. Item: the diamond ring "left to me by my grandfather, Cavaliere Ufficiale Rutilio Valdarena, as a sacred legacy: and the gold watch chain with the semi-precious fob" (*sic: nec aliter*) "which belonged to the same." Item: "tortoise-shell snuffbox with gold trim" and finally, some onyx acorns or balls of lapis lazuli, also of agnactic origins: "so that he may remember me, like a sister, who from Heaven will pray constantly for him, and may follow the luminous example of his Valdarena grandparents and the unforgettable Uncle Peppe" (Uncle Peppe, in fact, forced donator to the Fascio of Via Nomentana, was still taking snuff from the tortoise as late as 1925, in Viale della Regina 326) "and may he always follow the paths of goodness, the only paths that can win us, in life and in death, the forgiveness and mercy of God." She hadn't forgotten the old ex-domestic Rosa Taddei, either, a paralytic in the hospice of San Camillo: nor Assunta Crocchiapaìni (in reality Crocchiapani: it may have been an error of reading caused by the handwriting, or perhaps merely an oversight on the part of Doctor Fumi), the Alban maiden without any paralysis, crowned by her lofty silence and with dazzling eyes: "for whose flourishing young womanhood I desire and pray for, now and always, the supreme happiness of Christian offspring." She also left Assunta, among other things, six sheets, double-bed size, and eighteen pillowcases: and twelve towels, with fringe, specifying which ones. Various bequests followed, anything but negligible, for several women's charities and institutions: such as the bequest to the nuns of Saint Ursula, to some female acquaintances, to some friends, and to various little girls and babies, "today tender flowers of innocence, tomorrow, with the Lord's protection, blissful and holy mothers for our beloved Italy."

And at last a little purse of twenty thousand lire to the same, listening (without seeming to) Don Corpi, along with an ivory crucifix on an ebony cross, "that he may assist me with his good prayers through the pain of Purgatory to the hope of Heaven, as in this Vale of Tears he has supported me with his paternal counsel and with the doctrine of Holy Mother Church."

"Here's a woman whose like you don't find often!" cried Doctor Fumi, striking two knuckles of his right hand on those poor papers, where the gentle hand of the murdered woman had moved (he was holding them in the meanwhile with his left).

All were silent. Balducci, in spite of those donations, seemed the first to have tears in his eyes. In reality, without going that far, he was showing that he, too, was convinced. The warm, the deductive sonority of the voice, of the phrasing, had persuaded them all: some to accept, some to surrender: as if gathering the aghast souls under the mantle of God's will. A handsome, male Neapolitan voice, when it surfaces from the limpid depths of deduction, like the candid nakedness of a siren from the marine milkiness in the Gajola* moonlight, is free completely and, in every clause, of that angrily assertive manner of certain northern beasts, and their married-scorched *Führer*: (in a bonfire of gasoline). It is pleasing, pleasing to our ears to abandon ourselves to such happy argumentation, like a cork conquered by the gentle current of a stream towards the valley, towards

* La Gajola is a little island off the tip of Cape Posillipo, just outside Naples.

the call of the depths. The sonorous flow is but the symbol of the flow of logic: the source of Eleatic statement has been transformed into a moving course: boiling up in the disjunctions or dichotomies of the spirit or in the blind alternations of probabilities, it is perpetuated in a dramatically Heraclitean deflux πάνγα δε πόλεμος, filled with urgencies, with curiosities, with desires, expectations, doubts, anguish, dialectic hopes. The listener becomes able to form opinions in any direction. The objection of the other side is pulverized in that musical voluptuousness, coagulates with a new nose, like the herm of Janus, when you stare it in the face, and then, immediately afterwards, from behind.

All were silent.

At the reading of that text, or at hearing it read with such involvement, a text which, to tell the truth, was a little out of the ordinary, one would have believed that, at the moment she wrote her will, poor Liliana, prey to a kind of madness, or divinatory hallucination, already foresaw her end as imminent: if she hadn't positively been meditating suicide. The testament bore the date of January 12th, two months ago: her name-day, as her husband pointed out: a little after the Epiphany. It was "the unbosoming of an overexcited woman," someone opined tacitly. And the writing, too, to Balducci, Don Ciccio, Don Lorenzo, betrayed a certain jerkiness, a certain agitation: a graphologist would have earned the fee for his expertising. A strange ecstasy in this detachment from worldly things, and from their names and symbols: that voluptuousness of farewell which immediately distinguishes heroic minds as well as minds unwittingly suicidal: when one, not yet departed on the long journey, already finds himself with a foot at the water's edge, on the shores of darkness.

Ingravallo was thinking: he thought that even Christmas, that the Crib, the Epiphany . . . with their children, their gifts, their Three Kings . . . with that sunburst of golden rays under the Christ Child . . . straw in the manger, light of the divine source . . . could have concentrated, as in a mental storm-cloud, certain melancholy fixations of the signora: January 12th. The poor testatrix, at that moment, must not have had all her emotions under control. Damnit: and yet . . . and yet she had maintained the provisions: she had changed nothing afterwards, in February, in March, not a syllable. Therefore, indeed, she had trusted the will to Don Corpi, urging him to "hide it and forget it."

An enigmatic expression: already clear to Don Ciccio, however: to forget it for the duration of her life, as if she wished to see buried, as soon as possible, that guilty list of possessions: which, only in the final loss of herself, she was permitted to scatter: which at every new day led her back towards the obligations, the inane reasons of living, while her soul tended already towards a kind of expatriation (her dear soul!) from the useless land towards maternal silences. The city and its people would know the future. She, Liliana . . . Forgetful of markets and cries, with brief opal wings, in the sweet hour, when every farewell is necessary and every still-warm wall loses its color in the night, Hermes, appearing to her in his true being, would at last have looked towards the doors, with silent command: the doors through which one leaves, at last, as the populace continues talking, to go down, down, into a more pardonable vanity. *"Evasi, effugi: spes et fortuna valete: nil mihi vobis-cum est: ludificate alios"*: at the Lateran museum, a sar-cophagus: Liliana had remembered those words: she had asked him to translate them.

That giving, that donating, that sharing out among others! Ingravallo thought: operations, to his way of looking at things, so removed from the carnality and, in consequence, from the psyche of woman (a little woman, he thought of some, a little bourgeoise) which tends, on the contrary, to cash in: to elicit the gift: to accumulate: to save up for her-self or for her children, black or white or chocolate brown: or at least to waste and to squander without giving to others, consuming like wastepaper hundred-lire banknotes in the cult of herself, of her own throat, her own nose, or lobes or lips, but never—and Don Ciccio became heated, in a kind of pre-established delirium—never, however, in honor of her rivals: and still less of rivals who were younger. That casting away, that dissipating like petals in the wind or like flowers in a floating stream, all the things that count most, that are most carefully locked up, sheets! contrary to the laws of the human heart which, if it gives, either gives in words or gives what is not its own; these ended by reveal-ing to him, to Don Ciccio, the emotional state of the victim: the typical psychosis of the frustrated woman, the discon-tent, the woman humiliated in her soul: almost, indeed, a disassociation of a panic nature, a tendency to chaos: that is, a longing to begin all over again from the beginning: from the first Possible: "a return to the Indistinct." Since only the Indistinct, the Abyss, the Outer Darkness, can re-open a new spiritual ascent for the chain of determining causes: a renewed form, renewed fortune. For Liliana, it was true, the inhibitive powers of the Faith were still in force, and more the cohibitive ones: the formal proclamations of Doctrine: the symbol operated as light, as certitude. Radiated in the soul. Thus ruminated Ingravallo. The twelve *lemmata* had had the effect of channeling her psychoses towards the funnel of a holograph will, perfectly legal. The accounts of death were settled down to the last fraction of a cent. Beyond the confessor and the notary lay the limpid spaces of Mercy. Or, for others, the unknown liberty of not being, the eras of freedom.

The female personality—Ingravallo grumbled mentally, as if preaching to himself—what did it all mean? . . . The female personality, typically gravity-centered on the ovaries, is distinguished from the male insofar as the very activity of the cortex, the old gray matter, of the female, is revealed in a comprehension, and in a revision, of the reasoning of the male element, if we can call it reasoning, or even in an echolalic re-edition of the words circulated by the man she has respected: by the professor, the commendatore, the gynecologist, the smart lawyer, or that slob over on the balcony of Palazzo Chigi. The woman's morality-personality turns for affective coagulations and condensations to the husband, or to whoever functions in his place, and from the lips of the idol takes the daily oracle of the understood admonition: for there isn't a man alive who doesn't feel he's Apollo in the Delphic sanctum. The eminently echolalic quality of her soul (The Council of Mainz, in 589, granted her a soul: by a majority of one vote) induces her to flutter gently around the axis of marriage:

impressionable wax, she asks the seal of his imprint: for the husband, word and affection, ethos and pathos. Whence, that is to say, from the husband, the slow and heavy ripening, the painful descent of children. And when children are lacking, proclaimed Ingravallo, the fifty-eight-year-old husband declines, through no fault of his own, to the position of a good friend, a plaster idol, a pleasant ornament about the house, or chairman and general manager of the confederation of knickknacks, more image or dummy of husband; and man in general (in her unconscious perception) is degraded to puppet: an infertile animal, with a big, fake carnivalesque head. An implement that is of no use: a gimlet with its threads worn out.

It is then that the poor creature dissolves, like a flower or blossom, once vivid, now giving her petals to the wind. The sweet and weary spirit flies towards the Red Cross, in unconscious "abandoning the husband": and perhaps she abandons every man insofar as gamic element. Her personality, structurally envious of the male and only stilled by offspring, when offspring are missing, gives way to a kind of desperate jealousy and, at the same time, of forced sisterlike συμπατία in the regards of her own sex.

It gives way, one might believe, to a form of sublimited homoerotism: that is to say, to metaphysical paternity. The woman forgotten by God—and Ingravallo now was raging with grief, with bitterness—caresses and kisses in her dreams the fertile womb of her sisters. She looks, among the flowers of the garden, at the children of others: and she weeps. She turns to the nuns and the orphanages, anything to have "her" child, to "have" a baby of her own. And in the meanwhile the years call to her, from their dark cave. Enlightened charity, from one year to the next, replaces the sweet philter of love.

Another circumstance emerged, meanwhile, from the painstaking (of course) search, ordered and carried out at the lodgings of Valdarena: who lived in Prati, in a handsome bedroom-studio in Via Nicotera: in a little villa: while, in his place and in the bed of his youth, at home, or rather at his grandmother's (Liliana's Aunt Marietta) there huddled and slept—the bedpan, but not the foot warmer, having been sent away—that old bag of bones, Aunt Romilda: widow of the unforgettable Uncle Peppe. On the marble top of the dresser, in Via Nicotera, they "discovered" a picture of Liliana: inside, in the top drawer, a man's gold ring with a diamond: and a gold watch chain, very heavy, and quite long. "This is an anchor chain," Ingravallo said, showing it to Balducci, who recognized the two objects as fomerly belonging to his wife's "treasure." Without rancor, and without any particular amazement.

The chain, at one end, terminated in the characteristic spring snap (of gold link), and at the other, in a little gold pin, cylindrical, which could be stuck in a waistcoat buttonhole: one of the nine higher of the then regulatory twelve: *ad libitum*. (According to the choice of buttonhole the "personality is expressed.") And then, the hook for the pendant.

Balducci noted at once that the big, swaying fob had changed stone. It was a kind of reliquary, oval: a minuscule gold-bound peace held by a golden stirrup, so that it could swing and even revolve completely under that arc, since it was pricked on either side by two little invisible pins: gold, yes: it was all gold, solid gold, 18-karat gold, handsome, red-gold, yellow-gold, on the knobby hands, on the dry bellies of their grandfathers, who today are mere worn, disgusting parchment filled with poverty and plague, or empty chatter in the wind. Lousy wind of hardship, with soap costing three hundred lire the pound. In the frame there was set a beautiful jasper, with the tegument of a little plate of gold, on the back, when you turned it in your fingers. Also elliptical in shape, it was, naturally. A blood-jasper: a dark-green stone, its color gleaming like a swamp leaf, was made for certain noble cuts, or corners, or keystones in arches, for secret throne rooms in palaces in the architecture of Melozzo or of Mantegna, or in the marble squares of Andrea del Castagno in his murals: with delicate veins of a cinnabar vermilion like stripes of coral: almost like clotted blood, within the green flesh of the dream. In what was called Gothic lettering, and intertwined and interlaced in the glyptic work the two initials: C.V. On the other face, smooth, precise, the little plate of clear gold.

All these novelties instead of the ash-blue opal that Balducci had seen there other times: a stone with two faces, recto and verso, and also very good-looking, he explained to Ingravallo, but . . . A sublunar stone, an elegiac stone, with soft, suffused milkiness as in a Nordic sky (*nuits de Saint Petersbourg*) or perhaps of silica paste, set and frozen slowly in the cold light, in the twilight dawn of the 60th parallel. On one side was carved the monogram R.V., Rutilio

Valdarena: the other side was smooth. The name of the grandfather, the archetype of all the Valdarenas: who, as a kid, had been blond: a reddish blond, they used to say. When the grandfather died, the chain (with the fob) had gone to Uncle Peppe, on whose waistcoat of black velvet with yellow dots it had hung for a few months, on Sundays and Holy Days of Obligation. Her grandfather had meant it to go to Liliana, of course: to little Liliana: from her Grandad Rutilio: who, however, had temporarily left it to Uncle Peppe, in a kind of equitable trusteeship. And, when it came to Uncle Peppe the opal fob with the benign and beneficent warmth of all fobs and charms and coral horns, but with the sinister cancer-promoting aptitudes which *ab aeterno* had dwelt in the noble and melancholy frigidity of that gem. Seven and a half months after the grandfather's death, the uncle had not been able to evade his obligation, so nicely opaline, to transfer to Liliana the ownership of the gold chain, in accordance with the paternal will: with that toy attached to it. Because it was then, Balducci declared grimly, that the uncle had become unforgettable.

"Poor, dear Uncle Peppe!" the survivors wept. Balducci could see his features again in the remembering mirror of his heart, as husband of the niece. Allocated there, in his big chair, amid a soufflé of cushions, surrounded by his relations who hung from his lips; two fine, gray walrus-mustachios, and two large, yellow horse-teeth orchestrated his sad smile, the good yellowing smile of the "gentleman of the old school," former, distinguished client of the Baths of Chianciano. While in that posture so abandoned to the opinions of Doctor Beccari, and with that slightly Mongoloid tinge in his mustache and his cheeks, he celebrated within his immediate family the great virtues of the same and all the Valdarena clan in general, the bluish fob of the Lord's day used to rest on his black waistcoat on an axis with his liver and duodenum. Titillated by the thin, waxy fingers of the trustee, the gem covered both organs, duodenum as well as liver: alternating from one to the other a bit, perhaps: like a girl who is keeping at bay two swains at the same time. It was, to be precise, of cancer of the liver, supplemented by a similar affliction of the duodenum, that the bearer of the opal found himself forced to succumb.

O powerful emanation of the doubly ill-starred bioxide! to the damnation of the abdominal tract, by God! and half the tripes of Peppe! Witness-bearing presence of an invisible light, it was the son, that reverse talisman, of the unimitated elegy; a standard-bearer of the distant September dawn, page to the milky-blue reticence of the Polar semester. Worthy, in its nobility, to have bejeweled the finger of a count of the palace, who had fallen asleep at Roncesvalles, with seven windows in his heart: or of a viscount, suddenly gone pale in the September prisons. Bearer of a double curse, Ingravallo conjectured, given its double face. The double evil eye must come from the bioxide. The combined duodenum-liver cancer is one of those double numbers that the cancer lottery rarely comes out with, from the modern cancerological cabala: whether in Europe or abroad.

Everybody, then and there, took fright; they began to touch wood, some here, some there. "And as for Liliana, well, Doctor, it seems to me . . ." and this time, again, poor Balducci let out a sob, his voice shook. He wept. At Santo Stefano del Cacco he was summoned daily, you might say.

In the little writing desk near the balcony, in Via Nicotera, Sergeant Di Pietrantonio, assisted by Private First-Class Paolillo, found ten thousand lire: ten one-thousand notes, brand new. The members of the family, aghast at the death of Liliana, then at the young man's arbitrary arrest, as they called it, were unable to indicate the source of the money. At the Standard Oil they denied having given him anything beyond his usual salary at the end of February. Ten thousand lire! It was unlikely that Giuliano, even in a year, could have saved that much from his earnings: as a recent graduate and starting employee, a young representative, a good-looking young man. With the expenses of his marriage in sight, which is tantamount to saying, in part expended.

A salary, good as it was, and some percentage on the deals that he handled might allow him, in Rome, to eat, clothe and wash himself, and pay for the fine room and bath at Signora Amalia's: manicures and cigarettes extra: extra his grandmother's fettucine. His women, given his charm, the quality that made Don Ciccio so jealous, apparently didn't cost him very much. "He had many invitations," according to his relatives: and also from his landlady, not herself the owner of the little villa. "Yes, he brought ladies to his room. No, not the lady in the picture. Some ladies of the aristocracy . . ." (so she trilled). Ingravallo drew a breath "mentally" with great circumspection. The room's entry was private. In announcing this prerogative of the room, she, the landlady, assumed a serious, haughty voice, like a building contractor, when he says, "a fine view, three baths."

"Oh, he had invitations everywhere. Because everybody

was devoted to him." "Every *woman*," grunted Don Ciccio, within himself, gazing again into those deep, big eyes of Signora Amalia, circled by two blue crescent moons which were pendants to the two golden crescents she wore in her ears: which, at the first turn of her head, seemed about to go "ding-dong." Like an odalisque of the Sultan.

Ingravallo subjected Valdarena, who had already been heard once that day, to yet another questioning. Night had fallen, it was happast seven. He had lighted, as reinforcement, a "special" bulb, which hung down to his desk. He showed him all of a sudden, without forewarning, the *corpora delicti:* that is to say, the chain, the diamond ring, the ten one-thousand lire notes, not to mention among these exhibits the photograph of Liliana, which, for good measure, he had left in. Valdarena, seeing that money and those objects on the desk, along with Liliana's picture, suddenly blushed: Don Ciccio had removed a newspaper which was concealing them. The young man sat down: then slowly he stood up: he wiped the sweat from his forehead: he regained his composure: he looked his preyer in the eye. There was a sudden movement of his neck, of his whole head, with a sweep of his hair: as if he had resolved to cast himself into the worst of it. He entered instead the bold, almost eloquent phase, of his own stubbornness and his own apology; he was silent for half a minute, then, "Officer," he shouted, with the haughtiness of one who insists on the legitimacy of a deed, of another person's sentiments which, nevertheless, concerns him: "there's no point in my keeping silent any more, out of fear of what people might say or out of respect for a dead person, a poor murdered woman:

146

or out of shame for myself. Liliana, my poor cousin, yes, she was very fond of me. That's all there is to it. She wasn't in love with me, maybe . . . No. I mean . . . not in the way another woman, in her place, would have loved me. Oh! Liliana! But if her conscience" (sic) "had permitted her, the religion in which she was born and raised . . . well, I'm sure that she would have fallen in love with me, that she would have loved me madly." Ingravallo turned pale. "Like all the other women."

"Yeah, like all the others."

Valdarena didn't seem to notice this. "The great dream of her life was . . . was to join herself to a man," he looked at the glowering Don Ciccio, "to a man, or maybe even to a snake, who could give her the child she had dreamed of: 'her' child, the baby . . . she had waited and waited for, in vain, in tears. She wept and prayed. When she began to realize that time was passing and nobody could stop it, then . . . poor Liliana! In her emotional state she wouldn't recognize her own incapacity: no, she didn't admit it. And yet, without saying it outright, without putting it into words, she used to imagine, to dream that with another man, per-haps . . . Believe me, Doctor, there's a kind of physical pride, a vanity of the person, of the viscera. We men, of course, some more, some less, by nature, we're all a pack of . . . preening turkey-cocks. We like to stroll up and down the Corso.

"But women have their pride, too: a physical one, like I say. You probably know this better than me." Ingravallo was biting back his fury, black as a thunderstorm. "She . . . Liliana . . . when I talked with her sometimes, all alone, the way cousins do . . . you know, I could see . . . she lived on that dream of hers, you might say: that with another man . . . Another man! A tall order! with all that religion of hers! So . . . in that fantasy, she . . . in her guts . . . she thought . . . it seemed to her that . . . the other, that other man, could have been me . . ."

"Ah," said Don Ciccio, "my warmest congratulations!" A horrible grimace, his face like tar.

"Don't laugh, Doctor," the suspect cried, pompously, his youthful pallor all gleaming in the "special" hundred-watt light. "No, don't laugh. Time and again Liliana talked to me about it! She told me always that she had loved Remo . . . sincerely; I mean, she was kind of a goose about it, I'd say, poor thing." Ingravallo, in his heart, couldn't help conceding this: "an only daughter! without a mother! with no experience . . ." She had loved him "from the first day she saw him," naturally. "She loved him still, she respected him, poor Lilianuccia!": the voice hesitated, then got going again: "For nothing in the world, religion aside, would she have thought of betraying him. But when she saw the years passing in that way, the best years of her life, without even the hope for . . . for the fruit of that love . . . it was, for her, it was like a tormenting disappointment. She felt humiliated, the way they all feel when the baby doesn't come off: more than sadness, it's a kind of spite, to think that other women are triumphant, and they aren't. The most bitter of all of life's disappointments. So, for her, the world was nothing but weariness: nothing but tears. Tears that gave her no comfort. Weeping and weariness. A swamp. Enough to drive her mad."

"Let's skip the weariness, Doctor Valdarena . . . What about the chain, and the diamond? Let's get down to facts. It looks to me like we're wasting time here. We can do without these flights . . . these flights of fancy": he made a gesture as if dismissing some winged creature, urging the falcon up into the blue. "Let's talk a little about this anchor chain": and, taking it by one end, he swung it under his nose, looking him steadily in the eyes, blackly, "about this little gadget," and he weighed it in his other hand, "this tiny little thing." He seemed, at most, curious, wanting to observe minutely: like an ape into whose hand someone has dropped a toy whistle. Curly and black, that pitchy head, bent thus over the fingers and the metal that makes every mouth water, seemed to emanate tenebrous preconceived notions; and the procedural brightness of the room, as soon as the notions appeared, apparently forced them to curl up in that way, to become permanent, like a shiny, carbon fleece, on the skull: "We have read the will of the Signora Liliana, rest her soul, poor woman, and she left these to you," and he set down the chain, picking up the ring from the table and beginning to weigh it in the palm of his hand, "because old grandfather Romilio, Signor Balducci says— was that his name? Romilio? Have I got it right? Ah, Rutilio? Grandfather Rutilio wanted it to go to his grandchildren, to his own flesh and blood . . . all in the family, I understand, I understand, and therefore to you, their pride and joy. But how come we found the stuff in your room? And how did the opal turn into an onyx? a what? . . . Yes, I meant to say . . . a jasper?"

Giuliano raised his right hand, which appeared white,

vivid, faintly traced with blue, the flexible veins of adolescence: he showed, on his ring finger, the magnificent jasper which prison hadn't taken from him: the one Ingravallo remembered seeing on his finger at the Balduccis', after dinner on the 20th of February, as they were taking their coffee. "She wanted it to match this," he answered, "she wanted me to get married, to have a kid. You're sure to have one, she said to me every time: and then she would cry. When I told her I was getting married (at first she wouldn't believe it), that I was going to live in Genoa, as soon as I showed her the snaps of Renata, well, no, I can't say she was jealous, not the way another woman would have been . . . No. Isn't she beautiful? she said, but kind of with her teeth clenched. A brunette, isn't she? A pretty girl: just right for you, since you're as blond as an angel. And she started crying. As soon as she was convinced about the wedding, that it wasn't just a story . . . Doctor, you won't believe it . . . sometimes I think I'm going crazy myself . . . she made me swear, right away, that I'd have a kid, as soon as I could: a little Valdarena. A Valdarenuccio, she said, through her tears. Now swear! A darling little innocent. She was out of her mind, our poor Liliana. She would adopt that first one: because Renata and I, she said, would promptly make another, and a third, a fourth: and those would be for us. But she had a right to the first one, she said. Providence would give us, Renata and me, all the babies we wanted. Because that's how the good Lord is, she said: everything to one person, and nothing to another." And it is in this guise, indeed, that He displays His mysterious perfection. "You're young, she said, you're healthy . . . (like a bull, Doctor, I can tell you) like all the Valdarenas. The minute you're married, you'll make a baby: I can almost see him, almost hear him . . . If you don't have one on the way already. She laughed, and went on crying, too. And you've got to swear that you'll give him to me. I was to let her adopt it, in other words: like it was her child.

"What'll you give me, if I give you my baby? I said to her once. Christmas was already past, and New Year's . . . it was after the Epiphany. Why, it was past the middle of January. I was only joking. She bowed her head. Like she was thinking . . . tired, sad: like a poor thing who didn't have anything to trade me: as if she had to ask for charity. Love? No, no, I didn't want that: I didn't mean love—I said, joking. She went pale, and flung herself down in a chair, like she was desperate." Ingravallo paled, too. "She looked at me with those eyes of hers, imploring. They were clouded with tears. She took my fingers, my right hand. She looked at my mother's ring, this one here: and she began to slip it off my finger. You've got to leave this with me for a few days, she said. Why? Because I say so. Because I want to match something, the present I'm going to give you. So I left it with her. And the next time I went to see her—Remo was off on a trip, he was in Padua, and without knowing it, I went to the house to see her—the next time . . . as soon as she saw me, she gave me my ring back, then, without saying anything, she made like a sign to me . . . a smile, the way you smile at a kid. Here, she said, and she looked at me: here! She took my hand, and slipped that ring on my finger, her grandfather's ring;

this other one, my mother's, I wear on my middle finger, as you can see. Here, Giuliano, now take care of it, it's grandfather's ring. My grandfather. Your great-grandfather: what a good and handsome and strong man he was! He was a real man, like you! like you!" (That *like you, like you,* made the bulldog grit his teeth.) "And this is grandfather's watch chain . . . And she showed me that, too (it's this one that they took from me in Via Nicotera) and she turned her eyes to the portrait, you know? the oval one, in the gold frame with the ivy leaves, you know?"

"Ivy leaves?"

"Yes, bright green, in the living room: the big portrait of her grandfather, Rutilio: you can see the chain on his stomach. This very one." He touched it, extending his hand to the desk, sadly. "With the fob . . ." He shook his head. "Then she said to me. Lilianuccia . . . poor Liliana said to me: you told me you have to go to Genoa. Before you get married, you have to fix up your house: on the shore at Albaro, is it? You can't kid with those Genoese, you know. I know that. Look! So I looked. No, I said, no, Liliana, no, what are you doing? . . . Don't make such a fuss, she said, a big man like you. I know a man's needs, what a man needs when he's getting married. Take this, for now, take it. Take it, I tell you. Please, do me this favor, don't make me work so hard. You know I don't have much imagination along this line. Take it! I moved away, I didn't want to, I started to run off, I put a chair between us . . . Here! She grabbed me by the arm, and stuck an envelope into my pocket: that one . . ." and he indicated it, with his chain, on the desk, next to the banknotes: "the ten thousand lire . . . it'll soon be two months ago: the twenty-fifth of January, I remember. Then she wanted to give me the chain, too. At all costs. I couldn't stop her, believe me." Ingravallo had grave doubts about the whole story. "We were in the living room." Then, pensively:

"But there wasn't anything attached to the chain, I mean, that big bugger of a fob, that bad-luck piece. Tomorrow you must go to Ceccherelli, he's my jeweler. You have to leave it with him, just a couple of minutes, so he can attach the stone to it, you know . . . You know what? Of course, come now, you know that it had that stone attached to it: I've showed it to you dozens of times! But I've had it changed, she said. I had the opal changed for a jasper. It's to match this one, the one in your ring. That's why the week before she wanted me to leave it with her. She took my hand, and looked. She said: it looks so nice! they both look so well on you! the gold, too! it looks absolutely pure. They made such handsome gold things in the old days, before the war. But this was given me by Mamma, I said, a memento . . . after a while, when she had married a second time, the engineer, you know. Well, I didn't know, she said, with a kind of grumpy expression. I had a jasper put in. A bloodstone, green, dark as a pimpernel, with two coral veins . . . red! they look like two veins of the heart, one for you and one for me. I picked it out myself, she said, in Campo Marzio. He's probably finished engraving it by now: he was going to mount it this morning: with your initials, like the one you have on your finger. Because I didn't want to see that opal in the family any more. Touch wood! And she touched the top of the table there. She

153

made me touch it, too. She laughed. She was so beautiful!"
Ingravallo took this, grimly. "I don't want it in the family
any more, that opal. It looks like it's bringing bad luck
to all of us. No, enough; I don't want it. By now Ceccherelli's finished his work. The opal—no, it doesn't exist
any more! (And we both had to touch wood again.)

"It doesn't exist any more, because I don't want it,
even if it did belong to grandfather. They say it's bad luck.
And, in fact, poor Uncle Peppe . . . you see? Cancer. And
double, at that. Who would ever have imagined such a
thing? He was so good, poor Uncle Peppe! Believe me,
Doctor Ingravallo. I remember every single word: it made
such an impression on me. I can't forget that face of hers.
How she laughed, and how she cried! Those presents! A
scene between cousins. But it could have been a love scene!
No, no love, not on any terms!" he seemed to recover himself. "It was really laughable, too, poor Liliana! So you'll
go tomorrow, no, today, she said. Promise me! Yes, yes,
to Campo Marzio, to Ceccherelli. Remember. Just before
you get to Piazza in Lucina, where there's that pizzeria.
Yes, San Lorenzo in Lucina: now don't start playing dumb
on me, you know perfectly well. It's on the right, though."

Ingravallo didn't want to believe it; he couldn't But
he realized, little by little, that he was being drawn to
believe what he would have believed unbelievable.

"Doctor Ingravallo, listen to me," Giuliano implored,
"maybe she was crazy. I don't want to insult the dead, a
poor dead woman. And after the way she died, too! But
listen to me, please . . . I . . . for her I was . . . I realized . . .
I . . ."

"You . . . what?"

"I," Giuliano got a little mixed up, laughed nervously, laughing at himself: "I was, for her, like a champion of the race, this great old race of the Valdarenas. Seriously. If she could have, if she had been free . . . But her conscience, and then . . . her religion. No, she wasn't depraved" (sic) "She wasn't like so many other women" (sic) "It was just because of that idea, that obsession of hers, for a baby. It really was, believe me, a mania, a fixed idea, anybody would have understood that: something that made her think queerly. It was stronger that she was, believe me, Doctor."

Valdarena's affirmations had the timbre and the incontestable warmth of the truth. "And how do you explain the disappearance of the iron coffer? and the two bank books?"

"How should I know?" the young man said: "how could I know who did it?" He looked at Ingravallo. "If I knew, that monster would already be in jail for sure, in my place. The coffer? I've never even seen it. The chain and the ring, along with the ten thousand lire—she gave them to me: she forced me to take them. The envelope—she was the one who insisted on hiding it here": he slapped his hip with his hand: "For that matter . . . Remo must know about it, too, I should think."

"No, he didn't know anything!" Ingravallo contradicted him harshly. "Cousins' secrets!" under that pitch on his head, he was livid: "And you," he incriminated him with a forefinger, "you knew that he didn't know." Giuliano flushed, shrugged. "Well, like I said before, she was the one who gave me the ten thousand. She stuffed the money here, in my jacket," and he touched his side again. "That envelope, the one they took from my desk": Don Ciccio frowned. "Then I ran off, I ran away. I went into the dining room and locked myself in, playing, click. No sooner was I in there when she knocked . . . Then I opened the door to her: she went to the sideboard . . . to the buffet."

"Ah, in the dining room? Near the buffet? Right where you cut her throat?" Ingravallo's face by now was white, furious. His eyes were those of an enemy.

"Cut her throat? What I'm talking about was two months ago, Doctor, still in January, the twenty-fifth of January, like I said. About three weeks before . . . before you and I also met. You remember that Sunday, maybe a month ago, when you were at their house for dinner? well, about three weeks before that dinner. And besides, it's easy to check, my God. Why didn't I think of it before? Ask Ceccherelli, the jeweler in Campo Marzio. I went to get the damned jasper myself. He can testify to that. He had instructions from Liliana to give it to me, to me personally, the fob with the new stone with my initials on it, to replace that other one: she had told him to attach it to the chain for me himself, to her grandfather's chain," he pointed to it, on the desk, with his chin, "and she told him I'd bring it to him: me, in person. Liliana was so precise about everything; she had arranged it all: she had even showed him my picture. But Ceccherelli, when I went in, made me show him my identification, a license or something, he said: so I showed him my papers. He begged my pardon. But then I was bringing him the chain. What better identification could he want than that, after all. . .?

"So it was twenty days before the twentieth of February, even twenty-five days, all right. How is it that you didn't mention a word of it to anybody? To your grandmother. To your aunt? Why didn't you show it to the family? Wedding presents, according to what you've been saying. Family jewels. Grandfather's gold: which was to go to the grandchildren. Why hide it then? And how come Balducci, this morning, was so taken by surprise? A memento of your own . . . great-grandfather . . . you can surely show it to your grandmother: who is his daughter, if I'm not mistaken."

"The daughter-in-law would be closer: Grandfather Valdarena, Grandfather Rutilio, was my father's grandfather; that is to say, if you follow me, the father of my grandfather": Don Ciccio looked at him furiously with the suspicion that Giuliano was pulling his leg: in his situation? "That's why I'm called Valdarena, too. My grandmother, grandmother Marietta, who brought me up, was the *daughter-in-law* of grandfather Rutilio."

"The daughter-in-law, I know, I know. Aha? Wait. The daughter-in-law? Your father's grandfather—is that what you said? Then the Signora Liliana was . . . your aunt?"

"No. Poor Liliana was my second cousin. A generation behind. That's why, perhaps, I liked her so! That's why she was so stupendous!" Don Ciccio listened, glumly, bituminous: "she was the daughter of Uncle Felice: Uncle Felice Valdarena, who was my father's uncle, the brother of my father's father. Liliana and my father were first cousins."

"I see, I see. And so you hid everything? Very carefully?

157

You were afraid maybe you'd have to share the stuff? share the gold chain . . . with the poor? The way Amedeo II shared his Collar of the Annunziata?"*

"Vittorio Amedeo . . ."

"Vittorio, I know, I know. With your poor relations? With some third cousin once removed?"

"Some newly hatched ugly duckling of the younger generation," sneered the accused.

"Or were you afraid that Signor Balducci, the minute he got off the train . . . those presents, all that money . . . might be kind of a weight on his stomach?"

"No, no!" said the accused, with a pleading voice. "She was the one, poor thing. She! I really wasn't thinking of hiding them: but she said to me: mind you, Giuliano, this is between us, our little harmless secret, a secret between cousins . . . like in books! The secret of beauty: aren't we beautiful, the two of us? Of happiness, longed for and not fulfilled. Oh God, what am I saying! And she covered her face with her hands. You'll have happiness. And then the secret . . . let me think a minute . . . the secret of two good souls: who in a world a litttle better than this one . . . well, would have created other souls. In this world, though, the way it is (Doctor, if you could have seen her! At that moment!), we have to go our separate ways, like the leaves when the wind tears them from the tree. My goodness! she said, what nonsense is coming out of my mouth, today of all days. This is a fine way to wish you all happiness. And you have to have the baby, Giuliano! Forgive me,

* Vittorio Amedeo II of Sardinia once gave his *Collare dell'Annunziata* (a decoration corresponding, more or less, to the Garter) to a group of poor subjects—an episode included in all Italian schoolbooks for the edification of young students during the Monarchy.

forgive me. She was crying; then she smiled through her tears; in fact, she started to laugh. Happy, handsome—you have to make him, she said. And blond, mind you. Like you were, when you were a little tyke, laughing all the time, and wanting to wee-wee without turning your back, right in front of everybody!" Don Ciccio felt called upon to rummage among his papers for a moment, on the desk.

"She laughed, and she said to me: what would Remo say, when he comes back! If he knew I was giving presents to a young man! Even if he is my cousin, my handsome cousin who's going to be married. She laughed: who's marrying another girl, poor little me! No, no, you mustn't even tell your grandmother, poor old soul, or your mother, when you go to Bologna: you mustn't tell anybody. Swear! And I swore . . ."

Don Ciccio was in a cold sweat. The whole story, theoretically, smelled like a fairy tale to him. But the young man's voice, his accents, those gestures, were the voice of truth. The world of the so-called verities, he philosophized, is merely a tissue of fairy tales: and bad dreams. So that only the mist of dreams and fairy tales can have the name of truth. And, on the poor leaves, it is a caressing ray of light.

With his toothless grin, with that latrine-like breath that distinguishes him, Common Sense was already mocking the story, wanting to laugh, swine-like, in Don Ciccio's face, spit the round *no* of the smart-ass at his mop of a police dog not yet named cavaliere. But Thought will not be prevented: he arrives first. You can't erase from the night the flash of an idea: of an idea, slightly dirty, then . . . You can't repress the ancient Fescennine, banish from the old earth fable, its perenial Atellan: when aloft, happy and wicked, swirls the laughter from peoples and from the soul: just as you cannot charm away the individual aroma from thyme or horsemint or origanum: the sacred odors of the earth, of the barren mountain, in the wind. Up, up, from the packed cities, from the races, from every street corner, from the railings of every bridge: from the brown shores, and from the silvered, twisted people of the olives, which climb the mountains. When, over the houses and all the rooftops of mankind, a bluish air trembles a little, over their brims. When the warm dung heap smokes, above the frost, resurgent hopes: the fabling hopes of the truth! When every ridge dissolves, in the smoking plowed furrows! When the sharp descent of the billhook consecrates the olive tree to its fruit, and strips away falsehood. To Ingravallo, there came in a flash, between his grief and his contempt, that it was much more natural and much simpler, some-thing very logical, since it really meant so much to Liliana, this baby, that instead of giving him, this handsome crook here (who was before him) the gold chains of the dead . . . babies . . . from chains of gold, babies don't come, surely . . . it was much quicker if she made him give her, instead, another little plaything, much more suited to the purpose. That story, really, smacked of lies. A lot of nonsense, all made up.

And then, no . . . there wasn't a word of truth in it. Her husband, Balducci, was after all a husband: a great hulk-ing husband. If the baby hadn't come out, so much the worse for him, that ugly bastard. It was no fault of men. He clenched his teeth, livid, collected his papers into the red folder. He had the prisoner taken back to his cell.

V

B UT the statements of Ceccherelli, of his "boy in the shop," one Gallone, a handsome old fellow, thin as a rail, with eyeglasses, and of an apprentice, a certain Amaldi, or Amaldini, were entirely in Giuliano's favor. Ceccherelli, backed up by the other two, confirmed in every detail the orders he had received more than two months before from the poor signora, the various stages in the preparation of the fob: "It's for a relation of mine who's getting married, so do your very best." The signora had shown him a gold signet ring, heavy, yellow-gold, with a blood-jasper, very handsome with the carved initials G.V. in what you might call Gothic lettering: "I want the stone for the chain to match this one." She had left him the ring. He had taken an impression in wax: first of the monogram, then of the whole stone, which projected from its setting. Liliana Balducci had then come back to the shop two more times, she had selected the stone from five he had shown her, after he had laid in a special stock from Digerini and Coccini, the wholesalers; he had dealt with them for years, so they hadn't raised any objection to giving him the stones on loan. It was also fully confirmed, from the same source, that the opal—very handsome stone, but with that curse on it like all opals—was to be taken over by Ceccherelli, who had in fact, taken it over, adjusting the price accordingly, despite that R.V., which was faintly engraved on it, "because, as far as I'm concerned, if you'll pardon the expression, I don't give a good goddamn about all these old superstitions. Why, you'd think you were in the Middle Ages, indeed you would. Now, in all conscience, I'm interested in doing business, in as straightforward a way as possible. In the forty years I've had my shop, believe me, Doctor, there has never been a word, not a shadow of a doubt, even for so much as a pin. And besides, just to be on the safe side, I stuck it right in a special drawer I keep for such things, as soon as I took it out of its setting, with pincers, not even touching it with my fingers, so to speak. As for the pincers, I stepped next door to the barber's and disinfected them with alcohol: and as for the gem in question then, I locked it away in that drawer, the last one on the way to the bathroom. You know the one, Alfredo; and so do you, Peppino: it's so packed with coral horns that if that opal decided to put the evil eye on the shop . . . on *my* shop? Poor opal. It's like a capon in there, in the midst of so many roosters! . . . with a sharp beak too, I can tell you."

As for the ring, he had given it back to the signora after a couple of days, "if I remember rightly, it was when she came back to the shop to look at the jaspers." He was to give the fob to Giuliano in person, who was to come by and collect it, bringing the chain with him: "yes, that one": he recognized it perfectly. "That chain," Liliana had said, "You know? Signor Ceccherelli, you know it well. Remember? The one you estimated at two thousand lire? . . . That's the one I gave away. And grandfather's ring, too, with the diamond, you remember? You estimated it at nine thousand five hundred?" Ingravallo also showed him the ring. "This is the one, no question about it: a diamond of twelve and a half carats, to say the very least. A marvelous fire." He took it, turned it around, looked at it: he held it up against the light: "Time and again grandfather used to say to me: remember, Liliana, this must stay in the family! You know to whom I mean!" The words of her grandfather, a sacred formula almost, for her: that was clear: well, she had repeated it twice, there in the shop: "isn't that so?": in the presence of Gallone, and in the presence of Giuseppe Amaldi: both of whom nodded their confirmation. To Amaldi Liliana herself chose to explain every detail: what the two intertwined letters he had to engrave were to be like, and how she wanted the stone set: jutting out slightly from the oval setting: Ceccherelli, with his little fingernail followed the firm binding of the green stone, mounted as a seal, that is to say, projecting a bit from the setting: and with a little band of gold on the back, to conceal the rough side, and to enclose it.

In addition to the jewelers, who were heard in the morning, it must be said that the Valdarena family and its ramifications, that is to say Giuliano's grandmother, Balducci himself, and the two aunts from Via dei Banchi Vecchi, and Uncle Carlo, Aunt Elvira, and more or less all the kinfolk had been groping around for three days, some in this direction, some in that, seeking the road to salvation, the way to get Giuliano out, out of the mess in

163

which he found himself, poor boy, through no fault or sin of his own. Easier said than done. But after the three clarifying statements of the three jewelers, which were one good thing, there came immediately the even better statement of the head cashier of the bank, the man from the Banco di Santo Spirito. From the master file of her account (the savings account) it turned out that she, Liliana, had withdrawn the ten thousand lire, right on the 23rd of January, two days before making the present, which she had given him on the 25th, at her house, when he had gone to visit the Balduccis and had found her alone. The head cashier, Public Accountant Del Bo, knew Liliana: he had done as she requested, that time: he happened to be at the window, number 8, full of paternal smiles. A few minutes before noon. Yes, yes, he remembered perfectly: at the moment when he was snapping out those ten notes on the glass counter—ten filthy, freckled old blankets, they were, the mangy kind, that have come from the accordion-like wallet of some sheep-trader from Passo Fortuna or from the wine-damp counter of a tavern in the Castelli— she had said to him, with that soft voice of hers and those deep, deep eyes: "Please, Signor Cavalli, see if you can't give me fresh, clean bills, if you have them: you know how I like new ones . . . ," she had called him Cavalli rather than Del Bo. "Like this?" he had said to her, taking away the dirty ones he had in his hand; and he showed her a fresh pack, in the air, against the light, holding it by one corner, letting it dangle from two fingers. "Nice and shiny, look! . . . They just arrived yesterday from the Bank of Italy: the mint has just spat them out. They have a nice odor: sniff. The day before yesterday morning they were still at Piazza Verdi.* What? Afraid of germs? You're right . . . a handsome lady like yourself."

"No, Signor Cavalli . . . the fact is that I have to make someone a present," Liliana had said. "A wedding present?" "Yes." "Ten thousand-lire notes make a nice present, especially for a young couple." *"It's a cousin, who's like a brother to me. You've no idea . . . I was like his mother, when he was a baby."* Those were her very words: he remembered perfectly; he could swear it on the Bible. "Best wishes to the happy couple: and to you too, Signora." They had shaken hands.

Sunday the 20th, in the morning, further information from Balducci to the two officials: then to Doctor Fumi alone, when Don Ciccio, shortly after noon, was led to "concern himself with another matter" and preferred "to go out for a moment." In all truth, there was no lack of other matters on his desk. Indeed, the desk overflowed onto the shelves, and the shelves to the files: and there were people coming up and going down, and more waiting outside: some smoking, some throwing away the butt, some hawking and spitting against the wall. All heavy and smoky, the genteel clime of Santo Stefano del Cacco, in a syncretic odor, a little like a barracks or the second balcony of the Cinema Jovinelli: between armpits and feet, and other effluvia and aromas more or less of March, which it

* The Italian Mint is in Piazza Verdi, Rome.

was sheer delight to sniff. Of "other matters" there was
enough to wallow in, to swim in: and people in the waiting
room! Madonna! more than at the foot of the great Tower
of Babel. They were hints (and better than hints) of "an
intimate nature," the ones proferred by Balducci: in part
spontaneously, slipping into them, one would say, the
hunter-traveler abandoning himself to that kind of logor-
rhea to which certain suffering souls succumb, repenting
a little perhaps of their past behavior, as soon as the phase
of softening sets in, as the bruise follows the blow: post-
traumatic cicatrization: when they feel that forgiveness is
theirs, from Christ and man: and a part, instead, drawn
from him with the gentlest oral string, through a civil
dialectic, through a passionate peroration, a vivid flashing
of the eyes, an extracting maieutics and that charitable
poppy-heroin, the voice and the gestures of Parthenope and
Vesuvius: the action both bland, and the same time, persuasive, ahah! of an amiable type of forceps. And out
came the tooth. Liliana, by now, had got it into her head
that, with her husband . . . she wouldn't ever have any
babies: she considered him a good husband, of course,
"from every point of view": but when it came to a baby
in view, no, not a sign. In ten years of marriage, almost,
well! not even the hope: and she had married at twenty-
one. The doctors had spoken frankly: it was he or she.
Or both. She? To prove it wasn't her fault she would have
had to try with another. This is what Professor D'Andrea
told her, too. So, from those continuous disappointments,
from those ten years, more or less, where her grief had put
down such deep roots, her humiliation, despair, tears, from

those useless years of her beauty dated also those sighs, those "ah me's," those long looks at every woman, at those who were full, ah! . . . (When hearts heave a sigh, then sorrow is nigh, as the saying goes.) . . . at children, at plump maidservants, all leafy with celery and spinach, in their shopping bags, as they came from Piazza Vittorio in the morning: or with their asses in the air, bending over to blow a kid's nose, or to touch him, to see if he's wet through: for those are the moments when you see her at her best, the maidservant, all health, all thighs, from be-hind: now that it's the fashion to wear such short under-pants—if they wear any at all. She looked at the girls, she returned, for a flash, with a note of profound melan-choly, the bold glances of young men: a caress, or a benevolent license, mentally bestowed on the future be-stowers of life: on whatever seemed to her to contain the certainty, the germinal verity, the kernel of secret growth. Hers was the limpid assent of a fraternal spirit: to those who outlined the pattern of life. But the years were rush-ing past, one after the other, from their dark stables, into nothingness. From those years, as her educational restric-tion operated, the first evidence then the gradual exacerba-tion of a delirium of solitude: "rare in a woman," Doctor Fumi interjected softly: "and in a Roman woman even more . . .": "yes, we like our company, we Romans," Balducci agreed: and that need, quite to the contrary, to rest in spirit against the physical image of another, on the visible geneticizing of people, and of the poor: that mania . . . for giving double sheets to the maids, giving them a dowry at all costs, urging to marriage those who wanted nothing more: that notion of wanting to cry, then, and to blow her nose, that gripped her for whole days, poor Liliana, when they really did up and marry: as if, when it was done, she felt envious. An envy that gnawed at her liver: as if they had done it to spite her, marrying, and to say then: "Look at me: after four months, a kid on the way! Our little boy weighs eight pounds, he gains two pounds a month." On certain mornings all it took was for some woman friend to say: "Have you seen Clementina? What a stomach she has." and Liliana's eyes would be red. "Once she almost made a scene with me, her husband, over a girl from Soriano al Cimino: a peasant who came to Rome on the bus from Viterbo, to bring me a slice of wedding cake. I don't even want to see her, that shameless thing! she yelled. The bride, poor kid, came in with her husband, and with a belly on her like a balloon on the feast of San Giovanni, when they send up fireworks. They said: we brought you some wedding cake. Of course, they were kind of embarrassed. So I said to them, laughing: it looks like the air is plenty healthy, up there on the Cimino: she blushed and looked down at her stomach, like the Virgin when the Angel explains the business to her in the Annunciation: then she got her nerve up, though, and answered: well, Signor Balducci, that's how it goes. We're young. We kind of hurried things . . . When the baby comes, nobody will remember any more, whether there was a priest or not to bless us. But don't worry, now we've been blessed, all three of us." The years! like a rose wasting, the petals falling one after another . . . into nothingness.

It was at this point, with a face the color of ashes, that Ingravallo asked to be excused: for reasons of duty. Information and reports from subalterns: words and written paper: orders to give: the telephone. Doctor Fumi followed him with one eye, as he went towards the door, head bowed, shoulders bent, in an attitude that seemed weary and pensive: he saw him take a pack of Macedonias from his pocket, a cigarette from the pack, the last, plunged into God knows what griefs: the door shut again.

To Don Ciccio, it was as if he had known it, that whole story, for a long time. The impressions and memories that Liliana's cousin and her husband were drawing out, in a kind of tormented salvage operation, from her days now so horribly dissolved, confirmed what he had already sensed on his own, though in a vague, uncertain way.

Also that idea of wanting to die, if a baby didn't come to her: hadn't he "imagined as much," Don Ciccio, or didn't he already believe it a little? Through his acquaintance with Signora Liliana: a little of it had come to the surface with the admissions of the cousin, and now, from the talk of her husband, made loquacious by the tragedy, and by feeling himself the center of attention and of the general compassion (a hunter he was! he felt he had come back with a fine hare, gun on his shoulder, boots muddy, and hounds exhausted), wanting to unburden himself, after the blow: and disputing, freely, on the delicacy of the feminine soul and, in general, on woman's great sensitivity: which among those poor creatures! is something widespread. The word "widespread" he had read in Milan, in the *Secolo*, in an article by Maroccus . . . the *Secolo*'s doctor: smart as a whip!

This posthumous medical chart of Liliana was then filled in by the pity of her woman friends and those whom she had benefited: orphan girls who wept, nuns from the Sacred Heart who didn't weep because they were sure she was already in Paradise by now, they could take their oath on it: and Aunt Marietta and Aunt Elvira, in weeds, and a pair of other aunts from Banchi Vecchi, also rather black: and diverse acquaintances, numbering among them the Countess Teresa (la Menegazzi) and Donna Manuela Pettacchioni, as well as some other neighboring ladies from two hundred and nineteen: the two antagonistic trios: Elodia, Elia Bolenfi, Giulietta Frisoni (Stairway B) on the one hand, and on the other la Cammarota, Signora Bottafavi and Alda Pernetti (Stairway A), who also had a brother that counted for an extra six. All of them women with *widespread sensitivity* then: though of the kind that Liliana . . . kept at a distance. A widespread and delicate ovaricity, that's the word, permeated the whole stalk of their soul: like ancient essences, in the ground and the meadows of the Marsica, in the stalk of a flower: pressed at length until they explode in the sweet perfume of the corolla: but their corolla, these women's, was the nose, which they could blow as much as they pleased. Women all, both in their memories and their hope, and in the hard, obstinate pallor of their reticence and the purple of their non-confiteor: which Doctor Fumi elicited in those days into a mindful analysis, with the tact and the diplomacy which distinguished him throughout his hard-working career (and which have made him today, deserved reward! subprefect of Nucanaro, *adnuente Gaspero**: or rather, no, better still!

* A reference to Alcide de Gasperi, Prime Minister of Italy at the time this book was being written.

of Firlocca, a delightful little place, where he has ample opportunity to display all his fine qualities) and with that warm voice . . . the voice that indicated his presence immediately, even before the sound of the bell (room number 4), to the ears of every corporal and every thief, the moment he set foot inside the office.

The funeral, against the expectations, or more precisely, the pale hopes of the police, didn't carry the investigation a step forward; it only increased the gossip. The newspapers wouldn't let up, the thousand, pitying glosses crackled like flames through a field of stubble in October, without arriving at an idea. The cortege left the morgue at the General Hospital at eight A.M., Monday, March 21st: a rather chilly day, considering it was the official beginning of spring, neither foul nor fair, the sky cloudy. The obsequies were respectful and quite private, not to say hastened, in compliance with the desire of the authorities, who in the end were getting annoyed with all that mess. A few priests in the lead, and a bunch of little girls and some nuns, but with "a large affluence of people," as the papers put it, and especially of women, who formed a line that never ended, they took the shortest route along Viale Regina Margherita, which had been extended in that direction about a year before, and at eight-thirty or eight-forty they reached San Lorenzo, Verano, stirring up a bit of dust, since the street there hadn't yet been asphalted, though barrels of tar were already on the site. The authorities were annoyed at the thought that in Rome, in broad daylight, and in the same building, two crimes like that had taken place, the second more terrible than the first. And then, and then: the arrest of Valdarena, seeing how things were going, wouldn't hold water: and the taking into custody of Commendatore Angeloni . . . that hadn't added up to anything either, since the Commendatore, poor man, had nothing to do with it. In justification of the work of the police and of the higher authorities in the ethic state, it must be said, on the other hand, that the very day before, Sunday the 20th, there had disembarked at Naples' Beverello pier, at eleven or half-past, the Maharajah of Sherpur, coming from the banks of the Brahmaputra on a visit to the Artificer of the Fatherland's new destiny, and possibly the grave of the two procreators and the birthplace of the same, which is a two-bit hovel, however. With him he had six or seven slobs with chocolate faces, in white silk pants where their legs were lost, despits the fact that the men, too, in those parts, are fat, unless they do penance and fast for a couple of months every now and then, to gain their Paradise, since they have one of their own. This Maharajah of Sherpur, on his forehead, right in the midst of his turban, had had sewn two diamonds that sent off sparks and a spiky plume that was the longest of all Asia and Europe put together, but the plume of our Chief of State was even longer: and he, the Indian Maharajah, had expressed for some years, through the normal diplomatic channels of our consuls, whom our Chief had sent even to India, the hope of visiting our General Hospital and our Milk Center. The Center didn't exist yet, at that time, and the typhoid of the Year Fifteen* hadn't yet occurred: as for

* Mussolini numbered the years of the "Fascist Era." The Year Fifteen would be 1937.

the general hospital, he wanted to build one just like it at Sherpur on the banks, more or less, of his native Brahmaputra: a slightly smaller one, of course, but not for that less beautiful than our own: at Sherpur, the city where he was born twenty years ago, and where the Treasure is located, the State Mammon. The visit was arranged in this fashion: it was scheduled for Monday, March 21st at eleven, by which time it was presumed that the damn funeral of the poor signora would long be over. Whence the justified haste of the Authorities, which about ten o'clock turned into a headlong rush. Don Ciccio, once he reached San Lorenzo, slipped into the crowd—his ears pricked up—as it entered the church, and his bloodhounds did the same. And the same again, half an hour later, at the exit. With small results. Signor Remo had followed the hearse with his hat in hand, his face haggard, in a group with the aunts, who were almost all there, and with the close relatives. When the Mass had been said, and final absolution given the coffin, and then, inside Verano, when the grave had been blessed, where white lilies and carnations fell amid desperate sobs "good-bye, Liliana, good-bye!", the black Ingravallo stuck to the side of Don Lorenzo, like a boxer at the side of a giraffe, suitably dressed, and didn't let go of him till they were in the sacresty. He allowed the priest to undress, then loaded him into his car (if his old tin can could be called that!) and took him off to Santo Stefano.

Where, taking him into the office of Fumi, the latter expressed the opinion . . . that the distinguished man of God could give them some additional light on the condition . . . the spiritual condition of the lamented lady: in

173

order to assist the police authorities in a deeper examination of the case and the final redaction, "of what you might call the psychological report." A comma or two, a dot on an *i*, the brokenhearted prudence of Don Corpi did add to the report-synthesis. The visits and the implorations of the Signora Balducci to the church of the Santi Quattro, at certain happy seasons in the celestial calendar, or at the less sad ones, were, one might say, daily. Both to the Confessional and to Our Lady's altar: or else to the rectory, along the portico, all around the "fine cloister of the thirteenth century." The square sky was all light, as if through the eternal presence of the confessors, the sainted four: one on each side. The poor soul sought help in her suffering: the sweet word of hope, the compassionate word of charity. Of faith she had more than anyone. Don Lorenzo remarked, without of course losing sight of the seal of the sacrament, basing his words exclusively on extra-sacramental confidences and on the invocations of the person who had chosen him as the confidant of her private anguish, he remarked that he could fully confirm what was written above, that is to say, what had emerged from the amnesic uncertainty of *afterwards*, encouraged by the police to become certainty, verified, and from the intuition and complementing wisdom of the cousin and, why not?, the husband. Authoritative and massive, after that early and now overcome embarrassment of the first time (trip to Roccafringoli, delay, however voluntary, in "presenting himself to the authorities," and in "producing the will of the deceased"), with his hair cut short, in a tone of clairvoyant pity that asserted full lucidity in any value judgment, he affirmed, almost swearing to it, that the poor dead woman was the most chaste of souls, of the most pure, intentionally speaking . . . "What do you mean by that?" Doctor Fumi said. He went on. The long, black, and super-shined shoes seemed to convalidate his testimony: such an investment in Shinola, such energetic work of the elbow (of whomever) cannot be superimposed upon falsehood and disorder. The idea of divorce or annulment of the marriage, apart from all canonical difficulties, seemed abominable to her: no, Liliana wouldn't think of it. She "loved" too much and respected her husband, the man she had chosen: given to her, at the time, by God. Her desperation and her hope (vain) had coagulated into a melancholy madness (Don Ciccio understood this at once, Doctor Fumi a little later, and only approximately): they seemed to find their salvation in that intention, in that mania (the word escaped him), in that great charity of adoption: the legal adoption of a child. But at the same time she seemed to wait, to wait, as if she hoped, one day, to be able to have something better: from day to day she was waiting for a child, from year to year: and whose, after all? A future child, a future god-child: at this point he, Don Corpi, couldn't figure out from where, or from whom.

"The cousin!" exclaimed Doctor Fumi.

And in the meanwhile, as if to while away her desperation, she *did* adopt. She adopted "temporarily," adopted after a manner of speaking. She spoke of adopting: although, however, she had already replaced one will with another. Three times she had asked for the yellow envelope back, with its five wax seals. Three times she had torn away the seals, then had re-created the monogram. "Holograph Will of Liliana Balducci." She adopted, by word, though with a true effusion of the spirit, with all the sincerity of a hope resurgent at every new encounter: at every new abandonment, disappointed. She adopted, temporarily, those fine figures of girls: a whole line, by now, a string of pearls. Each better than the last. Four, she had brought into the house, in three years, one after the other, including Gina, poor little thing.

With the full permission of Signor Remo, who used to say to her: "do as you please, do whatever you think best," each time, so long as there was a little peace in the family, for a little while. So long as he knew she was at home with some female company, while he slipped off with Cristoforo after a hare, to try out the dogs on the Cimino. And, in any case, always with the advice of Don Corpi. Though with so many souls around him, with so much to do in church and not knowing those girls at all (he didn't even know who they were or where they came from), he limited himself each time to counseling prudence, prudence—so he stated and it was likely that it was so—to warning her ("mark my words!": but she, to such advice, turned a deaf ear), to urging her not to dissipate in sudden adventures of emotion her gift . . . the treasure . . . of an ineffable awareness of woman's great mission: which had been given her, certainly, by God. Four! in three years! "A great heart, poor Signora Liliana."

And she patted the maids and always forgave them if they broke a dish. She comforted them and told them to hope in the Lord. For in their case, vice versa, it was not so much hope as fear, what they felt: fear of having the kid a bit too soon, perhaps. The Lord, she told them, and she was a hundred per cent right, never denies life to those who desire life, and the continual resurrection of life. "It's a desire many women have," Fumi thought.

Don Lorenzo, with all due respect for the living and for the poor "deceased," then mentioned the three young girls that Liliana Balducci had welcomed as daughters, and then dismissed: and the various motives which, in turn, had determined the secession, more or less easy, more or less spontaneous, of the three would-be wards. The fourth, now, this Gina from Zagarolo, who was the niece presently on active service, benefited in the place of them all. The *carabinieri* of Tivoli had already questioned the mother, and the butcher too; Irene Spinaci wanted to come to Rome: but when she heard that Gina was at the Sacred Heart, she shut up: after all . . . what was the use of her coming? Just throwing away money? When she didn't even have enough to get on the train?

Don Lorenzo, once he had overcome a certain hesitation, then opened his bag of . . . charitable prudence. First, he turned his hat around on his knees a couple of times, nice and slow: with those hands (and with those feet) that made him look like Saint Christopher. Caught, priest though he was, by the vivid and pathetic eyes of Doctor Fumi (for once, they, rather than his tongue, were on duty), he gave way to the magnetic traction of those bulbs, so gently rolling, each parallel to the other, in their respective sockets, that is to say in the binding of those lids: black irises, as of deep velvet, like two spheres of tourmaline under the velvety shadow, the slightly melancholy shadow of the lashes: heart-rent flames, yet glowing with persuasion and with sliding dialectics, in that white face, paternal, pensive, inviting: welcoming as a trap. Beneath that other snout hanging on the wall, the Predappian* fezzer, in his frame, making boogey-man faces at the dried flies on the wall opposite: lips extended in a booby's pout, a three-year-old macaroni, to make all the Marie Barbigie† of Italy swoon: with that fez on his head and the Emir's plume. An Emir of mardi gras.

Three girls. The first, Milena, a little freckle-faced thing, after barely a month of that good food at the Balduccis', with that pure wool mattress under her and a warm comforter over her in the bed, had promptly started putting on fat: two round little melons under her blouse, a neat hemisphere, behind. But with this calf-fat she had also developed a taste for stealing, and a proportionate one for telling lies. She stole from the sideboard, and from the purse on the night table: and she lied with her mouth. Her tongue followed her nails, without giving it a thought, like your tail goes behind your ass, if you're a horse.

One day, then, stripping her bed, the maid had found a candle: a Mira-Lanza candle, those stubby ones they made then: which she must have taken from the new package in the kitchen; they were kept on hand in the cupboard, for when the lights fail, sometimes. She—with her ready tongue —said she wanted to light it to the Madonna: because she had a special intention: but she didn't have matches: she had fallen asleep with the candle in her bed. Doctor

* The little town of Predappio was Mussolini's birthplace.
† *Barbisa* is the Milanese dialect word for the female organ.

Ghianda examined the girl, made her drink citron water, which has a calming effect for certain nervous fantasies, plus a few drops, three times a day, of the anti-hysteric water of Santa Maria Novella of Bologna, which the monks make there with a filter, a specialty of theirs. (This was, afterwards, confirmed: in the Merulanian tones of Sora Pettacchioni.) In any case, to avoid misunderstandings, the Professor was called back, was asked by Liliana for advice. He frowned for a moment, looking at her with a hint of a smile, his mannerism of a severe but kindly father, his usual way with kids. He was a very distinguished pediatrician. With three fingers he toyed with his gold fob, over his waistcoat. After a moment of suspense, he relaxed his forehead, drew a deep breath, and counseled "it seems the best thing, to me," that the child be sent back to her respective parents: who, however, didn't exist, neither the one nor the other. Whereupon, after a little while, when a reasonable pretext had been hit upon, she was restored to her "uncle and aunt," comforted, in the anticipation of receiving her back, with a nice bank order, of a sea-green color, the kind that have such a psycho-tonic effect on our beloved Comit.* "The Banca Commerciale Italiana . . . will pay . . . on the line, for this handsome little sea-green gent here, the sum of lire . . ." And the more they are, the better it is.

Don Corpi stretched his legs, holding his hat with his forearms, like a shield over his belly, clasping the big fingers of his two hands, which sank into his lap. The second ward, already twenty or twenty-one years old, was Ines, and she, after a little while, had gone off to be mar-

* "Comit" is the abbreviation for the Banca Commerciale Italiane.

ried: a wedding that was all in order. She had married a fine young man from Rieti, son of property owners, a law student in his eighth year of college: the full course lasted ten. One fine day, just when Liliana's tendernesses were condensing over her head, she had suddenly come out with the information that "she wanted to follow her vocation." And she followed it: with excellent results. From the daughterly, and urban, adventure, she had extracted a bit of a dowry, had collected a hope chest: two big suitcases full of lace-edged linen. Affected, as she was, by a classic form of wifely foresightedness, not, however, of the grasping form of her predecessor, she had been able to captivate wholly the stepmotherly heart, so maternal, or so gently sister-like (Liliana was eight or nine years older than she) and had acted with stubborn assiduousness in infallible determination, minute by minute, and in the systematized premeditation of her every gesture or smile or word or whim or glance or kiss: those which distinguish the tacit will of the woman, when she has "character": a past mistress, on occasion, in prompting the thought without even giving its outline verbally: with hints, lateral tries and counter-tries, mute waiting: setting off a process of induction, like the stator of a generator: with the same technique whereby she is wont to surround and protect (and direct towards the Right) the first stumbling steps of a little one: channeling it, however, where she wants, which is where he can wee-wee in the most seemly way, and with utter relaxation.

Ines! The urban adventure! From Galilei's* matutinal

* Alessandro Galilei (1691–1737), architect of St. John Lateran, the beloved "San Giovanni" of the Romans.

clarities, when the Lateran office and mystery, the green gaiety of the churchyard receive within the city's walls the hick with his devout Sign of the Cross, the ass hitched up for a moment, gee!, from the golden pomp, at vespers, or ruby-colored, and from the full *cavate* of Maderno, from whose archway the indelible hymn in praise of Mary Mother has burst into the centuries never to return; from the PV and the BM and from the ten holes in the disk of the telephone, and from the big box of the radio which she put out of commission four times, the cothurnate fore-thinker had taken home a certain brisk, cavalier manner in darning socks, that is to say, taking the hole in wide circles, with needle and thread: and then, after that rapid circumnavigation, she pulled it all together and snapped off the thread at once, with her teeth. A first-class darn! Not even Princess Clotilde herself could have done better. A swelling, a musket ball under your heel which warmed your heart, for the whole festive day. Like so many orogenic seams towards the peak of a cone-shaped mountain: from those cones that pierce the clouds, which are the socks of the Lord.

She had brought to her student-husband, in addition to serene days and nights happy in the communion of souls and tongues, she had brought him . . . everything that a girl can bring in the practical and welcome line, for a student-husband: a great nonchalance in ironing pants, after having scorched six or seven pairs of Balducci's. That, we know, had been her discipline, her *gradus ad Parnassum*. Nothing ventured, nothing gained. We learn by mistake. Trial and error.

The third, Virginia! Don Lorenzo lowered his eyes, looking at the ground, though he was a grown man; then he
raised his eyes to heaven for half a second, as if to say: be
still, my lips! He joined his pious hams in a brief swinging
beneath his nose, before his beard: a to-and-fro in the plane
of the azimuth, an Italic, decent gesture. "The less said
the better!" he seemed to be pleading with Doctor Fumi.
It had to be said. The two officers were waiting: Ingravallo,
indeed, was on his feet, grim, nervously tapping one leg.
The giant's ten huge fingers slumped in his lap, still tightly
intertwined: comb and counter-comb: like an apostle of
marble, the kind that stand on the balustrade over the big
cornice of San Giovanni Laterano. Twenty-five pounds of
finger bones, good for cracking nuts, in that black furrow
of the cassock: where, in rapid succession, the black caravan of the priest's buttons descended: which had neither
beginning nor end, like the catalogue of the centuries. The
two shoes, at rest, shiny gravedigger color, but no more so
than all the rest, priapated from beneath the garment, like
two forbidden objects, camping by themselves near those
of Doctor Fumi, under the rack of dossiers, among the
four legs of the desk; and inside them, no doubt, two hunks
of double feet like a stone Saint Christopher.

"Well, what about Virginia?" Little by little, her character emerged: her headstrong vitality, the impudent type.
It turned out that the charmer had charmed two souls: in
two unconnected directions. The neighbor women, indeed,
said that she had put a spell on both: and some of them
played the numbers on the lottery. Her provocative beauty,
her health, like a coral devil inside that ivory skin, her eyes!

one could really believe that she had hypnotized husband and wife: "those brash ways," that somewhat rustic air, which revealed, however, "a big, sincere heart" (Petacchioni), or as was said, with a smile and a frown at the same time, with the professional tic of Doctor Ghianda, "a case of violent puberty." To this same Professor Ghianda, without being called upon to do so, Virginia had displayed her tongue, with a very rapid expulsion and an equally rapid return to its place, as if automatic, and with the tip pointed in a special way that was her trademark: sustaining then with the cold authority of her full face, though with a spark of malice in her eyes, his irritated, sulphurous gaze, filled with wrath and pitchy emanations. Hearing him called— she thought—piedatrician, or piediatrist, with great respect, by all the ladies of Stairway A, but even by some of B, she had believed that the distinguished man of science, whom she had seen for years going up and down the steps of the building in that mortician's overcoat to worm the kids, was, at the same time, the Monsignor's callus doctor,* Don Lorenzo's, that is: that this, in fact, was the basic profession of old frock-coat. An idea which, once it had entered her head, nobody had been able to drive out. The dimensions of Don Lorenzo's dogs made her certain she was in the right, believing that for such feet you'd need a piediatrist of that high rank. For the rest, my God! she had a pair of hips, two marble breasts: two teats so hard you'd need a scalpel: and with her way of shrugging all the time, so haughty, and that contempt on her lips, as if to say: shit to you! Yes, sir.

* Virginia assumes that the word *pediatra* (pediatrician) has something to do with feet (*piedi*).

After hours of silence, her bizarre insolence, her cruel laugh: with those white, triangular teeth, like a shark's, as if she were going to tear somebody's heart to shreds. Those eyes! from below the black fringe of her lashes: they flamed up suddenly in a black lucidity, narrowed, apparently cruel: a thin flash, which escaped, pointed, oblique, like a lie revealing a truth, which still unspoken, preferred to fade already on the lips. "She was a spoiled girl, but all heart," the chicken-seller opined, after an hour, when he had been summoned in his turn. "A fine figure of a girl, believe me; she liked to act saucy," the grocer's wife from Via Villari confirmed: "Ah! Virginia, from the third floor? She was a bag of tricks!" "That girl? She had the devil on her side," her girl friends said. "She had a devil inside her." But one girl, who was from the Patrica hills, let out a different expression: "She had a poker up her ass": and blushed at once. Commendatore Angeloni, extracted from Regina Coeli for an hour, to let him get a breath of fresh air, too, poor man, when titillated at Santo Stefano del Cacco, promptly drew his head down between his shoulders like a frightened snail: "Well," he merely grumbled, showing a pair of melancholy eyes, till he looked like an ox in a bad humor: yellow, they had become, after only a few days on the Lungara*: "I remember bumping into her a couple of times on the stairs, but I don't know her at all; I can't tell you anything," he affirmed sententiously, "about a person I don't know. She was the Balduccis' niece, or so I was told."

Once, several times (Don Lorenzo went on to say), without being much aware at that point of the "figure" or "position" of mother that Liliana Balducci intended to assume,

* Rome's Regina Coeli prison is on the Via della Lungara.

she—that is to say, this Virginia—in the house there in
Via Merulana, when the husband had escaped to his trains,
and when the maid was out, she had embraced and kissed
the signora. "When she got certain whims in her . . . her
head." Don Lorenzo managed to recover himself: with the
steady voice of charity he reported: she, at those moments,
well, it had to be one of two things: either she was out of
her mind, or else she felt she had to play-act like that. What
was certain was that she used to embrace and kiss the
mistress of the house.

"Mistress?" interrupted Doctor Fumi, narrowing his
brows.

"Mistress, stepmother—it's all the same." She kissed
her, the way a panther might give a kiss: "Oh Signora
Liliana, darling, you're like the Madonna for me!" then, in
a low low voice, in an even more stifled tone of ardor: "I
love you, love you, love you; one of these days I'm going to
just eat you up": and she grasped her wrist, and twisted it,
staring at her: she twisted it like a vise, mouth to mouth, till
each could breathe the other's breath, tit to tit. Don Corpi
rectified, naturally enough: "I mean, moving close to her
with her face and bosom." But both Ingravallo and Doctor
Fumi had understood the first time.

One day, in an access of filial love, she really did bite
her ear: and that time Liliana took fright. Madonna! How
it hurt! She ran all the way to the Quattro Santi, at full tilt.
Pale, breathless, she had displayed the part known as the
lobule, still dotted by the little circle . . . of those teeth! My
God! All in fun . . . but nasty fun, just the same. If fun is
the word for it.

Then they had tried to drag her into the church, "to make

her say some prayers, as many prayers as she could. Prayer, you might say, is the ticket to Paradise: or to Purgatory, at least. If you're carrying a heavy suitcase, you don't get past the Customs in Paradise . . . not the first time. But her pray? Not on your life! She hummed them under your nose, till you wanted to slap her, like a song, those Roman songs they sing with the guitar . . . sad ones, between nose and throat: or else shaking her head all the time, with her eyes on the tips of her shoes, *avemaria avemaria, la-la-la-la gratiaplena gratiaplena,* as if to mock the whole lot of us, the Madonna included. The Madonna! Now really! A singsong that would have put a baby to sleep. Shameless! Because if there's somebody who can help us out in this world, it's the Madonna, and her alone: because the good Lord . . . it looks to me like we do our best to give him a pain in the . . . the heart . . ." Don Corpi recovered himself: a second time.

Or maybe she wore her veil, but with her head in the air, at the high mass, in a kind of happy asthenia or bored echolalia: she became distracted, with the mother-of-pearl rosary that Liliana had given her: she held the book upside down, so she couldn't read it, even if she had been able to understand any of it. The feast of Corpus Domini . . . would you believe it? . . . she had the nerve to ape the canons of San Giovanni, as they chanted their office? with a man's voice? which only the devil could have lent her, at that moment. Even the saints from their thrones seemed to protest, all of them, painted though they were, because she had really made them lose all patience. He had looked her in the face, stopping his chant . . . sitting at the right of

Monsignor Velani. Then, after Mass, he had told her a thing or two, on the spot, under the portico, when they came to say hello to him, her and Liliana! But her only act of contrition was to shrug her shoulders, that animal: "till you wanted to give her a slap." And he raised and opened his hand over the table; it was so big that both Fumi and Ingravallo were wide-eyed, at last.

VI

On that same afternoon of Tuesday the 22nd, while in
room number 4 the above-mentioned conference of the
three men was still in progress, later filed among the official
records as "fifth questioning of Balducci," there arrived at
Santo Stefano (Collegio Romano) a telephonic communication from carabinieri headquarters in Marino regarding the
investigations on the "Menegatti case." The message was
received by Sergeant Di Pietrantonio. The communicating
office confirmed, off the record and simply as a warning,
that the owner of the green scarf (no longer so radically
green by now) had been identified as a certain Retalli Enea
alias Luiginio, aged nineteen, son of Anchise Retalli and
Venere née Procacci, born and residing in the locality
known as "Il Torraccio" not far from Le Frattocchie:
Lui-ginio. That's right, yes, Lui-gin-io . . . present where-
abouts unknown. Yes . . . no . . . fine . . . perfectly . . . No,
no . . . they hadn't found him at Il Torraccio. In short a
fugitive from justice. From what Di Pietrantonio's auricular
diligence managed at last to salvage from the shipwrecked
text (the receiver's crackling and the line's inductance
sonorized the message: various interferences, an urban
crossed line, laced it with chatter, tormenting reception), it

seemed more or less that the uncautious Enea Retalli or Ritalli, *sive* Luiginio (but obviously Luigino) had taken the scarf to be dyed . . . thirty-six quintals of Parmesan! Heddo, who's sbeaking? shipped yesterday from Reggio Emilia . . . Lieutenant-commander Racace here. Heddo? Heddo? . . . Abmiradal Mondeguggoli's house! The Bavatelli Shipping Company from Parma, yes, by truck . . . carabinieri headquarters, Marino, we have precedence. Thirty-six quintals, yes, three trucks, left at ten o'clock yesterday. No, the condessa's in the hospiddle . . . in the hordpiddle, visidding the admiradal . . . via Ora-zio! Yes, sir. No, sir. I'll ask. Police here, we have precedence, Rome Police Headquarters. Get off the line. Thirty-six quintals from Reggio Emilia, Parma-type cheese, absolutely first class! The admirabdal was obberadated on Monday: gallbladder: *bladder.* Yes, yes, sir . . . no, sir, no . . .

What could be extracted from such a muddle was, in short, that Retalli had taken the scarf to be dyed, to a woman at I Due Santi on the Via Appia, a certain Pàcori, Pàcori Zamira. *Z* like in Zara, *A* like in Ancona! Zamira! that's right. Za-Mir-a! known to many, if not all, in the area of Marino and Albano for many of her merits: if not for all of them. Then the connection broke off, in honor and for the benefit of higher authorities: or so it seemed. When night had almost descended, there arrived at Santo Stefano on his motorcycle Corporal Pestalozzi, or Pestalossi it may have been, bearer of a written report and more than one verbal message from the carabinieri station, that is to say from Sergeant Santarella, who in the absence of the commanding officer in those days, or in other situations of the titular lieutenant, was his representative. It was eight o'clock, hour of the stomach and the spoon, almost. Balducci had already been sent away, Commendatore Angeloni with the fondest good-byes sent off, liquidated. By this hour he must surely have been in bed, and with his nose more drippy than ever, his stocking cap pulled down over his eyes and down his nape: stuffed into his grandmother's bed, under a fat eiderdown and under stuffy, but deserted cover, the most suited and the most desired by a stuffed-shirt like him. Fumi's voice: "Have Pestalozzi come in." Nausea at the Cacco's piles of papers was about to overcome even the hardiest . . . But that northern and carabinieresque name electrified them. Pestalozzi, who had taken special pains to track down the scarf, was immediately received and heard in number 4 by Fumi: Ingravallo present with Di Pietrantonio, Paolillo, and Grabber. The last-named, protected by the shadows from a kind of huge, extinguished stove, put into his mouth and hastily chewed the last remains of roast-beef sandwich, which to a great extent he had already managed to lacerate outside, in the corridor. Er Maccheronaro, in Via del Gesù, just a stone's-throw away, never overlooked a chance to demonstrate his friendliness: and he had paved it inside, with three such slices of prime beef that, on first seeing them, he had taken them for three terra cotta roof tiles on a roof in Sampierdarena: nestling one against the other, all three supported by that big beam of double roll, the size of a carpet slipper, Madonna! the kind you can't even remember nowadays, now that the Empire has put its oar in. The panacea of panaceas for his empty stomach, lacking its soup, but already dewy in the

190

gastric juices of an anticipated gratitude and no less predisposed peristalsis. The customers at the counter, seeing that miracle, had been bug-eyed: natural enough: who can say what they were thinking; "Hey, Pompeo, what are you doing over there in that stove? . . . Come here," Doctor Fumi ordered, "you've got to hear this, too." He began and continued in a loud voice, with musical vigor, reading the report of carabinieri headquarters, Marino. When he had terminated, he began to titillate Pestalozzi with questions and, alternately, Di Pietrantonio, with the aid of his great shining eyes, which in the not-bright light of the room, a little each time, he turned, on every face: he mitigated with parallel statements, more and more vivid, more and more narrated (like neighboring little streams) the carabinieresque, buttoned-up discipline of the former and the smart, police alertness of the latter. That discipline is well evidenced, generally, and is operative in a tacit, a hard and cautious resistance in the face of the rival organization of the police.* The fact is that, at Doctor Fumi's gently inviting glances, so black, so limpid and melancholy in his pallid countenance—even at night, and in the weak candle-power of Madam Mazda—even at night, and barely descended from the motorcycle, at the marvelous timbre of that voice, the most buttoned-up of carabinieri couldn't resist. Pestalozzi, moreover, having still to catch Retalli, whose scarf alone had remained in his hand, was, in turn, interested in eliciting as much as possible from the five

* The law in Italy is enforced not only by the police, locally, but also by the carabinieri (formerly the Royal Carabinieri), a national force with a long tradition. There is ill-concealed rivalry between the two forces.

experts of the Collegio Romano: in pumping out the best from Santo Stefano del Cacco's urban cistern: data, various illations, motives for suspicion, well-founded hypotheses, doubts, counsel, the latest news: the final dotting of *i*'s and crossing of *t*'s the final disjunctions of the great deductive wisdom. And then the bloodhound's *amour-propre*, his pride in taking part in the investigation of the great crime which was on every tongue, from Frascati to Velletri, whose numbers all Italy was playing in the lottery, in all the best and luckiest cities: the Royal Lottery, as it was then, nowadays Lottery of the Republic. So that a kind of police-carabinieri osmosis began and continued to be celebrated in that room number 4, and at that late hour, through the ass's skin membrane of reciprocal distrust, professional jealousy and *esprit de corps*: a two-way flow of information, a game of *do ut des*, with amiable phrases, or even lapses into gossip.

Di Pietrantonio was personally acquainted with Sergeant Santarella: not to mention Ingravallo, who was even a distant cousin via various old women, aunts, a chain of godmothers: the chain of relations, repeated in time along the chain of mountains, the harsh Apennine, had traveled up the bitter spine of the boot, up, up, from Vinchiaturo to Ovindoli. And, besides Santarella was the shining eponym of discipline: and of Latial duty. Di Pietrantonio, for his part, knew la Pàcori, and Grabber knew her, too: because they had stopped for a drink, in September, at her counter: Zamira! of whose name and whose actions, open or veiled, not to say secret or splendid, legend had become first discoverer or *trouvère*, then divulgator and trumpeter: from Marino to Albano, from Castel Gandolfo to Ariccia.

Meanwhile Retalli Enea, aged nineteen, son of Anchise and Venere née Procacci, it turned out, had as his *nom de guerre* Iginio, not Luiginio: "which doesn't make sense anyway," they dismissed it, in one accord. "Bah! of course not!" they agreed. Tricks of inductance, overloaded wires. Inadequate service. Work on the line. The change of management!

La Pàcori, oppressed then by an accumulation of rags, garments, heavy sweaters, and ragged jerseys to dye, which would need the caldron of Beelzebub, her patron, with some suspicion of animal life inside the stuff, at the height of anguish, had sub-contracted the dyeing work, including the green sash to the Ciurlani firm in Marino: which, two days earlier, in the fury of a stupid equinoxial wind with slanting rain, had sent a carriage to collect that rubbish: and the horse had arrived soaked, and so worn out, poor animal, that they had to unhitch him, then dry him off in a broken-down stall, where it rained in, patting his ass and giving him some hot wine to drink. It was there, in Marino, that is, that Pestalozzi had directed himself. There was some stuff already dyed, in a heap, on a table: and other stuff to disinfect or to dye again, in two sacks against the wall, on the ground: but when it came to them, Sora Mara warned the corporal to watch his step, you can't be too careful: "Those little beasts, once they get on to you . . ."

Pestalozzi, a man with guts, sharpened his eyes, but with his legs, he drew back at once: "two steps to the rear," snip, snap, with military vivacity: like at close-order drill. After some pecking around by the titular Ciurlani (that is to say Sora Mara herself) in that pile on the table, which was already cooked almost white, purified in the autoclave of any possible quadruped, from it, in fact, the scarf had emerged, tugged by one end, the sash: unfinished: like a serpent drawn from its hole by the tail, green, yes, once, black-green with dots: now green no longer, but not yet its new color which, ideally, was to be a pale brown, because to perfect the pale brown a second immersion was required. Thus spake la Ciurlani.

But how was it, asked the experts, that Zamira, the trouser-maker of I Due Santi, had dared offer the information?

Pestalozzi led them to believe that the idea of questioning her had occurred to him: and "only later on" to Sergeant Santarella. They were the station's two motorcyclists. And at his disposal, in the course of certain private exchanges of ideas with some stubborn types, he had arguments which were not wholly ineffectual, indeed rather convincing, against the great plague of reticence: (Di Pietrantonio, in his mind's eye, was already examining the leather belt): arguments which, in some cases, could succeed in counterbalancing and even overcoming, in doubting hearts, in hardheaded bumpkins, the opposing fear, the terror of vendetta. But with the good Zamira . . . there had been no need to go so far. Eh! A woman! And a woman of such stuff, of such form! Not even calling her to the barracks *ad audiendum verbum*, not even that had been considered necessary: a thing which, for that matter, "you might say," would have caused her more pleasure than fear. Oh! Sergeant Santarella, that is, in other words . . . the station, yes, the station had its trump cards, some here, some there: "all through the deck": and Di Pietrantonio, taking the words from his colleague-adversary's mouth, assumed the wisest face in the Cacco office. "In the midst of the theater of operations," Fumi added, serious, turning over a paper, with gentle gravity. A niece . . . a girl who worked for la Pàcori. A little bunch of primroses for the sergeant. Two knitted stockings for his little girl, the baby, Luciana, and a few words to go with them. Few, but well-chosen.

Fumi then recalled that a girl, that Ines, Ines . . .—and he started to search, with one hand, in the file of fine ladies, which he kept on his desk as a kind of mindful aroma, like lovely flowers in a vase—Ines . . . Ciampini, yes, from Torraccio, or Torracchio, on via Appia, the stop after Le Frattocchie, had been picked up a few evenings earlier by a patrol from the San Giovanni police station: the evening before the crime: picked up for loitering, no identification papers: and on well-grounded suspicion of prostitutional activity in a public place (Santo Stefano Rotondo!), activity for which she was not licensed (a mere amateur, in short). She had insulted the arresting officers, calling one of them "Sergeant Fathead." She had offended, "admittedly probably with only sporadic activity and, on that evening, in an entirely occasional form," she had been caught in flagrant contravention of the Federzoni orders for the reformation of the urban sidewalks under booted régime, "in accordance with that special regulation from the Minister of the Interior on February fourteenth, you know the one, Ingravallo, regulation number seven hundred eighteen—help me out on this—Ingravallo, with that memory of yours!—concerning the moralization of the Capital." Ingravallo didn't open his mouth. "And held for suspicion of complicity in a

theft," Di Pietrantonio reminded his chief. "What theft?"
"A chicken." "Where'd she steal it?" "Piazza Vittorio."
The morning of Wednesday the sixteenth, after the round-up
of the nymphs, Corporal Juppariello of the San Giovanni
station had shown her to the two women who had suffered the
robbery three days before: a chicken-seller and another
woman who sold slippers. A theft of an old pair of shoes
from this latter, and a chicken, too, nearby, from the next
stand: plucked and neckless, as it turned out, but in compensation with three feathers in its ass. And the ones who
snatched them, both shoes and chicken, were two characters,
a boy and a blond girl, "who had wandered around for some
time along the street, in that very crowded hour, then they
had separated, and had mysteriously disappeared with the
merchandise." The chicken-seller's wife, who was the one
who yelled loudest of all, "at first" had thought she recognized in Ines, Cionini Ines of Torraccio, the very blonde
who she believed had snitched the feathered creature, or
rather, de-feathered. "On second thoughts," however, she
seemed to hesitate. A sample chicken, to enlighten the police,
had been taken to San Giovanni, in every way similar to
its colleague which had vanished from sight three days
before—it was now Sunday the 13th—and the same with
the two shoes: accused and accuser were then coached together to Santo Stefano, the shoe lady with them. Questioned
at headquarters, Ines had sustained and sworn, with many
a "I hope to die if it's not true," that she knew nothing of
the fowl, in the first place: that she was an apprentice
seamstress, though without employment at present: and
that she had worked, as a trouser-maker at I Due Santi,

just beyond le Frattocchie. "And then what?" Then she had been reduced to coming to Rome, to look for work. "It's no shame to have to look for a job." The chicken let off a terrible stink: it, too, had been taken to the station, along with the two shoes, both lefts; once at Santo Stefano del Cacco, the bird had apparently taken fright and, though dead, it had shat, there on Paolillo's little table: not much, though, to tell the truth.

"Let's hear this Ines!"

Fumi swung around in his chair, pressed the button, and asked for Piscitiello, he charged Paolillo to have Piscitiello hand the girl over to him, if she hadn't already been shipped off to Regina Coeli. Paolillo, after a short while, brought in a rather well-supplied girl, with two marvelous eyes in her face, very luminous, shiny; but she was incredibly dirty and disheveled, and her stockings! her cloth shoes, half in tatters, with one toe sticking out. A gust of the wild, not to say worse, breathed into the room; a smell: "Mmm! get a load of that!" all of them said to themselves, mentally.

After a certain amount of preamble concerning her vital statistics, Ines . . . Ines Cionini, questioned a while by Doctor Fumi and some by Don Ciccio, examined from head to foot by Corporal Pestalozzi, Sergeant Di Pietrantonio, and Paolillo and, behind them, a little by Grabber, Ines understood at once what they wanted from her. They wanted to hear her voice. So she sang out, she spilled the beans. Without having to be coaxed. Had she perchance worked for la Pàcori? Yes, that was where she worked, for Zamira. Zamira? Yes, that was her name. And . . . how? And . . . when? And . . . for how long? Ah, for over a year! And . . .

what did she do, at Zamira's? What sort of customers did she have? Oh, all kinds. Just about everybody came to her, men and women: because of her cards. And . . . also, what did she have in her cellar? Cellar? Well, the floor below? Oh, she kept a demijohn of oil! And pecorino cheese, too! Oh, sure, of course. Un huh. And how many girls did she have working for her? How old were they? From sixteen up? There were some that were only fifteen. And the carters? And the horses? Oh, the stables . . . sure!

And what other animals did she have around? And who took care of them? Aha! Is that so? And they played cards, too, did they? Oh, but only on Saturdays. Naturally, of course. That's obvious enough. Saturday evening. Just about everybody came. The wine was good. Yes, she had a license: yes, for alcoholic beverages. Et cetera et cetera. It came out that on Fridays and Tuesdays she was also visited by the force, the Royal Carabinieri. Pestalozzi would have liked and, above all, *should* have tried, to protest. He thought, on the other hand, that it was preferable for him ἐξωτέρῳ, to let a little fresh water run on, from such a generous faucet: and he contented himself, at critical moments, with a shrug and a shake of his head: "nonsense! all lies!" But they all believed it, nevertheless. The police dote on nonsense: in their rivalry with the carabinieri. Each of the two organizations would like to have a monopoly on such stories, on History indeed. But History is one alone! Well, they're capable of hacking it in two: a piece for each: in a process of de-twinning, of amoebic splitting: half for me, half for you. The singleness of History is derogated into a double historiography, it is devolved into psalm and antiphony, it is potted in two contradictory certainties: the police report, the carabiniere report. The one says yes: the other says no. The one says white: the other says black. Dogs and cats get along better.

Ines Cionini had had her fancy-man, she admitted, a good-looking boy: a real and proper lover. Who, they all thought, must have met her and perhaps even . . . why not? . . . treated her with some tenderness . . . in a period far closer to her latest bath. She was very beautiful, to gaze upon, despite the squalor of the room, the moldy light on the brick floor: white of face and throat amid the pools and fringes of dirt: with swollen, red lips: like a baby sylph, precociously troubled with puberty: and rather undulant in her turning, in her leaning forward, pained by certain weights (a little in the manner of some saints, some nuns, believed to be Spanish) as if by an incontrovertible charge, a heavy burden, eternal: laid upon her by the ancient caprice of nature. Surfaces imitating the true, nucleal volume seemed to enfold her repeatedly, like circles surround the stone cast in the water, amplifying "in the minds of the witnesses," that is in male delirium that stupendous suggestion: from her there emanated, along with the above-mentioned aroma, the true and basic sense of the life of the viscera, of hunger: and of animal warmth. The idea proper to stables, to haystacks: and far from all lowly pragmatic sanctions. Her gem-eyes, a child's, enunciated to all those men, still without their supper, the name of a happiness that was yet possible; a joy, a hope, a truth superior to their papers, to the squalid walls, the dried flies on the ceiling, the portrait of the Shit. The syphilitic Swaggerer. Perhaps, poor creature, the adjective that so suited to the beshat Maltonian* was to modify her as well? No, she didn't look ill: if not with hunger, with beauty, with puberty, with filth, with impudence, with abandon. And perhaps with sleep, with weariness. Her fancy-man had led her into theft, after having had his will of her: because the soft whisperings at nightfall had concluded with "shift for yourself." Her erstwhile employer and mentor had clarified her thinking, or had enabled her to clarify it for herself. Love, after besmirching her, had handed her over to the whim of hunger. All, now, hoped to find in her the longed-for spy of whom they had need. She understood this; she knew it: and for that matter, hell, who gave a damn? the evil that the blue days had poured over her was such that she had to give it back, to her protectors. So she sang. About her mistress-teacher. "Teacher of sewing? Mistress-seamstress?" Teacher of sewing and not of sewing. La Pàcori: yes, Zamira. In parallel fashion Pestalozzi and Di Pietrantonio reported. Ingravallo shook his huge head also: three or four times.

La Zamira, yes: known to all, between Marino and Ariccia, by the lack of her eight teeth in front (her teeth began with the canines: Ines pointed to her own, as paradigms, opening and twisting with one finger her lovely lips), four above and four below: whereby the mouth, viscid and salivary, red as if burning with fever, opened badly, like a hole, to speak: worse, it stretched at the corners into a dark and lascivious smile, not handsome, and, no doubt involuntarily, coarse. Despite the face, there were

* Another reference to Mussolini, son of Rosa Maltoni.

murmurs, that rictus, that vacuum held for some of the Royal force and for some non-royalty a perverse allure. Sometimes on certain afternoons, her eyes were flashing, yet soft, swollen underneath, like two serous blisters, filled with a dazed and slightly baby-faced malice: she was a bit drunk: you could see it: you could smell it on her breath: then her wrinkles smoothed out as if by a breath of Favonius. At other times she seemed more herself: her, Zamira: the light must have struck then on something hard, like the flame of a witch's curse on the face. The harsh roughness and tempestuous dishevelment of her hair, and the parallel, profound wrinkles all over her face, which was brown and dark, wooden, and the greedy ambages of her gaze in those moments delineated better her aspect: like an ancient sorceress, priestess of abominable spells and roots, the stewed roots, in which the soul of a Lucan, of an Ovid is entangled.

Her official activity was that of a mender and re-weaver, trouser-maker, dyeress, and in some cases, notions-merchant empirical in curing sciatica through secret herbs, seer, clairvoyante, card-reader, licensed to sell wines and liquors at I Due Santi, and Oriental Wizardess with a diploma in the first degree: in her workshop-tavern where the carters of the Appia stopped for a half-liter of wine, precisely at I Due Santi. She was consulted in the exorcism line, for casting or removing spells, exorcizing the evil eye from infants in their bonnets, simple-minded babies, and preventive spells in general; gifted also in the branch of washing heads to drive away lice, and when some girl's monthly was overdue, whether through nerves or other troubles, of which there are many, as all know. An immunologist of great experience and rare knowledge, after the liberation of Italy from the menace of the bolshevik hydra thanks to the Great Balcony of the Holy Sepulchre (October 28, 1922) the cracking of the malocchio sive evil eye, whose infinite case-history was at her fingertips, more and more constituted the chief subject of the appeals to her art. But not all. She was also skilled, *sic et simpliciter,* another gift of nature, as authoress of propitiatory or even repellent potions, according to the requirements of the case, and of almost all the love philters and powders for both signs, that is positive and negative. She could make pedigreed dogs have a miscarriage, when impregnated by some mongrel stray. She knew how to inculcate, at a reasonable fee, a certain *quantum*—that is to say the necessary amount—of kinetic energy to the dubious, to the insecure: comfort them in the *pragma,* corroborate them in the act itself. With ten lire one purchased, through her medicine, the faculty of willing. With another ten, that of being able. She un-kierkegaarded little crooks of the province, channeling them "to work" in the city, known as the Urbs, after having purged their souls of any remaining perplexity, or of their last scruples. She set the bold on their path, showing them that the poor creatures of the weaker sex asked for nothing better, in those years, than to lean on someone, to attach themselves to something, that would be able to share with them a mindless emotion, the sweet pain of living: she catechized them in the Protection of the Homeless Girl, in competition with the better-known organization of the same name. And her catechumens looked upon her as a mistress, though dubbing her, from one drink to the next, filthy, when they thought she couldn't hear them, of course, and bag and witch: such is the foolhardiness of our time, and their personal coarseness: and even perhaps titling her the old sow, her, Zamira Pàcori! and old procuress, hah! a seamstress of her position! and Oriental wizardess with a diploma of the first degree! Some gratitude. And they even had the nerve to say that the Due Santi, the two saints of the locality . . . were . . . a pair of "if you follow my meaning," accompanying this assertion with an immodest manucaption—prolation of the pair in question, wrapped though they were in the crotch: immodest, oh yes, but not infrequent then, in popular usage. Slander. Foulmouths. Hick scum, that go out at night to steal chickens.

Oh! the clean thread of time, of the Alban time and her own, unwound from the distaff of her divining like truth from an oracle. Murky or serene, but all summoned to her foresight, the days and the events seemed to orbit around her, to rise and vanish in her. To her, then, from that so fearful expectation of the multitude it was only right to prick the long study of the believers, derive from every consultation her little lire, from every delay of the miracle an increment for the faith, from every most secret vapor the aurora borealis of an improbable summoned back to probability. Why yes, indeed, who would ever have thought that? Despite the gratitude and the scared respect by which she was generally surrounded—collective hope and religiosity, Orphic sense of mystery and of the transcendence in the great heart of the people—despite her diplomas and degrees, Oriental and Occidental, and after infinite séances, after all those abracadabras with the skull on her table, and the respected needlework of more than ten years, her girls around her, poor babies, mending or knitting or sewing on rows of buttons, why yes, that's right, who would ever have thought it? Don't do good if you are not prepared to receive evil. Even Zamira. The base skepticism of the carabinieri persisted in surrounding her with the usual, unseemly suspicion through which they . . . many times, succeed in ruining the lives of seers, embittering the souls of card-readers: and even of the most respectable seamstresses. And that is: they thought, indeed they were sure, that she was an ex-whore (and no one could shake them from this opinion), widow, from year to year, of about fifteen former reserve captains in retirement: whose traces, little by little, from one autumn to the next, had become evanescent, from Marino and Ariccia. Having given herself, as the years passed and her incisors with them, to an ever more sly and bold madamship, with its epicenter, in fact, at I Due Santi, in a kind of cellar under the workshop-tavern: cellar or half-basement room that had light, perhaps even sunshine, from the garden. The garden—a few turnip greens, also disheveled: an occasional cabbage, its leaves stripped off by the sirocco, made wormy by Pieridae: with a dour hen, flapping there from time to time, checked by a string that was all gnarls, to lay eggs out of season—was at a level lower than the normal altitude of the road, the Via Appia. The cellar, or half-basement room, was equipped with a urinal: and, more, with a cot: which however creaked at a mere nothing, the bastard, and had the tegument of a "counterpane" of faded green: damasked by undecipherable maculations which, in their authentic obscurity, had a baroque tendency: a full, pompous baroque of the first jet of imagination, though it was washed and dried in the garden, the coverlet: and it seemed to deny even hypothetically any belated, neoclassical restraint. Attached to the wall, to one side of the little bed, you could see a really sweet oleo: a nice bunch of naked girls, at their medical exam, and a doctor with a little black goatee, looking at them one by one, but dressed like an ancient Roman, without eyeglasses, and with sandals instead. He had stuck his thumb in the hole of a little board, and with the other fingers of the same hand was grabbing a bunch of brushes, to paint with iodine who knows what part of their skin, if he found some pimple on any of them. It opened, this little drawing room or examination room, through a door provided with latch and chain, into the sanctum or oracular receptacle, properly speaking. There bloomed the prophecies and the responses (after working hours) of the seamstreess-sibyl: when all the girls were upstairs, on the other hand, at that hour of sewing and clickety-clack, well, at that time, the magical apparatus was visited by some large rats, using all the caution due the situation. Rats half as long as your arm came tiptoeing in, sniffing, those sons of bitches! with mustaches on them! ready to scent a ghost's sheet two palms away in the dark, and the smell of cheese, at a mile, all the way from the house of the garbage man, who kept their whole family at full board. But they had to be content with a bare smell of that manna, unable to reach it in any other way than with their olfactory sense: they whiffed the Idea, an invisible Presence. The presence of good mountain pecorino, a whole cheese of the days before the Empire landed on us: yes, right on the neck. A trestle in the darkness. A cast-iron stove, A country fireplace: a kettle over it, hanging from a chain: and a fine pot, in one corner, in the midst of such rags! a kind of copper pot which, in a few years' time, would fall prey to the Immortal Fatherland, War-Bearing, shoulder to shoulder with the Twotone *Bruder*, at a mere sign from the Deuce, the adored Doochay: thief of saucepans and pots of all peoples: with the excuse of making war on England.

There was everything you could want. A place, in short, this workshop of Zamira's whose like you would never find, still less its better, for distilling a drop, a single and splendid drop of the eternally prohibited or eternally unlikely Probability. Jerseys to be dyed, trousers to be mended: the moths devour the owl: but some of it was always left, the eyes of the owl live, knowing topazes motionless in the night, in time, surviving the ruins of time. A point of contact of the vital compossibilities: magic, knitting, tailoring, trousering, wine from the Castelli and even from Bitonto (a keg, with a tap: two demijohns, rubber siphons), cheese and beans in April, the grandson of the mustachioed chief rat, rummaging inside the skull, in the cellar, that is to say in the "dyeing room"! in the cranium, where he had entered and where he would come out by an eye, an empty socket, naturally. Packs of cards on the table, the astrologicheral tarot cards: hourglass, cabala of lottery and pentacle: a stuffed owl, with a pair of eyes on him! And pecorino, in a big cupboard, and flasks of oil: ah . . . locked and barred so that not even a rat . . . no, not even with Zamira! they had had it. They could die of frustration, poor darlings! Abracadabra puffety-poo.

The Elysian gathering of the gentle shades, the summons, the evocation of the compossibilities! Poor, and dear, Zamira! She used to pour out wine for the carters on the Appia, for the carabinieri on their rounds. Standing, these last, having come in from the summer, guns on their shoulders: dusty, overheated, blinded by the immensity: stunned by infinite cicadas: with head and cap amid the cloud of flies, up, up, which gave out a humming at times as of an unseen guitar plucked by the phalanges of a ghost. She, after having brought the drink, took her chair again, wielding her needles, toothless (the front ones) in the circle of her tender novices likewise seated at their work: working with the needle, or knitting. Heads bowed, but raised, however, promptly, from time to time, one after the other, each after her neighbor: to thrust back with one hand, as if bored, the tangle of falling hair. But at that moment! they emitted a flash, those eyes: black, shining, emergent from boredom; then they lingered, bored, on the indifference of an object, a button, the butt of a rifle, the corporal's service revolver, or a little lower down, or a little higher, a little more to the right, a little more to the left. A scent of country women, in short skirts. What promises, what demographic hopes, poor darlings, for the eternal spring of the Fatherland, of our beloved Italy! What knees, Madonna! what big knees . . . Stockings—never even dreamed of. Underwear? Hm. The mountain women wore more, to hear the Bull roar in the stands.* Their plump legs held tight together, like they were

* The "mountain" is that of the French revolutionary Convention. The "bull" is Danton. An obscure reference, prompted by Gadda's wide reading in French history.

hatching an egg, or brooding over a treasure. Or else, the complete opposite: feet on the crossbar of the chair, so that, if one assumed a position of vantage, there were panoramas —you can imagine. What thighs!

A man's gaze plunged the penumbra, then in the shadows: it wound, it climbed among the passes of hope, as an explorer of caves dives and climbs, or a chimney sweep. Not to mention carabinieri! Grumpy, as their duty bound them to be, their eyes never stopped searching. And the eyes that came back to them! Eyes? Furtive arrows! Shots, that make the heart die in the chest, of those standing carabinieri: while at the same time the seamstress spoke to them about Libya: the fourth shore*: the dates that were ripening, exquisite, and the officers that she had known there and who had "courted" her with success. This remembering courting captains and colonels for the benefit of plain privates was a stratagem of seduction. Her eyes began to sparkle again then, tiny, pointed, black, darting: under the multiple furrowing of her forehead, under the rumpled pergola of her hair, which was gray and hard, like the fur of a mandrill. Considerable saliva lubricated the outburst of her speech, evocative or oracular as it happened to be: the lips, thirsting, fevered like her gums, dry or viscid, which, deprived of the cutting edge of the former ivory, seemed today the entrance, the free antechamber of every amorous magic. Of which, to be sure, the tongue was the chief instrument:

Énkete, pénkete, pùfete iné,
Àbele, fàbele, dommi-né . . .

* The "fourth shore," an Italian jingoist slogan, referring to the shore of Libya, Italy's onetime colony.

The devil couldn't resist this summons.

Yes, yes, Zamira had at her disposal a fine supply of niece-apprentices: and reserves, then, scattered along the Via Appia, the Ardeatina, or the Anziate, at this or that milestone, supplementary seamstresses: who, in any unusual situation, clickety-clack, were there to lend a hand: and they lent it: as for example, during the summer maneuvers of the Fourth Bersaglieri Regiment. For the patrols, for the carabinieri, patient upholders of law and order in the infinite summer, such organization was not required: the roster of the immediate employees and nieces was enough. All of them such, more or less, the nieces, to render those vinous visits sweet, and of the most joyous, the most disturbing, sheltered from the dog-day sun after miles, white miles, for the dusted and sweating bearers of guns. On patrol, after having walked their musket along highway and trails, or the heavy revolver, with all its bullets in it, and a couple of magazines in their cartridge box, the unconquerable servants of duty loved to cool off a moment in that harem of Zamira's, so warmly shadowed and silent: which was for all adepts the vestibule of the happy hypothesis, the sanctum of consultations, of Alban consolations. The moment of gentle anguish was fleeting, ah, what else can a moment be? but the following moment followed it: the integral of the fleeting moments is the hour: the unmatchable hour, where a precise thought was deviated towards hope and towards anguish, like a flashing shuttle, in the warp of furtive glances, mute dissent or mute consent.

The fact is that the carabinieri used to stop off at her place, la Pàcori's, the seamstress's: neither headquarters nor discipline opposed this: and at times, they had recourse to her. Little jobs of mending: when perhaps a button is about to come loose, and its stem must be reinforced. One morning, one of those overgrown boys had taken off his tunic, blushing, to have a tear mended: which he had picked up he couldn't remember from what berry bush or hawthorn. Another time, another youth, his pants: so people said: for a motive not entirely analogous, they went on to add. Zamira sent him down to the cellar to take them off: and after him she sent Clelia, or—according to other reports—Camilla, to take the trousers and bring them up to be mended, in the workshop. The divestment of the royal servant required some time: such a long, sweet time! Whereupon the girls, above, at a certain point began to cough, to snicker, to say ahem, especially Emma, that bold-face: until Zamira lost her patience, became angry and scolded them all, calling them a word that wasn't clearly understood, hissing drool from the hole.

Also the sergeant, Sergeant Fabrizio Santarella, hum, one of the two centaurs of the Alban headquarters, the higher in rank of the two motorcyclists, he, too, had taken the seer-dyer some jerseys to be dyed: big packages. He was heralded from afar, from Torraccio, from the last houses of le Frattocchie, from the Robine Vecchie at other times or from Cassera to Sant'Ignazio, or from the Sanctuary of Divine Love: he approached, scattering shots, he arrived, re-echoing, boom boom boom boom: the motorcycle was stilled at the door. They were women's jerseys, those packages: because Sergeant Santarella, who one day had been dragged to the altar by one woman (and not even a very swollen one), lived with nine: his wife, her old blind mother and her slightly feeble-minded sister, a sister of his own, unmarried and chaste, with all the psychic ornaments which from chastity descend upon sisters: three daughters, not yet of an age where chastity is a problem, and two tenants, twin sisters, once about to lose their chastity, but by now (after congruent skipping town of the hoped-for de-chastizer who, unable to make up his mind, had dropped both of them before turning his hand to . . . to the task) now definitively returned to chastity. Having one day decided to rent, because of the times and the opportunity and his pay, a small redundant portion of his penetralia, that which turned its mold towards Auster, he thought naturally of the paper with the widest circulation: and when it was time to nuncupate the offer in the *Messaggero* he hadn't had the heart to assert to the readers "no women," that cruel "halt!" of the landlady of Ingravallo. No, no, no, in his house . . . quite the contrary: women there were: and women there would be.

Of the male element, in his house, there was only himself: not counting the male *bouche* of the Douche, which from time to time resounded in the tympanic chambers, exciting tonic resonances, revitalizing his head no less than that of twelve million other Italians: more so, for his was a sergeant's head, clever as it was. From time to time, like winding an alarm clock. It came out, the dear voice, needless to say, it came from the box of the radio: with which Fabrizio Santarella had provided himself in Milan, when he had gone there on a "special assignment," to follow the trail of two gentlemen, both named Salvatore; and he had come back from Milan, with the two Salvatores, and in addition, with a radio with two valves: prodigious discovery of that prodigious civilization. Another male voice, and of the baritonal persuasion also, was that very rich and extremely sweet one of a gramophone, in the moments when it was playing male: because right afterwards, perhaps, it got the whim of being female. The marvelous gadget was transformed, that is, with the most perfect nonchalance, from masculine to feminine and vice versa: with disturbing alternations of *impasto*: from the Duke of Mantua to Gilda, from Rodolfo to Mimì. For the rest, in the home of Sergeant Santarella, there were women: and women there would be. Malicious-minded men and, even more, women, said that despite the nine women, the eighteen dainty shoes with eighteen women's heels that clicked about in the hours of domestic *loisir* . . . among the . . . domestic walls, in the presence of the domestic *lares,* who were two fine plaster cats over the unlighted fireplace, delivered, poor Toms, of a male from Lucca, they said, oh yes, while the gramophone from Via Zanardelli ladled into his soul for the twenty-third consecutive time the tiny frozen hand, for him and the whole neighborhood, they said, yes they did say, that he had a weakness for some of the niece-apprentices of Zamira, the dyer of I Due Santi. Well, he liked a bit of skirt, Sergeant Santarella did, like all sergeants.

An expert in the art: only logical. At the right moment he knew how to close his eyes. Or open the both of them, on the other hand.

A marvelous mien: his face full, reddish-tanned in cheeks and nose, blue-black where his shaven beard virilized it.

The generous skin of the Italics, in their baked harvests, in July, in the thresher's sun: scorched, to use Carducci's word. A health like a country horse trader. Those stiff mustachios à la Wilhelm II. That heavy pistol on his left hip, weighing six pounds. He made hearts fill with joy at the very sight of him. The girls, on certain moonlight nights, dreamed of the sergeant. Certain seedy bums with all the poverty of the imminent Empire upon them, certain down-at-the-heel bicycle thieves, dopes who lounged around the streets and dives all day long, at night to labor, were over-joyed to allow him to handcuff them, to be "put inside" by him. When he arrived, goddamnit-to-hell, they could draw breath: their anxiety was over, their danger: it was an end to sweating and running, to fiddling around, jump-ing at the slightest sound, at the suspicion of a gate's distant squeak: breaking locks, your heart in your mouth: there now, all suffering was at an end: they were seized with joy again, in their hearts, poor boys! their faith in the morrow was restored. They were so pleased, just to see him, that they forget their sad obligation, damn the judge: the obligation to escape with their haul, and—what was worse—with their tools, too, and overloaded: after so much labor, to have to take to your heels, too! So it goes. They greeted him with a glance, with a little laugh of under-standing, a laugh that means "between us . . .": they made him spontaneous gifts of whole bunches of picklocks, skeleton keys, whole assortments of jimmies. They asked him, respectfully, for his last match: to light, voluptuously, their last butt. Aaaaah! Ah! they said, exhaling, with voluptuousness in their throats, or expelling the smoke through the nose: "Ah well, all right, you know how it is," they said: and they held out their wrists: there was born in them a sudden longing for the chains on their wrists: as the weary, exhausted man wants only his bed. They held out two light-fingered paws: he could do what he pleased with them: dazzled by that darkened face, by those steady, black, piercing eyes: by those red stripes, on his trousers, those silver chevrons on his sleeve: by that white calfskin bandoleer like the banner of authority, inquiring, pursuing, handcuffing: by that V.E. in the silver grenade on his cap: by that paunch, by that ass. Yes, ass. Because he turned, he spun, raged, then again wheeled around, planted that pair of eyes on the face of one and of all, mustache erect, pointed, like two nails, and black: he acted, deliberated, telephoned, click, clickety, click, yelled into the receiver, asked for the reinforcement of the two privates from headquarters, imparted orders: which all obeyed, that's the beauty of it, and in a kind of algolagniac frenzy, of masochist voluptuousness: caught in the magic circle of the V.E., in the gravitational ellipse of that nucleus of energy so happily irradiated into its satellies: and, after them, into all thieves in general. Who longed only for this, as soon as they saw him: to be overwhelmed into the clink by a glance from him. Then, when everything seemed to be over, and when his women were whispering Papapapapapapà, there again came the explosions of the shudder-ing Motoguzzi, adding glory to glory, life to life. It set off amid clouds of dust, leaving behind murmuring girls: the brides: the nieces of Zamira, barefoot: fugitive demon of the red-striped legion, exhaled from crumbling castles:

where Night, surprised by these hours not his, ah, had forgotten to replace him in his cavern: when she extinguishes, instead, on the ruins of every tower, the two yellow circles of the owl. The belated wing becomes flabby, like a remnant of tenebrous velvet, in its nest of shadows and rock. Tapestries of ivy ward off the day. He, on the contrary, as soon as the sky was pink and gold: from Rocca di Papa to Castel Savelli, down, from Rocca Orsina to Monte Nuncupale, up: for already the hoe or the maddock was at work, in vineyard or among the olive trees. Bang, bang bang, off at top speed, reawakened, the motor shaking between his knees. Or he jolted on it with a restrained rumbling in the morning, where the little road penetrates cautiously into the brush: or where, proceeding up the mountain, it is lost to all solid ground, among thorny hawthorn thickets. Or where strawberries and snakes commingle, at Nemi, beneath the brush. He acted, an active agent: he disappeared, reappeared, like a genie summoned by a spell: immobile by the trunk of an ilex, perhaps, he and his Guzzi steed, one foot on the ground: and a little further on, erect, the pole-like private: the haunting presence with red stripes, with bandoleer of white calfskin over the shoulder, with V.E. in the silver grenade on the cap. Ornament, with handcuffs in his cartridge box, of the Alban headquarters: with two chains ready for four wrists and two packs of cheap cigarettes and a dozen shots of reserve, the centaur-arrow of Via Ardeatina and, even more, Via Appia: at a certain milestone on certain days, he overtook Lancias in full tilt, Maria Santissima, and after Her immediately with railroad crossings favorable:

he was up with them, there, they let him pass: not yet the red Lancia of Francesco Messina,* however, who didn't yet fly to Sicily, in those years, to kiss his Mamma. He took *au ralenti* the wicked curve of the Cecchina station: he only turned off the motor and stopped, the situation demanding it, at the station of Santa Palomba or Campoleone: where the Ardeatina and the Anzio road crossed, at the same level, the hurling advent of the Rome-Naples. Terror of hens on guard, the locomotive-leveler arrives with livid flashes on the pantograph and at the springs and joins: and behind it the whole train and the hammering din of the express, repeated, iterated, at every tie, as if to uproot all the points of the switches. And those hens went on clucking, flying up, strangling themselves in their tormented vocalises, showing feathers, and white plumes, in their vortex. What cannot fear do? It even makes geese fly. Or again, halfway through Le Frattocchie, he had to stop: at the Appia crossing, or at Ca' Francesi, at Tor S. Paolo, at the Ciampino station: heedless, at other times, of the peremptory assertions: *Dangerous curve! Railroad crossing! Bumpy road!* or of their symbols, imported from Milan. The Milanese, Luigi Vittorio, had sown Italy with the rare seed of their warning, of their "road signs."† Their outstanding signalism, one fine day, made, of the old boot, a new signal. To warn the people, to inculcate in the

* A private reference. The Sicilian sculptor Francesco Messina was, apparently, at one time the owner of a red Lancia.

† The Milanese engineer Luigi Vittorio Bertarelli was President of the Italian Touring Club and sponsored, about this time, a campaign to set up the standard Italian road signs all over the country, arousing Gadda's ire.

velocipederasts respect for disciplined ways, and, at the same time, for their own necks: to teach one's neighbor how to live in this world: erect iron stakes in all of Italy, hoist on to them "road signs" enameled, through public oblation, that desire made them water at the mouth: taking as pretexts the most innocuous, the most sleepy crossings, every curve, every fork, every bump, or, as they say, every dip. The technical memento of Bertarelli, of Vitori, of Luis,* in those years: then, on reblanched walls at the entrance to every hamlet, the totalitario-politico signs of the Turd: ("it is the plow that makes the furrow, but it is the sword that defends it . . . in a pig's ass"). Sergeant Santarella, Cavaliere Fabrizio, was, was a "great enthusiast" of the Touring Club; as a "life member" he knew its anthem by heart: "The Touring Hymn," born in Valtellina to the hypocarduccian-hyposapphic† Muse of Giovanni Bertacchi: a nobly caesuraed hymn, like the Marseillaise, and like all anthems in general, with a bold impetuousness in the refrain, that *ritornello* so dear to the hearts of all the life-member motorcyclists:

Forward! And on we go!

Which eliminates, as one can see, any possibility of going into reverse.

Santarella, setting to a hypothetic melos that life-enhancing meter, went along humming it and savoring in spirit—as one might gnaw on a toothpick after dinner—

* Vitori and Luis are Milanese dialect for Vittorio and Luigi, the names of the hapless Bertarelli.

† "Hypocarduccian" is a reference to the patriotic poet Giosuè Carducci (1835–1907).

in its fugitive pregnancy, along the rumbling and the rush of the succeeding miles: from the dusty trapeze of the road. Then, near Ciampino or La Palomba, he raised his eyes: up and up: white caravans of clouds, crossing the sky in mid-March, pursued by no royal representative: but they too, had somebody who saw to hooking them: and this was the silvered peaks of the antennae, like the teeth of a curry-comb biting into cotton into the fleece of the fleeting, the snowy flock was ripped by a perpetual deformability, then was gathered in an unreachable alternation of presages, with the wind high, cold shreds of blue.

VII

Ines Cionini . . ."

"Yes, Chief?" Paolillo asked.

"To be kept at our disposal! . . ." Poor girl, she was to await the dawn on the flat board of the night tank, wrapped in a tan army blanket under the Sign of the Louse: in the company of other Nereids fished from the ocean by the patrol, wrapped in similar double vicuna, and similarly involved with the relations of the Same, and from time to time sighing or even eloquent in their sleep: and in the presence of a pan mute, uncovered, in a corner: known as the "Commendatore": an authoritative sort, in fact, the Lord Treasurer of excrements. It brought the spirit back to certain Roman abundance and looseness of living and acting, to a certain pre-forty-eight (or pre-forty-nineish)* and quite Gregorian† "*loisir de sieger.*"

Poor girl: when, however, that order was given, well, Sor Paolillo came for her again at ten.

As to Pestalozzi, at a certain point he had asked Doctor Fumi leave to go, begging him for time to take a bit of re-

* References to the Italian revolution of 1848 and the brief Roman Republic of 1849.

† "Gregorian" has a faintly Papal flavor, but in Roman dialect *gregorio* also means the "behind."

freshment, after the long and not perfect day's work: an idea Fumi also found excellent. Having plunged down from the most salubrious hills, the super-sergeant centaur had interpreted the desire of one and all. They agreed to meet at quarter-past nine, or half-past. Before going off again, logically, Pestalozzi wanted to agree on the sequel: the conclusion of what had already been accomplished. In a shuffling along the halls and stairs, the assembly broke up.

In the meanwhile, having gone to Palazzo Simonetti in Via Lanza, Ingravallo ripened what the Deuce on his throne in the Palazzo del Mappamondo would have called "the instructions to be imparted . . ." to the inferior levels of the hierarchy: that is to say, to the earthenware vessels, one below the next, which drank in gulping, the cascades of his truculent foolishness: each from the behind of the other. It was late. Drizzling. Everything was still topsy-turvy in the night. Don Ciccio ladled into his mouth the lean broth, but not really so lean, emphasizing in a brothy trail the poverty of the proteins and the peptonic ingredients: then, fed up, he chewed and gulped down a few morsels for better or worse, without a word, his big head over the plate of that stew of rubber gristle, poor Don Ciccio! the amorous target of an occasional "But what's on your mind this evening, Doctor?" from his unequaled landlady, all anxieties, all concern: who wouldn't stop spinning around him, him and what he had been served. "A nice piece of cheese? Some of that Corticelli stracchino that you like so?" And, when he grimaced: "Just a little piece, Doctor. Try it: it's so good . . . It can't hurt you . . ."

Under the glass spotlight rimmed with pleats and green-and-white ruffles like salad, his pate seemed more tenebrous, more curly than usual. No automobile! No help in moving away from his base. There were automobiles, bah! "but only for those bastards in political," that is to say, the political section. The excursion he had missed, that horrible Thursday: "the seventeenth of the month! The worst number there is," he sighed, "seventeen, lousiest of all! . . ." he grunted, through clenched teeth.

Now all the merit went to the carabinieri of Marino. "Those big-hats, those Punch-and-Judy cops." Pestalozzi dined with good appetite off the marble-topped table in Via del Gesù, at the Maccheronaro's, where Pompeo had taken him: Grabber, as he was called, who also acted as master of ceremonies, at Santo Stefano, when the occasion demanded.

Pompeo, for his part, didn't see what obstacle could oppose the introit of a reprise of that shoe-sized sandwich he had had at seven: with paving this time, of roast beef and mortadella, in alternate slices, gently laid in that sofa of bread, by the expert, pudgy fingers of the Maccheronaro himself: who tegumented the slices at last, after a checking, dismissing glance, with the precut and set-aside roof top or lid (the upper half of the roll): the lower lip sticking out, but by a bare millimeter: while his double chin compressed and, so to speak, flattened against the collar, if one could believe he had a collar, ended by hiding entirely his spring-like tie, a bow, with polka dots on a green ground.

The customers present, envious, were stunned. A full-scale torpedo boat, something exceptional. To see it from the outside . . . quite decorous: but ponderously stuffed, within. Er Maccheronaro raised his eyelids, deeply serious, his lip still extended by that fraction of an inch, fixing without a word his beloved client, in the moment and in the very gesture of handing him this trophy. "Is this it, or isn't it?" his gaze seemed to signify. Pompeo allowed himself to be fixed. He set his tooth where it deserved to be set. After a couple of cavalierish bites, his mouth resembled a grinder, an eccentric millstone. He couldn't manage an answer, if anybody asked him anything. He looked towards the person in question, his big eyes wide, with the air of having understood.

At ten-thirty they were all gathered in Doctor Fumi's office. Paolillo brought back Ines. Who was—and where was—the young man? And that girl friend of her girl friend? Why, what girl friend? The one . . . the one that she had talked about, Mattonari, Camilla: "the one, if I'm not mistaken," Doctor Fumi said, "the friend who worked with you at Zamira's," at I Due Santi.

Camilla Mattonari, Ines admitted, had spoken to her of a girl friend, who had been in service in Rome, but not an all-day job.

"Half-time, you mean."

"Well, I don't know if it was half: she worked for some people who had given her a dowry, and now, she had to get married."

"Married to who?"

"Married to a gentleman, a businessman in trade: the kind that live in Turin and make cars: who had given her two pearls. And on Candlemas Day, for that matter, she was wearing them in her ears, those pearls. Everybody saw them." And she had also met her one evening . . . what a pair of eyes!

"What eyes!": and Fumi was annoyed; he shrugged.

"Well, yes, her eyes . . ." Ines rebutted, "were . . . different. Different from the eyes like the rest of us have. Like she was a witch, or a gypsy. Two black stars, right out of hell. At the Ave Maria, when it was getting dark, she looked like a devil disguised as a woman. Those eyes were scary. It was like they had an idea, in them, of getting revenge on somebody."

"So you know her then."

"No, I only saw her once . . . after dark."

"Where?"

"Well . . . it was on a road, in the country."

"In the country where? . . . Look here, girl, don't think you can fool me . . . You're trying to pull the wool over my eyes."

"It was a dirt road: where there was a field . . . and a church, but without any priests in it, it has a long name with *tondo* in it."

A liar, who got all tangled up in her own lies. Fumi wondered whether she was crazy, or something like it. The tortuous, winding notions of a stupid peasant girl who's lying. After having snapped at her, the four of them, like four dogs at a doe, pulling her and pushing her this way and that in the torment of easy and nonetheless repeated objections, they succeeded in the end in wrenching from her lips the calming lie, the plausible lie: the one which, contradicting or resolving all the previous ones, seemed finally the truth. The "country road," it was discovered, must have been a street (in those days still countrified and solitary) on the Celian hill, amid silent umbrella pines, fields of artichokes and some stables, and crumbling walls and an arch or two, trod, at nightfall, by the wondrous steps of solitude, so dear to lovers: perhaps it was Via di San Paolo della Croce, or more probably Via Della Navicella or Santo Stefano Rotondo. The arch was that of San Paolo, if not the archway of Villa Celimontana to the side of Santa Maria in Domnica. The "*tondo*" . . . "without any priests in it," wasn't, could not be, the Temple of Agrippa, where the bloodhounds had traveled in their thoughts, immediately rejecting is since it doesn't stand "in the country." It was instead Santo Stefano Rotondo, deconsecrated, in those years, to permit certain restoration work.

With all these logistics Doctor Fumi had rather lost sight of the gypsy, the bride of the Turin industrialist. The bloodhounds seemed to sink deeper into the mud.

"Tell us about these earrings."

"I didn't see them. But everybody knows about them: two long earrings, like a real lady's." And she repeated, in an obstinate singsong: "her fiancé gave them to her, a businessman from Turin: he buys and sells cars: how can I make it any clearer than that?"

"Just skip the clear and the dark . . . clarity is our worry," Doctor Fumi scolded her, his eyes now sleepy in their wrath. Who was she? Yes, this witch, this gypsy. . . Where did she live? What was her address? "Her address. . ." Ines hesitated again. Well, she must have lived somewhere around Pavona: that's what la Mattonari had told her. And that's what everybody said, at I Due Santi. "That girl's lucky: Rome is where girls get ruined: and instead she even got herself a dowry, that's what. And now, whenever she gets the notion, she can marry herself a real gent."

The officials, Doctor Fumi, Ingravallo, Sergeant Di Pietrantonio, the corporal exchanged glances. Grabber, perceptive young man that he was, read in those glances a thought: "This girl's trying to screw us. She thinks she's stealing candy from a baby."

Ingravallo seemed tired, upset, annoyed: then absorbed behind a chain of thoughts. Strange analogies, Grabber suspected, unknown to the others, were at work in that brain. There was no apparent connection, but who knows that one didn't exist, who knows but what Ingravallo would guess it, black and silent in his reflecting; there was no trail from the aproned delivery boy, to the thief in overalls, to the unknown murderer, to the big eyes of the gypsy.

"And what about the boy?"

"What boy?"

"Your boy friend, that *guappo*, that little crook: what do you want me to call him?" Doctor Fumi seemed to encourage her, to invite her to see reason, to speak. Then Ines took fright: she seemed tired, all of a sudden, in her filthy attraction: she seemed to withdraw in shame, to cloak her suffering: with sunken, hollow eyes, her white brow swathed in sadness under that blond hair, so hard, hardened with a bit of dried rain and crassament desiccated in the dust (that hair, all of them thought, from which a green celluloid comb would have extracted gold in the sun), with her lips a bit swollen and as if still chapped, by every gust of March wind.

"His name is Diomede, my boy friend. But I don't know where he lives. He's always moving around."

"Moving around how?" He moved around in the two best senses of the word: often changing his room or rather lair or cot: and strolling idly about Rome from morning to evening: looking for you never know what. The last time, she had run into him at the Tunnel of Via Nazionale. He lived here for a while, then there. But he wouldn't tell her where he was staying. On a couch at some relative's: in a room rented from a seamstress. In the empty bed of an uncle who had died, a couple of weeks ago . . . that is, the uncle of a friend of his, who had lost his uncle. And when he couldn't manage any more, couldn't pay up, then he had to get a change of air, you see?

"Obviously," Doctor Fumi concurred in a low voice. And he wandered around the city with no particular place to go, or else with slow and perhaps meditated itineraries: he shifted softly from one neighborhood to another: Monti at ten, Trastevere at four, at Piazza Colonna or Piazza Esedra with the lights and the red-green *réclame* of the evening, the night. The residential districts? Yes.

"He also used to work Via Veneto, Via Ludovisi every now and then, where it's a little darker, because of the women."

The girl blushed, raised her head, and her voice became spiteful, irked. "He went out walking, walking: he had to have his shoes resoled every month: he walked, and disappeared, and you never knew where he had gone."

Either to cultivate his beauties, or to escape his beauties: certain beauties, at least so it seemed to Ingravallo, looking for him, eager to find him, to catch him, with long, examining looks beyond the flow of the cars, from one sidewalk to the other, or along the sidewalk crowded with tables and chairs, with ladies and gentlemen drinking or in the process of sucking, in cautious, disinterested sips, the pallid fistulas.

"They'd go to the end of the earth to hunt for him," she stated: her eyes steady, calm.

"He too! He, too!" Ingravallo's feelings ached. "In the roster of the fortunate and the happy, even he!" His face became grim. "He, too, persecuted by women!"

"So he kind of wanders around, you know what I mean . . ." and, after some hesitation and with a certain amount of emotion in her tone: "so all those women looking for him won't find him at home, so he doesn't have to trip over some girl every step he takes."

With one hand she threw back the evil mop: she was silent.

"I understand," Doctor Fumi resumed. "Now, tell me: what's he like, what kind of a face does he have, this Diomede? By the way, is Diomede his first name or his last name?"

"His last name?" Ines lowered her eyes: she blushed, to gain time, to fabricate her seventy-third lie.

"His last name," Ingravallo followed up. "Yes, we may need him."

"To learn a few things from him, too," Doctor Fumi added.

"Well, he didn't want to tell me his last name."

"But he finally did tell you, though," Ingravallo insisted. "Out with his last name."

"Listen to me, girlie. The bunch of us, here . . . it's best for you . . . we need his help."

"But officer, sir, how can you need a boy like him? He's never done any harm to anybody."

"He has to you! . . . Seeing as how the vice squad has run you in."

"Well, I mean, that's between me and him: the police haven't got anything to do with that: it's our business."

"Aha, so the police have nothing to do with it, eh? Honey, you're not talking sense. We're the ones who know what the police have to do or not."

"He hasn't done anything."

"Well, then tell us his name."

"And I don't feel like I've done anything wrong, either": her eyes became damp: "Let me go, too."

"Diomede, eh . . ." and Doctor Fumi's gaze had the unswerving quality of a request to see identification papers, urgently.

"Well, they told me his name was Diomede . . . Lanciani, Diomede." And she burst into a sort of stifled, soft weeping.

"Don't you worry your head. We want to get hold of him because he has to tell us . . . something: something interesting. That's why we have to find him."

"Hurry up now. What sort of a mug does this Lanciani have?" Ingravallo insisted, hard. "Is he big? little? blond? does he have dark hair?"

Torn between distrust and pride, Ines dried her eyes with the back of her hand. "This Lanciani's an electrician," she said proudly: and took to sketching his likeness. Her voice, after pauses of fear and suspicion and admissions filled with belated caution, became animated to the point of a heedless gaiety, almost joy. She resented Ingravallo's choice of words. "If you want to know about this mug," she resumed, turning to Fumi as to the more benign of her two principal inquisitors, "there's more than one boy who'd be glad to have it, that mug; believe me, sir, chief, that you wouldn't mind having it yourself, a face like that." "Sure, sure." "A boy this tall": and she made the usual gesture, raising and extending horizontally her hand. She bent her head to one side, the better to glance at her palm, to evaluate, from below, the accuracy of that indication of height. "A handsome boy. Yes, he's handsome. So what? Is that against the law? He's smart, too. Yes, blond. It's not his fault if his Mamma made him a blond. Eh? Was she supposed to make him dark, when she felt like making him blond?" In her bag she even had his picture. Paolillo went straight off to the storeroom to dig out, from those rags, that miserable little purse: the identification card of the poor girl, which she had refused to the patrol when she was picked up, was already on Doctor Fumi's desk and under the light, open, crumpled. Paolillo returned, with the vagabond's purse and, in his other hand, the photograph of a young man painfully autographed crosswise with a scrawled signature: "Lumiai Dio . . ." he spelled out, as he walked, and he was about to hold it out. "Hand it over." Doctor Fumi tore it from his hand. "Lunci-a-ci Di-o . . . God only knows what he's written here. Diomede!" he exclaimed, victorious. A character! A face of the kind that the bimonthly "The Defense of the Race,"* fifteen years later, would have published as an example of splendid Aryanism: the Aryanism of the Latin and Sabellian peoples. As an exact copy, yes. He was blond, certainly: the photo asserted that: a virile face, a clump of hair. The mouth, a straight line. Above the life of the cheeks and the neck two steady, mocking eyes: which promised the best, to girls, to maidservants, and the worst to their dejarred savings. A bold sort, made to be surrounded and fought over, followed and overtaken, and then given presents more or less by all the girls, according to the possibilities of each. A type to represent Latium and its handsomeness at the Foro Italico.†

That photo, Ines explained, had cost her an incredible number of slaps: because he, one day, had wanted it back. Yes, he wanted it back at all costs. It was night, almost. He had turned mean, as she refused: he seemed out of his mind. He had yelled in her face, called her one thing and another, he even had the heart to slap her around: and, as if that weren't enough, threats. They were alone, between two walls, under a broken street light on the Clivo de' Publicii at Rocca Savella, where the knights are‡: it was

* *La difesa della razza* was the publication of the Italian racists, sponsored by the Fascists after the special (i.e., antisemitic) laws of 1938.

† The Foro Italico—formerly Foro Mussolini—is a complex of stadiums, swimming pool, and other sports buildings on the northern outskirts of Rome. It was—and still is—decorated by pseudo-heroic male statues, each representing a city or a region of Italy. Latium (Lazio) is the region of Rome.

‡ The Priory of the Knights of Malta is on the Aventine Hill, just above the Clivo de' Publicii.

growing dark. But she had taken the slaps, not batting an eye. She had held fast. At least that memento of him! of all the love they had felt for each other! and she loved him still, for her part: even if now . . . they forced her to turn informer. "But there's nothing to inform!" she yelled. "So he gave me a couple of slaps, what of it? That's our business: you can't put him in jail for that."

"A couple of slaps!" and Doctor Fumi, shaking his head, looked at her. "Before, you told us another story: but it doesn't matter!" and he drew his head down between his shoulders. He was about to tell her again that she had nothing to fear: they only wanted to question him, not to arrest him, still less, to lock him up. "Well, anyway I'm sure you'll never make it: you won't find him, not him." She spoke with her head bowed, pensive. "And besides, if you do find him, I'll be glad. That'll be the end of things between him and . . . that American woman." She seemed to be excusing herself, a woman, to herself.

The photograph of Diomede passed from hand to hand. Ingravallo also gave it a sidelong peep, as if reluctantly, though in reality with a certain secret annoyance: he passed it to Fumi, carelessly: a gesture meant to signify boredom and fatigue, and the desire to go and get some sleep, since it was high time: "one of a thousand like him." Finally after a few more ahas and a few more ahems, after a "But I've already seen it," it was knocked down to Pompeo, author of this last exclamation, who sheltered it in his wallet of simulated alligator, and the wallet he placed over his heart, agreeing in a loud and ringing voice: "Well, we'll do our best." The chief, meanwhile, had motioned to him: "Here," with the little rake of his four fingers of the right hand: and Pompeo had therefore approached: bent, now, he gave ear to the whispers of the seated official, and had already nodded his head repeatedly, looking far into the distance, that is to say, against the papered or opaque panes of the window: which the night's gaze, outside, observed, fearing, venerating. That ear listened, with its habitual zeal: and the doctor dropped those whispers into it, like so many drops of a rare henbane: and the movement of the lips was accompanied by a lively digitation, like a closed tulip, index and thumb in disjunctive oscillation.

At seeing the photo of her beloved take shelter against Grabber's heart, Ines, poor kid, blanched. Over her little nose her saddened eyebrows thickened in a frown that seemed wrath but wasn't: tears glistened, suddenly gleaming, under the very long and golden lashes (through whose comb, once upon a time, to her childish gaze, the glowing Alban light, the light of morning had been broken and radiated). They ran down her cheeks, leaving there, or so it seemed, two white streams, down to her mouth: the trail of humiliation, of alarm. She had nothing with which to blow her nose, nor to dry those tears: she raised her hand as if to stanch with the gesture alone what might have bubbled up from the wretched solitude of her face, to perfect the cruelty of those moments, the chill and derision of the hour which is their sum. She felt as if she were naked, helpless, before those who have the power to pry into the nakedness of shame and, if they don't mock it, they pass judgment on it: naked, helpless: as are all sons and daughters without shelter and without support, in the bestial arena of the earth. The stove was damp. The big room was cold: you could see your breath in it: the light bulbs of the Investigation Squad were governmental. She felt upon herself, shuddering at it, the men's gaze, and the rips, the tears, the wretched bunting, the sordid poverty of her dress: a tramp's jersey. To God, she could surely not address herself, not in these clothes. When he had called her by name, the name of her baptism, three times: Ines! Ines! Ines! at the beginning of her life in the underbrush, three times! like the three Persons of the Holy Trinity . . . the oaks writhed in foreboding under the gusts of the mistral: they opened the path of the underbrush to her, behind the deliberate tread of the boy. When the Lord had called her back, with his gaze of golden rays in the evening, from the round window of *Croce domini,* she, to the Lord—who had the heart to answer Him? "I'm going with my love," she had answered that gaze, that voice. So as for the Lord, now, He had to be left out of it.

She bowed her head, which, falling over her face, her dry or gluey hair put in the shadow, threatened to hide altogether. Her shoulders seemed to grow thinner, more skeletal almost, in the jerks of a silent sobbing. She dried her face, and nose: with her sleeve. She raised her arm: she wanted to hide her weeping, shelter her fear, her shame. A gap, at the beginning of her sleeve, and another in the undershirt below it, revealed the whiteness of her shoulder. She had nothing to conceal herself, but those torn and discolored remains of a poor girl's dress.

But the men, those men, blackmailed her with their gaze alone, afire, broken at intervals by signals and flashes, not pertinent to the case, of a repugnant greed. Those men, from her, wanted to hear, to know. Behind them was Justice: a machine! A torment, that's what Justice was. Hunger was better: and going on the street, and feeling the rain drizzling in your hair: better to go and sleep on a bench by the river, in Prati. They wanted to know. Well? What sort of dealings did this Diomede traffic in? She shut up. And they: come on, come on, talk, spill it. They weren't asking her to do any harm to anyone, after all: only to tell the truth, they begged her. Some truth! Putting people in jail for it. People . . . who have to shift for themselves: they have to live the best they can. Talk, spill. And be quick about it. No harm, after all. And, in the contrary case, bad papers for her. They needed him for the law, because a big crime had been committed, in all the papers it was. They showed her some of them. Rubbish. She waved the newsprint under her nose, slapping a hand on it as if to say: there you are. (She drew her head back.) For the law: "not to hurt you or anybody else," Grabber added calmly, persuasive, with a deep voice that came right straight from his heart. He was one of the Brothers of Happy Death, Grabber was, the ones who wear hoods over their heads and accompany the deceased: when it came to consoling widows there was nobody like him on the force. "Diomede," the girl said to herself, "is bound to be innocent. Giving a girl a slap or two, the coward, doesn't mean he cuts women up with a knife." She was reserved. She hesitated. "With these cops, a girl never knows." Maybe it was better to satisfy them, she thought. Better for Diomede, and better for herself, too. That would be an end of it, at least! They'd quit their nagging. Pompeo would take her back to the dormitory. She'd throw herself on the planks; hard as they were, she could still fall asleep there. Maybe even those four-legged relatives would fall asleep too, poor babies! She was dead tired: her head swam: worn out.

"What did Diomede do?" she started. "What were those women he had hanging around him? What sort of women were they?"

She, between humiliation and the fury of the great jealousy she suffered, her face still plunged into her elbow, her hair falling lankly even beyond the elbow, hiding her whole forehead . . . ended by saying, sure, he was capable of going even with old bags, as long as they . . .

"As they—?"

Well, of course, yes, no: she didn't want to insult herself, since she also went with him. It was . . . it was for his own interest. Because he had been out of a job for two months: and he couldn't find work: another job, a little better, to keep going.

"So what does he do?" asked Doctor Fumi, mildly. "What would his job be, if he wasn't out of work?" The great eyes of the inquisitor widened, a little yellowish at the corners, they rested sadly on that tangle of hair, which streamed, like a fountain, from the girl's elbow. "Electrician!" she sobbed, without raising her head entirely, only extracting it slightly from that defense of arm and elbow, and allowing its voice to escape. Now, with softened tears, she was dampening the sleeve, where there reappeared a hole, at the point of the bone, and the rip of the blouse and jersey and the white of the skin, at the shoulder. "And now he has an English woman," she stated, resuming her sobs, in that bath, with bathed words: "an ugly American, he has, but what do I know about it? She isn't old, though, not this one, but with hair like straw!" She wiped her nose on her cuff. "She has money, that's what she has": and again she burst into sobs.

"And who is she? Do you know who she is? Where does she live? Can you tell us? Speak up. This American, this English woman . . ."

"What do you think? Who do you think I am? She's probably there, in one of those swell hotels, where rich people stay . . ."

"There? Where?"

"There, in the fancy part of town, Via Boncompagni, Via Veneto. How should I know? I know the name is Burger . . . Borges . . ."

"I know. The Pensione Bergèss," said Pompeo, pronouncing the foreign name after his fashion.

"Pompeo," said Doctor Fumi, turning, "tonight I want to see the hotel lists."

Pompeo looked at his wrist watch. Ingravallo moved from his desk and began to pace slowly up and down the cold tile floor: his head bowed, sulky, he seemed to be meditating on all these complications, as was his wont.

"The Foreigners' Bureau, Pompeo, the file. Pensione Bergèsse. And good hunting. Since we've got a clue here, go straight to the night clerk and see what he has to say. Reports! Doormen! Information! What are all those porters for in hotels, anyway?" He hesitated a moment. "And in *pensioni*, too, Pompeo. Ingravallo, you better have a look, too . . . into this mess with the American." Don Ciccio nodded his assent, with two-tenths of a millimeter of movement: of that great head.

"And tomorrow morning, Pompeo, you're going to take a little stroll along Via Veneto. You've got to meet this English girl by accident, you get me? And then—we understand each other, eh? . . ." Great eyes on Pompeo. "Follow her, trail her: and catch her with the boy!" index finger towards the abyss, "after the rendez-vous," triumphant tone: "you've got to bring her in with the boy, not before": a singing note. "After they've met! You understand me, Pompeo? Straw hair!" he frowned. "English, English," pensive, thoughtful, or rather . . . why not?" thoughtful, "Scotch, or American!" Brief silence: "after the rendez-vous!"

"I understand, chief, but . . ."

"Straw hair!" eyebrows and lashes turned inexorably up towards the stars: a tone that admitted no appeal: palm extended, repelling, resisting any objection, licit or illicit: fingers splayed like a monstrance.

"And the photograph of the boy photographed here": he slapped one hand on his head, with pathetic emphasis: the good-looker, the picture of . . . of Diomede Luci-ani . . ."

"Lanci-ani," corrected Ingravallo.

"All right, all right, Ingravallo! Lanci-ani, Lanchy Annie." Then, turned to the others present, over the circle of whom he moved his eyes, and with the pacified tone of one who is speechifying *de moribus, de temporibus:* "Those girls land at the Immacolatella, a hundred and fifty at a time, at the Beverello pier! From the Conte Verde!" he stated: and drew his brows back half across his forehead, index and thumb joined authoritatively to form a circle: "the largest ocean liner of the Italian Counts Line!" They come flying out in droves, in fact, from the belly of the Count, like so many hens from a cage: which, after a long trip across the world, is finally set on shore, opened: coming down the gangway in groups, with bags, some with eyeglasses, they scatter over the Beverello: amid trunks, hotel agents and men from Cook's, with words written in gold embroidery on their caps, and porters, and people waiting open-mouthed, and vendors of ices or coral horns, offering services and addresses, and inventors of needs which are not needed, meddlers, curious bystanders of every kind, women.

"But . . ." and Doctor Fumi waved the hole of his two fingers, extending his little finger, "hens that lay golden eggs! when they lay them. Their father, the mother, back in Chicago, think the girls are coming to look at the pictures in the museums, to study how the Madonna is dressed up, how pretty she is: how handsome San Gennaro is, too": and he was shaking his head, at the certainty of those fathers and mothers: "The Beato Angelico Chapel! The Raphael rooms! The frescoes of Pinturicchio!"* He sighed. "Those little things have other rooms on their minds," he murmured. "The Assumption of the Virgin!" he exclaimed: "by Titian, Tiziano Vecellio!" and the last name, in that dirty room of police headquarters, lent an added propriety to the first name: as if this Titian were a fellow with all his

* Pinturicchio (or Pintoricchio) was a nickname, meaning "little" painter; Doctor Fumi is making a pun on the name.

documents in order, a person whom suspicion couldn't even graze. "The portrait of the Madonna—the spit and image—with those seven wax angels over her head! . . ."

When he was assistant chief at the Frari station in Venice, the five scarlet Cherubim of one of the six Enthroned Madonnas of Giovan Bellino (Galleria dell'Accademia) had become impressed on his memory, his genteel however bureaucratized memory, like the seven seals of the Apocalypse, in a lead-colored sky. And he had thrown in the Assumption: which has a dance of *putti* all around the Virgin's head, vice versa, some with doves' wings, others without: one, wingless, with a tambourine: singing hosannas.

"That's what their parents think, back in Boston, in Brooklyn." He tapped his index finger against his forehead, hammering. His eyes assumed a knowing look, the sly face, reproducing the slyness of those relatives. "They think these girls travel around Italy in herds, a hundred at a time, like little kids in a boarding school. A hundred at the museum, a hundred at the opera, a hundred at the aquarium, you know, where they keep the fish, under water; a hundred at the Baths of Caracalla, a hundred at San Callisto following that monk with the candle, which then goes out. Those girls—Ingravallo—not in a pig's eye." He turned to his inferiors. "Those girls, as soon as they get off the boat, Ingravallo, you follow me . . . bzzz bzz": he fluttered, with his hands, casting them here and there like thunderbolts, with the eyes of the Thunderer.

"One slips away here, another there, you understand me?" and his eyes, luminous in their sadness, gathered assent on all sides. "Each on her own, and God for all! Taormina, Cernobbio, Positano, Baveno," he was becoming stubborn: "Capri, Fiesole, Santa Margherita, Venezia," his tone hardened, with stern emphasis in its crescendo, a vertical wrinkle in the middle of his brow: "Cortina d'Ampiezzo!"

"D'Ampezzo," grumbled Ingravallo.

"D'Ampezzo, d'Ampezzo: all right, Ingravallo, you're our philosophy professor." He frowned: "Cortina, Positano! And—see you later!" he waved his hand in the air, a farewell to somebody who wasn't there: "See you here, six months from now"; the index plunged. "Here, here on the dock, Beverello. In exactly six months." He was silent. He sighed, knowingly. "Raphael my foot!" he exclaimed, in a new jerk, in a return of his contempt: which contempt rolled and died away beneath his preceding statements, like thunder after a storm in flight. "Rooms!" and he became agitated. "Pinturicchio! The room they're after is another kind, Pompeo, and you have to hunt for that room, if it takes all night!" Stilled at last, to himself: "And the Pinturicchio they want . . . is another man, too . . ."

The girls, no sooner were they dished up on to the Beverello from the tenebrous belly of the Count, felt at once, in their hearts, and since they were girls one couldn't say they were wholly wrong, they understood, they sensed suddenly that in the land of the fine arts, and of the fine artisans, they would prefer a live painter to a Pinturicchio deceased. Ingravallo, too, had read Norman Douglas as well as Lawrence: and had distilled Calabria, Sardinia (growling) as from a phial of super-effective elixir. He remembered that one of the two great erotologists, but he didn't recall which one, had become transformed into a geodesist, and had considered the wisdom of drawing up a map of the male contour line, extending it to all the surface of the earth. He had then triangulated, in his geodesy, also the Circean territory, extracting from it the documented certitude that Circe had not chosen badly the site wherein to exercise her art, which was the art of putting young men to sleep. This territory of the most profitable drowsiness, that is to say, of the highest level of male potential was, according to Norman Douglas or according to Lawrence, a spheric triangle, or rather, a geodetic one. And the vertices, the extreme geodetic strongholds of the unmatchable triangle, he, Norman Douglas, or he, Lawrence, saw as emerging from the three cities of Reggio (Calabria), Sassari, and Civitavecchia, to the great vexation of the citizens of Palermo. "He could have moved a little farther north, this sonovanologist," Ingravallo thought, silently, clenching his teeth in anger: "and a little more to the east," his unconscious prompted him, "to the top of the Matese mountains."* He shrugged: "It's his business!" And, teeth still clenched, he drew the conclusion: a conclusion probably unjust: which, in any case, is of no interest to the present report.

The girl's broken but explicit admissions continued trickling out until eleven, or thereabouts. The annoyance, or the wrath, at some points, in her spirit seemed to over-

*That is to say, to Ingravallo's native Molise.

come her love, the ardent remembrance of the flesh. Diomede, at the beginning, had come to see her at Zamira's, every day. Far from her eyes, and from the greedy exercise of his own, the enflamed young man, it seemed, could not stay for more than a few hours. Or else he accompanied her, burning, trembling, at times, for a good stretch of road, or a dirt track which turned into the fields, solitary, hesitating in his walk, between two thickets, with every hesitation, both of his person and his heart: and of his senses. They took the path that followed the oak thicket, in the direction of Tor Ser Paolo, or the little road of the Fountain of Health, towards Casa del Butiro. Ines, now, seemed to be thinking. Her lips parted, as if in the intention of uttering a new word: "Zamira, she liked him a lot, in her way. She sort of confided in him." She whispered to him, in fact, certain long tales, under his nose, looking him in the face, staring hard, devouring him with her eyes, her too, oh yes, why not? with a cackling voice, whispering, like in the confessional. A psspsspss like she was saying a prayer to him, or giving him good advice: good only for him, since he had special need, for the health of his soul. She wouldn't stop that psspsspss . . . : sometimes, for greater security, after looking all around, and maybe even standing up on her tiptoes, she would put her mouth to the boy's ear: the exquisite secrets were not for the nose, but for the secret privacy of the tympanum. "Like she was saying a prayer, one of those long ones, that gives you a stomach ache. Worse than the double Rosary of Christmas Eve . . ." As if to give him secret instructions, hah, concerning undertakings, or deeds, or obligations, or opportunities, or troubles, or dealings, or expedients . . . of considerable moment. Zamira spoke to him then, to Diomede, with a rolling of the eyes and a galloping of the tongue like a foreign minister new to his frock coat, but already smart,* when he feeds new words to the beloved ambassador in a low voice, in a selective "aside": and keeps vigil, at the same time, and maintains at the proper distance and in the proper awe the others: who seem to be mocking him by their gaze alone, with their calm foxy confidence, consummate in their art: the thin beak saturated with subtle initiatives: the tail with provident experience, and the back with unforgettable lashings. In the toothless mouth, the hole, black: from which, between one word and the next, she sucked back in the already erogated saliva, with a kind of slightly damp sibilance where her *r*'s wallowed backwards, like one who, cast up by the wave, is pulled back by the undertow. A hesitation of tiny, sweet bubbles, on the lips, accompanied this salvage: which, with a sudden sweep, shortly thereafter, the pointed and scarlet tip of the tongue was assigned to conclude. Yes, a sparkle of the eyes, in her face, when she so much as spoke to him, to the boy, to Diomede: yes, within the two serous blisters beneath her eyes, two black dots, her eyes, two pinheads. You'd have said that Old Nick had finally revealed to her where the treasure was to be found, buried, the long lost pile of gold doubloons: or the elixir of requited love for lovers. A livid smile distorted her mouth, to one side, diaphragming the hole: over the skin of half her face a yellowish cast—something fearsome— like certain unhealthy fires, of Beelzebub's mint.

"You might say, she was in love with him, with Diomede, that ugly old hag." Fumi looked Ines in the face again,

* Another reference to Mussolini.

dropping his jaw, his tongue hanging, as if he were in a spell. "And he used to listen to her secrets, then. And sometimes she even took him down to the cellar with her, so she could talk to him more in private, like. I bet she had something important to tell him all right, the shameless thing! at her age! The girls . . . kept telling me I was a dope. I used to get nervous! But if you don't have the tin, you can't eat. No, I couldn't make ends meet, not at home, with that no-good dad of mine. Even the jailhouse won't keep him. So I had to swallow it, like it or not." Zamira and Diomede disappeared down the little stairway, one after the other. As to the motives of all that mysterious parleying, "nobody knows. I don't know."

"Come on, out with it. What's all the fuss about?" Ingravallo said, hard. "Stop that sobbing!" The girl under questioning, poor creature, admitted, then denied, then doubted, then supposed that the subject must have been— and she felt there was great probability of her hitting the nail on the head—a string of suggestions, or of advice "about how to make us girls fall for him, without him falling for any of us." A code, an etiquette of canny love: an initiation to controlled, bookkept gallantry, if not even to profitable gallantry. And if this were so, it meant profitable for both, "for him and for her": her, Zamira. Pestalozzi, at times, smiled, shrugged slightly, as if to say: "I realized all this long ago: only natural: of course."

The officials, in view of the hour, decided to understand that Diomede, the fancy-man, must act—was he charged by Zamira to do so?—as a clay pigeon, or like the decoy owl on a stick, for the beauties. The beauties, the poor

Venuses of the countryside: those robust, solid girls, whose every cheap garment is to dream, in the dryness and in the unplacated light of the day, amid the brambles and the stubble, in the August sun. "Every cheap dress," Fumi thought: "grace granted by the mystery." And it was, he thought, the gilded, the vaporous mystery of the city. Clothes, ornaments, smells—from a bottle . . . A golden lamina, giving off such light in the night, like a symbol, like a pass to an Orphic rite: to enter there where it is celebrated, at last, the rite of living. An emotion unknown which can be known without initiation, but foretold and dreamed of (with perfumes of garlic on the breath) by the heart, at evening. A mute "thou livest! Thou shalt live!" after rapid forkfuls of fodder: from the kindled clouds of the evening, from the warm horizon's promise.

"The wicked mystery of this world," thought Ingravallo, instead. He already hated, in his heart, that character, blond though he was: and the familiar clenching of teeth, the clamping of jaws, accompanied the appearance and the not-immediate disappearance of the image. It was, in his skull of diorite, an abominable image. A filthy, a wretched thing, that braggart, that gigolo! "Ah," he brooded, "Diomede then must have acted as the persuader, the initiator: for the sacred rites of the abracadabra: the beater: the pointer, pointing out the quails and the partridge, on the hill: a young terrier, flushing the hens from the bog." At least that was how everyone there understood it, in the great room where you could see their breath under the pears of light, drawn into a circle around the palpitation of a partridge, between the big cops and their attendants: Doctor

Fumi, Ingravallo, Sergeant Di Pietrantonio, Pompeo, and Paolillo, known also as Paolino . . . Pestalozzi, "the cyclist." Ines did not speak out explicitly, but it seemed to them that they could nevertheless infer from her highly appreciated tale of the descent into the cave (of the enterprising blond with the more-than-Cumaean* sibyl), from the many though hesitant and repentant "I don't know's, I couldn't say's," it seemed to them that they could actually write in the report that Diomede Lanci-ani had bestowed his violent comfort (this, the girl allowed them to deduce always, was the nature of comfort, from him), also on the mature hostess-seamstress and and dyeress, cleaner of garments both military and civilian.

Yes, bestowed his comfort: despite Venus the Snooty and all the swarm of her powdered Cupids. "That old, toothless ex-cow!" thought Pestalozzi, in his sylloge, rather northern in accent, to tell the truth. It was evident by now: the blond had given repeated proof of his wisdom and valor, to the old woman: even though when it came to the obviousness, the enticements and the itineraries, Pestalozzi opined, modifying, forever known and traveled through the ages, this wisdom had proved superfluous, and the valor more necessary than ever. A valor heedless to all repulses by adverse circumstances. He had granted her the best, or the worst, of his own spirit of initiative. Yes, it was clear, now, the spirit of initiative . . . he had boldly insufflated it, into the sorceress: perhaps, in fact certainly, after suitable remuneration. "Because he didn't have any cash before," Ines blurted, "and then he had some."

* The sibyl of Cumae (just outside Naples) was renowned in ancient times, described by Virgil in Book Six of the *Aeneid*.

246

Corporal Pestalozzi seemed indeed to remember, without difficulty, the tacit existence of Diomede: whom he had met at the wine counter of I Due Santi. He frowned. It seemed to him, at a certain moment, that he would recognize him. What? Can it be? Yes. But that very day? The silent and unexpected appearance of the youth from the stairs: a young man of singular attractiveness, to be sure, blond as an archangel, but without sword: returning from the incursion into the Abyss. The Abyss, that time, must have received the blow. A blow that deserved praise. He had in his face, a steady and pale face with slightly prominent cheekbones, he had in his clear and steadily blue gaze that sort of insolent, almost hysterical volition with which a painter, in the Marches, had studied (and taken pleasure) in perfecting the natural physiognomic notes of the winged celestial creatures: when he charged them with slightly awkward missions. Such volition, if it had to be described in words, would be graphicized in the well-known terms: "Everything has to go the right way, which before it is 'right' is *my* way, seeing as how I'm an archangel. And if anybody thinks different about it, I'll settle his hash right away: with this cudgel here."

Then and there, however, he hadn't seemed too convinced, exceptional creature though he was, finding himself face to face with a carabiniere corporal: a figure that didn't suit his taste, so red and black: and which upsets everybody a little, under certain circumstances. But sly, he saw at once that the corporal had downed an orangeade: well, that was all right then.

Having come to Rome to work as an electrician, Ines reported, he had found work in a shop at sixty lire per week:

"but then they fired him." Whereupon, afterwards, he worked here and there: on his own: "he went to people's houses to fix wires when they were worn out, or to wire a room, in a new apartment: or maybe some old bag's place," she insinuated, and became annoyed. "Or to change the fuses or make the bells work, when they broke down and wouldn't ring anymore, because some ladies, and their husbands, too, are afraid to touch electric fuses. *Mamma mia!* Afraid of getting a shock. And then, if you stop and think about it, who would ever have the nerve to climb up to the top of a ladder, till you touch the ceiling with your head? Except some poor kid who does it to earn his living? standing on that ladder for hours and hours too? Putting all those wires together, that's what I say . . . well, if we women do it, you can see everything . . . I mean, garters and all the rest": she turned two magnificent eyes, two gems. "No, nobody wants to do that kind of job." She seemed to hesitate for a moment. "Well, maybe the Milanese, everybody knows what they're like: they get a kick out of that stuff: they're all engineers." She was repeating, or so it seemed, in these words, an affirmation of the young man.

Ingravallo scratched himself lightly, tick, tick, with the back of his thumb, on the black Angus mop. "So he worked at odd jobs then. Can you tell us where?"

"I don't know where; he never told me. He went to work for people, in their houses. Sometimes he went to work even for a countess, he said: she spoke Venetian"; she assumed her spiteful little mask, adorable. "And I have a feeling that with her, he . . . or maybe I'm wrong": and she broke off.

"What's this feeling of yours? Out with it," Pompeo said, in a kindly tone.

"I have a feeling that . . . that he made a thorough job of it. He's a wide-awake kind of boy. When something's broken, he finds the trouble right away. And then, in Rome, with his living expenses. It couldn't be any other way."

Fumi turned his eyes on Ingravallo; at the very moment that Ingravallo had raised his own, more clouded, to look at him. Then, to the girl:

"This countess then? Where is she? I mean," he clenched his lips, "where does she live?"

"Somewhere near the station, I think: past Piazza Vittorio though. But I . . . I don't know that part of town very well." She blushed faintly: her voice seemed to dissolve, to vacillate: to tremble towards weeping. "I . . . What is this? Now you want to make a spy out of me? I . . ."

"Talk, talk, talk, eh girlie? Make up your mind. In or out. You take your pick . . ." menaced Ingravallo, anything but amiable: and he stood up, black.

"It's a long wide street," she said, hesitating between shame and remorse, "a straight one . . . that goes all the way to San Giovanni."

"I get it," Doctor Fumi said, "I get the whole thing." He glanced again at his colleague, who looked back at him.

Diomede was in need of money: when he had it, he spent it: and he procured more: he spent that, too: coffee, cigarettes, neckties, ball games, movies, trams: he even played the lottery.

"He even wanted to drink an *aperitif*: Carpàno, it's called" (she explained, mistaking the accent). "At Piccarozzi, in the Gallery. Before he went to eat." But she said this with pride, as she might have said: "and a shirt of real silk, yes, sir!"

"And where does he go to eat?" asked Fumi.

"It depends. If he's by himself, he makes do with a sandwich maybe. He might even drink straight from the fountain: a gulp of Aqua Marcia in Via della Scrofa or at the little fountain in Piazza Borghese. But if he's with some of those young ladies, with fancy customers . . ."

"So he wasn't all yours, then," Pompeo pricked her, with a grin. And touching her shoulder: "Come on, baby, you got to get it off your chest, console yourself!" she moved away, spitefully, as if disgusted by that contact. "Yes, yes," she wept, "I do want to console myself."

She dried herself with her hand, sobbed, changed her mind: "Well, what do you think? He's not the only fish in the sea." And she started, at a new sob, to look for a handkerchief: to dry her face, her nose: until, as usual, she rubbed it on her sleeve. Poor creature! The elbow revealed the hole, and the sleeve the darns and the tatters. The poor wrist, the arm, the shoulders jerked in desperate sobs. But she raised her head: and with her wet face she looked at them again. "When he finds a woman that'll come across, I mean one of those women . . . who don't make any fuss about it, because that's what they're out looking for, then he makes her go to a fancy place: to Bottaro in Passeggiata di Ripetta: or to the Quattro Cantoni to L'Aliciaro, behind San Carlo: or maybe in Via della Vite, if he catches on . . . that she's from out of town, that she's maybe a foreigner, something special: and he has a sharp eye for them. Even to the Buco in Sant' Ignazio, sometimes, where they're

Tuscans, he told me: from Tuscany. And there, you have to drink their wine, and it costs more because it's famous and fancy and all."

"I understand," murmured Fumi, his great head on the desk.

"Tuscans!" she resumed: and throwing her head back, with one hand she thrust back her hair, those blond locks on which drops of glue had rained: then she whispered, bored: "they're a bunch of stinkers, too, goddamn 'em." The imprecation was lost in a murmur, in the apocope of the pronoun, in an ever less benevolent stammering of the tongue, of the lips.

"Stinkers? What have they ever done to you?" Grabber pricked her again, with a tinkling laugh, as a novelist would say; but which, given his gullet, was instead the thunder of a trombone.

"Nothing. They didn't do nothing to me. I just happen to know they're stinkers, that's all."

"Take it easy, Pompeo, and don't bother her," Doctor Fumi said, contracting his nose: and to the girl: "You were saying?"

"I was saying that, with women like that, he picks them up right off, without having to work too hard to make them catch on. 'I beg your pardong, could you direck me to Villa Porghesay?' When they're on Via Veneto, a foot away. Or even at the arches of Porta Pinciana! the pigs. 'It's not far away from here.' I'll say it isn't. All you have to do is cross the street. He lights her cigarette maybe. 'I can show you the way, if you want!' And they want, all right. With me, it's different, with these rags I have on . . .

dying of the cold. With me, now, he doesn't even want to come: he says I'm stupid, that I look like a beggar. But with them! From Porta Pinciana, to the lake, to the Belvedere—it isn't a walk that makes your feet hurt, either. A little chat, as they go, turning to look at each other every now and then, looking her straight in the eye. Oh I know, I know how he does."

"And what about you?"

"Me? They've screwed me, that's what they've done, so's I don't know which way to turn for a crust of bread: I'm just about ready to jump in the river. With them, they have a nice hot meal, a dinner—or supper, anyway."

"And the ready?"

"The ready?"

"The money, I mean: who puts out?" Pompeo interrupted again, rubbing his thumb against his index finger in the classic gesture.

"Shut up, Pompeo, you're getting on my nerves," Fumi admonished him. Then, to her: "These dinners, or let's say these suppers: who pays for them?"

"He pays, of course," the girl replied with *hauteur* and envy: "but she passes him the cash under the napkin: or when they go into Bottaro's" (envy of the disbursing rival) "while they're looking in the window . . . at the list of the day's dishes. To see if there's chicken, or lamb. They've worked it all out along the way: and he's got a driver's license and everything, he took the exam, and all he has to do is collect the license in Via Panisperna, but he needs certain papers still, certain official stamps: and he knows all the restaurants in Rome by heart, but it wouldn't look good for him or for her either, to let them see that she's the one who's putting out the money. Rome isn't like Paris, he says. Because we've got the Pope here." They laughed. In her weariness, in her tears, erect, at the end, in the mucid light of the room, she had spoken, resplendent: her lashes, blond, turned aloft, radiated above the luminous gravity of her gaze: her tears had cleansed the irises, a dark brown, the two turquoise jewels they enclosed. Her face appeared stained and tired.

"And he made his aunt, too, if she is his aunt, give him a hundred lire. One time when he was in a hurry to go someplace, I forget where. And I have a feeling she never saw it again, that hundred note. Her husband's a scar-face; she says he used to be a baker, but he never comes home."

Zamira had had a fight with him: "Maybe because he talked me into coming away: and she was furious. You'll regret this, she said to me: the old witch! Listen to me! you'll be sorry, baby! With those dragon eyes of her's! He made me touch a coral horn*: and he touched it, too. Yes, he was the one who talked me into it. So they had a fight. Maybe that was the reason, or maybe—who knows—because there was no more money in it for them. She's an old witch, a lousy hick whore. Even in Africa, she went whoring. Fifteen years ago. And when it comes to money, she'd skin her own father alive. He took me away."

"And that's why they fought?" asked Fumi, not convinced. The girl didn't hear the question. "You can understand how he looked at it, too. A boy like him! For nothing . . . too little! He told her to find herself somebody else. He

* To ward off the evil eye.

said he wasn't working just for the fun of it. You women, he says, don't have to do anything, just have a little patience. You just have to be still for a couple of minutes. A couple of sighs. And in the meanwhile . . . *domino vobisco* . . . so long . . . till next time! But us men, he says! and he swells his chest: with us, it's a different thing, altogether!"

"Did you hear *that?*" said Doctor Fumi, deeply depressed, as one who hears or sees torpedoed or mocked, by unforeseen jest or torpedo, the most sainted, the most deeply rooted belief in the goodness of human nature. He turned his great eyes around sadly, as if to ask aid of the gentlemen co-inquisitors. His neck was stuffed into his shoulders: as if an apostle of ill humor had pressed a heel on his head. The cynical boldness of those remarks of the young man, reported by Ines, seemed to put a full stop to her tale.

They were about to dismiss her, and Paolillo was already moving, an uncoercible yawn having engaged his jaws, which for over an hour had been longing for another occupation: when, tears dried, she threw out another few words, as a supplement to what had already been said: with a calm, ringing voice, like the reprise of an aria which she had previously paid out towards the bliss of the listeners: "He has a little brother, too, named Ascanio: he must have hung around the same building, where that countess from Venice lives. A cute little kid: smart as anything! always scared, though, like he was afraid he wouldn't get away with something. He looks up at you, and then shuts his eyes: he reminds me of a cat when it wants to tell you it's sleepy, when instead it's done something dirtier than usual, and knows it, but doesn't want you to know. A quick kid, like his brother: but a different kind: something between an altar boy and a delivery boy from that baker's there."

"And this would be the younger brother, the little one, Ascanio Lanciani," Fumi said, pensive, inviting, forcing his whole tongue into the *cia* of Lanciani, exceptionally. But the cats were all out of the bag, now.

"Yes, Ascanio," she spilled on, nevertheless, "Ascanio."

Ingravallo had a start, which he contained, a growl of his soul: like a dozing mastiff in his professional suspicion, which rewakens, at night, the muffled and cautious footstep of the Probable, the Improbable. "A kid who worked in a shop, at a grocer's . . . Moving here and there, like his brother. Then I think he traveled around, from town to town, with a peddler. I saw him just last Sunday, the thirteenth of the month, he was with his granny, selling roast pork . . ."

"Where?"

"At Piazza Vittorio, and he even slipped me a sandwich: from under his apron: he knows how to do tricks: with those eyes of his, scared stiff, for fear his granny would see him: with that mop of hair he has. He said to me: don't tell anybody you saw me here. I wonder why. Always mysterious, that kid. A sandwich with a slice of pork. Big enough to last two days. But without letting the old woman see him. That old witch would have slapped him good, if she'd seen. She'd already given me a dirty look, when she saw I was talking to the kid, whispering . . ."

"What time was it?"

"It must have been around eleven. I was so hungry I

couldn't see straight. The big bell, at Santa Maria Maggiore, kept ringing and ringing . . . to bring us the grace from San Giuseppe, they say, who's so good: because Saturday was his feast, but I was already in here. In fact, he made me run into Ascanio, who gave me that sandwich. That bell, when I hear it, it sounds like my granny on the swings: up and down, down and up, drrring drrring, every time you give her behind a push, she lets out a word or two from even from there: brrr brr frrrfrrr . . . I was so hungry! I told him right out that I was hungry, that I was a good customer: while he went on yelling 'Get you roast pork here! Nice roast pork (that nobody wanted, not at that price) golden brown.' He understood me: he had already caught on, the moment he saw me. That was the last good food I ate: something to stick to my ribs, before I ended up in here. I was lucky!"

Chance (*non datur casus, non datur salus*) well, on the other hand, it seemed to be chance itself that night which succored the puzzled, straightened out the investigations, changing the turn of the wind: chance, luck, the net, a little unraveled, a little frayed, of the patrol, more than any artful wisdom or hairsplitting dialectic. Ingravallo had them call in Deviti (he was there, this time) and charged him, the next morning, to look for the kid, Ascanio Lanciani. The features of the boy . . . could be furnished him at once by Ines, a proper little portrait. And she also had to explain the location of the stand, and the grandmother, who sold roast pork: yes, at Piazza Vittorio, yes: where they had their counter. Pestalozzi was furnished with a copy of the list, typewritten, of turquoises and topazes, in which all the o's (opals, topazes, onyx) figured as so many little holes or dots in the onionskin paper, round just like an *o*: ulcers of a precision and of an operative deliberateness not adequately comforted by the budgets. Some were topazes, properly called, others were *topazos*: the jewels of the broken-and-entered and detopazed Menecazzi, who returned, this time, to the definitive possession and full enjoyment, by right and by might, of her own *z*'s: her Venetian *g*, for the rest, joyfully commuted into a central-Italian *c*. So it happened, in the documents of the implacable administration by which we have the honor and pleasure to be ministered with the papers and rubber stamps necessary to life, that the recovery of a Carlo Emilio from a precedent Paolo Maria, preceded in turn the name of the great dead of Cannae, is offset by a Gadola: which, meanwhile, is permitted to glow in civic execration in place of a Gadda.* The sheet of the Menecazzi list was supplemented (Ingravallo, handing Lance-Corporal Pestalozzi the second sheet, took a look at it) by another list, more grimly horrid and splendid: of those other jewels, kept in a little iron coffer, in the first dresser drawer, by Signora Liliana.

* A complicated and typically Gaddian aside: he refers to the bureaucratic confusion which once had him registered as Paolo Emilio. (Paulus Æmilius, in 216 B.C., advised Varro not to fight Hannibal; Varro did and was defeated at Cannae. Paulus was killed, having refused to flee when the opportunity was given him.) Then he was registered as Paolo Maria, before he succeeded in having his name entered properly, correcting also "Gadola" into "Gadda."

VIII

THE sun still hadn't the slightest intention of appearing
on the horizon when Corporal Pestalozzi had already left
(on his motorcycle) the barracks of the are-are-see-see* at
Marino to hurl himself on the tavern-workshop where he
wasn't for one moment expected, at least not in his capacity
as functioning corporal. The girls, and before them, the
sorceress herself had sniffed in the air, yes, a certain, indefinable interest, then perceived a certain circumscribed
buzzing of carabinieri (like the ugly horseflies when, of a
sudden, a new miracle is scented, in the country), of the
sergeant and the corporal, in particular, all around the
sweet fragrance of the knitting shop, and finally to the very
door of the tavern and even inside, at the counter: an attraction which wasn't the usual, for from the 17th to the 18th,
from Thursday to Friday, in the space of twenty-four hours,
it had become objectified in a scarf of green wool: yes:
probably, if not surely, pinched: whence the urgency, for
the beneficiary of the change of ownership, to take it to
Zamira to be dyed. The new and, perhaps, even a bit intensi-
fied buzzing of the huge men in olive drab or black-and-
red wasn't ascribable to private urges, that is to say to the

* R.R.C.C., the Royal Carabinieri.

exuberance of the eternal lymph from within the straits of discipline. No, no! The alert and ever closer circling of the workshop, or better of the little hovel that housed the same, had become, in the last couple of days, a royal, carabinierial buzz, obviously to be imputed to a determined case in point of the pinching variety: in short, a police-style buzzing. So that they, the girls, were? Silent! Lips sealed. And knitting, cutting, plying their needle: zum zum zum at the sewing machine. The two bechevroned men, sergeant and corporal, one after the other, and almost in mutual rivalry, had tossed out with effective nonchalance, as if it were a matter of mere passing curiosity, a couple of unforeseen questions, then foreseen and expected, concerning the scarf: and what was it like, and what color was it, was it made of cloth, or knitted, by hand or machine-made? An old lady had lost it, according to what they said . . . as she got off a tram. Zamira blew little bubbles of saliva from her hole and beaded her lips, at the corners: it was her way of palpitating, of partici-pating. She had, one might say an invitation in her eyelids, the most melting, the most edulcorating invitation of *mi-carême*. But that other girl, that quasi-bride, the one who to the paternal heart of the sergeant was the opened, purplish rose in the bouquet of the white and still-closed buds, had shot into his eyes "her" eyes. A rapid, luminous adept's glance: and that arrow shot, so dewy with intelligence, had been more than sufficient for the sergeant. To concert with immediate parapathia an encounter, vespertine and casual, oh very casual indeed, halfway along the little road to Santa Margherita in Abitacolo: at an hour when no living soul was to be seen. Then and there the scarf was brought back

to him (ideally): so green: and in the welling-up of whispers also there came to the surface the buggy, March, the
horizontal rain and the new moon and all the strong March
winds, and the offering of hot wine, poor horse! in a water-
ing bucket: and, what was more important, the Ciurlani
Dyers in Marino. And finally the first name, last name, alias,
fixed abode of the denominated male or "boyfriend": with
some further information, some hints about his appearance,
his character, type, manners, figure, shoelaces. His overall,
for that matter, not to mention the cap, were missing from
the portrait: a precise question of the sergeant remained
unanswered. In the workshop-tavern at I Due Santi, all the
girls, every time, and Zamira also, on the other hand, had
become lost in a dreamy innocence, had remained silent, or
had answered in questions, with their eyes, their questioners:
or else they had shrugged and had contracted their lips in a
moue of ignorance.

Towards Monday, then, that rather rascally zeal of the
carabinieri had become completely stilled. A private or
two, true enough, had dropped in, descending from his bike;
to order an orangeade. The swaying of the handle of the
door with glass panes (colored ones) had given the swaying forewarning of a customer: and he had appeared: a
carabiniere passing by. The orangeade having been in-
gested, when its respective gas, as usual, had erupted back
again in the kind of nasal crypto-belch which follows a
beverage of that kind, then the soldier had unbuttoned his
tunic, had opened it slightly, for greater comfort and the
drawing of breath: and had drawn out a kind of hamburger
swollen with papers more than a generous salami sandwich:

a rotten wallet: an organ indispensable, to the sweating, to the wretched, to effect the laborious payment of a "soft" drink. His fingering his buttonholes, restoring to a freer splendor the noble buttons of his uniform, had granted the girls—not to say to the mistress-seamtress—occasion to eye, in a furtive glimpse, but surely a connoisseur's glance, the vivid outlines of his chest, to appreciate the mood of the quenched man: peace, vigor, relaxation, inhibition, pride, and, to record it, this mood, on the positive side of the ledger of humanity's general heritage: excluded, in practice, any dutiful assignment any "causal motive" or rationale of service.

March the 23rd, in the carabinieri's barracks, at Marino. Having risen in the night, come down at daybreak, a private was waiting in the courtyard. Pestalozzi appeared, a dark person, from the shadows, from beneath the archway: he walked to his machine: his bandoleer stood out, white, to underline the dispatch of his actions in an elegant apparatus of authority. A few words to the subaltern, a brief inspection of the beast, splashed with mud up to its muzzle. Once he in the saddle, with one foot on the ground, the left, he gave the kick to the motor: with his right. The sentry had opened the doors, as if for the exit of a great coach, of some Roman Apostolic Prince and Duke of Marino. Pestalozzi seemed lost in thought. Wednesday the 23rd, he thought. In fact. He raised his eyes to the tower, which a spout of almost-yellow light, from a screened bulb, tinged at its top, in a stripe, a little below the surviving roughness of the cordon at the pinnacle. Six twenty-five by the clock in the tower: the same as his own, exactly. To accompany him he had summoned this private, who was already weighing down the rear part of the seat with his behind and was about to draw his feet into the boat, too, clasping his superior by the waist, with both hands, and awaiting the motor's first explosion. Pestalozzi with his right foot, pressed down: he reiterated the starter. The cylinder began at last to gurgle, the whole machine to tremble, to beat its wings. The sentry saluted, at attention: the threshold was passed. The turn did not occasion falls. But they weighed, the two of them, on the tires. The cobbles were slippery, a steep slope: a little skin of mire, in some places, made it even more dangerous. The mare with the two riders on her withers rolled down, under restraint, grumbling, it bore to the right, then to the left towards the gate of the town, between black peperino walls and shadows, beneath little square windows, armed with rusty iron bars to incarcerate the darkness. An occasional civic lamp swayed its greeting to the fleeting men, in that dark and stony poverty of the village: a bracket coming from the lichened walls, which sloped back, like the curtains of a fort: electric flower of the willing budgets, ultimate sob from the bowels of the vice-mayor for the antelucan solitude of a street from which the north wind precipitates, whistling, at night: or the sirocco slows there and dies, three nights later. They descended to the gate of the town.

Once past the arch, the road started spreading out towards the Appian: it went among olive groves barely silvered by the dawn and the prone skeletons of vines in the vineyards. Then it was thrown back, like a stole, over the damp shoulders of the hill. At the first curve the view also turned back.

Pestalozzi raised his head for a moment, cut the motor, put on the brake, stopped their course, with a certain caution: he paused for a couple of minutes, to cast the morning's horoscope.

It was dawn, even later. The peaks of the Algido, the Carseolani and the Velini unexpectedly present, gray. Soratte, sudden magic, like a fortress of lead, of ash. Beyond the passes of Sabina, through small openings, portholes that interrupted the line of the mountain's crest, the sky's revival manifested itself in the distance by thin stripes of purple and more remote and fiery dots and splendors of sulphur yellow, of vermilion: strange lacquers: a noble glow, as if from a crucible of the depths. The north wind of the day before had died away, and here, to alternate the auguries, the hot slavering on skin and face, the gratuitous and now subsiding breath of a sirocco's lashing. Further on, from behind Tivoli and Carsoli, flotillas of horizontal clouds, all curled with cirrus, with false ribbons of saffron, hurled themselves, one after the other, into battle, filed joyously towards their shredding: whither? where? who knows? but surely where their admiral ordered them, to get it in the neck, as ours orders us, all their little sails within the range of the winds. Labile, changing galleys, tacked at a high, unreal height, in that kind of overturned dream which is our perception, after waking at dawn, tacked along the ashen cliffs of the mountains of the Equi, the whitened nakedness of the Velino, the forewall of the Marsica. Their journey resumed, the driver obeyed the road, the machine addressed the curves, bending with the two men. The opposite half of the weather there, above the shore of Fiumicino and Ladispoli, was a brown-colored flock, shading into certain leaden bruises: gravied sheep pressed, compact, meshed in the ass by their dog, the wind, the one that turns the sky rainy. A roll of thunder, rummm, son-of-a-gun! had the nerve to raise its voice, too: on March the 23rd!

The sergeant pressed down with his foot, accelerating towards the fountain. From the right, where the plain was dense with dwellings and went down to the river, Rome appeared, lying as if on a map or a scale model: it smoked slightly, at Porta San Paolo: a clear proximity of infinite thoughts and palaces, which the north wind had cleansed, which the tepid succession of sirocco had, after a few hours, with its habitual knavishness, resolved in easy images and had gently washed. The cupola of mother-of-pearl: other domes, towers: dark clumps of pines. Here ashen: there all pink and white, confirmation veils: sugar in a *haute pâté*, a morning painting by Scialoja. It looked like a huge clock flattened on to the ground, which the chain of the Claudian aqueduct bound . . . joined . . . to the mysterious springs of the dream. There, stood the general H.Q. of the force: there, there, for many moons, his dreamed-of application lay waiting, waiting. Like pears, medlars, even an application's ripening is marked by that capacity for perfectable maceration which the capital of the ex-kingdom confers on all paper, is commensurate with an unrevolving time, but internal to the paper and its relative stamps, a period of incubation and of Roman softening. Bedecked, with silent dust, are all the red tapes, the dossiers of the files: with heavy cobwebs, all the great boxes of time: of the incubating

time, *Roma doma*; Rome tames. Rome broods. On the hay-
stack of her decrees. A day comes, at last, when the egg of
the longed-for promulgation drops at last from her viscera,
from the sewer of the decretal labyrinth: and the respective rescript, which licenses the gaunt petitioner to scramble
that egg for the rest of his natural life, is whipped off to
the addressee. In more cases than one, it arrives along with
the Extreme Unction. It licenses the applicant, now sunk
into coma—*verba volant, scripta manent*—to practice that
sleeping art, that crippled trade that he had surreptitiously
practiced until then, till the moment of the Holy Oil: and
which from then on, *de jure decreto*, he will make an effort
to practice, a little at a time, in hell with all the leisure
granted him by eternity.

The sergeant sped downhill towards I Due Santi. It was
a sultry day, the mugginess seemed to have drunk the
swamps. But the wind of their speeding and an occasional
rare drop, like a musket ball in the face, presaged the
alacrity of their investigation, and the fecund interviews in
the useful hours of the morning. Sounding the horn at a
gander, which lingered to duck its ass in the road, he ripped
a half-curse from his teeth: it was at that moment that
there came to his mind, in a flash, haunted by his wakening
at this early hour, the endless dream of the night before.

He had seen in his sleep, or had dreamed . . . what the
hell had he managed to dream of? . . . a strange being, a
topass: a topase. He had dreamed of a topaz: what is, after
all, a topaz? a faceted glass, a kind of yellow stop light,
which grew, and was enlarged from one moment to the
next until it promptly became a sunflower, a malign disk

265

that escaped him, rolling forward, almost beneath the wheel of the bike, in mute magic. The Marchesa wanted it, the topaz; she was drunk, yelling and threatening, stamping her feet, her face estranged in a pallor as she uttered obscenities in Venetian, or in some Spanish dialect, more likely. She had raised hell with General Rebaudengo because his carabinieri weren't bright enough to overtake it on any road, or path, the awful topaz, that yellow glass. So at the railroad crossing of Casal Bruciato, the glass sunflower . . . by the right flank, march! It had fled along the rails, changing its form into a yellow rat and snickering top-as-ass-ass: and the Rome-Naples express raced on and on, full speed after the sunset and almost already into the night, into the Circean darkness, diademed with flashes and spectral sparks on the pantograph, luminous stag saturated with electricity. Until, realizing that the mad rolling along the fleeting parallels was not enough to save him, the topaz-ass-rat had turned from the track and had sped into the countryside in the night towards the mouthless ponds of Campo Morto and the underbrush and the thickets of the Pometian shore: the women signal-keepers yelled, shouted that he was mad: they were to stop him, handcuff him: the locomotive chased him through the swamp, with two yellow eyes searching everything, cane brake and the darkness, to that point where place names become sparse, at the foot of the mountain of Contessa Circea, where Japanese lanterns and garlands swayed above the terraces on the shore, in the evening breeze from the sea. Nereids, there, freshly emergent from the waves and immediately denuded of their garments of seaweed and foam, amid the bustle of waiters in white jackets and of damp siphons and fistulas, were wont to make merry the enchanting night of Villa Porca. The Contessa, amid languid dirges, asked for a phial for sleep, for oblivion: for the vain arabesques, the bewilderments of dreams. Of the dream of not being. At Villa Porcina, under festoons of yellow ten-watt pears and drunken balloons, sweetly obese in the breathing and dying of every melody, the sorceress of the (perpetually) open snuffbox elicited at her scent the imminent swine, those who, at that philter, and that perfume, were to turn into snouted pigs, after having become eared-asses at the school: of the machiavellian club's hard knocks. Already the female pupils writhed, stark white except for the thicket triangle, from every austere veto of fathers, they wriggled in silent offering: which, from slow, restrained moorish saraband gradually was exalted to the trochaic rhythm of an *estampida*, where the resolute beating of the foot bestowed a fierce arsis on the floor: while the prompt erection and the shaking both of neck and head gave their hair back to the abyss, signifying the untamed pride both of the cervix and of the spirit, reiterated by the ta-ta-ta-tum of the castanets. Then as the aggression of the naked (but not for that hebefied) males broke into the chorus, the *estampida* was exacerbated to a sicinnis, to a dance simultaneously exozcizational: a swarm of frightened and bosomy nymphs pretended to abhor a herd of satyrs, to shield themselves and take shelter both with their hands and in flight towards their rubescent and fumigant thyrsi, already half-dazed, to tell the truth, by their excessive officiating: with their noses. Falling at that point among their legs, like the black thunderbolt of every prompt and every black happening, the crazed topaz had suddenly frightened the beauties. Shards of an exploded heart had flown off in every direction, to every corner, stopping—at the very sight of that possessed sewer rat, their hippy and mammary ritual. And there were shouts and shrills not to be told as the mustachioed one darted here and there like an arrow's notch, black, sharpened meatball. Many of the priestesses, forgetting their nakedness, had made a gesture as if to draw skirts down to their knees, protecting a defenseless delicacy: but the skirts were only a dream. And so was their delicacy.

Thus, in this delirium, they had sought safety in flight, in the ponds of the swamp, in the shadows of the canes, in the night, the silvery thicket of ilexes and pines on the shore, in the free wash of the beach, lorded over by a seething swell: others, poetesses and sea-creatures diving from the lunar rocks of the circeum, had plunged into the foam of the breakers. But the Contessa Circea, drunken, threw her head back, tossing her soaked hair (as yellow balloons laughed and swayed in Chinese) in the torpid benignity of the night: soaked in a shampoo of White Label: the cleft of her mouth, like an earthenware piggy-bank, arched, open and vulgar, till it could touch her ears, splitting the face like a watermelon after the first incision, in two slippers, in two soles of clogs: and from her rolling eyes, where you could see the white below the iris like that of a Teresa repossessed by the devil,* down her face dripped ethylic tears, bluish gouts: opalescent pearls of a contraband Pernod. She in-

* A reference to the Bernini St. Teresa in Ecstasy, in the church of Santa Maria della Vittoria in Rome.

voked the flask of *ratafia,* called for the subventions of Papa, Pappy, the great Aleppo, the invisible Omnipresent, who was, on the contrary, the Omnivisible pig, hailed savior of Italy, omnipresent in his tickling, in every kind of tickling: impotent as he was to achieve anything whatsoever, and even less his verbose braggings. There dripped azure pearls, tears of aloe, of terebene and vodka: the head thrown back, the hair lost in the night, with the two fingers, thumb and index, each with a yellow topaz, raising her skirt, in front, revealing to one and all that she was wearing underwear. She was wearing it, the sainted woman: yes, yes, she was. The wild rape had taken that path, which was the path of duty, for him and for his scenting scariness, climbing up her thighs now like ivy, fat and trembling in his terror, making her laugh and laugh in silly cascades, raving at his tickling: there: they were made of cardboard and plaster, her underpants, that time. Because once, in life, they had put a plaster cast on the trap.

The sergeant sped on, with a dry crackling, in the direction of I Due Santi, with the private grabbing his waist, blinking his eyelids at the oncoming wind, bothered by the dust. Disappointment wakened him abruptly. The time in which we would say that dreams extend has, instead, the diaphragming rapidity of a Leica's click, is measured in lightning segments of time, by fractions of the fourth degree on the orbital time of the earth, commonly known as solar time, the time of Caesar and of Gregory. And lo, now, beyond the flotilla of clouds that was skirting the rocks of the east, the opal became rose, the rose thickened and was stratified in carmine: the lividness everywhere, to the north, of broken day: then, at last, from the ridge, the splendid eyelash: a dot of fire, in a peak of the ridge of the Ernici or the Simbruni the unbearable pupil: the straight, arrowing gaze of the handsome Apollo, the spotlight. The gray latitudes of Latium were clarified, made plastic, emerging, purple-clad, almost like crumbling milestones of time, fragments of towers without names.

When the bam-bam-bam died out at I Due Santi, in a brief skid of the wheels, which the brakes quickly hindered, then blocked, the private found himself on the ground standing, as if he had fallen there: a mountain bear: stretching, from right to left, the lower edge of the olive-drab tunic, which was revealed to be an extremely short garment, over the rotund opulences of his anthropological type. To the right of the Appia, for those who went on in the direction of Albano, the door of opaque or colored panes to a little store, whose threshold of gray and worn peperino, on the outside, was at the level of the still damp asphalt. Opposite the door, to the left of the road that ascended straight and calm, between the mouths of the two connecting roads, one of which had brought them here from the barracks and the town, the low wall of a garden or a vineyard or something of the sort: above which there protruded, somewhat disheveled in the muggy dripping of the morning, the tops of some dried reeds. The wall was broken by a tall shrine, with two eaves and curlicues of pale stucco on the front. Two tumblers, and in them some primulas and periwinkles, consecrated to devotional use, flowered and colored the stone of that kind of window's sill: from which the Divinity, a bit stunned in the head, leaned out as if from a pulvinar over the bustle of the Appia. Framed by the jambs and the slightly cockeyed arch, the old painting, its color quite faded and chalky, demanded all one's attention: the Fara Filiorum Petri* gazed at it, though stupefied by sleep and dazed by the novelty of this excursion. Two figures, surely saints—he argued from the data: that is, dressed in clothes that weren't the pants-and-jacket of ordinary men, and their pates behaloed: of which the one, without beard, smaller, was dark and bald: the other, hard and boney, with a white blob on his chin, like a spoonful of lime, and thick hair halfway down his forehead, white, or once white, inside the halo's yellow circle. Those two little short cloaks, bunched like a bandoleer on the left shoulder of the two partners, did not cover the calves and still further, below the calves, the repainted malleoli: and that had allowed the first painter, their "creator," to bring on to the scene four unsuspected feet. The two right ones, enormous, had come to him in a flash: and they were generously tentacled in toes, stretched forward in their stride, to puncture the foreground, the ideal plane (vertical and transparent), to which every visual occasion is referred. With particular expressive vigor, in a remarkable adaptation to the mastery of the centuries, the big toes were depicted. In each of the two extended digits, the cross strap of otherwise unperceived

* Fara Filiorum Petri is the peculiar name of a small town in the Abruzzo from which, apparently, this carabiniere private comes. Gadda refers to him at times by the name of the town, at times by combined forms of it ("Farafilio"), and at times by his surname, Cocullo.

footwear segregated and singled out the knuckled-toe in that august pre-eminence which is his, which belongs to the big toe, and to that toe alone, separating it out from the flock of the toes of lower rank, less suitable for the day of glory, but still, in the osteologues' atlases and in the masterpieces of Italian painting, toes. The two haughty digits, enhanced by genius, were projected, hurled forward: they traveled on their own: they almost, paired off as they were, stuck in your eye: indeed, into both your eyes: they were sublimated to the central pathetic motif of the fresco, or alfresco, seeing as how it was plenty fresh. A bolt from heaven, a light of excruciated hours blanched them; however, when you came right down to it, the light seemed to rise from underground, since it struck them from below. The distant bray of a donkey, as the wind rose again, with the tinkle of bells. The glorious history of our painting, in a part of its glory pays tribute to the big toe. Light and toes* are prime ingredients, ineffable, in every painting that aspires to live, that wants to have its say, to narrate, persuade, educate: to subjugate our senses, win hearts from the Malign One: insist for eight hundred years on the favorite images. Not even the saints, then, so laden with so many gifts of the Lord— not even they could avoid the indispensable gift of feet: and still less these two, who walked the Appian Way together to Babylon,† towards decollation or upside-down crucifixion. They had, indeed, in their feet, the physical instrument of their itinerant apostolate: they trod on the

* This whole passage is underlined by an untranslatable play on the similarity of two words, *la luce* (light) and *l'alluce* (big toe).

† Babylon, in this case, means Rome.

feet of Ahenobarbus. Who, however, remained less than persuaded. No, the saints must not lack their full complement of toes: as soldiers must receive their full issue of tins: and even less when an Italian painter of the sixteenth or seventeenth century or, of the eighteenth, or worse, kneels before them and prepares to depict them, from below, with the soul of a pedicurist. Light, in Italy, is the mother of toes: and if one is an Italian painter, it's nothing to joke about, as Manneroni didn't joke at I Due Santi, neither with the light nor with the toes. The metatarsus of Saint Joseph has been peduncled with an inimitable big toe in the Palatine *tondo* by Michelangelo (the Holy Family): which huge digit, for a minimal portion, to tell the truth, has its pictorial tegument from the little toe of the Bride: a livid and almost surreal, or perhaps eschatological light, proposes the Toe-Idea, loftily incarnating—or in ossifying—it, in the foreground of the contingent: and salvages it promptly for the metaphysical bruises of eternity. The same metartarsus protuberates, the foot's thumb, rival of the Michelangelan-Palatine (to signify the miracle, or rather the audicle, of male chastity) in the Urbino master's Sposalizio, today at the Brera. The divarication of the solitary, bony toe from the remaining herd of other toes is rendered prominent by the perspectively charming joints of the cleansed pavement, where there is no husk or skin, neither orange's nor chestnut's, nor has any leaf or paper settled there, nor has man urinated there, nor dog. And the master toe, though disjoined from the others, at its root is spurred and gnarled: and then it converges inwards, as if forced by gout or by the habitual constriction of a shoe momentarily removed, or I'd say *domum relapsa* as if too fetid for the hour of the

273

wedding. And it responds, made august by its divarication, it responds to the tall, erect ecstacy of the slender stalk or staff which, overnight, miraculously flowered with three lilies, instead of the customary white carnation: and it picks up, from the rather rare juncture of carpenterial innocence with carpenterial poverty, the testimonial value of an artisan connotation: more than a toe of more than a barefoot carpenter, in that fashion.

As to the iconography of the two saints, and of the holy apostles in general, ah, didn't Manneroni dedicate to them the unspent energies of a velvet-bearded forty years of his own life? assisted on his scaffoldings not only by his believer's fervor, but by the tragic qualities of his genius and an iron constitution: by an athlete's physique, a prophet's appetite: and by a handful of cash, from time to time, given him, however, reluctantly, by the commissioner of those miracles. In the shrine of I Due Santi, adorned and curlicued with cheese-pale stuccos, he was finally enabled to collect and employ all of his talents: the talents which had been swelling his brush, in twenty years of initiation and pictorial apprenticeship, and of obstinate discipline through twenty more years of bearded mastery. Ejaculated impetuously and with free hand on the mortar, still fresh —that is alfresco—the two big toes, the Pietrine and the Pauline, display all the vigor and the urgency of their creation . . . inderogatable, of the enunciation . . . by coerced squeezing, as if splattered there by some source or spring . . . *"ch'alta vena preme."** The "creator" couldn't bear

* "At prompting of the Eternal Spirit's breath," Dante, *Paradiso*, XII, 99 (Binyon translation).

another moment's delay, before creating. *"Fiat lux!"* And there were toes. Plip, plop.

Also of the painter Zeuxis, for that matter, it is rumored that he made a mountain, of lovely foam, at the mouth of a horse, splattering we don't know what sponge on his muzzle, at a whim, but catching it a little too low. And it worked out well. While Pestalozzi had taken to fiddling with his machine, bent over and absorbed, the short-tunicked young man, having crossed the road, moved under the shrine as if for a prayer or a vow: hinting, with his thumb alone, at the Sign of the Cross, he looked up, open-mouthed, and noticed that, with one hand, they held the edge of their garments, the two walkers, inasmuch as, if they didn't, their clothes would have been muddied along the way. It was muddy, in fact, towards the mire of the plain, even the road or row that they still had to travel: that same one, perhaps, that the Farafiliopetri now saw descending towards Le Frattocchie. A light must have spread from above, at one time, but the years, the decades or the centuries, had equated it to the squalor of the general wash: overcome by the light from underground. The bald saint, a little gnome with black hair at his temples, looked like somebody who knew a thing or two: able to read and write as smart as a lawyer, maybe even better: but he seemed to be slowing his pace, now, not even reluctantly, to allow his colleague to go ahead. A kind of right of primogeniture haloed the cervix of the latter, kindled and sharpened his pupils, it circumflowed, like rough beard, the mug that was greedily thrust forward to discern, a fisherman peering at his line: his nose was hardened to the task: granted the title of a

Princedom which made his gray hair seem of stone, woolly as it was, to the forehead minimized of the harder. Beneath the figures of the two men, in the two waving scrolls one upon the other in exergue, the tubby Farafiliopetri managed to read, in silent parting and closing of the lips, barely forming the words without uttering them: *"Crescite ve-ro in gratia et in co ... co ... coccione Domini Preti Sec Ep."** The sergeant, in the meanwhile, had taken it into his head —despite all prearranged plans—to medicate his machine on the spot, bent over her greasy viscera. He persisted in titillating obstinately it wasn't clear what hot nipple or what teat, withdrawing his fingers immediately, every time, with a "damn" or a "Jesus Christ!" in a whisper, and snapping them each time in the air, as if to shake off the burning. *"Saepe,"* the Farafilio read on, *"proposui venire ad vos et pro-hi-bitus"* (still mentally) *"sum usque ad kuk Paul ad Rom."*† Whereupon he was certain that he had truly deserved his diploma: from grade school. He had received it the year before, as a Baptist received Baptism after his twentieth year, and immediately added it to the already presented and certified papers: hair, brown: eyes, gray: nose, straight: height: 1.74 meters: chest: 91, circumference of the behind . . . not required. And now, at last, after the diuturnal assistance of the goddess of learning (and penmanship), spreading even to within the range of Pallas

* *"Crescite vero in gratia et in cognitione Domini. Petri Secunda Epistula: (III-18)."* (Author's note). ". . . grow in grace, and in the knowledge of our Lord . . ."

† *"Saepe proposui venire ad vos et prohibitus sum usque adhuc. Pauli ad Romanos: (I-13)."* (Author's note). ". . . oftentimes I purposed to come unto you, but I was let hitherto . . ."

the Speller, now, behind, the "certificate of studies": diploma, yessir, yes, elementary.

La Zamira, for it was truly she, so disheveled and ungirt, pushing a broom, preceded by a conspicuous cluster of domestic fluffs and straws and indefinable rubbish, received the two men with the salivary lubricity of her professional smile and the peasant falsity of her gaze. The resultant grimace, made livid by the window and the uncertain whiteness of the weather, then kindled by a sudden dart of the sun was meant to disguise as extremely welcome this most unwelcome visit.

"Come in, come in." Was she expecting it, this visit? Or did she guess its reason, if not its immediate purpose, then and there? The hard corporal wanted to bring his motorcycle inside, too well known to be left out in the road. When he had persuaded it to descend the step with both wheels, like an uneasy horse, he set it, with some difficulty, near the knitting machine. He looked at the *femme fatale*, at the sorceress. She hadn't yet combed her hair. Her bangs were a tangle: a gray clump of stubble and roots. Beneath the bumps of the forehead and the rain pipe of the two orbital arches, the pointed flashing of the irises, black, or almost: authentic fear, suspicion, reticence, derision, deception. Flanked by the four surviving canines, the barrel vault, obscene: her lips, at the corners, drooled revolting little bubbles, amid the irradiation of a thousand wrinkles, not yet smoothed or dispelled by cream. It seemed, that vault, the evil door whence like a snake, the head had to come blackened forth, followed then by the whole neck of an unforeseen stratagem, a cavil of the whoring peasant woman. The two dopes perceived, in alarm, the spell that misted towards them with her breath, like that of a gecko or a dragon whose experience in duel is not known. Pestalozzi had—and wanted—to make an effort in self-control: with one hand he seemed to dry his eyes, that is to say his eyelids, under the vizor, to clear his soul and his sensory faculties, which were commanded to pursue the investigation. "Goddamn whore!" he argued mentally. With this ejaculation he felt himself sergeant once again: "The below-named Farcioni Clelia, from Pozzofondo, and Mattonari Camilla, resident at Pavona, work here. Where are they?" The Farafiliorum, meanwhile, was scratching his behind with sweet leisure: or lifting from it, perhaps, the too-sheathing underpants. With both hands, and with two parallel and symmetrical gestures, he proceeded to press his tunic along his hips. It was still like a too-short undershirt: he was ashamed: that insufficience was embittering his whole day.

"Come right in, Corporal. They'll be along any minute. Who wants them?" Zamira counter-asked, insinuating, insolent. The handle of that filthy old broom, all burs, was now clasped in her two hands as if she leaned on it, in repose, and to listen. Pestalozzi, now master of his soul, gave the vile woman a thunderous look: "lousy old whore" was its meaning, mute, his lips closed, straight, "you can see for yourself who." She seemed to dissolve into attentions, pushing aside as best she could the filth to the flank of the sideboard, and allocating the broom there too, as if to guard what it had collected. "I'll go call them, if you'll mind the store for me: I can trust *you*!" she smiled, turning: after taking a shawl from the rag pile: and she started to go out, wagging her tail, for their joy as desiring but abstinent youths. He clenched his anger in his teeth, Pestalozzi did: and held her back promptly by one arm. A wink! and she whirled around suddenly, like a garter snake when you step on its tail.

"If they'll be along any minute, then we'll wait for them here. Don't move. Sit down," he fastened her to a chair, pressing her into it: "There. But if they don't come . . . we'll take *you* in, this time." The good dyeress paled: the harshness was rather, in him, descended from the hills, despite the noncommissioned officers' school. Santa Maria Novella had not shed on him the grace, oh no, of excessive refinement. The respectful glands were gadgets of the future, then, for a noncom; hopes, in the heart of evildoers, of a brighter morrow: the brighter morrow of those days. Harshness, at that time, was borne as a duty: the "courses in human relations" had not yet been set up. The chevrons of sergeanthood, a long promise waved under his nose like a shredded meal beneath a cat's, demanded wisdom, firmness: harshness, when required. Then, once sergeant, he could play the kindly man, the gruff bear with a heart of gold . . . full of understanding. So harshness it was: in that moment made even heavier by his annoyance. That breath, those mocking eyes of the sorceress, those lascivious *double-entendres*—their witchcraft had to be dispelled, the coils of her hypnosis had to be broken. "You, move away from that window," he ordered Cocullo, "hide over there." The motorcycle was now under cover, sheltered from the curious and from the rain. But along the provincial road, after the descent from Torraccio, its crackling had been heard more or less by everyone, and by some, he thought, seen, from the little window of the privy: at the hour of rising, when they yawn, in their trousers, wandering about the house with a train of suspenders at their shins, towards the sink, scratching the head in the prickly luxuriance of black hair, a ninth jawbreaking yawn, a rub of the eyelids with the most diligent knuckles and phalanges: whence sleep, so sweet in the morning, is dissipated and vaporizes away slowly, almost despite itself. Consciousness then identifies with itself, resumes its own skin, its lousy cloak. It begins to count again its chickens, the foolish events of the day-light hours. A motorbike on the road. The corporal seemed to reflect: "Have they come to work regular, these last few days? Or have they had justified absences?

"Worked . . ." the sly old bag hesitated, "absence? justi-fied?" she stammered, to gain time. No, with such legal language she couldn't, in all conscience, and therefore dared not pretend to be familiar. She was the sincere type, all heart, a woman of few words: deeds, rather, actions . . . to the succor of souls, of needful hearts: who had recourse to her . . . for disinterested advice. And hearts, as we all know, by their own nature . . . tend to fraternize. In pairs. Nor could the corporal, from her, insist on law-court style. He had no reason and still less any right to demand it, with all the subtleties and circumlocutions and cavils that be-cloud it, on the lawyer's tongue. Oh! lawyers! they were so nice! And such good customers! She dreamed for a moment.

But woe that she should be a customer of theirs, she pondered.

"Justified absence of who . . ."

"Don't play dumb. Don't pretend you don't understand; you know very well what I mean. The two girls I told you. Who?! Farcioni and Mattonati . . . Mattonari, that is. I have a feeling that last Tuesday, the fifteenth that is, I suspect . . . they didn't turn up. They said they were sick." He invented that "said" out of the whole cloth. He had never met them nor sought them: he also dropped that Tuesday instead of Saturday, to provoke a denial, and the consequent correction. Zamira seemed to be racking her memory.

"Come on, answer. You've got to answer right off, dear Madam, not think about it a year. If you have to think so long, it's surely to make up some lie. Have they come to work regularly? This is what I'm asking you. Or did they stay home some morning? I want to hear this from you, from your own lips. We know it already ourselves, never fear: the carabinieri know everything!"

"Why, what do you know? Why are you asking me, then, if you already know?"

"I told you. Because I want to hear it from you, from you in person, what you think about it and what you have to say. Yes, you, Signora Pàcori, Zamira, with your diploma in fortunetelling": and he sought it, on the wall, with his gaze: hanging like an engineering degree in a surveyor's office. But it must have been downstairs, with the Death's Head, in the consulting room, near the padlocked cupboard where the cheese was also stored.

She tried her smile again, her most lascivious one: she

recalled her dribble, sucking in from the corners, despite the vault in the midst. She dried her lips, moving her little tongue in a rapid, scything motion, which then rested, for a moment, at the margin of impudence, of sluttidence, as Belli* might have said. It was, in general, a slimy and dark red tongue, as if it had also been painted: and at that moment it crouched down among the canines, nice and docile, in a posture of waiting and perhaps of relaunching, since the fence of incisors had rotted away in the wayward years.

"Well, Sergeant dear, what can I tell you? You let me know . . ." and she swayed her head, here and there, looking like a silk moth, very coy: and she was careful, at the same time, to wriggle, with the larger part of her profferings, poorly concealed in this early hour, on the edge of the chair: to which she felt nailed. "You let me know, because I imagine, you know too, he he he, that we women, he he he, since we *are* women, he he he, have our little troubles . . . every so often . . . a punishment of the Lord, he he he, to try our patience, poor us! It isn't our fault if we're not like you men, he he he, who are always able to stand up!"

This time, revolted, it was he, the corporal, who played dumb.

"What troubles? Leave troubles out of it!"

She went on, haughtily:

"Well, Sergeant, just think a minute—with that kind heart of yours! You can't deny that it's so. My poor little girls, poor things!" Then, imploring: "You mean you don't have a wife?" shameless! "Or a couple of sisters? Not even one? . . . everybody has a sister, you might say. Where's

* Gioacchino Belli (1791–1863), Roman dialect poet.

the man these days, with all the men around, who doesn't have a couple of sisters to marry off? Even that big poet, the patriotic one, had one: the poet who made everybody cry, at Christmas, in Libya, at Ain Zara, with the Sixth Bersaglieri . . . what was his name? he's dead now, poor thing! What was his name? Giovanni . . . you know . . . those places where there's grass," and with her hand she drew the name from her forehead, "Giovanni . . . Giovanni Prati! No, no . . . not Giovanni Prati, wait a minute," and she continued, with her hand, "How can I have forgotten? It's all the trials I've been through . . . they've ruined my memory. Giovanni Pascoli!* There, now I remember: I knew he had a name like the places where they make hay."

"Skip the grass and the hay, and the meadows and the pastures. And forget about the dead. Just answer me."

"But, Sergeant dear, let me get a word in. How can I answer you, otherwise? I was saying, how everybody nowadays has a sister, no? And if you have one, then I'm sure . . . that day comes around for your sister, too, poor lamb; maybe she has a little headache. We women, he he he, have our headaches here." And she touched her belly, almost caressing it. Her eyes flashed satanic, intoxicated. The black oven between the incisors' gap. The tongue drawn back, now, like a parrot's when he gurgles in his throat, in spite. Her hair seemed to be summoned aloft, by electricity, as if it were about to burst into flame and crackle like brambles, when a spark, on the baked earth, kindles them.

"Yes, I understand, you women here get a headache from

* A pun on the words *prati* (meadows) and *pascoli* (pastures), surnames of two Italian nineteenth-century poets. Pascoli, a bachelor, lived with his sister.

all the knitting you have to do. But don't start nagging me with headaches now. Cut it short. Enough of this chatter. You have to tell me when it was that they stayed home, these two girls: Mattonari and Farcioni. I already know, but I want to check with you, to see if you're telling the truth, or if you're lying. If you're lying, if you're lying to put the investigation off the track, here, here are the handcuffs, all ready for them and for you." And he took from his pocket and dangled before her nose an example of the ill-famed hardware. Seated, the witch didn't bat an eye: those armillae, in any case, didn't concern her. "Well?"

"Well, let's see . . . it must have been last month, the one before this. Now that I think of it, we're just at the new moon." Obstinate, she harped on this theme: "How can I remember the monthlies of all the girls? I think that's asking too much . . ."

"Too much? Moons? Now look here, Zamira Pàcori! Have you lost your mind? Who do you think you're talking to?"

"But last month . . ."

"Last month my ass! Watch what you're saying. Last month! I'm asking you if they were absent on Tuesday the fifteenth, or Friday: one of the two." (He didn't dare bring his Saturday into play.) "This is what I'm asking you. And this is all I want you to answer, because you know very well."

At that point, as if summoned from the darkness, from the slightly opened door of the little stairway which led into the store (of which the young boys daydreamed, others mythicized, and more than one, because of the palm-reading, knew from experience), there peered in, then hopped onto the chill tile floor, here and there, with certain cluck-clucks of hers, among two piles of sweaters, a surly and half-featherless hen, lacking one eye, with her right leg bound by a string, all knots and splices, which wouldn't stop coming out, coming up: such, as from the ocean, the endless line of the sounding where the windlass of the poop summons it back aboard and yet a fringe of beard decks it out, from time to time: a mucid, green seaweed from the depths. After having hazarded, this way and that, more than one lifting of the foot, with the air, each time, of knowing quite well where she meant to go, but of being hindered by the contradictory prohibitions of fate, the pattering one-eyed fowl then changed her mind completely. She unstuck her wings from her body (and she seemed to expose the ribs for a more generous intake of air), while a badly restrained anger already gurgled in the gullet: a catarrhous commination. Her windpipe envenomed, she began a cadenza in falsetto: she pecked wildly at the top of that mountain of rags, whence she sprayed the phenomena of the universe with the supreme cockledoodledoo, as if she had laid an egg up there. But she fluttered down without any waste of time, landing on the tiles with renewed paroxysms of high notes, a glide of the most successful sort, a record: still dragging the string after her. Parallel to the string and its chain of knots and gnarls, a thread of gray wool had caught on one leg: and the thread this time seemed to be unwoven from a rhubarb-colored scarf, beneath the dyed rags. Once on the ground, and after yet another cluck-cluck expressing either a wrath beyond cure or restored peace and friendship, she planted herself on steady legs before the shoes of the horrified corporal, turning to him the highly unbersagliere-like plume* of her tail: she lifted the root of the same, revealed the Pope's nose in all its beauty: diaphragmed to the minimum, the full extent of the aperture, the pink rose-window of her sphincter, and, plop, promptly took a shit: not out of contempt, no, probably indeed to honor, following hennish etiquette, the brave noncom, and with all the nonchalance in the world: a green chocolate drop twisted *à la Borromini* like the lumps of colloid sulphur in the Abule water: and on the very tip-top a little spit of calcium, also in the colloidal state, a very white cream, the pallor of pasteurized milk, which was already on the market in those days.

All these aerodynamics, naturally, and the consequent release of chocolate, or mocha, as may be, were exploited by Zamira to avoid answering: while some surly little feathers, snowy and delicate as those of a baby duckling, lingered above, in midair, softly swaying, till they seemed the dissolving rings of smoke from a cigarette. In this new wonder Pestalozzi's imperative faded away. She got up quickly from the chair with all her bluish behind, and started kicking her slipper and waving her skirt after the sulky beast, since she had no apron, and screeching at it: "Get out! Out! dirty, filthy thing! The idea! Of anything so nasty! To the sergeant here! Filthy animal!"

So that the filthy thing in question, still trilling a thousand clucketyclucks, and spewing them, all together, towards the ceiling in a great cackling résumé, doubly anchored though she was by string and yarn, took flight up to the top of the

* The soldiers of the *bersaglieri* (sharpshooters) regiments wear hats with special plumes of cock tail-feathers.

sideboard: where, pissed off, and resuming her full dignity, she deposited, on the pewter tray, another neat little turd, but smaller than the first: plink! With which she seemed to have evacuated to the full extent of her possibilities. Fear (of the carabinieri) brings out the worst in all of us.

And there, at the glass door, the brass handle began also to show signs of restlessness. The door opened. A young girl, from the March outside, burst into the large room like a gust of wind. A dark shawl around her neck: umbrella in hand, already closed before her entry. A wave of handsome chestnut hair from the forehead back, almost in a cascade over the shawl: March had invaded it, with lunatic arabesques. At the sight of the olive drab, as soon as she had come down the step, she stopped, lips parted, dumfounded. The two soldiers and Zamira, all three, sensed an unexpected emotion which had flamed up from her uterus through the lymphatic glands and the vaginal tracts into the fullness of her boobs: in a faint gasping, but certainly a vivid palpitation. Her face paled, or so it seemed: it was, at this point, the slightly hysterical white of a desirable girl. She remained with her lips parted, then said: "Good morning, Corporal": and hurled a larboard glance at the other one, whom she had already discerned on coming in and descending the step, but whom she saw for the first time, cornered in his corner as if in a modest penumbra: over whom prevailed, in any case, the chevroned dazzle, that is to say the hierarchical precedence of Pestalozzi. After the glance at the other simpleton, she made as if to look around for a place to set her umbrella: but the lynx-like gaze (lynx was the word he used to describe himself) of the above-named sergeant . . . no, the lynx-like gaze did not miss a movement of her left hand (which held in the ring and little finger that scarecrow of an umbrella), to the charge or benefit of the other hand: a kind of scratching or massage inflicted or practiced with the thumb, from below, and externally with the index and middle finger, on the long, central fingers of the right hand: as if to warm them up, foreseeing the work to come. In the apparent casualness of the gesture there was an insistent, a premeditated quality: it was the gesture, not casual, of one who wishes to remove a ring, with some effort, and who proposes, at the same time, to conceal the not-easy operation from others present. The corporal glared at the girl, approached her by two paces, bang, bang, gently but firmly took her right hand by the fingertips: an invitation to the dance which admitted no refusal. He seemed to be pressing and squeezing them, one by one, those fingers, one after the other, as if to feel if there was a pimple, or a callus, as he went on looking into her eyes, fixed and perplexed, with the manner of a magician on the stage in a demonstration of hypnotism. Finally he turned it over, that hand, and stood there looking into its palm, to read her fate, one would have said. A handsome yellow stone, a topaz?, glowed like the headlight of a train, a hundred facets, on the inner part of the finger, the ring finger, after her surreptitious half-twist. It gave forth, from itself, the bumptious and slightly silly gaiety, at moments, of colored glass, under the sudden appearance and alternate fading, among the March clouds, of the sun, also seized with a uterine languor: for in that first month, when he has barely caught a whiff of the rain in the skies, he too is seized with the vapors and palpitations: like that Apollo that he is.

"You . . . who are you?" Pestalozzi, radiant, asked her, recognizing in his own desire the stimulating identity of the face, the eyes, the genteel figure of the girl, though not yet her name, in the filing cabinet of his mind. "Are you Clelia? Clelia Farcioni? or Camilla Mattonari?"

"Why, Corporal, what's all this about? Yes, my name's Mattonari, all right: but I'm not Camilla. My name is . . ." she hesitated, "Mattonari Lavinia."

"Then where is Camilla? And who is she? Your sister?"

"Sister?" she pursed her lips in disgust, "I don't have any sisters," disdaining the hypothesis of such a kinship.

"But you know her. She works here: you said her name, Camilla's. So you're friends." And in the meanwhile he was still holding her hand. She had set down, at last, the umbrella: she frowned: "Did I say that? Camilla? I just repeated the name you said, corporal." Pestalozzi thought he had caught a use of the article, in Tuscan or Lombard fashion,* which hadn't been spoken at all.

"Friends? I don't have any friends." The violence of this denial, a second time: no more than the corporal was expecting: "Well, if you don't have any friends, so much the better: you can speak out then: and no foolishness, because I don't have time to waste. Who's Camilla?" he continued to hold her hand, by the fingertips.

"She's . . . yes, a girl who . . . she's learning to be a seamstress, too . . . she works . . ."

"She works here?"

---

* In Northern Italy proper names, in indirect reference, are often preceded by the definite article. Pestalozzi thought he heard her say *la* Camilla.

"Well yes," she admitted, hanging her head.

"She's her cousin: a distant cousin . . ." Zamira said calmly, in the tone with which the *Almanach de Gotha* asseverates, and all believe, that Charlotte Elisabeth of Coburg is the fourth cousin of Amalia of Mecklenburg.

"And where is she? Why isn't she here? Isn't she coming to work today?"

"How should I know?" the girl shrugged. "She'll be coming."

"You can see for yourself, Sergeant," Zamira insisted, haughtily. "We're out in the country. We work when there's something to do . . . to make or to mend: when there's need, I mean. Every other day, more or less. But in the winter, with the weather like this," and she took advantage of a fading of the sun, through the panes, and nodded towards the outside, "with these storms, you can't tell from one day to the next . . . whether it's spring or whether it's still January, with this weather maybe we work one day out of five. You know better than me, Sergeant, since you must have studied all about the weather and the signs of the moon, the way I did, when I got my fortunetelling diploma," she recited in a sententious tone:

> "Candlemas, Candlemas!
>   Winter's end has come at last.
>   But should rain fall or north wind blow
>   Winter then has weeks to go.

and three weeks ago, if you remember, just like today, the weather was something terrible; the water came right down into the shop, and that lousy hen," she sought the hen with her eyes behind the machine, "even stopped laying. Today maybe we have nothing to do, and tomorrow there may be a whole heap of stuff."

"It looks to me like you have a fine heap of lies, enough to last a month," and he indicated with his chin the little mound of things, piled as if in two peaks, like the back of a camel. Still holding the young girl by the hand, he abandoned the clucking hen to her doubts and the double train of yarn and string and the relative knots.

"Now . . . tell me something: who gave you this?" he raised his hand of the palpitating Lavinia, now clasping her by the wrist, and looking at the topaz which, from the inner part of the hand, she had turned again on her finger.

"Who gave it to me?" she made an effort to blush, as if at a tender secret.

"Signorina, hurry up. Take off the ring. I have to confiscate it. And tell me who gave it to you. If you tell me, all right. And if you don't tell me . . ." and he took from his pocket the familiar plaything: presenting it to her.

Lavinia blanched: "Corporal . . ."

"Skip the corporal. Take that ring off right now, and hand it over, make it snappy, because if you don't know, I'll tell you: it's stolen goods. It's in the list of jewels and gold objects stolen from the countess in Via Merulana, from Countess Menegazzi: it's here, in the list of jewels." And, to motivate his demand which, in spite of everything, he knew smacked a bit of bullying, he replaced the handcuffs and removed, from another pocket, Ingravallo's paper. The procedural timidity of that which in the *Barber* is marked in F sharp, the "force," had not yet sunk then, in 1927, into the present Oceanic depths: but it already knew certain aspects of today's taste. Even the most harsh official, alone in the countryside in the midst of the populace, deferred to it, as they defer to it today. Having therefore extracted the list, squaring off the two sheets as if he were reading a warrant, Pestalozzi pretended also to look there . . . for the legitimate authorization to proceed. "Mmm . . ." he went down the first lines, muttering, and stumbled at once at what he was seeking: "gold ring with topaz!" and his was the voice of victory. He waved the letterheaded paper, put it under her eyes, the girl's. She, Lavinia, didn't even know how to read it.

"Police Headquarters, Rome!" he chanted in her face, in a tone of importance, and of ironic detachment towards the rival organization, which, just because they could type a couple of sheets of paper, gave themselves such airs: "Police Headquarters, Rome!" He took the ring held out to him by the girl, her face pale with spite, livid, with the air of submitting, helpless, she, poor country girl, to this abuse of power. Zamira, silent, looked on: and listened. "Aha! this is the very one!" Pestalozzi ventured, examining the ring with a connoisseur's eye, turning it over and looking at it closely, as a fence would have done in Via del Gobbo, tending to sequester it at once: meanwhile he clasped the two sheets of paper in the other hand, between little finger and palm: "this is the topaz I've been hunting for for two days: this is it!" as if his professional wisdom, operating in his cranium *ab aeterno*, had allowed him to recognize it instantly. In reality he was seeing it then for the first time, and he had been hunting for it for two hours, if, after all, it really was a topaz, and not a piece of bottle, perhaps: "Who gave it to you? Tell the truth. He did, Retalli. You don't have the money to buy it: a ring like this! Enea Retalli gave it to you: he already confessed it yesterday to the sergeant." (Retalli was still a fugitive from justice.) "He's your lover, we know that: and he gave you this topaz"; which was rather a naïve remark. "Nobody's my lover: and Enea Retalli is out working somewhere: I don't know where; and it's not true that you caught him last night, or that he confessed anything."

"So much the worse for you then. Come on. Let's go," and he motioned to Farafiliopetri: and grabbed her by the arm.

"Corporal, you've got to believe me," the girl protested, freeing herself, "a girl friend of mine gave it to me; she's promised to buy it off a woman; she lent it to me for a couple of days, because today . . . today's my birthday. She gave it to me just for two days."

"Ah, and how old are you?"

"Well . . . I'm nineteen."

"Are you sure?"

"Yes, I was nineteen last night."

"So you were born at night then. And who lent you the ring, for your birthday? Speak up."

"Corporal, how could I know . . . that it belonged to the contessa that they murdered in Rome, or whose it was? The peddlers that go along the road on horseback, from town to town, you know? You think they know who owns or who made the stuff they sell?"

"That's enough fibs!" and he squeezed her arm, which he had taken again and was holding.

"Ouch!" she said: "You're bullying me."

"Who gave it to you? Come on. You can tell it to sergeant. He'll make you spill it, all right." He drew her towards the door. Fara also started to move, in compliance, he uprooted himself from where he was, left his corner. The hen had settled down, God knows where.

"I got it, Corporal, from a girl . . . A girl who works here gave it to me. We've been talking for ages about corals to wear around the neck, or earrings . . . And I was always saying that I didn't have anything to put on for my birthday."

"Then say who she is. You know her," Zamira prompted, pale.

"It's Camilla," she answered Zamira.

"Ah! Camilla Mattonari then? All this fuss to give us the name of Mattonari Camilla, your cousin, whose lover is a thief, or even a murderer, maybe. Come on: take me to her."

"What about the motorcycle?" Zamira stammered; to her the very thought of that machine in the shop without its master annoyed her unspeakably. She had got up from the chair. She wrung her hands before her belly, a little ball that made her look three months pregnant, considerably stained below her belt, where there were certain rivulets of dishwater or coffee; she had no apron. Her lips pursed, forgetting now every invitation and all her winks, with the foresighted and deducing gaze of one who guesses from a single movement the motives and intentions of the mover, with intent and glistening eyes, she followed the motions of the two men in their somewhat embarrassed footsteps between sideboard and bike, machine and table, counter and chair, between the heap of sweaters and the door: the door to the road. The light in her eyes changed, became evil, malevolent and almost sinister, at times. She seemed to see oscillating, like the oscillation of a charge, a tension in the spirit, as if it meant to break the sequence of acts and inacceptable deeds, the procedural validity of that carabinieresque miracle. Which she saw, at a given point, in its true light: in its certain meaning, compelling recognition: a gray and scarlet devilment of the Prince of Demons: he of the sergeant's stripes: he, in any case, whom she had been able to recognize on many occasions as the sworn enemy of I Due Santi: who took shelter in the fortress, at night, in Marino, when the mountain wind howled, to meditate before the bluish circle of the lampwick his malefactions for the day, ubiquitious then in the great hours of the sun like the view of the falcon, who peers and sees over all the land, in farmyard and meadow, on mountain or plain. A red-and-black, chevroned malefaction, filled like the September night with a thousand sophists' persistences, which from day to day press ever closer around the person of one who, perhaps, works honestly, who tries to get along as best he (or she) can, with the first expedient that comes to mind, to fight off the many tribulations of life. A duty though vain and maleficent, suited to justify, as well as to determine, one's corpulence, one's rubicund health, one's pension: an arbitrary and therefore illicit intervention into the private operations of magic, or of simple palm-reading, such as to spoil the outcome of everything: disputable then, on good grounds, with augural looks on the order of her own, zamirian gaze, as well as by a summons for help to the great king with the straight horns, Astaroth: the very one that she, Zamira, had to call. So that she busied herself now, with her fingers, making on the sack of her paunch like the pharmacist on his marble counter, certain movements, certain twirls, certain jokes not comprehended by common ratiocination, as if she were shelling invisible peas or crumbling or snapping some invisible pill in the direction of the unaware Pestalozzi who had his back to her, still unsure what was to be done. Her lips began, little by little, to bubble up again, to twitch, and her cheeks to vibrate, to boil *motu proprio* in a grim contempt, which was being sharpened into the fideistic peroration of certain witch doctor–priests of Tanganyika or African Kafirs or snub-nosed, kinky Niam-niams, their heads all curly, dusted with coal, gold rings hanging from their noses, their behinds like terraces, when they implore or imprecate from or to their animal gods in their monosyllabic-agglutinate language and in homologous and rather nasal chanting: "Nyam, nyam chep, chep, i-ti, i-ti, give that lousy missionary a humpback and get him off our balls." Mennonite missionary, of course. And meanwhile they give him a drink, their spit whipped up with coconut milk in a coconut shell, a sign of subtropical honor, or Tanganyika reverence.

"You, Signora, keep still with those fingers!" the Filiorum commanded her indignantly. His cheeks had become red, the red of tomato sauce, whitened to cheese color in the lower portion of his jaws. The objective clarity of ratiocination, in him, got the upper hand of the unreason of the powers of darkness: as if his elementary diploma had been countersigned by Filangieri himself with his own hand,

Don Gaetano Filangieri, Prince of Arianello, Minister of the Realm.* He wouldn't admit, couldn't tolerate that the "superstition" of past centuries should rise again in magic, in the art of fashioning hunchbacks for one's neighbor, carabiniere as in this case, by that fingering of the witch. There is a uterus in us, always, a reasonable one, which is disturbed by a wink, a hint, a kneading of fingertips with which, despite every new enlightening of the Realm and every diploma on outsized paper, the most enlightened certainties are poisoned.

"Let's go," repeated Corporal Pestalozzi, making up his mind. "I'll leave the machine here," and he turned, "watch out for it: put a chair in front of it, and don't let anybody touch it."

Signora Pàcori smiled at him, a little automatic smile, though black in the center: a dry little smile, silly, the kind she was used to dispensing from the counter in gray moments, a habit of her art, of a saleswoman who knows how to look at smokers: she revealed, as usual, the hole: she could do nothing else. Her eyelids closed a moment, as if in foretasted voluptuousness: foretasted out of duty, out of professional obligation. Her little eyes signified, with a moment's flashing, the usual permission: to whom? to what? The malevolence meanwhile, on her forehead, had waxed and polished the two bumps, two strongholds still held by the devil.

"Where is Retalli?" the corporal was saying to the girl.

"Corporal, I don't know," she said: her face distraught.

* Gaetano Filangieri (1752–88), enlightened political thinker and author.

"And your cousin? Where is your cousin? Take me to her. Come on." He seemed seized, really, by the mania to catch somebody, not to go back, empty-handed, to the barracks. A ring—and what a ring!—he had. All right. But now a suspect was needed, an accomplice, male or female, if not the guilty party in person.

"But I . . ." the girl whimpered again, forgetting the umbrella where she had placed it.

"Come on, that's enough. Show me where she is": and he opened the door, inviting her, with the other hand, to make use of both the step and the exit. Lavinia went outside first.

"At the railroad crossing," Zamira then hissed into his ear. But the private also heard her. Still, under her malevolent forehead, the pernicious light of her gaze was not spent. "She's the niece of the signal-keeper: at the crossing. That's where she lives."

"Which crossing?"

"The road to Castel de Leva, to the bridge; then to the left, the crossing at Casal Bruciato": she seemed a deaf-mute, explaining herself with her fingers, with the aphonous movement of her lips. She didn't want Lavinia to hear her, from the road. Farafilio stumbled over the step: "Careful!" she said, maternally: and repeated: "On the road to Divino Amore. Almost to the bridge. Then to the left."

And with that little thrust, with that viaticum, she succeeded in getting off the two comrades, with their four great boots. They would have plenty of dust to swallow! Old Nick had heard the boiling of her prayers, had graciously listened to her reiterated invocations and her pleas.

"Take care of the machine!" the corporal shouted to her again, from outside: as her gaze sharpened in meanness: "at the bridge of Divino Amore!" she shouted, as if to strike again at the rear guard of the vanquished. What fireworks exploded in their wake, what ejaculations, while the glass door was still open behind the departing men, history, past-mistress of life, has not troubled to record.

IX

THE Divino Amore bridge! Easier said than done! a mile and a half, and even more: a good forty minutes' walking: and with the girl, and with the shoes she was wearing. An apparition of the sun, a disk, an ephemeral or faint sphere, with fleeting veils of vapor on its face, so that it looked like the yoke of an egg seen through the white: tepid, at times, or soft; then, in some sudden yawn of the day, between one cloud and the following, reawakened, restored and randy, astride that gallop of the sirocco: flight and journey, from the Pontus, of all the cloud bank, huddled, slapping its flank against the spikes of the Apennine. The road was only one, luckily, except for the first part, however: the highway, the Appia, then at a right angle, the local road, for Falcognana. Taking the opportunity of that angle, a path went off diagonally into the countryside: too muddy an itinerary still, through the fallow fields that were of a damp, new green, water-soaked: and, here and there, as if sugared by the frost. If she came up this way, Camilla Mattonari, so Lavinia said, they were sure to run into her, walking along the asphalt, or at least on the dry part, to be precise, of the road from Falcognana. A buggy, which overtook them after they had turned in that direction, al-

lowed the corporal to make Lavinia climb in, and the private
after her. When the happy couple had been seen aboard, he
turned back towards the little tavern at the corner, to ask
somebody for the loan of a bike: otherwise, he would go
back up to Zamira's, to recover his steed. The Farafilio,
serious and round of face as of bottom, didn't seem wholly
displeased by his superior's inspiration, which spared him
the walk, however hygienic it may have been, and granted
him the tepid contiguity of the girl's thigh, though, *hélas!*,
keine Rose ohne Dornen, the thrill was shared with the
driver on the other side, that is, the side of her other thigh.
Despite the odor, promptly perceived and appreciated, of
feminine vitality, and the disturbing co-seating in the vehicle,
of such a "supple" and "nice" young lady, the stern
soldier, be it said to his praise, was obdurate, yes, obdurate
in being, or at least seeming, the most legally and
militarily agnostic of carabinieri of the whole legion, in that
wakening March of the Castelli. The descent was slow,
among the new plantations of some vines (still barren)
which broke the meadows. They reached a crossroads, with
the horse, already in sight of the bridge known as the Divino
Amore bridge, with which the above-praised local road
passes over the Velletri line of the railway. Divine Amore
proper, a little church of ancient date, here and there
replastered, and two hovels leased to the sun by the Latium
of the guardian Princes Torlonia, and Castel di Leva, which
flanks and dominates them, and looks around through the
empty eyes of the Torraccio tower, and girds or girded them
with a wall, are about three miles from the bridge. There,
at the crossroads, Pestalozzi was able to overtake, on a

bicycle, the excursion companions he had sent on ahead, displaying on his outstretched arm his chevrons which seemed a patent, a driving license exceptionally granted him, for such an unfluent vehicle. The bike was a music box, with a creak-creak in its hubs. It was like a machine with broken teeth for eating torrone: but there was not much in the way of torrone around those parts! The driver went ah to the horse, to hold him back a little and, in the meanwhile, leaning to the right, he was wringing the brake handle, as more and more, on the rims, the two brake blocks slid until they creaked. The horse, going downhill, disputed as best he could, then finally having sustained with his scrawny rump the successive jerks of the harness, when they arrived, one after the other, on his two buttocks, like the slaps of the sea against the innocence of the beach; he aimed definitively at the solid part of the road, without raising again in a trot, now spent, his forelegs; he skidded a little on all fours: and stopped, turning his head only slightly at the tug of the reins, as if to say: "I'd like to see you pulling a buggy! you have to try to stop me *now*, just when we're going so well." Plunged forward the three heads of the travelers, the brimming jiggling teats, the desirable throat and the face and slightly hysterical pallor of Lavinia as if in an attack of vomiting: as happens to everything that is not properly packaged, crated and nailed into a system: and travels, however, on its own, as if forward at random. Pestalozzi got off the bicycle. From the Falcognana road, which crosses, with the Divinio Amore bridge, the half-trench of the railroad a few hundred yards further down, at that point the road for Casal Bruciato broke off: which descends, even today, with a broad curve, to cross the same train track on the same level. On the roof of the yellow signal-man's house there weighed, uncertain and broken in parts, a smoke, though they could not see if it had come from a chimney: it was dispelled, as if with effort, in March: to depict, in that rising search of its own nonbeing, the poverty that had generated it: or to dissolve in the rustic solitude that pang of daily need that those who feel it are wont to call hunger. The perennial, insisted name, the desperate diphthong of the horned owl had fallen silent in the night: had died with the dawn. From an unseen elm, now, perhaps from a Roman oak surviving the axe in the emptiness of the countryside, the intermittent appeal, the unreachable, imploring iambus of the cuckoo. In foretelling the new fronds to the earth it seemed to recall the eternal, lost seasons, to ache with spring.

Lavinia begged the corporal to leave her "outside," to wait. "Outside where?" There, or rather: "here. Otherwise they'll start thinking that I . . . that I turned my own cousin in."

After some negotiation the corporal consented, reluctantly: and he added a word or two suitable to the occasion: cards on the table. He engaged the buggy for the return trip: set the bicycle against the bank, which at that point, beyond the dip in the road, marked the rise of the grassy land again: he charged the driver to guard it. Having arrived with the trusty Farafilioro, at milestone 20, they were received by the furious barking of a lousy mutt whose eyes they could barely see, but whose spare, canine teeth they saw with fear, he was so fanged and hairy, half-spinone,

half-Maremmano hound* and half sonofabitch (this was
Cocullo's ideogram), but fortunately, on a chain. An old
woman appeared, contrary to all credible hypotheses, in
that panorama of deconsecrated railway; she tried to calm
him, to silence him, then came to the bar: which interrupted
the road, to signify, if not quite the imminence, at least the
expectation of an extraordinary phenomenon: that is, the
black passage of the train, the puffing of steam above and
below, marvelous fluid, which confers virtue and locomotory
quality to freight, even in ascent, as well as to train 181,
half-freight, half-passenger: which, in fact, already gasping,
announced the slippery play of its crankings up up up pup
pup pup from le Frattocchie, overwhelming the distant
imploration of the cuckoo: and at signal kilometer 20, it
would be equally victorious over the grade: a miracle of art,
an unterminated four per cent incline, but all curves and
countercurves, of the late nineteenth century. At the house,
known to some as Casal Bruciato, it was awaited every day,
once a day, with the algebraic certitude and the trepidation
of spirit that, at the speculum of Arcetri or the Mount
Palomar Observatory, every seventy-five years, attend the
recurrence of Halley's comet. The old woman, decrepit
though she was, must have understood at once that this unwanted olive drab-and-black visit . . . looked for all the
world as if it were aiming at her house! so she sewed up,
without parting them again, the two bloodless rims of her
lips, the two curly hairs embellishing here and there the
jawing of her chin, and left to them, to the Brothers Grim,

* The spinone is an Italian hunting dog; the Maremmano is a
large white sheepdog.

304

the initiative of paying their respects, to the older and higher in rank of the two. In the meanwhile, without giving any outward sign nevertheless, she made an effort to swallow the event, this, of the three arrivals, which she most feared and abhorred in the torment of her viscera: by hastily recommending herself in prayer to Sant'Antonio di Padova loving miracle-worker for all of us, and also, however, in another plea to the good offices (automatic in her former days) of the *plexus haemorroidalis medii.* She arrived, in fact, at the deliberate constriction of the more celebrated rectal rings, extenuated though they were by advanced age: not entirely inoperative, though more and more crumbling with the years, were the so-called Houston valves, chiefly the super-valve of Kohlrausch, nor the semilunars of Morgagni. The desperate attempt to block the ampulla, whose constricted extreme ahi ahi ahi already the olive drab–black–silver trauma was affecting, in concomitance with the shrill whistle ahi ahi of the arriving engine, achieved nothing more than the release of a few drops, rather phobic, plonk, on the platform of Casal Bruciato: free on board, yes, F.O.B. Casal Bruciato, though some may say and, however, write C.I.F. (cost insurance free) and some P.L.O.P. The providential lack, under the crotch of the old woman, of that pair of tubular correctives of nakedness which our most exquisite reporters today habitually call "intimate garments," allowed the event to fall out on to the pavement, unobserved by the Grims. Filing forward, one after the other, by the pedestrian passage to one side of the bar, the carabinieri advanced in silence on the platform with heavy, nailed footsteps to the door of the house: as if they were unaware of the woman, believing her engaged in the exercise of public duties and by now dealing with the train. But they were deceived: they encountered there the potato-white face and the resolute bursting forth of a girl who had taken up, from a bench, a kind of rolling pin for preparing pasta in the home, but wrapped in a red and green cloth: and at that moment more green than red.

Meanwhile there approached, really, the puff-puff at full tilt: its headlights aglow even in this daytime hour against the darkness of each new tunnel: the only train of the morning, in that direction. It was coming up from Ciampino, all black, with the self-importance of a nasty fireman, sending up into the heavens cannonades of brown smoke from its spout and then, all of a sudden, white steam, certain comical foof-foofs which seemed so many shots inspiring one to say, "but what's come over you? What have they done to you?" and below, from a pair of cylindrical bags, one here, one there, as if it had a mustache on the ground floor. Whirled and somersaulted, gleaming and greasy, the connecting rod and, like a maddened knife grinder's, the crank, with an odor of burnt oil, in the tragic ascent of the grade constructed by Engineer Negroni. It was like a man who plants himself in front of you, wants to call you a bastard to your face, and unable to run because of gout, he spurts out his anger at you from his nose, and at the same time, from his feet. Beyond the house then, on the gray path flanking the flight of the gravel, two or three highly frightened and yet— *more insolito*—unhurried hens prepared to follow the track in accelerated fluttering: to cross it then, in flight, at the most opportune moment, with the cowcatcher upon them, and above the cowcatcher, the headlights, with that suicide premediation that distinguishes their species. The Maremmano hound or spinone hurled himself forward: one could believe he wanted to choke or self-guillotine himself with his collar, a slender ring of iron where his hair stood up, in wrath: and, the chain taut, he began to yelp and bark again in reiterated, frenetic explosions: as if he declaimed impetuous verses of Foscolo without understanding their sense, nor even their nonsense, to a public overcome with sleepiness; meaning to reawaken them all and to summon them to repentance and vigilance, nor to forgive sleepiness to the least of them. The demoniac idiot, in doing this, became lost between his sparse, distorted incisors and the ferocity of his canines and omitted from his lips, in whitish ribbons at each new jerk of his head, a pulpy drool like béchamel: in the arsis of such dewy rage, raising bloodshot bestial eyes to heaven, as if to invoke the approval of the supernal Beasts, the gods of his race, and to propitiate their chief divinity, and to encourage their consent to new and more foolish hendecasyllables. That which, cretin that he was, he considered his inderogatable duty amid the shoes and the puttees of the carabinieri. Those bilious petards of his rancor were lacerating his accursed gullet, of which—at moments—to the soldiers' hesitation, he exposed the cavernous flush, like the gaping jaws of hell: and seeing the fowl running before the streaming black monster, his vehemence was redoubled to the point of paroxysm and seemed, at a certain point, resolved to follow and even to compete with the hysterical biddies: but solidity of chain and charity of cord, or indeed string, restrained him, though not without effort. For which the hothead went on bobbing, without idea and with no gain for himself or for others, at every explosion from his throat: cerberus on leave upon earth and on the hills, where he had planted himself to work, guzzling their unmerited light, the gentle air of their open sky: *coeli jucundum lumen et auras.* The puff-puff was just about ready to pass. The wind which rose from the swamps seemed tired, its wing drooped in the daylight: but a whirr, again, of a wren, from a bush up to the rusty rainspout, or the broken flight, higher, and the conjugal cries, in reply, of two nestless jays. The girl with the potato face brushed the two characters aside, as if they were cards with a low face-value, and in a gesture of intolerance like a maiden rudely accosted, twisting her head in a grimace, she advanced with her instrument, to the platform: where, having grasped the implement with a steady hand and in a posture of attention, she planted it against her belly, at precisely forty-five degrees. That rolling pin with green skin now blossomed from her person, and it was, from its rough trunk, a sprout of exceptional vigor, and to hell with who might or might not see it: it was a standard not hers. The engine driver's blackened face was already thrust from his cab, to note the color of that bud. A stage Moor, an Othello with a black skier's cap. The puff-puff was the mixed train: the only one that came by in the morning: pieced together with three freight cars, of various age and structure, and two passenger cars: where the faces, the mops, and the shining eyes and mouths of the more impudent and the happier, or of some dope with more prestige than usual, gleamed at or hung from the windows, snickering. Or they leaned out, some of them, with half their chest and arms, in the gallant farewell of a waving hand. They mouthed with shining, lascivious mouths fugitive madrigals to the girl: their words were indistinct, but certainly filth: they were a swarm of soldiers discharged at that time, in that era, but even in another era, the same would have occurred. "He has his stick straight!" Cocullo was able to reconstruct, after a moment, in the rattling of the train that was already passing, and he clenched his teeth, paling with contempt and reddening higher up, between cheeks and chin. And they would have added another refrain for the carabinieri: if the train, which seemed utterly out of breath, hadn't gone so slowly. It was heard now creaking in the brake block and grating in its undergreased threadings, in descent: the Negroni grade, number 71, was followed, after the straight stretch of the station, by the counterslope of grade number 73, still Negroni's work: which had the fame of offering itself like a moorish odalisque filled with participating consents to the untangled enthusiasm of the mechanism whereby the puff-puff, freed from suffering and now silent in whistle and piston, would abandon itself, freewheeling, to the Mussoline glory of a first-rate derailing with consequent disabling of its own features and others', if it had not provided for the contrary, in fact, with its brakes. The air had become somnolent and seemed to stagnate over the ground. The little train was disappearing, made smaller, towards tall caravans of clouds: among the reminiscent shadows, fragments, crumbling walls, of a history not its own. The plumes of smoke which it had left behind after the bridge (of Divine Love) and before reaching the station, at the altitude,

barely, of a swallow's flight, had been dispersed a bit from
their track and hung now, white and useless, on the damp
green of the unploughed fields. The hens, as they did every
day, had survived the drama: for years, now, the ex-pupils
of Melpomene had arranged in an algolagniac, theatrified
ritual, in a scene "for Nordic tourists" the most foreseeable
and preventative breaches of their first and youthful error
of clucking and squawking for a mere nothing in an
hebephrenic crescendo: and they had adapted themselves,
instead, in a carefully chosen poetics, to silence and to the
vagotonic pallors of the mystes. Their orphic initiation,
little by little, had become perfected to mastery: it had
reached the climax of a pictorial wisdom, forgetting the
acoustic bravuras of puberty. A half-extinguished or dozing
and nevertheless always available and recovered voluptuousness reawakened them every day, with the toiling up of
the train and with the whistle, to the familiar fiction: to the
artificial excitement of the victim whom no one threatens, to
the precipitous fluttering and dash along the track and the
breach, to the attempt at flight (will Delagrange fly?),*
to the simulated suicide with the headlights upon them and
the concomitant dispensing of a couple of bonbons, puff-puff
passing. Though feigned was the orgiastic movement, the
little gift could not be feigned: thus, as in the theater,
feigned passions release kisses that are not pretense and the
cuckolds of the stage seem to be, a majority of times,
cuckolds in fact. Every day, every morning. Then, no sooner
had the locomotory entity completed its apparition, released
its huffs, then, having unwound the reel of their obligatory

* Delagrange was a French aviator who gave flying exhibitions in
Italy. "Will Delagrange fly?" was the headline of his publicity poster.

fright, they went on scratching about as if nothing had happened: and as if they were uprooting a weed, with a plunge and a prompt recovery of the head, the neck, pecking from the earth the rare worms.

The brief caravan of the tympanic importuning, railroadward, having passed, and almost extinguished the mad animality in calamitous growls and snarls, teeth clenched in rage: I'll show you, I will, Pestalozzi also forgot the old woman: behind or within whose empty and badly hung skirt, tatters with appendices of threads, he had seemed to hear some devilment grumbling, or some toad gargling. There was no evil spell, as at the sorceress's shop, but perhaps *jactura*: preterintentional. Yes. And he interpellated the girl directly. "Are you Mattonari Camilla?" He recognized her as a seamstress of I Due Santi, but hadn't known her name: the least elect, the least "friendly." He drew from his pocket, twice folded over, and slowly unfolded with official decorum, the sheet: in legalitarian justification of his question: the list of topazes already displayed in the shop. "Yes," she said. She was a medium-sized dumpy girl with pale gray skin that looked like greasy paper: a flat, rather potato-like face, little eyes, tan, drowned in the redundance of suet. "Do you recognize this?" and he put the ring under her nose.

"How should I know? Why should I recognize it?" she shrugged.

"Your cousin Mattonari Lavinia states . . . that she was lent it by you."

"No, no, she's a big liar. I don't have anything to do with it."

"That she picked it out," he improvised, "from the others that you have."

"That liar! The nerve! She probably got it from her boy friend. I've never had a ring like this in my life . . ."

"Like this! You mean, however, that you have others, or some others, different from this one. I want to see them. Show me where they are. And who is your boy friend?" but he neglected to linger on that quite ordinary image of the boy friend, completely gripped, now, by the idea that the fat girl was lying to him, that an almond or two, in some hole, she kept hidden. "And, while we're about it, why didn't you go to work this morning?" The girl, lips white, with the gesture of a robot, raised the pin with its double skin, and with eyes avoiding the corporal's glance, as if to say: "through the fault, or merit, of this here."

"Yes, I see that you've got that flag in your hand: but . . . are you the signal-man? Is that what you're trying to make me believe?"

"No, my uncle had to go down to Ciampino, to the office. He's the chief here. But when he has to go someplace, then I stay here for him."

Chief, in her lexicon, meant signal-man.

"Let me have a look at the other rings, if there are any: at your corals: all the jewelry you have: your Sunday earrings."

"Jewelry? I don't have any corals, not even earrings. What do you think? Poor as we are, hungry all the year round?"

"Your uncle is a government employee: you work as a seamstress, when you work. Let's not waste any time. Show me what you have. If the stuff is yours, nobody's going to touch it. And if it isn't, I have a search warrant. And if we start searching and then something funny turns up . . . Seek and ye shall find: and if you find, you have to report to the superiors. I hope I'm making myself clear. I don't know if you know the regulations . . ."

"What regulations? I don't know what you mean . . ."

"The re-gu-la-tions," he shouted, "the law! what the law says!"

"Sorry, Corporal, I don't follow you."

"There's a law, right? And a list of regulations, where it tells us what to do, how we're supposed to proceed. We . . . have to obey the regulations. So watch out. Don't force me to search the house," which was, really, no more than a cabin, "or the room where you keep the stuff . . . your things. It would be an aggravating circumstance for you: Article 788": (788 my ass: he invented it on the spot): "the article is clear as a bell." The girl peered at him, now that she was a little more self-confident in answering, her big tan eyes set in the pork fat of her eyelids, with the miserly hesitation of the peasant who demurs at opening her mouth, between fear and suspicion. The old woman had acted as if she had things to do in the garden: and had gone down there with a little hoe which was heard intermittently striking the ground. The dog, its snarling passed, still stared fiercely, with that zeal peculiar to the stupid.

"If we have to do the searching," Pestalozzi added again, "it'll be worse for you. I told you. Seek and ye shall find. You understand me?" The squat girl, as if the corporal had pointed a pistol in her face, shook herself and turned, walked away like a somnambulist, went into the house—or cabin, as may be. The two men followed her. From that telephone booth-*cum*-kitchen which was the ground-floor room, they went up, on steps of gray peperino, to the floor above, into a smaller room, irregular, as required by the stair well. It was occupied by three beds, and ill-furnished for the rest. Pestalozzi and Cocullo, after the girl, could barely squeeze into it. A smell of clothing, if you call clothing the lipoids, the amino acids, the urea, the sweat, in short, in which the clothing of the poor is steeped: a window with a grille and mosquito net: no furniture, beyond the three beds, which seemed three pallets for dogs, and a minimal little cupboard with a scalene fragment on it, of a mirror long since broken forever. On the wall, over one of the little beds, with a little olive branch with shriveled leaves, in its dark frame, a two-lira oleograph, yellowed at the edges, which Pestalozzi recognized on the spot. It was the Madonna del Divino Amore, over the postern of Castel di Leva, who had appeared to the tormented man lost in the night, pursued by ferocious, barking dogs who were about to claw and tear him apart, but who at the sight of Her fell back: and the fence enclosed him.

The cupboard, half-wardrobe and half-dresser, emerged from beyond the third bed, between the edge of the mattress not of sweet-smelling corn husks, but responsible—with the other two—for that so "human" sultriness, and the recently whitewashed wall. It looked as if it received, collectively, those futile items, those tangles of yarn, those odd buttons, those lozenge-shaped rags, of which the good women of the *campagna* and of every other part of the fatal peninsula are cautious collectors, fussy savers towards the improbable needs of a tomorrow where neither yarn nor string is, since there will be nothing to bundle up. Pestalozzi glanced at it, the humble item of furniture, but without special interest.

"Well then?"

"There," murmured the potato: more with a jerk of the head, since she had little chin, than with a movement of the lips, motioning below the bed, the second one. Moving around it, they discovered and, moments later, brought up a coffer: a little wooden box, bound with dark tin at the edges. The girl armed herself with a key, produced as if by magic, then crouched to reach the chest with both hands, from under the bed. Her face and the full part of her bust lay slightly over the tan blankets: she groped like a blind woman, and a knowing one, gazing straight ahead until she had mastered the removal of the parallelepiped, then as if guessing rags, at random with the divining gestures of a blind musician gifted at striking on the piano the right keys, to erogate from the keyboard the pathetic squadrons of his blindnesses. She took out the chest, opened it. "Go ahead and search, Corporal: there's nothing there." And then, since the corporal didn't move, displaying in his face how much the goatish hovel already disappointed him, and how much his nose was repelled by it, she raised the lid, scraped up a blouse or two, a shawl, some black stockings with white heels, a cardboard box, a man's shirt, the best one. "And the ring? Where is *your* ring?" Annoyed by the chief deduction of the corporal: "you mean to say you have another one": she opened the little bicarbonate box under his nose: raised from it, as from a nest of cotton batting, a poor little chain that seemed of gold, with a light cross which also seemed gold: a brooch with a fake coral, another metal pin with an enamel four-leaf clover.

The corporal took the chain with two fingers, spread the others to hold it out, and let the cross dangle: then the green-enamel pin, as you pick from the hawthorn hedge a butterfly resting with its wings closed, to restore it to its flight. "You mean to say you have another one." She had told him no. Now she didn't consider it licit to contradict herself, or in any way to recede from that negative stand. The oily, motionless, stubbornly statuary quality of her physiognomic attributes helped her meanwhile to leave her tongue in repose. Pallor, suet, and potatoship, those two buttons were stuck in it as if into a mound of dough, two round cheeks which looked as if they'd been hit by a good pair of slaps, all her best features, in other words, allowed her to stand there silent and mindless without a word: simulating only an apprehension which, perhaps, disturbed her but slightly. The corporal had eyed the cupboard. He was about to say to her: "turn over the mattresses! let me see under the mattresses! And instead he navigated about the beds and came, after his not-easy periplus, to take his stand between the last bed and the wall, in an attitude as if he were going to interrogate the bedside table. He pulled at its door, noticed that it was provided with a lock, an incredible thing for a night-table: it was a *sui generis* commode. He asked for its key. The Signorina Mattonari looked under a mattress, found it: she opened the cupboard with a greasy sadness in her face, like a loyal citizen harassed by abuse of authority. Rags again, woman's stuff, a waistcoat, a pair of worn pants spilled down onto the floor, for the disappointed knowledge of the noncom: they had been placed in there all anyhow, pressed in at random. He picked up with one hand a knitted bodice, a rabbit's skin, a pale blue undershirt with lysol-whitened zones. Two or three walnuts rolled out. Then, from the rags, there emerged, all decked with worn socks, a chamber pot. Filled with walnuts, and with more than one dent in its enameled convexity, one saw at once that it wasn't a piece of Capodimonte, nor even a Ginori. "Ah Gesù, my grandmother's walnuts!" la Mattonari cried, as if to bestow value, in an expression of possessive anguish, on this treasure: which the autumn had deposited in the capaciousness of the vessel, *en passant:* pilgrim who pays without farewell, before dawn, the debt of the hospitality benignly received. And she started, at the side of the standing corporal, to bend over and take up the recipient and to remove it, animated—so it seemed—by the best of intentions. She meant, with that gesture, to smooth the path for the Requisition, for the Aggravation, for the hard Cross, the Law. But the bloodhound's evil phlegm had already scented the Hiding Place. "Stop! You take it!" he ordered Cocullo. The girl stood up. The trusty Farafilio bent down. He introduced both hands into the cabinet: to seize, with the one, the brimming chamber pot by the handle, to press it respectfully from the opposite side with the palm of the other, as if caressing its kindliness. so rotund on the opposite and non-handled hemisphere. And he extracted it from the tabernacle (and it was heavy as it rarely had been) in the position proper to the user, or even to the owner, who prepares at night to employ it for its lower purpose. An eighth, a ninth walnut rolled out. Too scarce, then, for the almost boyish opulence of the brave soldier, the olive-drab tunic freed for public view his posterior rotundities, properly covered with cloth of the same color. Emphasized by the crouching position, they seemed to emulate and to surpass completely the smooth rotundities of the pot, as if a pump had swollen them, the kind on a tripod, that bicycle mechanics have. The incredible fullness was about to burst—so it appeared—the median rear seam of the trousers: which seemed, instead, only to loosen, in the taut zigzag of a line of reluctant thread, of a blue-green color, darker than the green of the cloth. The seam being pressed beyond its capacity, the breaking point was not reached. A sharp shot re-echoed in the room instead. No: it wasn't a revolver's bullet. Farafilio, poor boy, very probably blushed, with that patchy manner of blushing that he had, in his good, but severe face. Crouched as he was, his face against the commode and the pot in his arms, the purple did not spread. The humble duty had expressed itself: that was all: certain postures favor certain nomenclatures, as if eliciting the sound from the very sources of the same. The girl remained silent, amorphous. The corporal's brow became clouded: in the silence. Brimming, meanwhile, and heavy with every most dried gift of Vertumnus, the lousy pot was elevated to the honors of the top (of the commode), whence the gleaming fragment of mirror had been slightly removed. The maneuverer stood up, without turning around. "Dope! empty it on the bed!" the corporal said, harshly. The maneuverer obeyed. In his half-turn, the visible side of his face was shown papered with alternating zones, islands of flush and pallor: the flush a bishop color, the pallor the color of cheese. He also proved to possess, to an eminent degree, that property of the good, the generous, the honest: the faculty of blushing all the way down the neck. He set slowly, then quickly overturned the vessel where he had been told: with his hands then, all around, diligently confining. Of that treasure of nuts, the silliest, not yet unleashed, would have jumped down with multiple hops and cretinous festive rolls, going to earth, one here, one there, in God knows what corners under the beds: had it not, in fact, been for the hole, that is to say the imprint of the body in the bed itself. But they were screwed. All together, they fell into it, as into a casserole, making a neat pile. On the peak of which there was a little paper packet. Of blue wrapping paper, as if from the grocer's. Sugar, probably: a secret store of granny's. Moving from the other side of the bed, with impatient fingering, the corporal unwrapped it himself, that little packet. There appeared, then, a tiny sack of rough canvas: not swollen, and yet heavy and variously nutted at the bottom, in which there was merchandise: hazelnuts perhaps? or a little collection of buttons? or a rosary? choked, towards the mouth, by the tight turns of some string, then knots and double knots. Pestalozzi felt it. His face became illuminated: by the dawn of "this is it." The punishment that he had mentally comminated to his pupil evaporated from his thoughts. Half a lip curled, upwards, in a grimace of contempt: as if to render more explicit the features of irony: of his irony. The tangle of the many

319

knots was untangled by persistent use of nails: the tightness of the twists of string loosened to clear the path: from the undone sack, overturned, in turn, with every precaution, but on the grandmother's bed, the middle one, there landslided down, as if comforting one another in this unexpected exit and fall, little green balls, medals, brooches and carnelians, gold bangles, chains, crosses, filagree necklaces, tangled one in the other, and rings and corals: rings distinguished by rare stones, or shining with a single gem, or with two of different colors, before the open mouth of Cocullo, to the pounding of the corporal's heart: who could already feel the new chevrons climbing up his sleeve, to replace those now there. Sergeant's chevrons, this time. The objects froze, like little frightened animals, ladybirds who fold their wings, not to be seen, in the wretched lap of poverty; and instead, they were seen: they were seen as so many unmasked lies, recognized by the jeweler with the hooked nose, on the counter, after theft and recovery: of every most curious color and every form: a little cross of some semiprecious dark-green stone, which the fingertips of the future sergeant could not stop savoring, turning over and over: a handsome, shining little green-black cylinder, for interpreting horoscopes by the shitty priests for Egypt more than Pythagoras drew ravings from the apothegm of the pentagon, standing towards the west to blather, to gaze at the tops of their baked pyramids: mysteriosophic candy, concealed in the ancient womb of the earth, seized from the earth's womb, one day geometrized to magic. A poor little egg between pale-blue and milk-white like a little gland of a dead pigeon, to be thrown in the refuse: and

two earrings, with two big drops a sky-blue, isosceles tri-
angles, rounded at the tops, dangling and weighted, with a
marvelous felicity-facility, for the lobes of a boobified
laughing girl dressed in blue: who in one of their almost
transparent striations laughed enriched, as if by wisps of
gold enclosed there, to freeze. And a heavy ring, a gold-
bound cylinder which had circled the thumb of Ahenobarbus or the big toe of Heliogabalus, with a big caramel
orange-green, then a moment later, lemon-color: pierced
by all the rays, slightly, of the equinoctial morning as the
tender flesh of the martyr by his hundred and ninety arrows: perfused by pale-green lights, like the sea at dawn,
to the brightness of flint: which made the two men dream
at once, spellbound, of a mint syrup with soda in Piazza
Garibaldi at noon. And a little ring of golden thread, with a
red pomegranate seed that a chicken might peck: and a
final bangle, a tiny bauble, like a little ball of methylene
bluing to get the yellow out of the wash, held by a little
gold cap and by a pimple: and through this, attachable, by
a golden link-chain, to another and equally essential organ
of adornment, whether to the swelling beauty of a breast,
or even the male fold of a lapel or the paunched and gold-
watched authority of the protector of this breast, adminis-
trator, moderator and, in the last analysis, husband, "and
damn fool!" thought Pestalozzi, his teeth clenched. A
garnet cross, dark red moments of domestic shade. Rings,
brooches: unbelieved marvel. And the ruby and the emerald
shone and lay in the trench of the little mouse-skin bed,
fellow tenants of the moment with the verecond ambages of
the pearl, on the worn and almost ragged tegument of that

old woman's couch: amid the precious gleam and the twists
or polygons of the gold objects that kindled the minds,
after the pupils and the retinas. Pins and earrings were
tangled in the little chains, or mixed up with one another,
like twin cherries amid the twinned stems of their sisterly
couples: the pendants, in the immediate cataract, had taken
the rings with them. Ruby and emerald took on a name
and a body on the gray poverty of the cloth, or of the
tatter, in the closed mute splendor innate in certain beings
and signifying their rarity, their natural and intrinsic dignity: that mineralogical virtue which through false fanfares
and winks is trumpeted so often, in trumpeting carnivals,
by so many bits of bottle-bottoms, as, in said *derrières*,
the quality is totally lacking. The corundum, pleochroic
crystals, revealed itself as such on the rat-gray of the
ambience, come from Ceylon or from Burma, or from
Siam, noble in its structural accepting—splendid green or
splendid red, or night-blue, also—of the crystallographic
suggestion of God: memory, every gem, and individual
opus within the remote memory and within the labors of
God: true sesquioxide Al_2O_3 truly spaced in the ditrigonal
scalenohedral modes of its class, premediated by God:
despite the value-work of the Gadfly.* Gadfly di Revello
who was to last in his chair for an hour, chief economist
of the Turkey and cock-minister of his screwed nonfinances:
which, at a wink from the Big Cheese himself would have
revealed to the Italians the new heaven of the flaskable

* Paolo Ignazio Maria Thaon di Revel, Mussolini's Minister of
Finance, 1935–43. "Gadfly" is a play on the words *tafano* (gadfly)
and Thaon.

values, substituting in the zodiacal band of credit and monetary circulation, for the gold standard which then went to Hell to be liquified, the scorpion of humbug which we'll never be rid of again. And the Italiener from that fiasco-flask, drank greedily in big gulps.

Pestalozzi, no, he wasn't a Minister of Finance of Italy: and neither was la Menegazzi. Both of them had a certain sense of value and nonvalue: she, if for nothing else, to be able to satisfy the whim of forgetting in the bathroom all about value (the topaz) inasmuch as she wouldn't have got any pleasure, in any part of her dithyrambic and trembling body, in forgetting in the bathroom nonvalue: a bottle-bottom. Jewels they were, those resplendent rubies, that was obvious, incubated and born in the originative millennia of the world. The expert could check and guarantee this, despite the cuts, the faceting, the polishing of art. Gems crystallized naturally from fused sesquioxide, following the principles of the system: and not a crystallized pretense in a light, a glory of falsehood, from a basin of excrement. As the impetus, the grief of a soul freezes in a cry, coagulates in notation, following the formal processes of thought: in a frozen cry! which is its own, and not the bawl of another, or of the market place of bawlings and of souls. The corporal scattered them with his fingers, with the gesture of a cook sorting rice before throwing it into the pot, scattered the stones, the jewels, the gold ornaments, the fabulous caramels, shining gems of the Maharajah in the depression of the miserable blanket. Of those appearances, wisps of gold or luminous grains on the dark color of the drapery, a dotted line stood out, like a string (seen, however, from above, and from afar, from a mountain or a plane) of electric globes in the curve of the Riviera: such as the illumination of Botafogo beads, in the bananiferous nights, all around the base of the Pão de Azucar. Those jewels, at that moment, seemed to burst and play over the bed from the mingled amassment of diverse thieving coups. But Pestalozzi, with a certain applied hesitation at first, then with smug certainty, thought that he could gradually recognize, in that scattered splendor, the debatable and ultradesired pearl necklace, two or three bangles, an amethyst, the garnet cross, the ball of lapil-laruli (so it was written), the corals, the jewelry, possessors of the names and the descriptions which figured, colleagues and brethren of the topass, in the first and following lines of the first and second sheets of the Martinazzi list, or rather, to be more precise, the Mantegazzi. Owners of the names and the titles, in general use, in some cases a tiny bit difficult: ring "of" ruby with two pearls, brooch with small black pearl and two emeralds, pendant "of" sapphire, as one might say of pastry, "surrounded" with brilliants, carcanet typed as carcanot, then corrected to carcano, of garnets in old (sic) style, string of (the *o* a hole, of course) white pearls (quite fake) et cetera, small ring et cetera, large brooch with onyx stone et cetera. A good reading exam for the aspiring carabinieri's course, thought Pestalozzi.

Time, meanwhile, was pressing: that very morning, before noon, he had to return to Marino with the topaz in his pocket and with everything else he had managed to recover, in his wanderings so intensely fruitful of gems, gold, false pearls, girls pretty or ugly but all equally lying. Of the recovered, the found or not found, he had to render an account to the sergeant, list in hand: the names were strange and difficult, with something magic about them, mysterial, Indian: with all those holes, like so many punched railroad tickets, in the place of every *o*. The second list, incomplete because a sheet was missing, but no less pocked than the first, seemed to him, on the other hand, a pain in the ass, a lousy pain that didn't concern him at all, a job deferred to another, since officer Ingravallo, that big head who instead of brilliantine used tar, had said "expressly" that he wanted to deal with it himself. So that was Don Ciccio's business. Typed on a red ribbon, as if the ribbon had been dipped in blood, the list of the "Balducci stolen property" seemed to him materialized from a nightmare: sheeted and reported in pages from a secret horror which was not, on that mad equinox morning so filled with prognostications, no, was not the carabinieri's responsibility. No, the solitary country outside, dampened by the squalls of rain, barely eyed by the sun awake from time to time, no, it didn't want the horror re-created: which clothes, after the sudden flashes of the knife, all condonation denied life by the beast, the immobility of the funereal relic. Before the eyes of the concierge and the police (even before the ascertainments of the law) or of the terrified cousin who had come in without knowing, so he said, then among the carpet slippers of all, men and women, a whitened simulacrum for the wax museums of death: and that putrid ichor, down from the rent throat, the days following, in an odor of morgue. What he had recovered were jewels and gold "from the door opposite," the jewelry of the blond countess, in any case: and in the successive flashes of a dreamed (not seen) image, the corporal sighed. And fantasticating already that he would appear before her in his sergeant's stripes, in the guise of recoverer-savior, he tried at the same time to untangle himself from all the serpents of doubt: ". . . but perhaps some of the others, too, from the iron coffer of the murdered woman." He didn't waste time checking. By now he was in a hurry. Over any possible gems of Signora Balducci, with that half-recovered list there, the ambiguity of hypothesis hung still: the recognition and division of the individual items were to be carried out in the barracks, up at Marino, or perhaps in Rome at Santo Stefano del Cacco, while the jewels of Countess Mantegazza, which were individualized in the relative list, claimed each one, with prompt evidence, its stolen identity. And then, to tell the truth, his reason began to compute the remaining probabilities: in an hour and a half two lucky coups like this, a topaz on a finger and a chamber pot full of topazes, were even too much from the miserly cornucopia of Luck. A third stroke was not acceptable to the precogitative statistics of the mind, eager but still hesitant, dubious. The girl and Cocullo were waiting, immobile, as if drained of any capability of following: the corporal shook off his hesitation.

"Who gave these to you? Who brought them here? He didn't give you these as a present! Not you!"

"I don't know. This is the first time I've seen them. I don't know who put them there, in that place."

"Tell me who gave them to you. You know. Or who gave them to your grandmother . . . your uncle. The cabinet was locked. You put a lock on it. And you found the key right away."

"The lock's always been there. We keep stuff in there."

"Some stuff! Tell me who brought it here. You know. We already know: we've known who did it for a long time. In Rome, too, the police officer knows. Talk. You'd better confess, tell the truth; we don't have much time. If you won't make up your mind to talk here, then you'll talk to the sergeant, in Marino."

The girl remained silent, pensive, her eyes in the void: the potato of her face, the two tan marbles of her irises, the colorless lips betrayed no inclination to utter a word: like a rustic sibyl, or like a jurisprudent citizen, from whom a previous oblation had not elicited response. She was silent, in the silence, outside, of the country, of all the solitary countryside: the personification of an irreparable refusal. A stone hysteric, to whom the uttered falsehood has become truth and so will remain even under red-hot irons.

"Come to the barracks then. There they'll get it out of you, you'll see. Want to bet on it? The sergeant'll make you spill it."

The jewels were re-sacked, a nice handful: and plucked one by one the evasive ones, the centrifugal, peripheral ones. The corporal did it with his own hands, then with his fingers, paying careful attention not to abandon to the blanket a single grain of the "stolen property." His lips slightly parted for the task, and breathing heavily through veils of catarrh, the Farafilio, like a chilled lamb observing a laparotomy, held the bladder of strong canvas: introducing into it, to guarantee exhaustive reception, two gynecologists' thumbs. They tore up the comforters as if to unmake the beds, covers, sheets: not white, and even less smelling of corn, as the poet Pascoli would put it. She had collected the walnuts with the pot, like bailing water from the bottom of the boat, or as if emptying the trough. They also looked under the beds, made her overturn the mattresses ("Come on, Signorina, the air's good for them"), empty completely the cupboard of pants and worn socks, and the top, moving them. They groped at the mattresses, pulling them to a sitting position on the springs and, the first, over the two benches on which it was normally extended: with the little finger they broached the meatuses, with the big, or middle, finger, the rips. The Croesus chamber pot, from one bed to the other, was like a new mother, so thin and diminished, after having been so full. On the wall the green-reds of the Miracle, last year's little sprig with the dry and curling leaves, some silver-gray, others gray or greeny-brown or even havana color, as if the charisma that filled them had evaporated with the changing year. And below, at last, on the platform the light of a desolate knowledge, or at least, of glimmering. The evil, to the two dressed in gray clothes,* seemed to exist: to ripen days and events: since always; silent force or presence in a pandemonism of the country or of the earth, beneath skies or clouds which could do nothing but look down, or flee. It had evidenced itself in that sensation of alarm, of loosening of every just bond, which gripped their

* Cf. Dante, *Purgatorio*, XX, 54: "Save one, who gave himself to the grey dress" (Binyon translation, a reference to the last of the Carolingians, who became a monk).

hearts as they came out: at the sudden reappearance of the
town, of the racing cloud-bank, in the sky. The devil, for
the girl, had turned into a hen: the one that, in the garden,
plays ignorant, and cautiously lifts its foot, then replaces
it, to peck, to shit a bit here and there. One of the three
hens, but which? And so, near home, between one stubble
field and the next, the devil tempted with an egg per day
(and it could never be known which, of the three, had laid
it on that day) in the poverty and the solitude of the countryside without grange, tempted souls: then he reported
them to the sergeant, to the informers of the Lord: pretending, he the devil, or she, hen, pretending all day to be
merely intent on scratching, on hunting for grubs. Certain
roaches, certain worms. And as soon as the train was heard
puffing, he let himself be seized by that fear and hope of
having it upon him, and on the girls, too: to keep from
understanding which of the three, and *who* it was: being
the devil. Devil, there was no doubt about it, and spy,
imagined the girl holding out a horned hand towards the
chickens: spy, spy: having insinuated himself, in disguise,
into the home, that rural, railish home, there it is, there
he is: he swaggered around like a chicken, with a chicken's
manner: like a gent with yellow gloves on the Via Veneto, a
glass in his eye, a white flower in his buttonhole: he de-
loused a shoulder, with his beak, all proud of himself, then
the other one: he shat along, like it was nothing, but he
took advantage meanwhile of the convenience of being a
chicken, looking to one side, just the way chickens do,
making bold to peek into the kitchen, if the door was open.
He even came inside, maybe. And nobody sent him away:

the uncle was telegraphing to Ciampino or to Cecchina, tap taptap tap sitting at his machine. So he could spy around at his ease. He recorded with his mad pupil and retained in his retina: with that lateral eye that chickens have, like it was invented by Picasso, a bathroom porthole, a toilet void of understanding or any intention of spying to starboard or to port. And instead they're looking at you. Yes, he was the devil: worming his way into the kitchen, on the helpless tiles of the domestic poverty: or in ambush beyond the cane fence: little canes artfully stuck into the ground, with two opposing slants to make the figures of rhombs, ripped by the pouring rain and by the wind, half-broken and half-rotten, now, at the end of winter: a worn girdle, now: which does not isolate the domestic indigence, at kilometer 20. 25, from the open access of the country. The grandmother, amid the hens and the stubble, was like a humpbacked tree in the garden, a sorb already skeletal in death: set up as a scarecrow, one day, and then torn to black tatters by the north wind. She gave the earth a blow with her little hoe, then left off, tired, without straightening up. With four strides the corporal reached her. "I found what I was looking for," he said to her. "If you were the one who hid them, you'll have to give me an explanation . . ." She raised her face, which seemed carved from brier: she looked at him without understanding, without even hearing.

"She's deaf," Camilla warned him. They telephoned to the uncle. They wanted to tell him: Camilla had been "called in" by Sergeant Santarella, so they said: she had to "report" to Marino, as a witness: the signal-house would be left unguarded. The old man expressed no opinions and still less raised protests, over the phone. He made no comment on what they let him know. He was already about to come back to Casal Bruciato. There wouldn't be any more trains going by, Camilla knew that anyway, until the mixed train for Ciampino-Termini at twelve fourteen.

The old man, in reality, at hearing an unknown voice, was seized with panic. At the telephone, the girl explained harshly, when it wasn't a question of service communications or calls, he was infallibly seized with a paralysis of the basioglottis, or as she put it, he was tongue-tied: like an engineer, little inclined to speechifying, who moves perfectly his abacuses and yet hasn't at his disposal the "sufficiently appropriate words" not to say sufficient Italian verbs to be able to petrarchize over news that is far from good. A typical *aphasia coram telephono*, reverence, spite, incapacity of expressing himself properly, and the suspicion or indeed the obsessive certainty that one can be overheard and naturally mocked by third parties, by unknown imbeciles, and finally, the loss of one's own personality and the pulpifying of the logos in a flushing stammer, flowed or stagnated, endemic, in Europe, and, therefore, in the Italian peninsula of those years of *telèphone avec la manivelle*. In the campagna, in the country, you can imagine! Her uncle was a railroad man, ha! like the daddy of Lucherino.* And, rustic widower flabby though still fierce in the face, before he had his hut beside the tracks.

* A Gaddian private joke. Originally the phrase went, "like the daddy of Vittorini" (the novelist Elio Vittorini is, in fact, the son of a station-master). Then, afraid of offending a fellow-writer, Gadda changed the name to the mysterious "Lucherino."

He was born illiterate, like all of us; but where there's a
will there's a way: and by strength of will he had learned
his letters: he could read the tape like it was nothing at
all and he could tick away with his key. He mastered and
shot from his belly the multiskinned banner, like a lordly
esquire, at the Palio, the banner of the Torre, the Tartuca,
or the Oca.* Born timid, yes, vis-à-vis the black vulcanite
cup, he gulped saliva, rather than pour into it the clamorous
chatter of the day: he emitted cautious monosyllables: and
few even of those. The grandmother was left alone to await
him: alone, not counting the dog, the hens. She would have
waited also, in the full assumption of official position and
in the exclusive manipulation of the green club, good for
signifying proceed, for that little train from Velletri at
noon. The girl, one would now have thought her no less a
deaf-mute than her grandmother, was led to the crossroads:
where, awaiting the return of the carabinieri, the buggy was
standing: and Lavinia, above, seated, huddled, throat and
cheeks in her two hands, and her elbows set evenly on her
knees, her chin extended, lips drawn, and her mouth in
an attitude of contempt. Such a posture granted her, beneath
her arms, sufficient room to lodge there and almost conceal,
disdainful now and intolerant of glances, the tepid weight
of her teats: though the arch of each armpit still allowed
their profile to be seen, if one glanced there, perhaps without seeming to: as did Farafilio, in his palpitation, a little
later, as soon as they came up to the buggy.

* The Palio is the famous Siena horse race, where different sections
of the city are represented, each with a special name and device:
Torre (tower), Tartuca (turtle), Oca (goose), etc.

The proprietor of the horse was seated, beyond the ditch, on the rather high edge of the field in which the road, even today, is sunk, looking pensively at the ground: mouth open: his shoes in the dry culvert. He seemed to be speculating on human destiny and forebodings: he allowed his mind to graze in the limitless meadows of nothingness as utopists and lanternists are wont, having created the void there: that sweet Torricellian vacuum that the disturbed mists and the fogs of the equinoctial morning heighten, if anything, to an inderogatable condition of the life of the psyche. Curiosity had pricked him at once, on seeing Lavinia with the soldiers, then had been calmed and completely satisfied when, left alone with her and her horse (but the horse couldn't follow well the discourse of more than one voice), he had asked her about the case. Lavinia, bitter, had annihilated him in a few words, a process in which she excelled, and had huddled down in the position described. So, he, now, was mindless in peace, staring agape at some blades of grass: a thread of saliva was about to come from a corner of that unretentive meatus, filtering, from below the inert tongue, to drop on to the cobbles. His two shoes planted on the cobbles of the culvert, legs apart, his˙elbows on his knees, his whip extended from his ten basketed fingers, which held it slackly: and it seemed the staff of a flag from its socket on a balcony, or the tacit pole of the fisherman over the lake's silence: not did its handle rest on the ground, but instead of the ground, in a superfluous fold (immediately beneath his waistcoat of rawhide) which his trousers formed at jointing: so that it jutted from his lower crotch, like a faunesque stump gradu-

333

ally lengthened into a bending twig, in a thin and dropping splinter: like a patented contrivance, a private and personal organ, antenna or pole, disjunctive attribute of the radio-amateur-fisherman, or conductor. And all around the hanging twitching of the splinter (swaying with the wrist) a horsefly abandoned himself to his habitual goings and comings, which indicate a greed for footstuffs, perpetually awake or reawakening, and of the achieved spotting, that is, scenting, of the same. It buzzed nosily in a metallic vibration which reached top notes with certain swervings or counterswervings in figure 8's: drunk, almost, at having forced itself by the renewed fatality of a *sui generis* field of gravity: a field excogitated, for the new history, by the Buck of the young horseflies: where the ellipse of the Newtonian orbitation had been replaced by the lemniscate. He was one of those handsome green ones, with wings of metallic ash-green that recall burnished steel, devoted, as soon as he has it made, that is, when someone had made a turd, devoted to sumptuous pauses, and to ineffable epulations in the meadowed paths, in the unlofty corners of the territory: *du vieux terroir.* Wracked by precocious puberty in the muggy weather and by pubic nose in the equinox, in that cosmos of prescient odors (foretelling the spring fertilizing) he restored himself with the idea: of the tail of the whip. Who knows, the lout, what he thought it was?

The two cousins had glimpsed each other from afar. The trio, the new hope of Regina Coeli and her two great angels a little behind and almost at her sides, proceeded as a group. When they had approached the buggy, the proprietor stood up, and briskly raised his whip high as if a fine mullet had taken the bait: Camilla faded to a greeny-white: "It was you," she said softly to Lavinia, as she came within knifing distance of her, with the Brothers Grim at her ribs: the driver cracked his whip in the air, to reawaken the horse, and prepared to climb in after Camilla, in whom a hysterical malice from moment to moment was deflating the resultant inflation, *empâtée*, of the various volumes of the face, that abscessed consistency which with puberty, the two oily balloons of the cheeks, had assumed in her, to become all one with the cushions of her cheekbones. Her eyes, carved into the potatoish oval, had begun to react, gleaming in a white ground, to make themselves seen. Rage was giving her a gaze, lending her a face: "Me?" said Lavinia, "have you gone crazy?" Hatred, contempt, and also fear in that voice, in those words, which corporal Pestalozzi made an effort to intercept, then, in vain, to interpret. A slight breathiness, in her speech, a shy caesura. Her breast palpitated, most desirable, like a magnetic blade between the two poles: but this was not the magnetism of Maxwell, and the blade was instead of milk-colored skin, trepid and dear. "Me?" and she shrugged, "they're taking me in, too. We're going to have a little trip to Marino, to be witnesses." She raised her neck, haughty. "I have to tell you how it happened, when he, the corporal here, thought I was engaged, with the ring on my finger." The explosions of the whip reannounced, almost gaily, the advisability of being silent, of leaving. A little further on, at the high edge of the field, two little open-mouthed girls were looking on, with long underpants and shoes, without laces, that had belonged to their big brother. A strong man,

335

a peasant, was trying to light and to draw, twisting his neck like a plebeian painted by Inganni,* half of a half-cigar. "Get in," the corporal said to Camilla, "and stop talking: and don't try to work something out between the two of you, because it won't do you any good anyway. We already know the whole thing, how it went: and who gave them to you." The pocket of his tunic could be seen swollen, over his hip, on the right, as if to create a symmetry with the holster, as if to counterweight the encumbrance. "Go on, get in!" he repeated. Camilla obeyed. The owner got in after her, on the other side. The springs, perceiving his capacity, creaked again, and this time with their habitual zeal: then they were silent, quite flattened, crushed. The corporal, bicycle in hand, prepared to follow the buggy: which turned to the right, after a suitable turning of the wagon brake, like the pommel of a coffee grinder, after a last crack of the whip, a geeee from the master, a straightening of ears and a pawing of hooves on the part of the quadruped, a slap of the tail between the buttocks, after which it did not fail to start off. At a walk, that is, the walk of an old jade, going uphill, with three people. The road, in fact, rose: the bicycle, as soon as Pestalozzi pressed the miracle foreward, began again to chew, to gnaw on its torrone. The faithful Farafilio was to chew the road on foot. To enter that basket, with their full endowments, the two girls had to pack themselves in with some effort, so that they leaned, one against the other, at the shoulders and their respective thighs, like two fat quail, twinned on the stick, in the pan, to make a single generous portion: the driver

* Angelo Inganni (1807–80), a painter from Brescia.

supporting them on the one side, Camilla—as a counter-thrust—on the other, had clutched the lateral iron bar of the seat, fearing to fall out onto the road: that iron which was an available anchorage, the only one.

"Yes, it was you, you lousy spy," she said in a low voice, in a wrath greener still than her face. "You're good at flirting, I know. For a moment it suited him to see you every now and then, that pimp of yours."

"My fiancé, you mean," and Lavinia raised her head, resolutely, with the sudden dart of the snake, looking straight ahead, as if to avoid even the sight of her traveling companion of whom she yet perceived the hateful warmth, the odor. She twisted her lips, slightly, continuing to despise.

"No, no, fiancé my foot: he's not going to marry you, that's one sure thing."

"You want to take him away from me with money, you're so greedy, nasty snake, you. To get a taste of a man, you have to buy him, like the schoolmistress. But you won't get him away from me. You're too ugly, with that face like a potato of yours. And you're too tight: with that two cents you've saved up—you want to get him away from me?"

"*They'll* take him away from you, don't worry."

"You can leave them out of it. And yourself, too. I made him swear. I had a fight with him. 'With her? You think I'm crazy?' Go on, you potato, you. Go hoe the field, you ugly witch." The owner of the buggy kept his mouth shut: from time to time, to assume a casual attitude, he carefully cracked the whip in the air like a postillion in a cloak on the box, humbly clad in his flea-colored jacket as he was, inciting the horse with a a-ah! After each crack, on the contrary, he seemed intimidated: like the feeble-minded or certain children who fall silent when their parents quarrel because they can't understand it all, except for a frightful aversion, a hatred whose motive is hidden. He didn't know much about women. Woman is a great mystery, he used to say, on Sundays, at Le Frattocchie, at the Marinese's, sitting astride the bench, or in the summer under the arbor, with his elbow and with the half-liter of wine on the table. You have to study women carefully before you start anything, he would asseverate at I Due Santi, his glass half-drained, before the bar of the striped white marble: because Woman is a mystery. And Zamira pitied him, from aloft, with all the blackness of her mouth, half-disgusted, half-compassionate, drying her hands on her apron, which she sometimes wore, though dirty. And once she even answered him: "It's a mystery you can understand right away, if you just have a little imagination." He didn't understand them much, he said. And perhaps he didn't understand anything very much. With these, with one of them at least, but which he couldn't recall, he must have played when she was a kid. But he hadn't understood anything even then. He stood there, crestfallen, waiting to be fed. Now, when he came upon one on the road, sometimes, but never on his own initiative, he agreed to give her a lift.

"You're a lousy whore and a spy," Camilla resumed, anxious that the fight shouldn't end. She was enraged by the love of which she had been defrauded, even more than by the treasure that had been confiscated from her: what she already was calling "the jewelry for my wedding," the pledge of love, in any case, there, had ended up in the hands of the carabinieri, "damn the person who ever invented the stuff," she cursed, clenching her teeth.

"A lousy spy, that's what you are, bitch. Stinking bitch." The man in the tight jacket fired his whip aloft, said "aah!" to cover this altercation with his voice.

"They can hear you," he warned, without turning, in an attempted whisper that came out grainy with catarrh: and at that he became more timid than ever. He kept his eyes on the road, beyond the tips of the horse's ears which served him as sights, though double ones: because he felt, suddenly, the corporal's burning: eyes and ears alike.

The horse, at every new crack, did its best to seem to be engaging in a trot, which remained brisk for a few paces, then slowed down. The girls were silent. Lavinia, finally, was weeping: her beauty, her arrogance: crushed: so expert in the pride of loving: indeed, in being sought after for love. The young man who had given her the ring, that stone all light which seemed to be sublimated from the buttercup—where was he? where was her boy friend, at this hour? A knapsack over his shoulder, a knife in his pocket: a flash, a clump of light hair in the wind, like a handful of straw that suffers no comb: after having betrayed her and despised her, *her*, poor thing (and her tears, almost, were sweet), to go down to the station at Casal Bruciato and put gold all over that shit.

"That shit who's warming my thigh now."

Oh, Iginio. The carabinieri had caught hold of him by the scarf, but he, quick as a wink, had already slipped from their hands. That lousy pistol of his, he never dreamed of

339

shooting it, but just kept it to defend himself: and now, as if the rest weren't enough, he had hidden it, buried it. Thank God. But now it's not buried any more. Some gun! Good enough to scare the countess. The cap? Ha! He had it in the pocket of that sack thing he was wearing. The law, no, they couldn't put him in jail three years because of a green scarf and a cap, and an old pistol, all rusty and useless. The knife . . . *Madonna Santa!* he had been wrong to use it, on a married lady . . . in her house, if it was true that he was the one who did it. And a chill sweat, a shudder of revulsion and anguish now gripped her again at the thought: it was horrible. And she dried her cheeks, her eyes with a filthy rag. The fat sergeant from Marino—and she wiped her little nose—how had he figured it out? How had he guessed everything?

Because of the scarf, all right: but that scarf can't speak. And the ring with the yellow stone, how had he learned that it had been Igi who gave it to her? All of a sudden? And that she and Igi had exchanged their promises three days before, after almost a year that they had been going together, so that the ring . . . he had been the one to stick it on her finger, forcing it on her? "The ring's mine, isn't it? And you're my girl, aren't you" he had said, and had kissed her with a fury! . . . it was enough to scare you, almost. But the corporal, though, how had he managed to guess? Ah! Could he of been hiding behind a tree, behind a bush, right there, when they had said yes to each other? Or had somebody else seen them and told him about it? Had Igi gone around telling about it, the way men brag? (and her heart leapt with pride). Well, it wasn't too good for him to talk, either. And besides he wasn't the kind who likes to do much talking. You couldn't get much more than an um or an uh out of that mouth of his, that mean-face. Well who? Some girl from Zamira's? There were three of them now, sewing there: she herself went almost every day: Camilla and Clelia, maybe every other day. Camilla hadn't opened her mouth, for sure, with her dirty conscience at having taken the goods, all that gold and those stones: sooner than talk she'd do better to jump in front of the train. Clelia? Clelia liked those big carabinieri: to her they seemed like so many handsome devils, she could dance with them all and say yes to one every month, that was obvious: even a blind man could see it. But to turn informer to the soldiers and tell on a girl friend, a fellow worker! "Or maybe it's another lousy lie of that corporal's," and she glanced at Pestalozzi who was struggling upon his musical bike, "that lousy northerner, who wants to make sergeant no matter what? No: it would never pop into Clelia's head to inform on anybody. She walked her legs off to get a bowl of soup at night, and a cot, all the way to Santa Rita in Vitacolo: she was too far away, and in a place that was too open. It was already dark when she got home. And besides what? She'd be risking something herself. If Igi—just supposing—if Igi happened to find out, that she had talked! He wasn't above breaking her bones for her." And she recalled in a kind of somnolence barely illuminated by flashes, in a leap of her blood, in the hammering of the blood in her ears, she remembered that the sergeant's bike, the fat sergeant's, they heard it spluttering a little all along every road and path, raging at the closed crossing, annoyed, as far as Torraccio, Ponte,

341

as far as Santa Palomba, where the radio poles are, and sometimes yes, even as far as Santa Rita in Vitacolo.

But what did that mean? It was his job, running around on his motorcycle day and night, to go and visit his poor, to see how they were getting along . . . his chickens: that's why he wore those double chevrons of silver. "That's all he can think about, tearing around the day and night with his bike, you might say: and when he's done, he goes to bed: he plays the radio: and he has seven women who listen to it, besides himself."

Spies were not lacking, certainly, closed in the torpor of her mind and senses, from which Santa Rita had already evaporated. The sergeant, from confidences gathered the day before, had, according to her, succeeded in extracting (now she dreamt) how one Retalli Enea alias Iginio had become engaged to the beautiful Lavinia from whom with his infinite promises and a face that made you scared, he had obtained some advances. "Advances?" "Yes, some paper," answered the spy, without a face but with every certainty of the feminine sex, since she wore a shawl and skirt, "and especially . . . don't make me come out and say these things, Sergeant, you know what I mean better than I do." The ring—it had been he, Retalli Enea, who had given it to this beautiful Lavinia in a strange moment, as if he were going away: clasping her to him, kissing her furiously on the mouth, on the eyes. Or perhaps, that faceless apparition went on to say, and exhaling a word not human, to be rid of a trinket that was too risky to carry on his person, in those circumstances, and with the intention of collecting again one day, when he could move more freely. "But where were you when you saw them?"

"I saw them," answered the phantom of the lonely road, "I saw them from that pink house where you come up from Torraccio, where I go and do some odd jobs every now and then." "But if you were inside the house, and they . . . they were about their business outside, on a path. No, it doesn't work out right." "Sergeant, I saw them from the window." "From what window?" "From the window of the toilet": and Lavinia's mind was lost: real images become deformed, filtered through a tired, yet clairvoyant drowsiness. "You should go and look. It's a toilet, where you can see everything: motorcycles, the men working by themselves on the vines, and the carts, and the donkeys . . ." "And what were you doing in there?" "Sergeant!" He took her hand. "You swear?" "I can swear to that, all right, don't you worry!" she said then, and it wasn't clear with what lips she spoke, this fearsome mannequin: over which a shawl had been thrown, on which a skirt was hung. A girl, she was: and for a face, an oval, like the wooden egg for mending socks. The topaz had appeared two days earlier on Lavinia's ring finger (of the right hand) amid the amazement of all the girls. "My God! what's that on your finger?" to whose questions, to whose exhortations, "come on, tell us!" she had smoothed her eyebrows, "wouldn't you like to know?" and had shrugged her shoulders, piqued, then blushing as if content with this praise, this expression, all too clearly, of envy. "Don't show it around too much, Lavinia," Zamira had warned her, "with all these horseflies, we have buzzing around here, these days, buying smokes."

Pestalozzi had stored away, that morning, not only his immediate superior's commands, but also this hypothesis:

the engagement ring! and, naturally, the double list of the Rome authorities, as he called them in moments of detachment. His superior was careful not to say "I have been told that . . .": he had limited himself to the formulation of hypotheses, few and limpid: one more reasonable than the next. He found himself now, as he chewed along the road, forced to integrate one of these hypotheses, that topazesque engagement, in the light of the new as well as unforeseen results. The topaz, in the possession of Mattonari Lavinia, all right then, "supposing that Retalli gave it to her." But why and how had all the rest gone, instead, to the potato, to Mattonari Camilla? A pledge of some kind? Not so much a pledge of love, perhaps, as, for example, for some small loan of money, of which Retalli Enea was always in need? "Other than the job of being unemployed—he's no good at finding other kind of work," he thought, brutally, like that sociologist he believed himself to be, like that carabiniere he was. "And besides, he must have been in a hurry to get away!" the sergeant had postulated this, too. He must have got off the morning before: he had certainly gone into the country. Or had he, instead, headed for Rome, along the roads? How did the sergeant know that Retalli had flown the coop that day? They had spoken in the evening, in the barracks, when he, Pestalozzi, had come back from Rome, almost at midnight. Ha! He knew a thing or two, the sergeant did; he had pawns everywhere. A sixth sense! A nose! If only he, Pestalozzi, in time, could succeed in having a scent like that! "Let's see now," he brooded, to himself, his eyes on the ground, forgetting the two quail, "let's take a good look. It's time to pass the exam, Guerrino:

use your head, Guerrino. If you work things out right and carefully, this is the time that some silver'll drop on your sleeve. You'll be transferred, that's for sure: to Gerace . . . Marina's likely too. It's a little further from Orta than Marino (Latium) is: but they say, they swear, that the air is healthy there, too. And they have figs . . . and prickly pears. Ah well, moving around Italy, is our life. Let's see. Let's use the old head." And he plodded along. The sight of that countryside, so desolate in March, which with the return of the sirocco and of the wandering rains, from the shore, now, reached a cleansed clarity at the Castelli, at the houses of humankind, suddenly fascinated him as if it had appeared magically: the cubes and dihedrons of the houses crowned it at the peak, the cenobia, the towers. A moor for the mirages of solitude, a moment. But on high, ahead of him, the populated villages, the tram: along the consular road. Behind, he knew, the clay hills drained to-wards the dune the lashing rains: there, fear: the closed horizons of the little valleys, their weary marshes, the reddish mire where the canebrake thickens, a cold green color, a chill without shelter. Here and there, unforeseen, on the withers of the hill, an old tower, to scrutinize and recognize one who for months hadn't passed that way, but today, yes: with a roof of a single slope, like a cap over the eyes, walls baked by the relentless summer, faded by the brothy gusts from the southwest. Dried again by soli-tude. The signal-man's house, where shortly before he had so copiously harvested, the corporal thought on his bicycle, could have offered to Retalli Enea alias Iginio refuge and shelter, if only for a moment, on the first lap of a flight that

345

was anything but impossible. Along the main highways, like the Appia or the Anzio road, there was police surveillance: motorcycles: patrols, perhaps, from other carabinieri stations: and then the coming and going of the red-painted wagons which came down, in those days, with the barrels of new wine loaded in a mountain-like pile (for those who saw them from the side). And gardeners, early in the morning, and men carrying fresh ricotta on their donkeys with their gay bells: and trucks, from time to time, all spattered with mud and the night's rain, with their gross drivers in the cab like helmsmen, behind the pane, in their black oilskin jackets, their grappa-red faces, in their fox collars: those could clearly see anybody on the run, even if they don't look like they're watching. All of these, by now, had read the papers, with the two crimes in them. Resting, on the other hand, only a moment at the signal-man's, Iginio could then reach Casal Bruciato, cross—or not cross—the Ardeatina, slip off unseen under the sandstone ramparts which create the invisible security of Ardea, and create also, for the goatish lupercal god, a cave and a home: or, a divergent hypothesis, he could reach in any case the Rome-Naples train, at Santa Palomba Station: like a day-laborer looking for work, wait for the train, the poorest of trains, a *diretto*, the poorer of the only two that stop there. Or else . . . Pestalozzi suspected at last, doubling the horns of the dilemma, if he was out of breath or lacked money for the train, he could take to the country towards Solforata and the great thickets of the prince,* in the direction of

* The prince would be Prince Torlonia, owner of much of the land in this area.

Pratica di Mare. From there, come out on the shore: and, in easy stages, begging bread from the fishermen's huts, reach Ostia . . . or escape to Anzio. And then who could ever find him? Right. But couldn't he have taken the train to Rome? And money, at the ticket window? Who could have given him the money? . . . Lavinia? . . . What about Camilla, why not her? It was more likely that the ugly one had given him the money."

Musing in this way, he was finally aware of the road: they were almost at the Anzio crossing. He concluded then, leaving all his doubts open: it was his sergeant's exam, this; in the barracks the beans would spill forth. But the spirit, or the devil, of the "reconstruction of the events" hammered at his temples. Retalli . . . here's why he had left the stolen property at the signal-man's house. It was a place . . . which no one, perhaps not even Sergeant Santarella, would have been capable, of guessing: there was the ugly fiancée, there: ugly and sure. And the countryside all around, deserted. He must have decided to flee on the spot, after having caught some random word, in the discussions of the people, or read a headline in a paper they were reading. The jewelry . . . no, he couldn't leave it at his place. (A few hours after he had become "a fugitive from justice" they had searched his house.) They would have found it. It would have been the proof, imprisonment. To take it with him, if they should stop him, was no less dangerous than shutting it in a drawer. And so, there. To escape, to keep a safe distance, took money: and for the train, too! Camilla, perhaps, had some, could give it to him: she could cough up . . . a bit of the ready: and he would leave her, as a pledge, all those sapphires and topazes, of course, he would have given them to her.

But Camilla whimpered about being so poor? The corporal's mind became confused. Every hypothesis, every deduction, no matter how well-constructed, turned out to have a weak point, like a net that is unraveling. And the fish then . . . good-bye! The fish of the impeccable "reconstruction." Retalli, in a far shadier level, must work like that blond boy of Ines', like the Ganymede Lanciani, who had been the blond—and invisible—god of the interrogation at Santo Stefano: and in this rather withered collection, the greed of the search was stilled. Ganymede was a more easily filed denomination, in the archive of his memory, than Diomede was.

The girls, in the buggy, seemed to be quarreling again: they went on, in fact, exchanging vituperation in low voices: with cheeks like she-devils, hysterical witches: but the upper hand seemed to be hers still, the more furious in the eyes, the more contemptuous of lip, the more beautiful. Dying of curiosity, the severe Pestalozzi listened, but did not hear: the creak of the springs, the rasping of the bike, an occasional exploded admission from the ass of the tugging horse, prevented him from enjoying that altercation, as excited to see as it was in fact, in reality: without counting the disturbing snaps of the whip, and the aaaah's of the simple-minded driver, who seemed every time to wake with a start, from his diver's lethargy, to emit his voice, quite uselessly: since the horse, poor beast, more than what it was doing, could not do, nor its kindly ass explode. No, he couldn't hear, the corporal.

"Because you have a bank book with a couple of lire in it," he heard all of a sudden, and put one foot on the ground, "that's the only reason, ugly as you are. That's why Igi lets on he's engaged to you. Go on. You're one of those girls that if she wants a boy, she has to buy him with money." And she spat, overshooting with her projectile, the helpless knees of the driver, who said aaah! but in vain, because his intervention was belated: and then because the horse had stopped and had already planted his legs apart for an unforeseen (to him, the master) need. The corporal's face relaxed; his spirit was consoled.

"Yes," Lavinia shouted, venemous, "you were fed up with giving him money, after all you had given him before, so he thought he'd leave that stuff with you. A guarantee. You bought it for two thousand lire—you told me so yourself!"

"Liar, witch, whore—if you want to be a stool-pigeon after all, you've got to tell the truth—because lousy spies like you are no good to anybody, not even to the people who pay you." "Ahoy, girls," Pestalozzi said, resenting the slight respect in which the cousins Mattonari seemed to hold him: "now what's got into you? You can fight it out at the barracks. The sergeant will be overjoyed to hear you both talking at once: he'll let you go on arguing till midnight and after, don't worry. Once you're in the coop, you can peck at each other all you want. But that's enough presently. Cut it out." Where he comes from they say "presently" rather than "now." They say it in Rome, too. So the argument of the two furies died down, faded, like thunder that becomes calm, fleeing, on the marvelous lips of

Lavinia. The Farafilio, on foot, arrived overheated, his face flushed, except for the cheese-colored patches which whitened, as if for a belated confirmation, his jaws: just above the neck. He dragged after him, with some difficulty in the climb, that little balloon, so *court-vêtu*, so uncovered to the caprices of the equinox, that it recalled the old story, of the regiment confirmed (not to say baptized) by fire.

> *Le bon vieux grenadier*
> *qui revenait des Flandres . . .*
> *était si court-vêtu*
> *qu'on lui voyait son tendre . . .*

The horse, in the meanwhile, had finally regained his composure; and a definitive aaah brought him back to his job of tugging, before the good soldier came to learn the cause of the stop: which, from the distance, might have seemed a wait, ordered of the driver through the kindliness of his superior, and thus an act of clemency and total pardon granted him, Farafilio, in person. But, having glanced at the little hippuric lake, and sniffed the sweetish and still tepid steam that emanated from it, he displayed in the rubescent skin of his neck and the *ad hoc* zones of the face his reproof, his contempt. That little equine stop had been demanded by rude nature, but a blow of the whip might even have obviated it: there were two women present!

X

Iɴ the same hours of the morning of that same day, Wednesday, March 23rd, when the search for Enea Retalli alias Iginio had proved vain at Torraccio, where he lived when he lived there, Sergeant Santarella cavaliere Fabrizio was riding on his motorcycle over the provincial highway from Marino to Albano, so stupendously shaded, or flanked by trees, in the gardens and the parks which cover the slope. March finds a part of them bare or tattered, the elms, the plane-trees, the oaks: others have green fronds by the Feast of San Biagio or San Lucio: the Italian pines, the ilexes, the serene and almost domestic friendliness, in the villas, of the laurel, where, in other sites, the academician is crowned and, in some cases, the poet. From more than one indication, or clue, there was reason to believe, or at least not to reject the idea that the young man had headed (approximately) towards Pavona and Palazzo, moving down along sideroads and paths, when the roads proper seemed, in their way, unsafe. He also had a soldier on the rear seat, the good sergeant did, and armed, not to say embarrassed, with a musket. Having turned into a no-more-than-vaguely-indicative tune the seven syllables of the Touring's anthemer, his thoughts pursued the fugitive, who, with some advantage over him, had used the romantic "go!" proceeding by now at great strides beyond the confines of the "condition of unrecoverability." That phrase, that incitement, the sergeant-devil went singing to himself, between nose and mouth, yoking its bold (and equally imagined) rhythm to the explosions of his motor. Of the two soldiers stationed at the fort he had asked for reinforcements, by hand-cranked telephone, and knowing them to be equipped with a machine, that is to say a bicycle, he had ordered them to Pavona.

Quite different, on the other hand, and of a different life, crowded with a different and more densely settled people and populace, inscribed with other toponymics, ennobled with other names, amid the august ruins and the Umbertine grayness of the six-story houses, and the hindered and therefore bell-ringing rolling of the tram, was the working atmosphere of Blondie: his field of work and of leisure, of after-work and work-after, where he carried out his dandling and absent-minded (to hear him) technique, loafing, peering at random, sniffing, at a whim, a caprice, and the lucky wisdom of the urban idler who allows himself to be guided by the silence of every hypothesis and of every disjunction, like the sleep-walker on the rainpipe; he, instead, in the full agitation and the constant bumping into one another of people, as they go their way: after the bars, the shoe shops, the stores of soap and washing soda, along the fences of gardens with oblique palms beyond, yellow, whipped in the winter, tormented under arid skies, in changeable weather, by the very certain tridua of the north wind. The fountains, the basilica of Santa Maria della Neve, and the arches and the fornixes in the surviving walls, the cubes of peperino and of sandstone: recalling Tullius and Gallienus and of Saint Liberius Pope, among the invitations of the chestnut vendors, black-fingered over their braziers, their face serious, smoked, all wrinkled towards commerce, and the non-invitation of the waiting taxi-driver, huddled in his glass confessional: the charioteer of whom it might also be said that he is waiting (a call, an order) if his genteel snoring had not by now cut him adrift, far far from every less aware expectancy.

After the broad cantata, and especially, after the closing aria and coda of Ines, about the benediction that the bell of Santa Maria Maggiore had imparted to Ascanio's little theft, "I'll see that kid tomorrow morning," Blondie had said to himself: and he had liberated, at the exit, that huge yawn which had been wandering in his throat for two hours, like a caged lion, and right away he had sheltered it with his hand, as Doctor Fumi turned to him: "you take care of the boy. Have yourself a stroll on the Esquiline, and then in Via Carlo Alberto, go yourself. You're sure to pinch him in Piazza Vittorio, after those Faraglioni* there." Ingravallo had assented, grim: he would have gone himself, if he hadn't had better to do: and better he had: "You're sure to catch him. The girl was clear enough."

The following morning precisely at ten Blondie was on the spot (after having taken a little turn among the palms): that is the hour when the housewives are used to doing their marketing, with a view not only to supper, but more especially to the midday dinner which is their imminent

* Piazza Vittorio Emanuele, Rome's market square, has in its center some Roman ruins that resemble the famous *faraglioni*, tower-like rock formations near the shore of Capri.

353

care: the hour of the mozzarellas, the cheeses, the vermi-fugue onions, and the cardoon greens, patiently hibernating beneath the snows, the spices, the first salad, baby lamb. Of people selling roast pork there was a tribe at the stands in the square that morning. Starting with the Feast of San Giuseppe is its season, you might say. With thyme and the bows of rosemary, not to mention garlic, and the side dish or stuffing of potatoes with crushed parsley. But Blondie, his head hanging, allowed himself to be led among the cries and the red oranges by his loose-limbed optimism, whistling softly, or merely pursuing his lips, suddenly silent, casting an eye here or there, as if by chance. Or else he stood still, inconspicuous, his Homburg halfway down his forehead, hands in his pockets, his chilled back under a light-colored and rather lightweight coat, open, and with its two sides drooping in the back till it looked like the tail of a full-dress coat. It was a phony, between-season topcoat, which inclined towards the hairy, and to the soft, and proved worn in many places: it helped create the image of a drowsy wastrel, looking for a butt to smoke. Wrapped in the vortex of invitations and incitements to buy and in all the conclamations of that cheesy festival, he moved slowly in front of the lambish stands, passed carrots and chestnuts and adjacent mounds of bluish-white fennel, mustached, rotund heralds of Aries: then in short the whole herbarian republic, where in the contest of prices and offers the new celery already led the field: and the smell of the burnt chestnuts, at the end, seemed, from the few remaining braziers, the very odor of winter in flight. On many stands yellowed, now without time and without season, the pyra-

354

mids of oranges, walnuts, in baskets the black Provence plums, polished with tar, plums from California: at the very sight of which water rose in the back of his mouth. Overwhelmed by the voices and the cries, by the shrill comminations of all the lady vendors together, he reached at last the ancient, eternal realm of Tullus and of Ancus* where, stretched on carving boards, prone or, more rarely, supine, or dozing on one flank at times, the suckling pigs with golden skin displayed their viscera of rosemary and thyme, or a knot here and there, green-black, within the pale and tender skin, a leaf of bitter mint, set there as if to lard, with a grain of pepper which the cry praised in the hubbub: "a new little gland lent them in the kitchen, to other markets and to other fairs unknown." It wasn't hard for him there, given the stern wind of optimism which was driving him amid the whirl of women burdened with brimming shopping nets or bags, fringed with broccoli, it wasn't hard for him to recognize, from Ines' description, even at several paces' distance, the character, the trumpeting little kid that he wanted. He looked like a smart one, behind the stand, with a pair of eyes on him! the contrary, at that moment, of the fear and timidity that Ines had exalted, and with a thick mop of hair, supergreased, all to one side: he was standing with his grandmother. At the peak, falling a bit over his forehead, the strands of his hair had become curled like fresh salad after the capricious retouching of his comb, or like the roll of a choppy sea's wave, when it bubbles up for a moment before tangling and receding, and finally abandons the sand. A white apron bundled him up

* Tullus and Ancus, third and fourth kings of Rome.

slightly and while he yelled he was sharpening the knives, one long and one short, and at the same time looking at him, Blondie, but without any sign of seeing him: that big, dark blond head, with that Homburg like a dental specialist's which came down over his mug, who had taken his stand at proper distance, hands in his pockets: he was probably somebody who wanted to eat some pork, but if he didn't have any dough, poor bastard, he could die of hunger on the spot. "Get your roast pork here! Pork straight from Ariccia with a whole tree of rosemary in its belly! With fresh new potatoes, too, right in season!" (the season he had dreamed up himself, they were old potatoes cut into pieces, all dotted with parsley and stuck into the fat of the pig). "Potatoes of the season, ladies and gentlemen! better than hard-boiled eggs for salad! Better than capon's eggs, these potatoes, I'm here to tell you. Taste them for yourselves!" He rested for a moment to catch his breath. And then, exploding: "One-ninety the slice, roast pork! We're giving it away, ladies! It's a crying shame, that's what it is, ladies! You ought to be ashamed to buy it so cheap. One-ninety, easier done than said! Step right up, cash in hand, ladies! If you don't eat you can't work. One-ninety the slice! Nice, tender meat, meat for ladies and gentlemen all right. Taste it and you'll see what I mean: tender and tasty meat! If you try it once you'll come back for more, I promise you. You're the ones who make off of this deal. The lovely pork from the Castelli! We sent the pigs out there to wet-nurse, raised in the country, on the acorns of Emperor Caligula himself! the acorns of Prince Colonna! The big prince of Marino and Albano! who killed the worst Turks on the land and sea in the big battle of whatever it was. They still have the flags in the cathedral in Marino! with the Turk's crescent on them. Get your nice pig, ladies, roast pig with rosemary! and with potatoes of the season!": and allowing himself some peace after the spiel, as even the tragedian-actor rests after his role is played, he resumed, serious and composed, his sharpening of the knives. But after a couple of blows of the knives, he had a renewal of inspiration: a kind of jolt ran through him. It was the out-burst of another variation, or so it seemed to the policeman: "Try it, gentlemen, taste it! One-ninety: you can eat pig like a pig, and your wives will thank you for it!" Then, to a local beauty, lowering his tone: "What about you, pretty girl?" the girl, at that tone of authority, couldn't restrain her laughter, "a half-pound of pork?" And, *sotto voce*, to her, but with a glance at the penniless tooth-puller: "I'll give you the best part, that's a promise. You're my type, all right. You're too pretty! A nice little slice specially roasted for you, with a couple of potatoes!" Then again, eternally shouting and with eyes upraised this time and with cheeks of a senseless trumpeter: "Come on an buy this pork, every-body. Let's see your money; this is the time to buy it. It's a crime to leave the pig here on the stand, when it can rain again any minute, and I know you've got the cash on you. Don't be stingy now! The pork is yours, if you'll just dig out the old ready."

The grandmother, if grandmother she was, swindling merrily with the scales and with her chatter, now gave full satisfaction to the rubicund maidservant. And he: "One-ninety! This pig's pure gold!" But meanwhile that tooth-

357

puller of a Blondie kept on looking at him, after having pushed back his hat and bared his forehead, which appeared all aflame with a thick, unruly straw, somewhere between real blond and brown. At his sides two characters had turned up, two cops a lot darker than himself, one on his left and one on his right, like the silent gendarmes that Pulcinella notices after a while, in an alarm that is sudden, but belated in action. So that he, the kid, little by little, "ladies and gentlemen, one-ninety, get your roast pork, your pork, I get it!" he seemed to say to himself, his voice sinking lower and lower, "get your . . ." he muttered, cadaverous, "your . . ." and that little breath died in his throat: like a torch's light, more and more querulous and tawny, when it drips wax and dies, in a pool of stink, with the fried wick in the middle. With those headlights on him, all of a sudden multiplied by three. So, you can figure it out for yourself: when he realized who they were, it was too late to skip. He set the knives on the counter, muttered to his grandmother "they want me": and was already untying his apron. His legs trembled. He had to put a good face on it for Blondie, who, without letting the others see, had taken out a paper, a badge and said to him in a low voice, as he flashed it before his eyes, that fine talisman:

"You've got to come to headquarters for a minute; if you keep your mouth shut, nobody'll notice! These are two plainclothesmen, but if you'd rather, I'll take you in myself, without disturbing them to come along as escort. You're Lanciani, Ascanio Lanciani, if I'm not mistaken." So, to avoid any fuss, he had to abandon pork and knives, and leave everything to his aunt . . . his grandmother: she was there, hard, erect, with one eye, filled with uneasiness, on

358

the crowd, which went by, ignoring it all. He had an order to take the boy to headquarters, Blondie notified her briefly, and he displayed his document a second time: "Lanciani Ascanio" he added. The grandmother, the owner of the business, a middle-aged peasant woman, her hair still black, much thinner, in her wooden and wrinkled face, than her trade should have warranted, seemed uncertain what attitude to adopt: consternated no, but cross: "this boy hasn't done anything wrong, not a thing," she said, "why do you want to take him away?" Requested by Blondie in a low voice, she uttered her own name and surname, address, and showed him her license for the stand. She added, though without any enthusiasm, that she was a young aunt of Ascanio's Mamma. Blondie wrote this data on a piece of paper with a stub of pencil, then pocketed it. They looked like three cousins conversing: nobody paid any attention to them. They were from Grottaferrata, the grandmother admitted, reluctantly: the neighborhood of Grottaferrata, a little settlement known as Torraccio, after le Frattochie: but they had come to Rome eight years ago, yes, near Porta Latina, in the midst of the vegetables, you might say, a country road where there was barely a sign with Via Popolonia written on it, "it's where the truck farmers live, in the sheds. We live there, before the railroad tracks: this way," she gestured, "you can go down through the reeds to the Caffarella swamp."

"A little shed in the midst of the broccoli, and we grow artichokes too." Ascanio slept there with them. They kept him out of charity, in exchange for a little help there at the market. His father . . . ha, his father; his brother had been out of a job for two months. "We haven't heard anything from him!" Ascanio, they were trying to help him, poor boy, "the best we can." And she let him go with them, nice and quiet, upon assurance that they would bring him back to her, later. Equally anxious, on their part, to avoid scenes, not only for the customers but for themselves, the two dark-haired angels had moved away from the stand, were waiting farther on: the boy, white in the face after all his shouting, came around the stand, and his new cousin up to his side. This was Blondie's great art: with his head bowed shouldering his way through the crowd, he stumbled, as if by chance, over the character, *his* character: "Well, look who's here! What are you up to around these parts?" (*sotto voce*): "Tickling the ass of the working girls, or the men's wallets? If there's a button off their back pocket, then you've got it made: am I right?" Then, peremptory: "Let's go. The chief wants you: he's got something he wants to say to you." He took him by the arm, looking at the ground, as if he had a serious proposal to make to him.

They came out of the confusion towards Via Mamiani or Via Ricasoli: there was a passageway among the stands of the fish-mongers and the chicken-vendors, where they sell the squid and the cuttlefish and all kinds of eels and meals from the sea, not to mention mussels. The character, and Blondie himself, looked at those mushy polyps of a pale, silvery mother-of-pearl (so delicately burnished in their inner veins), sniffed, though involuntarily, the odor of sea-weeds from all the cool dampness, that sense of sky and chloro-bromo-iodic freedom, of bright morning on the docks, that promise of fried silver in the plate against the hunger that already could be called profound. Coils of boiled tripe, one upon the other, like rolled-up rugs, gentle anatomies of skinned kid, red-white, the pointed tail, but ending in its tuft, to signify—beyond contradiction—its nobility: "I'll give it all to you for four lire," the vendor was saying, holding it up in midair: all, that is a half: and the white clumps of romaine, or curly salad greens, live chickens with the eyes peering from a single side, and who see, each one, a quarter of the world, live hens, still and huddled in their cages, black or Belgian or straw-ivory Paduans: yellow-green dried peppers, or red-green, which made your tongue sting just to look at them, and made saliva come into your mouth: and then walnuts, Sorrento walnuts, hazlenuts from Vignanello, and piles of chestnuts. Farewell, farewell, a long farewell. The women, the plump housewives: dark shawl, or grass-green, a safety pin, undone, ouch!, to prick the teat of the neighbor a moment: *così fan tutte*. Self-moving pudges, they ambulated with effort from one stand and from one umbrella to the next, from the celery to the dried figs; they turned, they rubbed their respective asses one against the other, groping to open a path, with brimming bags, they choked, gasped, fat carp in a pool trap where the water, little by little recedes, jammed, wrung, trapped for life with all their fat in the eddies of the great comestibles fair.

Don Ciccio, in the meanwhile, had not been wasting time, either. Having got home at half-past midnight. "Monday March twenty-one, San Benedetto da Norcia," enunciated the calendar from its nail (year's end offering from the baker opposite) with the leaf of two days earlier which Sora Margherita had forgotten to rip off. A big drop of molten metal, the half-hour, from the clock of Santa Maria delle Neve. He went to bed, fell asleep, snored heavily, postponing all further deduction to the morning. When the angry trill broke loose, all of a sudden, in the silence of the sleeping house, bursting unexpected from that old turnip of an alarm clock self-moving on the marble (of the table) to announce the new headaches of the day, there, two knocks, discreet, from the landlady at the door, authenticated the furious admonition of the imbecile: despite the great longing that he had, in his head, to turn over and go on sleeping, they—clock and landlady's summons—dragged him to his feet at six. He slipped, hard-assed, and used to fall from the side of the bed, ker-plonk, like a peasant, on his heels. Stocky, and of sturdy legs, which appeared hairy from the knees down, from the straw-yellow nightshirt with little red parallel lines which bedecked him at night, he used also to repent *ipso facto*, even before he had appreciated it with his waking mind, that thud: which resounded on the plank floor, despite the wormy little rug, and announced his activist rising to the neurasthenic engineer on the floor below, by waking him with a start. Not even the north wind of the night, as he came home, nor, once in bed, the speedy breeze of dreams had been able to rumple the lambskin mop: black, pitchy, curly and compact: which re-resplendent in the new light, whatever Pestalozzi may have thought, did not require brilliantine. The knotty legs, the portion visible, emitted, indeed, arrowed perpendicular to the skin their hair, equally black, saturated with electricity: like lines of force of a Newtonian or Coulombian field. His eyes still closed, or almost, he slipped on his old slippers: which seemed to wait for him like two little animals crouched on the parquet: waiting for his feet to each his own. He stretched, looking like a *guappo* recovering consciousness, chain-yawned eight or nine times, until he had dislocated, or almost, his neverthe- less mighty mandibles. He concluded each time with a o-àm! which seemed definitive and yet wasn't, inasmuch as he began again, immediately afterwards. Tears dropped from his left eye, then his right, slowly slowly, squeezed one after the other by the consecutive yawns, like the two halves of a lemon successively used by the oyster vendor. He gave his head a brief scratching, a review with three nails of the occiput-jungle, zin zin zin, looking like a monkey: and with the automatic motions of a sleepwalker he headed for "the bath." Arriving there, and closing the door with its latch, he could finally unburden himself in the most radical and expeditious of ways of that annoying sensation of *trop-plein* which marks every morning, and every bladder however elastic and youthful, on the prompt awakening of the owner.

Which contributed, with the March draft from the badly closed window, that is badly closable, to clearing up his head completely, even though the draft was a gust of sirocco. He slipped off the nightshirt, still all tepid both with bed and sleep, and hung it on a hook: whence he saw it hang, empty, immaculate, the nocturnal skin of himself. Dawn was breaking. From Marsyas, after having so badly sung in his sleep, he seemed to have stepped out, an Apollo. An Apollo no longer twenty, a tiny bit hairy. He scratched his great head again, approached the basin, and giving free rein to its lymphs, he soaped his nose and face, neck and ears. He shook his mop under the high faucet of the basin, with those puffs and those nasal trumpetings, like a seal coming to the surface after its underwater twirls, which were, every morning, from the "occupied" bathroom, the unfailing sign of his bountiful ablutions. A sweet excitement from the other part of the door that the latch barred, a delicate trepidation used, in those moments, to overcome his genteel hostess, Signora Margherita: Margherita Antonini, née Celli, widow of the late Commendatore Antonini: no, no, no, not the keeper of a rooming house, ah!: a very distinguished lady, sister-in-law of his Excellency Barlani, president Pier Calumero Barlani: president, no . . . yes . . . she couldn't remember of what: it had been several years since he, too, passed on, poor man: a pulmonary emphysema with suppuration, septicemia: he was, you might say, the support of the whole family. She annulled the eternity of waiting in tiled hallways with the relative odor (cat pee and kerosene) with silent transferences, winged with improbability and with miracle, which seemed to be celebrated in a field of gravity now disused, and even unfunctioning, as if of a demagnetized magnet. She passed thus as far as the kitchen and the pots on flowing little steps, which her long bathrobe of pink flannel withdrew one after the other, from the perception of third parties; and there remained in the hall, like a belated trail, the very idea of continuity in the infinitesimal sense of the term.

Which fluidity and lightness as of a ghost shivering in cotton, though devoted to the mourned manes of the deceased, "my poor Gaspare," was applied (in truth) to not disturb in any way the strophic successions of the ablutional rite, and freeing, at the same time, of the nasal passages, to which Don Ciccio was wont to abandon himself. In a revitalized heart-beating, in her role of hostess (no, *not* landlady), oh no, with unperceived blushings as of a girl ready for confirmation, she devoted herself through all the house to the first cares of the day: which bore fruit, barely risen as she was from her bed, first of all in a canonical cup of coffee and milk, already prepared the preceding evening: the celebrated double coffee of Sora Margherita: a true folly, deprecated by all, and first by all the landladies in the building, oh yes, *they* were rooming-house keepers! Yes. "Poor man," she used to say, "could I send him on an empty stomach to Santo Stefano?" She couldn't bring herself to add "del Cacco," in the fear, perhaps, of becoming derailed from the Cacco.* Devoutly offered on a pewter tray, the coffee in a pot either of copper or tin (it wasn't clear), the milk in a pitcher lacking its handle, the sugar in an unemployed jar of peptone, a little, greasy cylinder, at the foot of the low-slung pot, little plates with toasted crusts and curls of butter, the frowning doctor, never you mind, threw himself on it every morning like a buffalo: with the excuse of his haste, crunch crunch, in a flash everything had disappeared. That morning, needless to say, that Wednesday March 23rd, Feast of San Benedetto

* The word "Cacco" is close, in sound, to several Italian obscenities (see footnote, page 57), unsuited to the lips of Sora Margherita.

the farmer, according to the calendar, "and with such anguirsh for that poor soul on your mind," Signora Celli made the sign of the Cross, "*ora et labora pro nobis,*" she margheritized. "Anguish," grunted Don Ciccio, highly offended, his mouth full of mush: "and the *pro nobis* you can skip." He choked, his face turned purple: any minute he would shoot it all from his nose, crusts and coffee. "Anguirsh, anguish," the donator trilled, "isn't it the same thing? You've had too much education, Doctor: you're like a school-teacher sometimes." And in the meanwhile she struck him twice on the back, practical woman, and like a sister, *hélas!* lovingly assisting: she, who had become a specialist in rapping (on the hard wood of the door). The doctor wiped his mouth, stood up. He had already intrigued yesterday morning, and then at night before leaving his office, for the car: by telephone, on the switchboard, by direct visit to him who could grant it, and by talk: and again on the phone at eleven in the evening, Assistant Chief Pantanella was discussing it with Commendatore Amabile: he had whispered into his ear, poor man, a whole wind: with considerable hail of angry electrons: he had raised his voice as if he had been speaking to a Turk (Amabile was deaf). The automobile? Yes, sir, he had already made a requisition. Yes! He had asked for it!

And he had—incredibly—obtained it: from a colleague of his: the chief of the political section. Who, foreseeing a slack day, well, two or three fezzes left over from the day before, he had let him have the sedan of the "P" department, albeit reluctantly, and giving himself great airs of having done him a very special favor, a rare gesture of delicacy "because it's for you, Don Ciccio, you realize . . . Ingra-vallo": as if to indicate that he would expect, one day, a favor in return. For another he wouldn't have done such a favor, no: "not by a long shot." An old hulk of a car, you'd be ashamed to go out in. Rattly and slow, two slabs of cor-rugated iron for fenders, hand-painted black, all wavy, with drops where the paint had dripped, which swayed and jolted as soon as the car moved, like two cabbage leaves hanging out of the cook's half-empty shopping bag: with one door that wouldn't open, and a handle that couldn't keep the other one shut: one window that wouldn't roll up, and a smashed headlight: so it was even one-eyed: the tires worn down like old shoes, and with so many buboes outside that it looked like an inguinal hernia. It had been, *illis temporibus!* the highly respected automobile of the Chief of Police of Rome. Fallen into the hands of the gang in the post-March days, and immediately defamed in pro-portion to the times, the events, and the learning of those young gentlemen whom it had driven around, it told of itself now, in unambiguous terms, its own record of service. Within, one sensed, one sniffed, they must have drunk and toasted, chewed salami, stained their lips with Olevano, "damn good, this red stuff from Rome, it goes down like oil" "sure, castor oil," smoked cheap cigarettes, sneezed, spat, vomited both Olevano and salami.

So that everyone, now, in that car, political or non-political, stuck his head in unwillingly and a cautious shoe after the head, the other shoe still on the ground, and a suspicious, examining eye, nostrils the same: as if, from such muck, vapors could steam forth, conjunctive to the odor, pallors of lemures of more than one three-months'-old dead infant, with the tail all coiled, and the little head of a donkey. Careful, frowning, uneasy. The idea that there had settled in the cloth (of the seats) some organic ejection of the more popularly known variety now obsessed every user: it made fearful the more cautious, and cautious even the bold and heedless, were there any. All of them hesitated a little (very little), scared, each, of his own basic decorum, that is to say the decorum of the seat, of the pants: those so dignified trousers, paid for in installments, month by month, in sums withheld from salaries, with the respective tightening of the belts of the same. Once stuck to the bottom, well, it's obvious enough, every least-deserved stain, in maculating the splendor like the most reputable spots of Father Secchi, stained the luminous rotundities of the photosphere.

And he had also obtained permission for gasoline, Ingravallo, playing his cards and then, all of a sudden, bang, ace of trumps, he screwed the whole lot of them: he filled it with gas enough to cruise to Benevento and back. Three armed policemen, two with muskets: but no Grabber, ordered off to the Pensione Burgess, nor Blondie either, ordered to Piazza Vittorio: but instead, all nice and thin with his mustache erect, Sergeant Di Pietrantonio, who makes four: and he, Ingravallo five: and six, the showfurr, in twenty-seven French words were still allowed.* So I don't have to tell you what the car looked like. The Barcac-

* One feature of Fascist nationalism was the banishing from Italian usage of all foreign words: *"ouverture"* became *"apertura,"* for example, and—in this case *"chauffeur"* became *"autista."*

cia from Piazza di Spagna out for a drive. It sped, as it could, with its tires swelling, soft as they were, and at the first stone they encountered, they already wanted to blow up: the clutch went crack at every street corner, at every dog that crossed their path. At Via Giovanni Lanza, under repair, it tangoed and rocked through the potholes for more than a hundred yards, spattered muck against the legs of the passers-by, even those on the sidewalk: parabolic slabs of liquid mud, opalescent against the pink lights of the morning which, nevertheless, was darkening: it plunged, re-emerged, and looked as if it had been repainted: a nice nut-colored bath, it had had. At Largo Brancaccio, as they were turning into Via Merulana towards Piazza San Gio-vanni, Ingravallo looked, grimly, to his left: he rolled down the window, Santa Maria Maggiore, with the three dark arches of the loggia over the narthex, seemed to follow, with the afflatus of charity of her plebs, a bier that had sprung from her own womb. Designed and constructed enunciation, artful, on the summit of what must have been, in the distant centuries, the "hill," the Viminal, the seven-teenth-century architecture of the basilica, as if of a sump-tuous dwelling of thought, had its roots in the shadow, in the darkness of the straight descending street and in the tangle of all its offshoots: a hint, the cuspidal campanile, beyond the tangle of branches and foliage that flanked it. But over the brick of that romanesque little tower, the sky was prepared for its decoration. Don Ciccio stuck out his head, tried to raise his eyes towards the clouds, for the day's forecast. All the clouds could be seen running: a flight of horses; they crossed the clear broad stripe, blue at moments, of the sky, between the two parallel rain pipes: they rushed off God knows where, prompt cohorts. The plane-trees and the boughs of Merulana were a forest, as the car turned, a tangle to the eyes, on the parallel descent of the lines which nourished the trams: still skeletal in March, with already a merely skin-deep languor, nonetheless, a kind of itch within the happy, street-lining clarity of their bark, made of scales and patches: dry leather, white calf, silver: the undergarment the color of a tender pea's skin, amid the bustle of the people, the coming and going of wagons and bicycles. And emerging then from the boughs, and already awakened at a hint of purple, the campanile "of the ninth century" seemed to warm in the sun's ray: to waken, at that tepidness, the dozing bronzes, which, at any moment, would then officiate. Trapped within its cage, the heavy bell of the scholars began to sway in its turn, slowly, slowly, with a trembling almost unnoticed at first, with a rumble still suspended in the heavens, like that of a metallic wing. The wave spread happily through one's thoughts, over the balconies, the closed windows of the houses vibrated with it, every most sleeping window. An old grandmother on a swing, who rhythmically took in air: and grated forth her soft whisper, a little watery at every new thrust, and one doesn't know from what guitar: to summon Lucianos and Maria Maddalenas to their classes, with their braids down. Where, in fact, a little later they ran, with a pack of dictionaries: and some were already out: and on foot, or on the tram, which meant they had a bit of money: alone, or in bunches, like so many little flights of sparrows, of little wrens: after drying their ears in haste, and perhaps even washing them a bit: yes, their ears: indispensable organ of all study. Dong, dong, dong, dong. The bell, the old woman on her swing, hurled out that bumblebee signal, from the pendulum, with all her heart, at every blow with full ass that she gave it, to be able to take the forward thrust. And gradually, it became more full-bodied every time, this admonition, emphasizing the air, magnifying the wave: until she, the grandmother, spun it out for you a bit *en sourdine:* to not stir too badly the little darlings, the Nanninas or the rumpled Romolettos: who from a nonentity of an alarm clock in angry trills would have got the scarlatina poor babies! A sweetness in her heart, to hear her, the old granny! That perorating cautiousness brought the evil closer by degrees, in a subdued modulation: no, *not oil:* the evil of re-awakening to knowledge: to recognition and to reliving the truth of every day: which is that, immediately after the cold water, there is school waiting, and the teacher with his zeros in readiness. She, the grandmother of all, uncovered with her slow caress the little heads, the black curls of the boys, of the girls: she parted their eyelids, just barely, drawing from them, with the clean tip of the counterpane, the veil of the fugitive dreams. It took her a half hour to wax, very slowly, and another half hour to wane. She descended, little by little, into her calmed silence. Which was the silence of the offices and the tasks at their beginning, the chilblains on the penmanship. With that great portrait of Him hanging on the wall: a mug, who because he was born stupid, seems to want to take his revenge on all.

A few curious faces, of two or three loafers with their hands in their pockets, and with three gaping mouths under the black questioning of their eyes, received and then surrounded, at Marino, the car "of the Roman police" when it honked twice, poh! poh! before the main gate of the fort. In the frame of a window, on high, behind a rusty grating, the face of a young man appeared, with two stars on his gray canvas collar, one here and one there. He vanished. A few minutes: and the gates opened. The willing and bumpy car, after some great pushing and reversing and turns forward, with several jolts and starts which one wouldn't have hoped for, even from her, finally drove through that arch of triumph, which it had devoured the countryside to gain. And it had been, the road to the fort, a narrow, climbing road, all compact cobbles, between spurred walls which retained the shadow patched with lichens, on the old peperino, of strange pools and cockades, blue-green, yellow. The cobbles slippery. A slab at the corner: Via Massimo d'Azeglio. Ingravallo got out of the car, imitated by his followers. The sentry said: "The sergeant is out on a search party; the corporal was sent to I Due Santi, on that crime business." Meanwhile another soldier appeared. Higher in rank, or older, after a not prompt and rather soft clicking of heels (these gentlemen were from the police) and a raising of the head which announced more explicitly and more elegantly that he had come to attention, he handed Ingravallo a bluish envelope which, on being torn open, produced a sheet of paper, folded over twice. Santarella, therein, communicated that he had sent Pestalozzi to la Pàcori, accompanied by a soldier, for further checking; he, with another man, was out to follow the tracks of the fugitive Enea, alias Iginio, which was how they called Retalli. He had some hopes of overtaking him, that is to say, of catching him and of handcuffing him, to bring him, handcuffed, to the barracks: not however, a certainty. Ingravallo, more than a little cross, took off his hat, to allow his head to get a bit of air, clenched his teeth: two hard knobs on the two jaws, halfway from the ears, gave him, under his black mop a kind of bulldog's muzzle, already illustrated on more than one occasion. The two carabinieri were not the least impressed. The carabinieri, in peace time, and nuns, at all times, know how to draw from their respective disciplines that durable steadiness which indemnifies them to the jolt of current events, if not even to the quakes of history, for which events or history, however, it may turn out, they give as much as any history merits: that is, not to damn. "Do you know whether Crocchiapani Assunta," Ingravallo asked, "about whom I sent a communication on the twentieth, has already been questioned at her home?"

"No, sir."

"And why not? Do you know where she is? I mean, do you know the locality?"

"Tor di Gheppio, the sergeant said."

"How long does it take to get there?"

"With a car, sir, about forty minutes . . . even less . . ."

"Well, we'll start there then. Let's go."

The noncom sent for some character, who was supposed

to be familiar with that zone: a thin little man, dressed in black as Ingravallo was. They welcomed him aboard. To get the car out of the courtyard, ass frontwards, along a narrow curve and uphill, to thread it into the d'Azeglio toboggan in a forward gear, took a number of pushes in the direction opposite to that previously described. Ingravallo, blackly, continued to clench his jaws: his teeth creaked. He was mentally cursing the tires, the springs, the Fascists. If he had a flat, wouldn't he look a fool? with this new man in the car. The whole legion would laugh for thirty years. The automobile of the Rome Police: with a hernia-ed tire that goes plof, at the climax, and it's only luck if the car hasn't driven off a bridge. But the car went: it would go. It sped against the wind, with rare seeds of rain on the windows: with unforeseen jolts at certain recesses, certain bumps not yet reported by the Touring Club. Olive trees, and their fronds of ashen silver, were still not much shaken: beaded by the night's rain, or dried at the first sun, they spoke of the clear continuity of the year already adolescent, already tormented into Aries, smelling a bit of manure in the vineyards, in the brown earth of the hummocks, the slopes. A cloud passed over the grain or the fields, barely grassy: and an immediate fear gripped them, as if they were to be spent again, in winter: to that shadow, swift and yet feared, they seemed to adapt themselves helplessly, to freeze, despairing. But the wing of the sirocco, quite to the contrary, tawny and tepid, in the pale humidity of the day: more than a calf's breath in the stable. The weather, muggy, gave the augury of grain,

of the battle of grain* and of corn and of the rearings of
the Jack-ass it cared little. A late-March frost, Ingravallo
thought, could upset, God unwilling, the presage: the eighty
million quintals were to come down to thirty-eight. The
Autarch Jawbone, for his forty-four million . . . subjects,
yes, fine subjects too, had to load on grain in Toronto,
where there were French become English in Canada, beg
maccheroni from the redskins. And Ingravallo clenched and
creaked, from rage and satisfaction joined together. They
went down to Torraccio, where the sirocco, dying, became
warmer: or so it seemed. They turned on to the Appia at
I Due Santi, having to travel over it, retracing their steps,
for a good half-mile, towards Rome, that is, to the turn-off
for Falcognana. After a short stretch of this road, they
encountered the Anzio road, and turned off again. The wind
dropped. With the Guzzi motorbike of Sergeant Santarella
and the motorized Pestalozzi, the carabiniere had suggested
that a meeting was not improbable, or even almost certain:
but they didn't meet at all. An ass, on the other hand, loaded
with wood, and with the respective peasant on his back, one
hand clutching the tail: or a little flock of about fifteen
sheep, the shepherd with his green umbrella, shut: no, no
dog, they cost too much. A buggy: "the vet from Albano,"
the little man informed. He drove calmly, ruddy, a cigar
butt spent in his lips, with threadbare gloves. After a little
more than a mile and a half on the Anzio road, they had
to take a right: "this way, this way, towards Santa Fumia,"
their guest said. Over the Santa Fumia bridge towards

* The "battle of grain" was Mussolini's campaign to increase the
production of wheat in Italy.

375

Tor di Gheppio and then towards Casal Bruciato. The muddy little road went downhill, then hardened: the tracks dilated into puddles, brimming, against the light, with livid water, molten blue-silver lead, where the wing of a dab-chick was seen, black, or of a scattered jay. It seemed that, a little later, they had to become lost in the lands, in the mire. They crossed instead the tracks (of the Velletri line) at a level, similar to the one a mile to the north, near the Divino Amore bridge. Blades of grass, between the two tracks, rose here and there from the breach, between one tie and the next (of oak), as if the line were of no further use, after having been used, for one year, by Pius the Ninth. Strands of smoke lay still in midair, motionless, clotted there by magic: remains of a barely dissolved apparition: white, like cotton batting, or of an unreal white, like steam. The smoked outline of the little train was diminishing at that moment towards a distant arch: it accredited in itself, in its vanishing, the perspective flight of the two converging rails: and it resembled the Prince of Darkness, and the cabin of the last car, the rail, when it is freed from the enchantress and disappears with a hiss through its portals, under the black vaulted arch, into the mountain; and in the silence of the countryside and in the mute stupefaction of all things, at a goat's hoof-print that has remained to seal the mire and a wisp of sulphur in the air. "Tor di Gheppio's over there," the willing little man said, pointing, "towards the palace farm. Crocchiapani lives there, in one of those houses you can see, the little bunch on the left." Emerging then from the undulations of that clay bare of trees, which the fallow land made green in patches, a tower's pointed tip stood out against the sky, like a shard, an ancient tooth of an ancient jaw of the world. The houses of the living, mute in the distance of the cultivated land, stood before it: but a little more in this direction. They drove down.

"Pavona? The station?" Ingravallo asked.

"The town of Pavona is there," the guest pointed again: "down there, see? That's the station. If you cross the fields it's maybe twenty-five minutes: if you walk fast. But we'd get all wet."

"And the Rome-Naples line?"

"There," and he turned: "it's two, maybe even three miles: you just keep going straight, with the car. On our way back, then, if you have to go to Pavona, after Tor di Gheppio, then we could do down to Casal Bruciato, and take the Ardeatina there. If we go off in that direction, towards Ardea, right away, hardly more than a mile, we get to Santa Palomba—where those antennas are over there (he pointed them out), you can see them everywhere, even from Marino. There, if you want, you cross the road to Solforata and Pratica di Mare: so, for Palazzo, we can come straight up to Pavona. The whole thing, from Casal Bruciato, is maybe four and a half, five miles, maybe not even. With the car, maybe fifteen minutes." "All right," said Ingravallo, in whom all this toponymy had produced more clenching of the jaws: "now we'll go to Tor di Gheppio." They set off, they went: to the spot where the little man said, after spurts of water and various jolts, they got out. They left the car with the driver, who also got out and went off to one side for a moment, on his own. They started walking along the path which proceeded straight and not excessively muddily towards the three houses. They proceeded in so-called Indian file, one after the other, Private First-Class Runzato first of all, then Di Pietrantonio, then Don Ciccio with his hands in the pockets of his overcoat: and they looked like a school of grave-diggers, all so black in the clear, open day, as if they were going to pick up the deceased: and with some reluctance, too. "La Crocchiapani, that stupid girl, has already heard us coming," thought Ingravallo, "and she's peeking at us, for sure." In fact, as they were later to ascertain, she was observing them from the window, behind the almost-closed shutters, where the sound of the car had led her to station herself. When Ingravallo raised his face and Runzato whistled, then shouted: "Police! Let us in! Open the door!" the house, the first and the smallest, had a policeman at every corner. Kids, chickens, two women, two mongrel dogs with tails curled up like a bishop's crook, revealing all their beauty: couldn't stop looking, barking. Gleaming, black eyes, stunned in the wonder of the faces, and the almost tattered poverty of the clothes. "Who's here?" Di Pietrantonio prudently asked: "How many people? Are there any menfolk?" "There's a girl, with her father," said the nearer of the peasant women, who had come closer, as if to save their children, or a hen more in danger. This house, of Tina Crocchiapani's, was a little square, slightly separated from the flock: a little, closed door with the number 3, on the ground floor. Before the threshold some slabs of stone, rather hollowed by footsteps, and shoes, and nails. No voice, within. Opaque, somnolent years, after the pink of the inaugural wash, had given the walls a faded squalor, and, on the side toward the north wind a dark rust, shadows: which was the corner to which these gentlemen had come first. At the eaves there was no pipe nor any wooden apparatus, known as gableboard: so that the roof tiles, along the edge, seemed to Don Ciccio, stumps, or depicted in cross-section, they made a sort of wavy pleating along the margin of the roof, a rustic ornate. A few blades of grass from the earth deposited here and there on the tiles, under the wind's auspices. An occasional drop fell, radiating, once detached from the tiles that had become black with the years; and dropped heavily, as if it were of mercury, to wound again, to penetrate, all around, the dampened compactness of the earth. A window was opened, then shut: the maddened hens cluck-clucked. Too yielding the roof's slopes, or too shapeless, they seemed to descend in waves, they had been softened by the rains and then baked again and as if swollen in the heat: they charged their masons with lack of skill in their art: or else, in the garret the tree trunk which served as a beam was twisted. One would think that, under the earthy insistence of that covering, all the rotten apparatus, one fine day, would give way and fall and crash in a ruin: or the whole roof fly away, rather, at a gust of strong wind, like a rag, no sooner than the squall hit it. The wooden shutters, at the windows, one closing, one slamming: without paint of any kind and already putrid or splintered in the weather, in the steady evaporation of the years. Instead of glass, greased paper, on a frame, or a rusty piece of corrugated iron.

The little door opened a crack. When it was completely open Ingravallo found himself facing . . . a face, a pair of eyes! gleaming in the penumbra: Tina Crocchiapani! "Her! Her!" he meditated, not without a composite beating of the heart: the stupendous maidservant of the Balduccis, with black gleams under her coal-black lashes, where the Alban light became tangled, broke, iridescent (the white tablecloth, the spinach) from the black hair gathered on her forehead, like the work of Sanzio, from the blue— dangling from lobes and on the cheeks—earrings: with that bosom! which Foscolo would have certified as a brimming bosom, in a troubadoric-mandrillian access, of the kind that have made him immortal in Brianza. At supper with the Balduccis, at Signora Liliana's! The field of the black and silent goddess, for her, who had been so cruelly sepa- rated from all things, from the lights and phenomena of the world! And she, she was the one, the one (the pathway of time became confused and lost) who had presented the filled and badly tilted oval of the plate, a whole leg, all the kidneyed syncretism of a dish of kid, or of lamb, in pieces as it was, had allowed to roll out, on the whiteness amid the silver and the crystal, of a goblet, or no, of a glass, the tuft of spinach: receiving, from Signora Liliana, that heartbroken reproof of a glance, and a name: "Assunta!" Tina, with her face, as in other times, severe, a little pale, but with an inflection of dismay in her eyes, looked at him nonetheless proudly, and he thought she recovered herself: two dark flashes, her pupils, again, bright in the shadow, in the odor of the closed entranceway to the house. "Doc- tor," she said, with an effort: and was about to add some- thing else. But Di Pietrantonio alarmed her, even though she had already noted him from the window, after the policeman who seemed to be leading the whole row of overcoats. Tall, and wordless, police-like in his moustache, was he not the punishment feared? comminated by the law? But for what guilt, for what crime, she argued to herself, officially, could they punish her? For having solicited too many gifts, for having received them, from Signora Liliana?

"Officer Ingravallo, sir, what is it?"

"Who lives here, in your house?" Ingravallo asked her, harsh: harsh as he was required to be, at that moment, his "other" soul: to which Liliana seemed to address herself, calling to him desperately, from her sea of shadows: with her weary, whitened face, her eye dilated in terror, still, forever, on the atrocious flashes of the knife. "Let me in; I have to see who's here."

"There's my father, sir; who's sick; he's bad off, poor soul!" and she was slightly breathless, in disdain, very beautiful, pallid. "He's going to die on me any minute."

"And then, besides your father, who is there?"

"Nobody, Signor Incravalli: who could there be? You tell me, if you know. There's a woman, a neighbor, from Tor di Gheppio, who helps me take care of the sick man . . . and maybe some other neighbor woman, you may have seen outside."

"Who is this one? What's her name?"

Tina thought a little. "She's Veronica. Migliarini. Hereabouts we call her la Veronica."

"Let me in anyway. Come on. Let's go. I have to search the house." And he examined her face, with the steady, cruel eye of one who wants to unmask deceit. "Search?":

381

Tina frowned: wrath whitened her eyes, her face, as if at an unforeseen outrage. "Yeah, search, that's what I said." And thrusting her aside, he came into the darkness toward the little wooden stairway. The girl followed him. Di Pietrantonio after her. It occurred to him, then and there, that Liliana's murderer, in addition to having received from Tina information which was useful to him "or rather indispensable: did I say useful?" could have also entrusted the jewels to her: . . . "to his fiancée?" They went upstairs. The steps creaked. All around, outside, the house was observed: three policemen, not counting the little man who had guided them there. Those two black and furious eyes of Tina—Ingravallo felt them aimed at his nape; he felt them piercing his neck. He tried, he tried to sum up, rationally; to pull the threads, one might say, of the inert puppet of the Probable. "How was it that the girl didn't rush to Rome? Didn't she feel it was her duty?": this was a compulsory idea, now, in his atrociously wounded spirit: "to the funeral at least? . . . Doesn't she have any heart or soul in her, after all the kindness she received?" It was the painful bookkeeping of the humble, the ingenuous, perhaps. The horrible news, perhaps, hadn't reached Tor di Gheppio until too late, and in that solitude . . . terror had paralyzed the poor girl. But no, a grown woman! And news flies, even in the jungle, in the wastelands of Africa. For a Christian heart the inspiration would have been another. Although, the father, dying . . .

The wood of the steps continued to creak, more and more, under the rising weight of the three. Ingravallo, once at the top, pushed the door, with a certain charitable prudence.

He went in, followed by Tina and by Di Pietrantonio, into a large room. A stink, there, of dirty clothing or of not very washable or seldom-washed people in illness, or sweating in the labor that the countryside, unremittingly, at every change of weather, demands: or rather, even more, of feces poorly put away near the illness, so needful of shelter. Two long tapers painted in the vivid colors, blues, reds, gold, of a coloristic tradition unbroken in the years, hung on the wall from two nails at either side of the bed: the dry olive twig: an oleograph, the blue Madonna with a golden crown, in a black wood frame. Some rush-bottomed chairs. A plaster cat with a ribbon around its neck, scarlet, on the commode amid bottles, bowls. Near the Illness was seated an old woman, her striped skirt halfway down her tibias, with a pair of cloth shoes, no laces (and, within, her feet) which she had rested on the crossbar of the chair, open like slippers. In the bed, broad, under worn and greenish blankets, covered in part by one good one (and warm, and light, gift of Liliana, Ingravallo deduced) an outstretched little body, like a skinny cat in a sack set on the ground: a bony and cachetic face rested on the pillow, motionless, of a yellow-brown like something in an Egyptian museum; were it not, on the other hand, for the glassy whiteness of the beard, which indicated its belonging, not to an Egyptian catalogue, but to an era of human history painfully close and, for Ingravallo, in those days, downright contemporary. Everything was silent. You couldn't understand whether the man was alive or dead: if it was a man or woman, who in proceeding among the consolations of offspring and of the hoe in a swarm of mosquitoes towards the golden wed-

ding, had sprouted that beard: a virile beard, as was wont
to say, even of feminine beards, the Founder of the five-
year-old Empire. The two tapers, here and there, seemed
to be waiting to be stuck into suitable candlesticks, lighted
by a match held in a charitable hand. Intolerant of this new
mess of the dying parent and yet cautious and pitying, the
imagination of Doctor Ingravallo kicked, bucked, galloped,
heard and saw: he was seeing and already dismissing the
coffin without drapery, of poplar planks, flowered with periwinkles and primula, surrounded by the absolving mutters
or the prompt insurgence of some phrase chanted, or perhaps nasalized for better or worse amid the murmurings of
the women and the good odor of the incense, issuing (*con
cuidado*) from the parsimonious sway of the censer: to
signify the great fear suffered and the repentance of the
deceased, and the imploration and hope, all around, of the
living and the surviving, once that coffin was closed and
nailed and well-hammered: and in short, a kind of convinced serenity in every heart (better to go like this than to
suffer for another month or more), in watching the planks,
the flowers . . . target of the reiterated spatterings of the asperges: between a shuffling of soles and a creaking of iron
on the cobbles, if there were cobbles. But the reality was as
yet different from the dream: those images of an almost
raving impatience regarded the future, however near that
future might be. Don Ciccio restrained the galloping of his
delirium, tugged at the reins of his pawing rage. The patient, so thin, seemed ripe for the last rites: Eternity, infallible physician, was already, bent over him. Lovingly,
she gazed upon him (and gulped some saliva down) with

the succoring and greedy gaze of a Red Cross woman or a nurse who was slightly necrophilic: concerned with wiping his forehead in a light caress with the more delaying hand: and with the other, expert one, maneuvering under the covers and even under the body, between the sacroiliac and the bedpan, had finally found the right spot to stick into him the little point, the ebonite straw, for the service of perpetual immunization.

Strange borborygms, under cover, contradicted the coma, and, more strangely, death: they gave the impression of a miraculous imminence: that the sheets and the blankets were on the point of bulging, swelling: of rising and floating in midair, on the paralyzed gravity of death. The old woman, Migliarini Veronica, was huddled in the chair, frozen in a commemoration of the ages that had, on the other hand, dissolved into non-memory: she had one of her hands in the other, resembling Cosimo *pater patriae* in the so-called portrait by Pontormo: dry, lizardy skin, on her face, and the wrinkled immobility of a fossil. There wasn't, in her lap, but she would have liked it, the earthenware brazier. She raised her eyes, gelatinous and glassy in their tan color, without interrogating any of those people who, to her, must have seemed shadows, neither the girl, nor the men. The spent quiet of her gaze was opposed to the event, like the mindless memory of the earth, from paleontological distances: alienating that face of a hundred-and-ninety-year-old Aztec woman from the acquisitions of the species, from the latest, quick-change artist's conquests of Italian eyeing.

A majolica pan, as if from a clinic of the first category, was set on the brick floor, and not even near the wall: and neither did it lack some undeciphered content, on the consistence, coloration, odor, viscosity and specific weight of which both the lynx eyes and the bloodhound scent of Ingravallo felt that it wasn't necessary to investigate and analyze: the nose, of course, could not exempt itself from its natural functioning, that is, from that activity, or to be more accurate, that papillary passivity which is proper to it, and which does not admit, *hélas*, any interlude or inhibition or absence of any kind from its duty.

"Is this your father?" Don Ciccio asked Tina, looking at her, looking around, and then taking off his hat.

"Doctor, you see the state he's in. You wouldn't believe me: but now you've got to believe me, finally!" she exclaimed in a resentful tone, and with eyes which seemed to have wept, the beauty. "I've given up hope by now. It'd be better for him, and for me too, if he died. To suffer like that, and without any money or anything. His behind, if you'll pardon the word, is just one big sore, now: it's a mess, poor Papa!" She was trying, thought Ingravallo harshly, in her grief she was trying to turn her father to use, his direct decay. "And he even has a rubber bedpan," she sighed, "otherwise his bedsores would have been infected. This morning, at eight o'clock, he was in pain again, it hurt him bad, he said. He couldn't stay still ten minutes, you might say. Now he hasn't moved for three hours: he doesn't say a word: I have a feeling he's out of his suffering now, that he can't suffer any more": she dried her eyes, blew her little nose: "because he can't feel anything now, good or bad, poor Papa . . . The priest can't get here before one, he sent word. Ah me, poor us!" she

looked at Ingravallo, "if it hadn't been for the signora!"
That remark sounded empty, distant. Liliana: it was a name.
It seemed, to Don Ciccio, that the girl hesitated to evoke it.

"Of course," he said, wearily, "the bedpan!" and he
remembered the unbosomings of Balducci, "I know, I know
who gave it to you: and that jar, too," and he indicated it
with his head, his chin, "and the blanket," he looked at the
blanket on the bed, "you were given them by . . . by a person
who promptly got paid back, for her goodness. Don't do
good, if you don't want to receive evil, the proverb says.
And that's how it is. Aren't you going to talk? Don't you
remember?"

"Doctor? what should I remember?"

"Remember the person who helped you so much, when
you deserved so little."

"Yes, the family where I worked: but why didn't I
deserve it?"

"The family! Signora Liliana, you mean! who had her
throat cut by a murderer!" and his eyes were such that,
this time, Tina was frightened: "by a murderer," he repeated, "whose name," he spoke, curule, "whose full name
we know! . . . and where he lives: and what he does . . ."
The girl turned white, but didn't say a word.

"Out with his name! yelled Don Ciccio. "The police know
this name already. If you tell it right now," his voice became deep, persuasive: "it's all to the good, for you."

"Doctor Ingravalli," repeated Tina to gain time, hesitating, "how can I say it, when I don't know anything?"

"You know too much, you liar," shouted Ingravallo
again, his nose to hers. Di Pietrantonio was stunned. "Cough

it up, that name, you've got here: or the corporal'll make you spill it, in the barracks, at Marino: Corporal Pesta-lozzi."

"No, sir, no, Doctor: it wasn't me!" the girl implored then, simulating, perhaps, and in part enjoying, a dutiful fear: the fear that whitens the face a little, but still resists all threats. A splendid vitality, in her, beside the moribund author of her days, which should have been splendid: an undaunted faith in the expressions of her flesh, which she seemed to hurl boldly to the offensive, in a prompt frown, with a scowl: "No, it wasn't me!" The incredible cry blocked the haunted man's fury. He didn't understand, then and there, what his spirit was on the point of understanding. That black, vertical fold above the two eyebrows of rage, in the pale white face of the girl, paralyzed him, prompted him to reflect: to repent, almost.

TITLES IN SERIES